THE
NURSE'S
SECRET

BOOKS BY LIZ LAWLER

THE NURSE'S SECRET

LIZ LAWLER

Bookouture

Published by Bookouture in 2022

An imprint of Storyfire Ltd.
Carmelite House
50 Victoria Embankment
London EC4Y 0DZ

www.bookouture.com

ISBN: 97801-80314-643-0
eBook ISBN: 978-1-80314-642-3

For my dad – a spinner of yarns who made me love stories.
And for Grace who loved happy endings.

PROLOGUE

Mary could hear noises outside the room, and wondered why no one was coming in. The pitter-patter of footsteps kept passing by her door. They must have heard her fall. Her water jug had come down with her. She could feel the wetness on the floor through her nightdress.

She had feared falling out of the hospital bed so many times, the bed being raised much higher off the floor than her bed at home. And along with the increasing level of disability and dependence on others, she also feared not being able to save herself. Until now, she'd been fortunate to have had only scares. When they moved her, they sometimes used a sheet to flip her over and would forget how light she was, and she'd come close to rolling over the edge.

The bed rail must have been left down this time. The abrupt landing had woken her, leaving her more startled than hurt. It was difficult to know if she had done any damage. She had grown used to the pain of the spasms in her limbs, so it was hard to work out if any bones had broken.

She moved her left hand feebly, her soft fingers tapping the floor in the hope of making some sound. Her voice was too weak to shout. Dysphonia, the speech therapist called it – her voice would come and go, but hers had not come back. It only got softer, just an airy whisper, and even that would cut out sometimes.

The saliva in her throat was pooling, and she couldn't swallow it away. She needed a pillow under her head to stop her from lying flat. Her chest felt weighty. She couldn't expand it to get enough air. Why didn't a nurse come? It was a hospital, for God's sake.

The doctor who came to see her earlier said he would be back, and maybe he had and she'd been asleep. She'd been tired out by her visitors. Trying to make them hear her quiet voice. Seeing her husband's martyred face and their pitiful looks, like it was his suffering, and not his wife's, they felt sorry for.

She managed a jerky breath and felt the immediate relief. She tried to calm her mind and think of something pleasant, and wished the audio tape on top of her locker was playing so she had something to listen to. *Silas Marner* had entertained her earlier, until Godfrey's childless state made her weep. She hadn't felt sorry for Godfrey, he hadn't deserved his daughter with his selfish manner. She had wept for herself and for her own wasted life – how much better it should have been.

She had been so in love. It was the only reason for agreeing to lie. They never spoke about it after that day. She had felt she couldn't mention it, which allowed the rot to set in. The rot is what destroyed her. Not this illness. In this last year, the truth had started to spill out. She couldn't contain it anymore. She suspected, though, that not many had believed her, with her mind damaged by illness, her ramblings a confused story.

The door opened, and Mary saw someone come into the room. She tried focusing on the figure, but her low vision only revealed to her a dark shape. She waited for them to say something, but the person stayed silent. Mary needed her oxygen back on and the saliva suctioned from her throat. She reached out a feeble hand, but it was ignored. Instead, the person moved away from her, and a moment later the dim lamp above the bed was turned off and the room went dark.

She heard breathing, and wondered what was going on. She couldn't work out what was happening. Fleeting thoughts were slipping through her mind, unable to pin down a reason.

Footsteps. Mary saw the door opening, a brief glimpse of light from the corridor before it closed again.

She knew then it was deliberate. The person was not going to come back. Someone had believed her after all. And this was the punishment. The light switched off. The door closed. She was left to die.

She stared into the dark, but it didn't matter anymore. The struggle for breath was passing. She hovered in her hazy memories and saw the rain diluting the red in the road. It was almost gone by the time help came.

Mary inhaled her last tiny breath, feeding her dying brain her last memory of the pale pink rain...

CHAPTER ONE

SARAH

Uncomfortable warmth enveloped Sarah. The plastic apron and gloves were holding heat against her skin, the face mask trapping her hot breath. In a rush, she yanked the mask off and breathed freely before catching a scent that made her queasy – the smell from the paper shroud. The camphor-like odour was similar to the smell that came with a jacket or coat from the dry cleaners. The whiff of dry-cleaning fluid was an odour she associated with death. She taped the notification of death to the shroud at chest level, to ensure easy identification of the body in the mortuary. She checked the information was correct: Time of death – 22.25 hrs. Date of death – December 9.

The man's relatives had left half an hour ago, his elderly wife supported by her son. She'd looked devastated, clutching her husband's jumper against her face as she left the cubicle. Night deaths seemed sadder, somehow.

All that was left to do was to wrap the body in a sheet. A task she had performed many times during her career as a nurse. At no point had it become just a duty. After more than ten years of nursing, giving her best care to the dead was the last and most respectful thing she could do for them. She covered the face, and then the feet, before bringing the sides of the material across the torso and around the legs, ensuring the limbs were held securely in position. She took another sheet to cover the shrouded body and then stepped away from the bed.

Sarah pulled her mobile phone out of her pocket to check the screen again. Nothing from William. They'd been married for twelve weeks and he hardly ever called. But this was different – it was her calling him and he wasn't answering his mobile or the house phone. It had taken a lot of effort and cajoling to find out why he was so quiet and seemingly depressed in the last few weeks. When her husband eventually told her yesterday about the anonymous letters and calls, she made him go to the police to report them.

On the other side of the bed Kathleen Price, a healthcare assistant, gathered up the soiled bedclothes from the floor and dropped them into the laundry skip. She was a well-built woman with silver in her curly black hair and had noticed Sarah checking her phone. 'The police will be busy. Checking up on a sleeping husband will hardly be a priority.' Her voice was brisk, but her Irish accent softened the mild rebuke.

Sarah sighed. Kathleen must be thinking that calling the police was extreme. The police were probably thinking much the same. 'You're right,' she replied. She stooped in front of the man's locker and started pulling out his belongings. She held up a tiny piece of cracked soap. 'Poor man didn't even have a decent bar of soap to wash with.'

'I'd still pack it with his property,' Kathleen said. 'His wife said he loved that scent.'

Sarah glanced over at her. 'I'm worrying about nothing, aren't I?'

It was Kathleen's turn to sigh. 'Just because your man hasn't answered his phone, it doesn't mean anything's wrong.'

'I'm not concerned because he isn't answering his phone, Kathleen. It's because he isn't answering the house phone. It's loud and I've rung it several times. He could have fallen down the stairs for all I know.'

The catch in her voice made Kathleen look at her with concern. 'He's a fit and able man. Why would he be falling down any stairs? He missed your calls, it's as simple as that. Maybe he was in the shower or putting more rubbish out to the bins.'

Sarah shook her head. 'It's not as simple as that. I'm not sure he should be at home alone. I didn't ring the police without reason.'

Kathleen stopped what she was doing and leaned heavily on the bed, causing the sheet to pull tight and outline the dead body. Sarah stared at the bed, wishing Kathleen had a bit more respect for the dead. Last offices was all about the care given to the body after death, all about maintaining dignity. It was not a time to have personal conversations and forget that the body was there.

Kathleen was waiting for Sarah to explain. 'He's been getting strange calls. Whoever it is hangs up without saying anything. It's put him on edge, because he has no idea who it is who's calling.'

'Huh!' Kathleen huffed, taking her weight off the bed to throw up her hands in exasperation. 'Well, there you go, you silly thing. He's not answering the phone for good reason.'

They both looked up when the door opened. Kathleen bristled as Staff Nurse Helen Tate came into the room.

'Bit late, aren't you? We've only his property left to do.'

Helen Tate was blonde and pretty and several years younger than Sarah. She seemed unfazed by Kathleen's remark. She gazed instead at the bed. 'It feels strange being in this room laying out a different body. I think of this as Mary's bed. She went so quick, don't you think?'

Sarah felt uncomfortable at the mention of Mary, a previous occupant of this bed, while Kathleen all but growled at the nurse. 'Did you want something? Or are you just bored, Helen?'

Helen gave a wounded expression. 'That was mean. I'm actually here to help.'

Kathleen glared. 'Sarah and I don't need your help. We're nearly done.'

As ward sister, Sarah should step in and address Kathleen's manner. Helen was a qualified nurse, and Kathleen shouldn't be allowed to speak to her like that. If Kathleen had a problem with the staff nurse, she should talk to Sarah about it, and Sarah should be the one to address Helen's laziness and her disappearing acts when there was work to be done.

Sarah wondered why Helen was in nursing at all, because she didn't seem very committed to it. She would be better off getting another job. She could go abroad or something. She could work for an airline, where she might meet a rich man on one of the planes, as wealth seemed to factor into many of her conversations. That, or get married.

'Kathleen's right, Helen. We are nearly finished. Five minutes and we'll be done.'

Helen stepped further into the room. She shook her head, while her lips curved up in an uneasy smile. 'There are two police officers here to see you, Sarah. They asked to speak to Mrs Shaw. You need to go and see them now.'

Her surname seemed strange spoken out loud. Despite being Sarah Shaw for three months, she was still usually addressed as Sarah James because most staff forgot she had married and changed to Shaw. For a moment she was stunned by the news, and almost missed the look of glee on Helen's face. Sarah brushed past her on trembling legs. This had to be about William. The police hadn't phoned, but came to her work.

Sarah made her way through the ward to the nurses' station, glancing left and right automatically as she passed the sleeping patients. A female officer was watching her as she approached, but Sarah managed to avoid eye contact. Her focus was on the man beside her. Sarah knew who he was, he was a friend of someone she used to know, though she'd never been introduced. He was a sergeant who investigated serious crime.

'Sarah Shaw?' he asked.

Sarah nodded, then noticed the hospital matron, Janet Langton, was quietly standing by, as if waiting her cue. Sarah expected the suggestion they all go somewhere private to have a quiet talk.

Her eyes fixed on Detective Sergeant Bowden. 'Is this about my husband, William?'

He nodded. 'Yes, it is.'

'Perhaps you should talk in the office, Sarah,' Janet Langton said.

Sarah shook her head. She consciously had to swallow to quench the dryness of her throat. 'Here is fine.' Her eyes stayed on Bowden. 'It's bad then, isn't it, if you're here?' she said in a tense tone.

'It is,' he confirmed. 'I'm so sorry to inform you, but we believe the body of a man found dead in your home is your husband.'

Sarah felt her knees shake. Behind her, she heard Kathleen's intake of breath. Then the woman was beside her, taking hold of her hand. Her head was spinning from his words. The body of a man found dead in her house was William's body.

'The police are at your home. Someone will come and talk to you again as soon as we have more information. But, in the meantime, it wouldn't be a good idea to go there. Best you stay elsewhere at the present time.'

Sarah nodded her head automatically. Her new home was out of bounds. Her new husband gone. They hadn't been married long. Their bed was new. The linen recently bought. It didn't matter where she went. It wouldn't change her situation. She was alone.

'I'll take Sarah to my house. I'll look after her there,' Kathleen said gently.

Sarah stood still for a few moments and heard a sharp cry. She realised the sound came from her. They hadn't said how he'd died, or suggested taking her to see William, which could only mean something unnatural had happened. Something that she could not change by going back to her address.

William was dead.

CHAPTER TWO

CHARLIE

Blue lights flashed silently from the police vehicles outside the semi-detached house, lighting up the faces of the people gathering on the open-plan gardens either side of it. The urgent sounds of sirens had woken them, bringing them out of their homes like startled rabbits, eyes blinking in shock, hands rubbing away sleep to make doubly sure that what they saw was real.

They were shocked because it wasn't natural. It hadn't happened to an old man or an old woman or to somebody who was ill. It had happened to someone who should still be alive. They were aware of this from simply staring around their street. A natural death wouldn't have brought this much attention, this many police vehicles and police officers from MCIT – the Major Crime Investigation Team – a two-force collaboration involving Avon and Somerset Constabulary, and Wiltshire. It wouldn't have brought the night owl reporters or a team of forensic investigators traipsing in and out of the house. A natural death would have left the street undisturbed and the people living on it unaware and still sleeping in their beds.

Charlie Bowden was watching the crowd, seeing their still-ness, and he wasn't surprised. They were waiting to see the body. In his experience, it would be a long wait. The pathologist still had to arrive, and the body would stay in that house for hours yet while Doyle carried out his examination. Crime scene investigation had advanced since Charlie joined the force. When he put on the uniform in 1987 he was eighteen, and DNA fingerprinting had only just been used for the first time in Britain.

Lighting his third cigarette, Charlie saw one of the para-medics through the open doors of the ambulance putting equip-ment away. Their job here was over; they were now needed elsewhere to help the living.

His fingers trembled suddenly as he wondered if, when his time came, he would make it into an ambulance. Or would he simply be found dead and transported in a body bag to the mortuary? He cringed as he heard in his imagination the sound of the heavy-duty polythene and the zip fastener being done up over his inert body. He could see his face was a little paler, his shirt collar done up, and his two-tone brown jacket cleaner than it ever had been. He looked clean and cared for as if someone had given him a good scrubbing and, in his mind, he heard a woman cry.

He inhaled smoke deeply, coughed sharply, and shook the morbid musings away. Through watering eyes, he saw Nick Anderson's car pull up.

Charlie suppressed the welcoming smile he was about to give to his colleague as a camera crew made a beeline towards him at the same time. He held a hand up to ward them off, and spoke sharply. 'Not now.'

'Well, when?' the female reporter asked quietly, her beau-tiful and well-practised smile full-blown. 'At least give me an estimate. Ten minutes, half an hour, all night? Waterproof mascara can only take so much before it runs a delightful black all down my face.'

Charlie repeated himself, hoicked his jacket up over his head to stop the cigarette between his teeth from getting rained on, and walked the route marked out for police personnel, crossing the neighbour's lawn to greet his colleague.

'Good to see you, Nick. How you doing?' He stepped back as Nick flung out an arm to get it in the sleeve of his leather jacket.

'I'm knackered, and can't believe I'm standing out here in the pissing rain in the middle of the night. Why am I here, Charlie?'

'It's like I said on the phone. We have a male shot through the mouth. There's no gun at the scene.'

'I meant, why was *I* called in?' Nick said sarcastically.

'Oh right.' Charlie sighed heavily. 'Ted Parry's broken his leg. Silly sod fell down some steps.'

'Pissed again, was he? I see. So you thought Nick would like an early start? No need of a day off – a bit of sleep considering he only just got back and didn't even get to bed Wednesday night. Is that it?'

'You're on standby this week, Nick. Sorry, but Naughton said to call you in.'

Nick nodded his head. 'I'll bet he did. Saves him from getting out of his nice warm bed. He'll probably give you a medal just for calling me in, Charlie. Probably shining one right now. A nice big gold one.'

'Sarky bugger when you're tired, aren't you?' Charlie mocked. 'Naughton's been and gone over an hour ago. It's him that deployed all this response. Police surgeon's been and gone as well. Naughton's notified the coroner. We're now waiting on a pathologist. He said to give him a call if you had any problems. Been treating you too soft up in the Smoke, I reckon. You used to have more stamina. You've forgotten what night work is.'

'Not forgotten, but not what I want right now. See how chirpy you are when... Great, I've just walked in bloody dog shit.'

Charlie tried not to laugh as Nick walked across the grass like a clumsy ice skater, trying to scrape his shoes as they both made their way to the house.

Crime-scene tape cordoned off the open-plan garden in front of the small modern semi. A narrow path bisected the lawn, and a forensic tent had been erected. A floodlight was angled to shine inside it and the silhouette of a person was clearly visible.

'What have they got in there?' Nick asked.

'Shoeprint,' Charlie replied. 'They're getting a cast of it now.'

A PCSO stood guard at the very outer cordon of the scene to prevent anyone getting too close to the house. She looked at Nick expectantly until he pulled out his ID.

'DI Anderson.'

She handed him a pen, the logbook was held up in front of him. He quickly scribbled his name and then started kitting up from the major incident box on the portable table beside her.

Charlie couldn't hold back his laughter as Nick pulled on a Tyvek suit. Nick huffed and puffed, struggling to pull up the long zip fastener over his bulky leather jacket, before putting overshoes onto his footwear. Bad tempered and impatient, he was finally ready for them to walk the pathway to the open front door.

Mark Steel, the crime scene manager, was coming down the stairs, his white suit softly rustling, wearing a white disposable face mask and with his unruly brown hair hidden by an elasticated white hood. His habitual humming stopped when he saw Nick and he blinked myopically from behind metal-rimmed glasses.

'Didn't know you were back,' Mark said, surprised.

'Just. And they've got me started straight away.'

The officer eyed Nick. His manner took on that of a head teacher bearing down on a loitering schoolboy. 'Gloves and face mask as well, please. You've got time. We've barely started.'

It was Steel's job to prevent contamination or destruction of evidence. If he was critical, it was tough – Charlie knew that every officer appreciated it when it came to court time. But right now, Nick was in a tetchy mood. Which was understandable, with him coming straight into a case, his first duty back. No one would be happy. Especially not at one o'clock in the morning.

'Give me a break, will you? I've just driven back from London, haven't unpacked, or had a cup of coffee. And nearly knackered my back getting into this Michelin Man gear.'

Steel sighed loudly, then disappeared outside for a few seconds and returned with gloves and mask. He waited while Nick put them on. He gave Nick the once over and nodded his approval before he walked away, humming a Christmas carol.

'For Pete's sake, Christmas songs is all I need,' Nick muttered, before turning his attention to Charlie. 'Right then. Bring me up to speed. What do we know?'

'He's a teacher. His wife's a nurse. She was on duty. I've been and seen her, and she's now staying in a colleague's home. No formal ID yet, but we found him in bed, and a photograph in the hall... It's the husband, William Shaw, up the stairs.'

'Who found him?'

'We did,' Charlie replied. 'Mrs Shaw alerted us at around ten last night when she couldn't raise her husband on the phone. He'd been getting nuisance calls, which he apparently reported to us. Anyway, a patrol car was in the vicinity. They tried to raise him on the phone, then banged on the front door. One of them went round the back and found the back door open, the house in darkness, so they went in.'

'Neighbours?'

'Uniform are getting initial accounts from them now. Also recording vehicle number plates around the area. They're seizing any CCTV images from the pub around the corner, and from the row of shops on The Hollow.'

'Any report of a gunshot?'

'Neighbours reported revving motorbikes from lads up the street. That's the only sound they heard. But the old boy two doors down says different. He reckons he heard a gun fired at about eight-thirty. Says he knows the difference between a firework and a gun going off.'

Nick nodded. 'Okay, good. So we might have a timeline.'

'He must be the sort who goes to bed early,' Charlie added. 'Mind you, there was a newspaper on the drawers. So maybe he went to bed to read.'

'And there's no chance the victim did it himself?'

Charlie frowned at him. 'I know you'd rather it was suicide, not homicide, to get you in and out, but unless he hid the gun afterwards, there's no way. We've got shoe impressions outside, and soil inside on the kitchen floor. And Steel's only just started.'

'I take it you've been up?' Nick said, nodding at the stairs.

'I have, mate, so it's all yours,' Charlie answered, leaving Nick to go up alone. He didn't need to see the body again. And Nick could do with some time on his own, to get his head in gear, to realise this was a murder investigation and not a suicide.

Charlie hoped the time away from Bath had done Nick some good, that whatever demons he carried were left behind. He'd been in a bleak place before he went, and Charlie could only speculate on the cause of his mood. As much as they were close, Nick didn't tell him what was wrong. He'd see it as a weakness to admit anything being the matter. Where matters of the heart were concerned, Charlie didn't go there. The subject was off limits. Charlie could wish all he liked, but Nick would settle down when he wanted and not when Charlie suggested. Charlie had wondered at the time if it was to do with Nick's mother, whether he had discovered her whereabouts. He was a bastard of a man to love when something was ailing him. And something big had been bothering him a year ago, before he went off to London. He never even said goodbye.

CHAPTER THREE

NICK

Upstairs, all the doors were open wide. Stepping plates had been put down on the carpets to walk on. Scene of crime investigators were concentrated in the main bedroom – recording, retrieving, extracting every possible piece of evidence. Nick waited. He stepped aside as an officer with a camcorder backed out of the room, giving Nick space to enter. Still images and video could later show what was not immediately visible at the crime scene.

The stench hit him as he stepped inside. Even through the face mask he could smell it. A large damp stain, ringed with a darker yellow, was drying on the bedsheet covering the man from the waist down. Beneath the sheet they would find the man's bowels had opened, either caused in life as the body betrayed itself in the grip of fear, or in death as the dying body simply emptied, unable to control itself.

Nick glanced around the room. There was no overturned furniture, no broken ornaments or pictures on the floor, no walls defiled by spray paint or faecal fingerprints that some sickos left as their calling card. But there was plenty of blood.

The victim's mouth showed upper teeth and lip injury, with

partly clotted blood in the oral and nasal cavities. The mucous surfaces looked slightly smoked, showing the marks from the discharge of a firearm. The brain matter blown out of the back of the head was splattered over a pale-blue velour headboard, and onto the wall above it.

Homicide by shooting through the mouth was rare. Putting the barrel of a gun into the mouth was more frequently associated with suicide. He pulled his gaze away from the body to assess the rest of the room – matching white furniture, duck-egg blue floor and soft-yellow walls, a white wicker chair between white-curtained windows with clothing laid neatly over it, marred only by the trousers on the floor. An IKEA wet dream for some, he supposed.

A book beside a folded newspaper on the bedside drawers drew his attention. He flicked it open to where a small card marked a page. The famous words 'Veni, Vidi, Vici,' jumped out at him. He wondered if the victim had read them before seeing who came to conquer him?

About to close the book, he saw printed words on the other side of the flowery card and realised it was a remembrance card – the type that came with a bouquet, or in this case a wreath – on which was written, *In memory of Ray.*

'Can we photograph this, please?' he asked.

The investigator closest gave a thumbs up. Nick then noticed small shiny patches of melted wax on the surface of the drawers, and pointed it out. 'And this. Can we keep an eye out for any used red candles? Up here or downstairs?' he added.

He gazed at the bed for more wax drips but stopped when he saw the dead eyes wide open. He stared closely as if to see who had last looked into them. But they weren't giving anything away. He wasn't a copper from a hundred years ago, when police photographed the eyes in the belief that the last image seen before death was recorded there.

He moved across the room and looked over the items on top

of the drawers: a bottle of Jo Malone, a Mitchum roll-on deodorant, a round blue bowl of hairgrips and hair ties. In the
wastepaper basket on the floor, an empty packet for Marks &
Spencer tights and a brown apple core.

He turned to one of the wardrobes and opened it. Instantly,
his stomach clenched. The scent filled his mind with a hundred
memories. He backed away from the women's clothes, and
quickly closed the door. Now wasn't the time to think of her, of
the little lavender bags hanging in the wardrobe. Now was only
for the dead man.

In the quietness of the room he heard a diesel engine
pulling up outside. He glanced out of the bedroom window and
saw a black transit van and a red Mini squeezing in among all
the police vehicles. Professor Doyle, the Home Office pathologist, levered his large body from the shiny red Mini while his
team climbed out of the van. Nick knew his own viewing time
was over.

Crossing the room to the door he heard shouting from
downstairs. Charlie's deeper voice carried over it. 'I understand,
Mrs Shaw, but I did say it wouldn't be a good idea to come here.'
Walking quickly out of the bedroom, Nick heard the woman's
voice clearly.

'I'm his wife!'

His mouth dried. His heart thumped. And for a split-second
he tried to make himself believe that the voice he heard wasn't
hers. Moving silently to the banister, he peered over and saw
the top of her dark hair and the slim shape of her shoulders. He
listened to Charlie soothing her. 'Calm down, Mrs Shaw. Let's
get you outside.'

Clearing his face of emotion, Nick walked down the stairs.
She looked up as she heard him and her eyes opened wide. She
made a move towards him, but Charlie put a restraining hand
on her elbow.

'You don't want to go up there, Mrs Shaw.'

Her eyes darted to Nick's. 'I need to see for myself what's happened. No one's telling me anything!' she said accusingly, glancing to Charlie. 'All I've been told is that William is dead, but no one's told me how!'

Nick took the last few steps towards her, his hands reaching out to offer some comfort. 'I'm sorry to tell you, the man upstairs has been—'

She wrenched herself free of Charlie and whirled past Nick at a speed too quick for either of them to stop her, the material of her nurse's uniform slipping through Nick's fingers as she raced up the stairs.

Nick stood helpless as her scream echoed down the stairwell.

Listening to her, he wished he had not come back. He wished he had stayed in London.

CHAPTER FOUR

SARAH

Sarah came out of the bathroom and heard Kathleen talking to her husband in their bedroom. 'The tea is weak. Why didn't you leave the bag in longer? Did you take Sarah a cup?'

Sarah wondered if she should cough to let them know she was on the landing. Their bedroom door was open, and she needed to pass it to get to the room she was staying in. Her hair was dripping water on their carpet. She hadn't wanted to use up all their towels, and planned to dry her hair with the one wrapped round her when she got back in her room.

'I did, and she threw it back up.'

'What! Jesus' sake, I hope she's not pregnant. That's the last thing she needs right now. Why didn't you call me, instead of letting her cope on her own?'

'She's all right, Kathleen. She's in the shower now. And a baby is exactly what she might be hoping for. She's lost William. Who else does she have? No one.'

'She has me! And you. A baby would only complicate her life. She needs time to get over this, never mind taking care of a baby.'

Sarah gave a silent gasp. Goosebumps sprang up over her bare shoulders and arms. The possessiveness in Kathleen's voice... It shocked her. They were talking about her like they knew her. She and Kathleen were work colleagues. Kathleen didn't know her, not intimately, and not even well, despite taking Sarah into her home.

Sarah had only met Kathleen's husband Joe half an hour ago. When she was sick in front of him, he let her know where the bathroom was, and said he'd fetch her some clean clothes.

She stiffened as she heard a light scraping of metal – the curtains drawing back – followed by a loud huff. 'Who was that on the phone? You let it ring long enough.'

'The police. They're coming to collect Sarah. They need a formal identification. And something about doing an inventory. See if anything's gone.'

'Jesus' sake, of course something's gone. William!'

'You know what I mean. A burglary or something.'

'I know exactly what you mean, but this was no burglary. William was killed by whoever's been phoning him.'

Joe's reply was terse. 'You don't know that. Don't go jumping to conclusions. Sarah will have enough to deal with, without you giving opinions.'

'I always put her first. I'd do anything for her.'

'Keep your voice down,' Joe hissed in a fierce whisper. 'She'll hear you.'

'I should have put fresh sheets on her bed,' Kathleen replied.

Joe sighed wearily. 'They are fresh, Kathleen. You changed them a week ago.'

Then Sarah saw the door close. Had Joe sensed she was there?

She tiptoed back to her temporary room, quietly shutting the bedroom door behind her, hoping no one would knock on it for at least five minutes. She needed a moment alone. Kathleen's words had stung.

A baby would only complicate her life.

Sarah wasn't pregnant, but Joe was right. A baby was exactly what she would have wanted right now. At thirty she had been made a widow. All she had left of her husband was his last name.

She spotted the clean clothes on the bed that Joe had left out for her to wear, and wondered whose bedroom she was in. In the early hours of the morning she hadn't noticed her surroundings, but now she was noticing everything. The peach walls, beige carpet, pine wardrobe and matching drawers. A large dolphin poster was on one wall. Indiana Jones on another. A small bookcase was packed with children's stories. The top shelf held all sorts of treasures: a green teddy with a shamrock woven on its chest, a blue jewellery box, open and showing its ballerina, and a large pebble, smooth, white and simple.

On the small dressing table was a wooden hairbrush, with dark hairs clinging to the bristles. The room belonged to a girl. A girl who liked dolphins and ballerinas.

She tried to recall if Kathleen ever mentioned her family. She would have struggled to remember Joe's name if Kathleen hadn't said it to her in the car after they left the hospital.

I've let Joe know I'm bringing you home. He's a great one for calming things.

Sarah shouldn't be here. Last night she hadn't been able to think. It was the easier option to just go with Kathleen. What else was she to do? The only clothes she had with her was the uniform she wore to work, now stained with vomit. In her workbag she had a spare toothbrush, some deodorant, a hairbrush, but no clean underwear. Without access to her home to get some of her things, her other option was on hold.

She had her debit card with her and could book a hotel, but

Kathleen had given Sergeant Bowden this address where the police could contact her. She was in a dilemma about what to do. She was Kathleen's manager, and she knew nothing about her personal life. She didn't even know if Kathleen had a daughter. Or a granddaughter for that matter. Kathleen was in her fifties. The room might be for an occasional stay. The décor suggested it had been a while since the paint went on the walls. The contents of the bookcase perhaps just a few random things brought out from the attic. Or the belongings of a grown-up daughter that were never moved from the room.

The situation was awkward. Kathleen clearly felt she had a place in Sarah's life. Which, thinking about it, was Sarah's fault. She should have sorted out how she was going to travel to work before selling Kathleen her car, and then she wouldn't have needed to accept Kathleen's offer of lifts when working the same shift. That could easily have led Kathleen to think they were more than colleagues. Sarah shouldn't have continued accepting lifts after she was married – her new home was much closer to the hospital. There was no need for her to have climbed into her old car for the occasional lift. She walked the mile and a half, there and back, on the days Kathleen was on different shifts or on days off.

But a natural friendship didn't grow between them. It was polite chit-chat to pass the time on the way to work. Sarah shared very little of her personal life, and then only to answer harmless questions about her impending wedding – the style of dress she was wearing, whether she was having a honeymoon. The most she ever revealed was last night when she told Kathleen about the phone calls to William. In the time she'd known her there'd been only one occasion where she felt uncomfortable with her – when she gave her negative opinion on Sarah getting married. Should that have alerted her to a worrying trait in Kathleen's character?

Sarah closed her eyes and breathed in deeply, her mind

returning to a bigger problem. Her thoughts had only wandered briefly. Seeing Nick last night had been a shock. When he transferred to work in London she thought she would never see him again. How was this meant to go now? Would he pull out of the investigation knowing it was Sarah's husband who was found dead? There surely would be rules against him being involved. They had dated for two years and, while not strictly living together, were with each other every day. If Sarah had not ended the relationship she might have married him. It hurt to think about how she finished it, to remember the shock on his face. She had never seen him look like that. The stiffness in his frame when he walked away had shown he was wounded. She felt sure he would not have forgiven her for that. But better that than tell him the truth.

Weary, she sat down on the bed and dressed in the clothes Joe had left for her. She couldn't stay in hiding forever.

When she arrived in the kitchen, Kathleen tutted as she stared at the grey jogging bottoms trailing over Sarah's bare feet. 'There are clothes in the wardrobe that will fit you better. I'll find something out when you've had breakfast.'

Sarah sat at the kitchen table. She didn't mind that the top or bottoms were too big. They were warm and comfortable.

'Joe said you were sick,' Kathleen remarked. She set a mug of tea down in front of Sarah. 'You can have coffee if you prefer?'

Kathleen was fishing, but Sarah wasn't going to be drawn. 'Thank you. Tea's perfect.'

'Did you sleep all right?'

Sarah nodded. 'I must have, because I woke when Joe brought me in some tea. Did I dream it? Or was it Joe who put me to bed?'

'It was Joe. You were in shock. He helped get you out of the car, and put a glass of brandy in your hand. But you just stood there until Joe lifted the glass to your lips. Then he put you to bed, fully clothed.'

Sarah sipped the tea. 'Joe said the police are coming to collect me.'

Kathleen nodded. 'Would you like me to come with you?'

Sarah shook her head. 'No. But thank you. After this... once this is done, I'll sort something out. Would it be all right if I come back here just until then? I need some things from home, but I think the police will have to collect them.'

Sarah didn't want to go near her house, even if allowed. Images kept playing in her mind. The blood on the sheets. His open eyes. *The smell of the room.* So different to how she left it when she went to work. She couldn't be on her own just yet. She needed to be around people for now. There was a potential killer at large, who may or may not want her dead too. She should be worried about this.

Kathleen's eyes turned glassy, signalling she was close to tears. Her voice was intense, not allowing Sarah to look away. 'Sarah, you need to stay here with me and Joe until the police know what's happened. This is your home for as long as you need. And Joe and I will be your family.'

Kathleen's reaction bothered Sarah. It was overly emotional. It was making her wonder about the bedroom. She noted Kathleen didn't say who the clothes belonged to in the wardrobe. Was there something more? Had her daughter become estranged from her? Had a daughter been taken away from her? Looking at Kathleen now, it was possible to think that.

Sarah was concerned she was being harsh. After all her head was all over the place. Kathleen was probably just lonely, and turned weepy-eyed at other people's plights. She might be one of those people who felt an immediate involvement and wanted to help. She was religious. Sarah had spotted a crucifix and a holy water font by the front door. At work, Kathleen couldn't do enough for the patients.

The doorbell rang and Sarah stood up. 'I'll see you later then.'

Kathleen nodded. 'That you will. I'll be here when you get back. So don't you worry about a thing.'

CHAPTER FIVE

NICK

The building assigned to MCIT, also called 'Brunel', was in Kenneth Steele House Police Station in Bristol. When Nick joined the police, his base was in Bath, and back then the city had a large police station and a custody suite. Now it had a front office desk in Manvers Street that closed in the evenings, and a yellow phone outside on the wall for out of hours use in case a member of the public needed to call the police. Developing technology meant a reliance on the public reporting non-urgent problems online instead of at a police counter. If Bath still had a police station, the Major Incident Room could have been set up there to save on the ten and a half mile drive back and forth from one city to the other, and would also have provided Nick an opportunity to go home and change.

He emptied sudsy water and washed the sink clean with his hands. He had given himself a strip wash, not only removing the imagined smells of the crime scene, but also the real smells of the sweat and grime of London. He had neither showered nor changed since leaving his rented rooms for the last time and his skin was beginning to feel uncomfortable. And in all his planning he hadn't given thought to practicalities such as hygiene and clean clothes when he dumped his suitcases at his flat with his suits in them.

Nick had spent an hour with the SIO and other senior managers to talk through the investigative strategy, and Superintendent Naughton had not looked one bit impressed with his deputy. His first appearance with his superior and he looked not only knackered, but unprofessional as well. The leather jacket was not right for the deputy senior investigating officer.

Nick would be managing the logistics of the investigation and implementing the investigative strategy, but at this first meeting he'd been struck dumb, leaving it to others to review the initial response, and discuss objectives, resources and forensic strategy. Elimination enquiries. Press releases. The whole shebang... All he'd done was stand quietly and watch the proceedings, making no contribution.

His sodden denim shirt lay on the floor, and he wished he had persevered with paper towels from the plastic box on the wall instead of using his shirt to dry himself. The clean shirt that Charlie had loaned him was a shade too bright and a shade too tight, but he now had no other choice than to wear it.

As he stared at himself in the mirror his appearance became unimportant. His eyes no longer hid what he was really feeling. Anguish and anger had darkened them to an even deeper blue. Why and when had Sarah married someone else?

As he was driving the motorway, all the pretence of his reasons for leaving London were left behind. It had nothing to do with his old job waiting for him here in Somerset, or that he never intended staying in London any longer than he had; it was because this was where *she* lived. He had dreamed their reunion down to the last detail, thinking through what he would say to her. But she had gone and put a husband in their way. A husband who was now dead.

The silver angel in his pocket mocked him cruelly. His pathetic hopes had blinded him so completely that any thought of her not regretting their break-up had never entered his head. How stupidly naive he was. He was thirty-five years old with a degree in psychology, and he still hadn't learned how to read people.

He pulled the key ring out now – a pure silver angel that spread only one wing. She'd given it to him, along with a key to let himself in if she was not home. He'd thrown it against the pavement after she said her piece, after taking off the key to give back to her, and the other wing had broken off. The broken angel epitomised what he had felt. She had crippled him and left him to wonder where it had all gone wrong.

Then yesterday he discovered why. She had met someone else.

An emptiness gnawed at his stomach, causing a dull pain, which had more to do with knowing what he had done than the fact he had nothing to eat in last twenty-four hours. Charlie could be a problem he hadn't factored in. With anyone else he could bluff his way into or out of a situation, but Charlie had known him since he was boy. He was usually the first to notice if something was up. Nick had to be doubly careful – to keep reminding himself he had never lied to Charlie – so Charlie wouldn't be suspicious of anything.

He took another look in the mirror and was disconcerted to see the deceit in his eyes staring back at him. He needed to disguise himself from ever showing that look. He needed to relax. No one knew Sarah was the reason he came back to Bath. Charlie had never even met her. No one knew about him and Sarah. Which now gave rise to a negative feeling Nick had never thought before.

Had she been embarrassed to be seen with him?

Was he someone she'd just liked to bed but who she didn't really see in her future for the long-term? Their dates were always about being alone together, which he never minded at the time, but now he questioned was it a sign that she was trying to keep the two of them a secret? He had convinced himself that she loved him. Had he misread other feelings and convinced himself of a happy relationship that was never there?

He had never seen her as heartless. But she had slain him without so much as a tear on her face. While he stared down at a broken key ring; she stood there silent waiting for him to go. How could he have misread two years?

He felt a deepening despair. What he was doing might all be for nothing if she still didn't care. He took a deep breath and gave himself a stern lecture. It was his decision to come back, in spite of what she had done, he needed to behave like a man. Not some snot-nosed teenager. He needed to behave like a police officer and not forget this advantage would keep him one step ahead of the rest of the team.

Charlie would grieve if he could see into Nick's thoughts. He remembered the time he first became interested in becoming a police officer. It was after Charlie visited his school. Charlie was wearing his uniform. While other pupils stared at him curiously, Nick already knew him by then; he'd been the policeman who first came to Nick's home when his mother disappeared. He'd become a regular visitor in the following few years, and the thing Nick remembered most back then, was Charlie had red fiery hair. Not like it was now, dulled to a yellowish copper.

A pupil sat crossed-legged beside Nick stuck her hand up in the air and asked Charlie if he thought it was sneaky that some police officers got to wear their own clothes. Because the 'bad-dies' won't know who they are.

Charlie softly laughed, but never really gave a proper answer. Instead he presented an image of what Nick would like to be. Nick hung on his every word. It became his mantra while kneeling at his bed in forgo of his nightly prayers

"The police are not just there to catch the criminals, they're there to protect the law-abiding people as well. The police are someone who want to help. They understand people even when those people do wrong. The police are someone you can trust."

Nick scoffed at the idealism of youth, while trying to ignore Charlie's voice in his head.

CHAPTER SIX

CHARLIE

Charlie balefully eyed the black clouds. He hated the rain. He was thinking about last night, when Nick got Mrs Shaw down the stairs. Then, to top it all, just when the house couldn't get any more disrupted, the pathologist's team had piled in, carting truckloads of stuff into the small hallway. Nick carried her out into the rain. Her face was as white as porcelain as the rain splashed off her cheeks. The only bright spot was finding out she had not come to the house alone. They were able to put her into the care of a colleague and have her taken away from the scene.

With a scene guard in place, she should never have been able to get into the house and see her husband dead. But it wasn't really the PCSO's fault. Mrs Shaw had snuck under the scene tape while the officer was distracted with a nosy member of the public. It was Charlie's fault. He should have left the police officer who accompanied him to the hospital with her until a family liaison officer could be found, so as not to leave her in limbo like that.

He fished out his cigarettes and lighter and offered them to

Nick as the man joined him. 'Here, it'll be easier if you light it yourself.'

Nick shook his head. 'Given up.'

'Glad to hear it,' Charlie said heartily, taking a step back so Nick wouldn't be tempted by the smell. His eyes screwed shut as wind blew the smoke back in his own face. It was too late for him to do the same. The damage had been done long ago.

The aroma of warm pastry and sausage meat tickled Charlie's nostrils as Nick lifted the cardboard lid. He held the box towards Charlie and made a face at the small piece of sausage roll Charlie broke off. Charlie wished he were hungrier. His shoulder blades and hip bones were jutting out, his ribcage resembling a washboard. He nibbled slowly while watching Nick tuck in.

'Everything okay in the flat?' he asked him.

'Didn't get a chance to see, did I? Turned on the lights, dumped my cases, then you phoned me.'

'Got back late, didn't you? Thought you'd have left London yesterday morning.'

'Wanted to avoid the traffic, and sober up before I drove.'

'What time did your farewell party end?'

'About five,' Nick replied, then added, 'yesterday morning.'

'No wonder you look terrible. So what did you do with yourself for the rest of the day?'

Nick's shrug was dismissive. 'What is this? Twenty questions? I grabbed a couple of hours' sleep. I said goodbye to a few people. Emptied my locker. What else?'

Silence resumed as Nick carried on eating. This was their habit of old. A snatched five minutes eating and smoking out in the cold. With half the sausage roll left, Nick was ready to talk.

'So, how did it go?'

Charlie pulled a face. 'The wife made it easy, probably because she's a nurse – knew why she couldn't touch the body.

The mother, less so. Wanted to go in and hold her son. Thankfully they'd covered the bottom half of his face. She was able to tell us that he had a scar down the inside of his left arm from an accident with a kettle when he was a child. But she recognised him anyway.'

Charlie folded his arms in an effort to keep out the biting cold, and saw Nick do the same as a gust of air swept in and found them in the sheltered area under the stone steps by the side of the building. The green shirt he had loaned Nick was riding up and Charlie watched him tugging it down impatiently.

'This shirt's going to drive me mad,' he grumbled.

Charlie stared at him for a second. The expression in his eyes seemed remote. 'Everything all right, Nick?'

Nick raised his eyebrow. 'Yes. Why shouldn't it be?'

Charlie shrugged. 'You seem a bit het up, that's all.'

'I'm knackered, what do you expect?' he replied huffily.

'Hungover more like,' Charlie mumbled. He stubbed his cigarette out on the sole of his shoe and out of habit pocketed the butt until he found somewhere to dispose of it.

Nick, busy closing the cardboard box, sounded amused. 'Charlie, I don't get hangovers. I get a set of symptoms as a consequence of drinking too much. Or at least that's what the doctor told me.'

Charlie walked behind him to the door. 'Bollocks. You just made that up.'

Nick glanced back and held his gaze. 'Truth, Charlie. I never lie.'

Charlie knew that to be true, but he wasn't sure right now if it was still the case. He wasn't going to point out that there was a question mark in Nick's story about what time he left London, because Nick would get annoyed. But Charlie didn't believe that Nick waited the whole day before driving back to Bath when, if he'd not been on call last night, he would be starting

work today. So getting back after midnight didn't make a whole
lot of sense.

Charlie wished he could get inside Nick's head to know
what he was thinking, because his answers were being delivered
piecemeal. This was probably not the right time to keep trying.
He'd give it a rest, choose a better moment, and now change the
subject.

'Have you been in contact with your father?'

Nick eyed him with intense surprise. His withering tone
conveyed disappointment. 'Seriously. We're not going down
that route, are we, Charlie?'

Charlie shrugged. 'I was just wondering. That's all.'

'Well, don't, Charlie. My feelings haven't changed. You
haven't forgotten what he was like? He nearly even had you on
your knees praying.'

Charlie gave a flippant response. 'It weren't all bad. I always
felt kinda holy when I left your house.'

Nick scowled, and Charlie was unsurprised. He couldn't
say he blamed Nick his feelings. Charlie had been contemp-
tuous of the man's inadequate parenting from the moment he
met him; the Bible, the only book he ever read, and his only
resource for teaching and nurturing a young boy through life. It
had been tough for Nick living with a man so short-sighted who
believed life lessons were better learned if simple pleasures
were denied at an early age. Like a full stomach, carpet on a
floor, a warm bed.

It was a wonder Nick turned out the way he did. Charlie
had known from the first day Nick walked through the station
doors more than a decade ago he would quickly rise through the
ranks. Fresh out of university he had it in him, and Charlie had
been chuffed to bits.

Nick tugged at the shirt again. 'Why have you got to have
such a short body?'

Charlie tutted. 'You're looking a damn sight better than

yesterday. And that shirt suits you – you look the business, that's all I can say,' Charlie said in a droll tone.

Nick gaped at him. 'You taking the mick? I look like a garden gnome.'

'No, you don't! It brings out the colour in your eyes. Makes your posture look straight and all.'

Nick self-consciously patted himself, bringing his shoulders back so that buttons strained against buttonholes. He glanced sideways and saw Charlie's shoulders shaking with mirth. 'Bastard,' he said, trying to stop his lips grinning back.

Charlie laughed loudly, his face breaking into a dozen creases. 'I know. Got you going though, didn't I? Just bung your jacket on and it'll be fine.'

Charlie was elated. He preferred to jeer him than talk serious. That was how they behaved towards each other. How it used to be.

He steered past him to hold open the door, carrying on with the banter. 'Come on then, Pinocchio, mind you don't hit your nose on the way in.'

To which Nick threw back a response that was music to Charlie's ears. 'Sod off, Bowlegs. You're getting on my nerves.'

As he climbed the short flight of stairs, Charlie felt smugly happy that Nick remembered the nickname he gave him. *Bowlegs.* Everyone else just called him Bowden.

CHAPTER SEVEN

SARAH

Sarah flopped into the chair with a weary sigh, which was enough encouragement to Kathleen to place a bowl of food down in front of her.

'You're exhausted. You're running on empty. It's only soup and bread. So let's have no argument. Just eat it,' Kathleen said in a firm tone.

Sarah did as she was told and picked up the soup spoon. She nibbled a corner of the bread and placed it back down.

'You need to eat!' Kathleen admonished.

Sarah shook her head. 'I have no appetite, I'm sorry. William is dead and all I can do is think about that.'

Kathleen dropped onto the chair beside her. She draped her arm gently over Sarah's shoulder. 'I know that, my darling. What else could you do but think of that? It's a massive shock. Anything I can do to help, just say.'

Sarah wished Joe was there, but he had gone to work by the time she returned from the mortuary. She was greeted by Kathleen, who didn't ask how it went, or how William had died, as she was more interested in showing Sarah the clothes she had dug out – T-shirts and jeans and hoodies from the wardrobe – that would fit Sarah, but only just.

Sarah would rather have just had cup of tea, and then gone for a lie-down. The mortuary had been all that she had expected, but made more difficult with William's mother there. They wanted two people to separately identify the body, which made it seem somehow worse that he had to be inspected twice to be sure that it was him. She would go and see her in-laws in the next day or so. Though she hardly knew them, it would be the expected thing to do.

She sighed inwardly. Kathleen's close proximity was making her uncomfortable. She had the feeling that Kathleen would like nothing more than for Sarah to turn and cry in her arms. Despite what had happened, Sarah's feelings were private. What she needed was for Kathleen to give her some space. She felt out of kilter already, and the offer of soup while it was still only morning made things feel even more abnormal.

She wouldn't ask about the bedroom, she decided, or about the clothes she'd been offered. Instinct was telling her to put up a barrier. During the conversation she overheard earlier, Joe's words disturbed her.

Who else does she have? No one.

Where did Joe get his information? It could only have been from Kathleen. But it was the way he said it that disturbed her most, as if Sarah was a familiar topic in this household. *She's lost William*, Joe had said.

As if he knew her and knew William.

William's name had tripped off his tongue like it was familiar, as if he was used to saying it out loud. Kathleen must have talked a lot about her for Joe to speak like that. And a lot of it was made up.

Sarah had other people in her life. She had William's parents, and she had her sister-in-law. Not that she knew them well, but she was not alone with no one, the way Joe seemed to think. Admittedly, she couldn't think of a single soul nearby who she could go and stay with, but that was through choice to not have many friends.

She was relieved when Kathleen rose from the table to answer her phone. Then, a moment later, she had to hide her agitation at hearing Kathleen arranging time off from work – to look after *her*. She was taking tonight off and tomorrow, and thanking the person on the phone for their help.

She beamed at Sarah when the call ended. 'Well, that was kind of them. They're letting me take compassionate leave, even though I'd offered to take annual leave.'

Sarah didn't know how to answer. She was shocked, frankly. Kathleen wasn't a relative or Sarah's carer. So why was she doing this?

'I think I'll go out,' Sarah managed to say. 'I need to get some things. Toiletries and underwear.'

'We can go to Asda,' Kathleen suggested quickly. 'They'll have everything. We'll pick something nice up for tea while we're there. You could do with a nice meal.'

Sarah could feel her scalp tightening. Kathleen's voice had got loud, bouncing off the kitchen walls. Was she always this excitable? Acting this swiftly, over nothing? Or was Sarah causing it just by being there? Sarah was going to lose her patience soon. Perhaps staying with Kathleen had been a mistake.

Kathleen's face got livelier as she delivered her exclamation. 'I have a better idea. We'll have fish and chips instead. We'll stop on the way home. There's a nice chip shop in Keynsham.'

Sarah was overwrought. The fuss was like a stylus on a scratched record. She was seeing Kathleen in a different light. The plaintive tone in her voice to Joe this morning had not gone unnoticed. Now this exuberant suggestion that they pop along to Asda, get fish and chips, and have something nice for tea was doing Sarah's head in. What was going on in Kathleen's head? She was behaving as if they were embarking on a day out.

Sarah did what she did best when she didn't want to give in – she sat silently until her silence was noticed. And when it was, Kathleen pulled a different face. A mixture of embarrassment and remorse, along with a conciliatory tone. 'Sorry, Sarah. I'm being over the top as always. I don't know how to behave with what's happened.'

Sarah exhaled slowly, trying to find the right words, to be tactful. 'If it helps, I don't know how to behave either. From what I've witnessed, seeing other wives losing their husbands, like the woman last night clutching her husband's jumper to her face, I should be sobbing, but I'm not. So what does that say about me? I can't feel anything.'

Sarah wondered if that's why she was finding Kathleen too much because of her own emotional state. Her nerves being sensitive to minor irritations like Kathleen's suggestions, while not able to feel what had happened to William.

Kathleen shook her head. 'You're numb, because you're in shock. Trust me, Sarah, you will feel it. And then you'll wish for this numbness again.'

Sarah held her gaze. 'Why did you think it was too soon?'

Her face went red, and she blustered a little. 'I don't recall saying that.'

Sarah was quick to reassure her. 'I'm not annoyed, Kathleen. You said it to me in the car a few months ago, after I told you I was getting married. I'm interested in why you thought it.'

Kathleen briefly closed her eyes as if to avoid Sarah's gaze. Then she spoke, a little formally, as if a little cross with Sarah. 'I suppose it's because I was used to seeing him as someone else. It felt confusing to see him with you. But you know that, don't you, Sarah?'

Sarah nodded, though she wasn't sure that was the sole reason for Kathleen's reservation. She sensed it went deeper. In the few hours she had been there, it seemed to Sarah that she had lost a husband and Kathleen had gained a project.

Sarah wondered what Kathleen would think if she knew the detective who was investigating the case was Sarah's old boyfriend. She might think it was karma. Because what were the chances of that happening – of Nick returning home and investigating the death of William. Sarah never would have imagined that she would have to face him and explain why she had married someone else. Or that after only a few months of marriage she'd be a widow.

CHAPTER EIGHT

NICK

Nick stared at the sea of faces in the Major Incident Room. Most of them he knew – or at least they were familiar. Every available chair was taken. The people standing at the back were at the earlier meeting – the Office Manager, House-to-House Team Leader, Interview Coordinator, and Mark Steel, the crime scene manager. On either side of the room, the Investigative Team Leaders and Community Awareness Specialists. A homicide brought together a large group of professionals to work together in a temporary team. The SIO needed a high level of management ability. But as Superintendent Naughton was focusing on strategic issues and was presently elsewhere, it fell to Nick to now lead the team.

'Okay, let's begin. For those who don't me, my name's Nick Anderson. I'm the Deputy SIO on this case.'

'Welcome back, Nick. It's hard to believe you've been gone a year.'

Nick glanced at the sergeant. Paul Robson was sitting right at the front, only feet away from where Nick was standing. So close that Nick hadn't noticed him.

'When you've time, I'm sure we all look forward to hearing whether you think our squad compares favourably?'

At the earlier meeting with Superintendent Naughton, Nick had been warned to be prepared for a sore ego. Paul Robson had hoped to step in as Acting Deputy SIO, as he was halfway through the development programme in major crime investigation. Nick eyed the man and wished he liked him better. Outwardly, Robson had all the right attributes to make a good colleague: he was confident and able. But Nick knew he was a palm presser and this made him wary of the man's true motives. Or maybe it was simply the clickety-clack sound of his hobnailed shoes, reminding Nick of his father.

Nick could have told him that this squad performed far more efficiently, but he wasn't going to stroke his ego. He had just spent the last year working with officers in London and saw crimes there that he couldn't imagine happening in their cities. Bath was safe, and Bristol had a twenty-five per cent lower crime rate this year. For which Robson should be thankful.

Instead he said, 'Good to see you, Paul. I look forward to that chat.'

He saw the man's nostrils briefly flare, but Paul Robson would be the least of his worries. Nick was putting his career on the line by keeping quiet about his past involvement with Sarah. This investigation could not fail, so Paul needed to get over his sulk and let Nick do his job.

DC Issy Banks broke the slight tension as she pushed through to the front shaking her head, mouth open in mock astonishment. 'My God, what did they do to you? Jesus, Nick, have you completely lost your sense of style? What's with the shirt?'

Nick was grateful for her outburst. He knew she had a soft spot for him. 'Charlie loaned it to me. He can't help it if he's colour-blind.'

''Ere, enough of that,' the man himself said as he walked

into the room and joined the group. 'I loaned you that out of the goodness of my heart. It suits *me*.'

'I'm sure it does, Charlie,' Nick softly jeered. 'With your hair, this shirt and a white tie, all we need is a St Patrick's parade and you could go as a flag.'

Officers laughed. Even Robson had a bit of a smile on his face.

Nick brought them back to attention. 'Okay. Let's quieten down now, please. Detective Sergeant Bowden will be giving you the brief about the victim.'

Charlie was ready and began straight away. 'The victim's name is William Shaw. Aged forty-three, married, no children. Profession – teacher. He was found shot dead in his bed at ten thirty-five last night by a constable. His wife, Sarah Shaw, rang the police when she couldn't raise her husband on the phone. She's a nurse and was working a night shift. Initially she was told her husband was probably asleep and couldn't hear the phone ringing, but then she said that her husband had been getting strange phone calls. William Shaw reported these calls to the police only the day before yesterday, along with something else, which the wife didn't mention. William Shaw received two anonymous letters, posted through his front door.'

Charlie opened a blue folder and pulled out two plastic sleeves, each holding a separate sheet of white paper. He held them up for the team to see. Each message was easy to read – the font size was large and in capitals. He read them aloud: 'I KNOW IT WAS YOU. I KNOW WHAT YOU DID.'

Charlie gave it a moment, then continued. 'There was no sign of a forced entry. The house was in darkness when uniform entered.'

'So not a burglary gone wrong,' Issy Banks stated.

'We have no reason to think it was that. Nothing in the house looked disturbed. An inventory will be done and Mrs Shaw will help with that. Shoeprints were found quite close to the downstairs front window on the little front garden, so we may have something with that. Mud was also found on the kitchen floor.' Charlie looked over at Nick. 'That's about it from me.'

Nick had been calculating the number of actions that the database indexers would have waiting for them. The trawl for information that busied the officers in the first days of any investigation. The names of neighbours, taken last night, would now be in the system, and all information collected would have to be checked. Reported times that witnesses saw or heard things couldn't just be rubber-stamped – they had to be double-checked. Before the advent of BBC iPlayer and Netflix, people mostly knew the time based on when they watched a programme. They remembered if they got interrupted watching *Corrie*, *Emmerdale* or *EastEnders*. But it was different nowadays. Fewer people were wearing watches and were more likely to get out a mobile phone and video a crime rather than note the time. The team would be using the Home Office Large Major Enquiry System to run this investigation, but not every piece of information would be in it, otherwise Nick would not be standing there right now.

Nick gave the team his input: 'This is a murder investigation. But what type of homicide is it? Did it happen in the course of another crime? Robbery or burglary, as Issy suggested. Revenge? Jealousy? It happened indoors so the victim and offender might have known each other. The method of attack – shooting. Did the offender choose the location to minimise disturbance and to avoid the attack being witnessed?

'The carrying of a weapon to the scene speaks of a planned killing. And, as most of you know, those who plan to kill generate less material to connect them to the crime. So we need to identify suspects as quickly as possible. How did the offender get to the scene and how did the offender leave? Car, public transport, on foot?

'And what of the victim? We need to know about him. His lifestyle. Hobbies, habits, routines. We need to know what it is he might have done to anger the killer. Was he targeted? Are the telephone calls and letters a link between the offender and victim? The messages are interesting, possibly blackmail. We need to keep a lid on that.

'This investigation will gain a high level of interest. The media will be all over it. This man was a schoolteacher. He might have taught some of you or your children. We do our job and we work hard at finding the person responsible. Every effort counts. Please remember that. Okay everyone, thank you for your attention. The time of the next briefing will be given shortly. See your managers in the meantime to discuss your tasks.'

He turned to Issy. 'Issy, I hear you volunteered to be FLO. Thanks for that. Charlie and I will be seeing Mrs Shaw later today, if you can pass that on, please?'

'Will do,' she said, smiling at him warmly, perhaps for a little too long.

Nick hoped she had found a boyfriend while he was away, and wouldn't be still casting an eye at him. He liked Issy, and nearly had something with her once, but that's as far as it went.

He had to hope that Sarah didn't say anything, that she would realise it was best not to mention their relationship to anyone. He could recuse himself. He had good reasons for not being the deputy lead on this case. And he would have done that if it was a straightforward *man is murdered – police hunt murderer* kind of case. But he couldn't afford not to stay on this one. It was probably going to be the most difficult case of his life. The better decision would be to come clean with Sarah. But that was fraught with difficulty, without knowing what she might do. The complication had created a conflict within him... he needed to protect Sarah, and simultaneously hide his feelings from her and his reasons for being involved. He had no

other choice. He made his bed when he crossed the line yesterday. He had realised that when he was outside with Charlie.
The man was like a bloodhound. He was risking a lot if he
failed to find a suspect. The stakes were high.

To win he had to outwit the hunters.

CHAPTER NINE

SARAH

Sarah felt her hair being stroked and opened her eyes in alarm. *What the hell?* Kathleen was beside her with a hairbrush in her hand. Sarah jumped from the bed, shocked. And was even more unnerved when Kathleen stared at the knickers she was wearing. Plain cotton with a print of tiny pink and blue birds, which she borrowed from an underwear drawer after showering. They hadn't gone to Asda to buy new ones because Sarah said she needed to lie down instead.

Sarah was mortified. She should have asked first. Underwear was so personal. 'I'll replace them with some new ones when I can,' she offered.

Kathleen sat still and quiet, her behaviour eerie. Her silence was making Sarah uneasy. Sarah grabbed Joe's tracksuit bottoms and quickly pulled them on. She was slipping her shoes on when Kathleen stilled her.

'There's a policewoman downstairs waiting to see you.'

'What—?'

'She'll want to know about William, I dare say. They'll want to know why he was getting calls,' she added grimly.

'Do you think so... I mean—? Do you think that's the reason he's dead?'

Kathleen shrugged. 'I imagine so. You said he was on edge. People do get strange calls sometimes, but most don't go to the police about them. William might not have told you everything. He might have known who was calling and had something to hide.' She gazed hard at Sarah. 'You'd better go and see what she wants.'

Her tone threw Sarah. Her warmth withdrawn. Perhaps she was beginning to view the situation in her home as a nuisance. Sarah usually felt the need to fill in the gaps that cropped up in awkward conversations. She had done so on many occasions during conversations with patients and doctors, patients and relatives, when something needed to be said. But she could find no right words to squeeze out now, and was left to say lamely, 'I was never there when the calls came. He was on his own when he got the phone calls.'

Kathleen raised an eyebrow. 'Well, it seems to me, then, that the person knew the best time to ring.'

Sarah waited for her to continue. That little cross tone had come back to her voice. Why was Kathleen cross? Was it because Sarah hadn't fallen in with her plans? The tone she had used with Joe showed that she was a bit of a bully. Is that what she was trying to do now with Sarah? Bully her? She'd made her views about William known already. Was she now picking the marriage apart?

It was a startling remark from Kathleen, that William might not have told her everything. Was she trying to make Sarah feel she didn't know her husband? Sarah was already aware that he hadn't communicated his concerns. She didn't need Kathleen reminding her. She didn't know what to make of it. Kathleen was an enigma. One minute kind, the next minute blunt. Sarah didn't know where she was with her or how she should respond. If she wasn't so aware that people would find it strange, she'd risk being on her own and go and stay in a hotel. But then she'd have to face Nick alone.

Leaving her in the room, Sarah made her way downstairs. She'd had enough of Kathleen.

The woman waiting for her in the sitting room introduced herself. 'Hello, Mrs Shaw. I'm Issy Banks. I'm a detective constable and also a family liaison officer. My role is to be here for you during this investigation, talk you through anything you don't understand, and keep you posted on any updates. Which is all well and good, but of course I wouldn't be here if this wasn't such a terrible time. I'm so sorry for your loss.'

'Thank you, and please call me Sarah.'

'I will. And please call me Issy.'

Sarah invited her to sit down, and hoped the pretty police officer wasn't going to be there for long, or that she was intending to stay with Sarah from now until the end of the investigation. Sarah didn't require a family liaison officer. Her husband had been murdered. He would have a post-mortem. The coroner would be involved. What more did she need to know, other than when a suspect was arrested? The police would let her know if that happened regardless.

She knew enough to know a FLO was there to support the family through the investigation, and gather information about the person who died. Sarah didn't want to talk about William to a stranger. She would have little to tell. Her husband had been a secondary school teacher, he liked to read in the evenings, he liked walks in the countryside. He'd enjoyed her companionship, but sometimes preferred being alone. He enjoyed sex with her, but was not needy of physical contact once the act was over. He was considerate of her privacy when bathing and dressing, always polite and respectful, and never asked her what she was thinking. She would let Issy talk, though, about why she was there.

Issy took a form out of her bag, and a pen from her jacket.

'I'm just going to jot down your details if I may. Full name, age, contact phone number, your job. That type of thing.'

'Yes, of course.'

She answered all the questions and Issy put the form away.

'I'm part of the investigative team, and my work is about helping to get justice for your husband, and any information you can give is essential to that process. It's important that you don't speak directly to the media, and let us handle them. I'll liaise with other family members, and let them know that as well. What I'd like to know is, what support do you need? I can put you in touch with Victim Support.'

Sarah shook her head. 'I'm not ready for that. I need to process everything on my own first.'

'Understandable. Are you getting support from family and friends?'

Sarah didn't feel it was necessary to voice her qualms about her present situation, or talk about her immediate plans. She hadn't decided what to do yet. Should she take Kathleen up on her offer to stay another night? She was so tired, it might be easier. She needed to think about it. She did not want to be in this house. She was with strangers because her own home was a crime scene, but she didn't have to put up with it. She had somewhere else she could stay. The flat she owned before she married William. It was still hers to do with what she wanted. The only problem was the keys weren't in her handbag with her new house keys, but in the pocket of the coat she was wearing when she locked it for the last time. She'd been thinking to sell it with getting married. She just needed to ask Issy if she could fetch them.

'The people I'm staying with are kind. Kathleen is a work colleague, she can be a little smothering, but only because she's caring. I don't really know her that well.'

Issy's expression conveyed sympathy. 'She's rather outspoken. But in a good way. She warned me twice not to upset you.

She's not going to let you come to any harm, which is the main thing. What about family? Or friends?'

Sarah shrugged. 'I'm a bit of a loner, I suppose. My job's always kept me busy, and after talking to patients all day I like to go home to the quiet. My mother is no longer with me, and I don't have siblings. I have my in-laws, but they're new to me.'

Issy sat with her hands in her lap, occasionally smoothing the material of her smart trousers. Her matching fawn jacket was buttoned up over a thin brown pullover. She looked poised and attractive, her hair pulled back in a stubby ponytail, with light make-up on her eyes and clear skin. She smiled kindly, seeming genuinely caring.

'Is there anything you can tell us at this stage that might help us?'

'No. Only what I already reported. I went to work and when I couldn't get him on the phone, I was worried.'

'Is there anything you want to ask?'

Sarah didn't want to ask for the flat keys. She might sound ungrateful, or even careless, for wanting to stay somewhere on her own. But she could ask for her black coat. Issy didn't need to know it was for the keys in a pocket. So at least she would have them for when she decided to leave. 'Actually, would it be possible for me to get some of my clothes?'

Issy cautiously nodded. 'I'll see what I can do. See if something can be arranged. If you make a list of what you want, I'll talk to the inspector.'

'Thank you,' Sarah replied. The conversation was winding down. She had warmed to her. She was doing her job, and doing it kindly. Her voice and manner were calm, which was a balm to Sarah's senses after being unsettled by Kathleen. Had she been brushing or stroking her hair? Either way, it was not normal behaviour.

'DI Anderson will be visiting you today, so is there anything else we can do for you?'

'No,' she replied. 'You've explained everything clearly. Thank you.'

Issy picked up her bag and rose from the chair. It had not been too long a visit after all. Less than an hour.

'Call or text me with a list of the clothing you want, and I'll try and sort it. And, of course, call if you have any concerns, or just need someone to talk to. You have my number for that reason.'

Sarah felt comforted. Issy couldn't be more perfect. It was like she had been given a friend on tap, which worked well for Sarah. The advantage of company but time alone if she wanted it. She didn't do well with having close friends. She would rather be by herself than with people who wanted to delve too deep. So long as Issy didn't try that, they would be fine. That way, the lie she was living stayed more like a dream. If she never spoke about it, it was never real. And Sarah never had, not in all these years, not since she was fourteen.

CHAPTER TEN

NICK

St Matthew's was a large modern L-shaped building three storeys high with dozens of flat windows and turquoise and grey panels laid over the brickwork. It was typical of many secondary schools in its colour scheme and design. The large, tarmacked car park was nearly full.

Nick and Charlie waited in the foyer, not wanting to interrupt the assembly, and looked quietly at the contents of the glass cabinets housing the school trophies. Long photographs showed all attending pupils in different years. In one photo, Nick read along the bottom row of names and found William Shaw sitting fourth from the left. He was a handsome man. He looked young and happy and would have been about twenty-eight or twenty-nine in 2007 when the photo was taken, and meant he'd been at the school for at least fourteen years.

Nick turned at a sucking noise as one swing door pushed open. An attractive fair-haired woman with slightly bulging eyes came out to greet them.

'Can I help?' Her face and voice were solemn.

Nick pulled out his ID. 'Detective Inspector Anderson, and Detective Sergeant Bowden. We're here to see Mr Simmons.'

'Of course. Mr Simmons will be out shortly. If you follow me to his office, I'll let him know you're here.'

Nick looked round the head teacher's room while they waited. He felt strangely very grown-up – he could choose to walk about and touch things or even lean against a wall if he so wished. He had liked school. It was the only place as a boy where he had felt life could be normal.

A large, scuffed desk in the middle of the room had a solid wooden swivel chair behind it. A small, solitary cactus boasting one tiny pink flower sat on a high windowsill. 'Doesn't change much, does it?'

Charlie raised an eyebrow. 'Maybe not from your day. Looks a bit different from mine. Canes were kept over in that corner and they were all well used. Good job they went.'

His cold voice surprised Nick. He wasn't aware that Charlie went to the same school as him. He didn't mention it on their journey or when they arrived. Although they were from the same area so it made sense. But when had Nick ever talked to Charlie about his childhood? Charlie was twenty years older than him. To his mind Charlie had always been a grown up and a cop he admired.

Before he could comment, the office door opened and a man entered with cropped, white hair and a high colour in his face. His pearl-grey suit made Nick self-conscious of his bright-green shirt and he buttoned up his black leather jacket discreetly, in an attempt to look smarter.

Nick offered his hand, introducing himself and Charlie. His fingers were crushed in a strong grip. 'You have our condolences, sir. This must be a difficult time.'

'Ron Simmons,' the man said. He slowly shook his head and gave a despairing sigh. 'I still can't believe it. It was only by chance that I rang William at home this morning. I got the shock of my life when a policewoman answered the phone. She wouldn't tell me any details of his passing. She said someone from the police would visit the school to let us know what's happened. I managed to get hold of Sarah on her mobile about half an hour ago and she confirmed that William was dead. I couldn't believe it. I've just let the teachers and pupils know. Half have gone back to their classrooms crying – and I'm not just talking about the kids. Very popular was William, very popular indeed.'

He walked over to his chair. It was a handsome piece of furniture. Nick could imagine it being in the captain's cabin on the *Cutty Sark*. It creaked as it took the man's weight. He indicated the chairs in front of his desk. 'Please, sit down. You'll have to excuse my manners. My brain is in a fog.'

Nick and Charlie sat down. The headmaster was trying to collect his thoughts, fleeting expressions crossing his face. 'So,' he said at last. 'How can I help?'

'By telling us what you can about William Shaw.'

The man raised his snowy head in further shock. 'Are you telling me that William didn't die of a heart attack or something like that?'

Nick shook his head. 'No. William Shaw died under suspicious circumstances.'

The head teacher looked deeply distressed. 'Oh God... not suicide?' He didn't wait for an answer. 'I can't believe it!'

Charlie interrupted him. 'No. Not suicide. Our enquiries into this incident are at an early stage—'

The man gasped. His high colour bleached away. 'You're talking murder!' he said in a deathly whisper. 'Good God! But who? Why?'

'We don't know yet,' Nick answered. 'What we do know is his death occurred sometime last night. You may start getting phone calls from reporters, or they might even turn up here, but I'd ask that you and your staff make no comment. If it becomes a problem, direct them to us.'

He nodded in agreement. 'Yes, the policewoman I spoke to

earlier mentioned media interest, it's why I let pupils and staff know of his passing. But I won't be mentioning this. I'll wait until it's public knowledge.'

'That might be wisest,' Nick replied. 'Especially for the pupils. We will, of course, be wanting to speak to staff, which we'll arrange in due course. I know that this has been a shock for you, but we need to know about anything that might be relevant. Anything that comes to mind that stands out. What was he like in the last few days? Or the last few weeks? Did he share anything that was troubling him? Any problems? Any enemies?'

The head teacher swept his hand down his face and gripped his jaw. '*Enemies!* William was a popular man, as I said. I never heard anyone say a bad word about him.' He took a ragged breath. 'This is so utterly sad. After Mary, I thought he'd found happiness.'

'Who's Mary?' Nick asked.

Ron Simmons looked startled. 'Mary? His first wife! Sorry, I assumed you knew.'

'Mr Simmons, we know very little about William Shaw. We haven't properly spoken with his current wife yet, so please bear with us.'

'Right, right. Let me start again then.' He looked around the room and then to Nick for help. 'Where would you like me to start?'

'How about 2007. I saw him in a school photograph in the foyer. Is that when he came here?'

'Yes. After the Easter holidays. William and Mary applied together. We had two vacancies. English and Geography. They had recently got engaged, it was a happy time for them both. Unfortunately, it didn't last. In about 2009, I think, Mary came to see me. She had been diagnosed with multiple sclerosis. She wanted to put me in the picture about the possible future for her – hospital appointments, days she might need off, things like that. I was fond of Mary and reassured her of my support.'

The head teacher paused, becoming a little overwhelmed. He pulled out a handkerchief and blew his nose before he continued. 'In the beginning, her illness wasn't really notice-able. For quite a few years. Then things changed. She was using a walking stick, experiencing extreme fatigue, and needing care. After that, William's life revolved around caring for her and coming to work.'

He inhaled deeply, as if hungry for air, clearly upset. Then the door to the office suddenly flew open, startling both Charlie and Nick, but mostly the head teacher as he grabbed at his chest.

A girl stormed in. Her face was wet with tears. Her big grey cardigan was dragged off one shoulder by the weight of a back-pack and her skirt barely covered her backside. 'Please say it ain't true! Please say he's not dead!'

Ron Simmons swiftly crossed the room to the distraught pupil. 'Amy, calm down! Come and sit outside. I'll find Miss Black and she can have a talk with you.'

'I don't want to talk! I want you to tell me it's not true.'

The regret in the head teacher's eyes made Amy cry harder. 'I'm sorry, Amy. I can't do that.'

Her face scrunched up tightly, then she screamed at him. 'Noooo!'

Ron Simmons escorted the girl from the room. He returned a couple of minutes later, even more shaken. Nick wasn't surprised. His own ears were still ringing.

'Sorry about that. Like I said, William was—'

'Popular,' Nick finished for him. 'A bit more than popular, I'd say. How old is she?' He watched the man's face turn cautious.

He chewed his lip for a moment. 'She's sixteen. Crushes on teachers are common. I only recently became aware that this was the case with Amy. Her father came to the school on Tuesday and said his daughter's teacher was a bit too "pally wally" for his liking. I assured him that Mr Shaw wouldn't be untoward with any pupil, but that I took his concern seriously. Wednesday I was at meetings all day. Yesterday, William was on a school trip in Bristol. That phone call I made this morning was to ask him to come in earlier so that we could talk.'

Nick nodded. 'We'll take Amy's address when we leave. And any contact details for the first Mrs Shaw, please.'

'Mary died,' he quietly said.

'When was that?'

'March seventeenth.'

Nick blinked in surprise. '*This year?*'

'Yes.'

Nick saw a fierce frown appear between Charlie's eyes. The short period of time since the first wife passed away had registered with him as well. He raised his eyebrows at Nick.

The head teacher read their expressions, and protested. 'Please. Don't go judging him on that. You don't know what it was like. I went to see Mary a few times in the hospital. She was a different person to the one I used to know. The change in her... she was *bitter*. And William put up with her ranting and raving that it was his fault, that he was the reason she was there. She raved about it being the hand of God striking her down, that she was being punished. To be honest, I was relieved for William when she died. He had no life with her.'

Nick could tell the man meant it. While most people hid such thoughts for fear of being judged callous, he was standing by his admission.

Nick did not have the freedom to admit to his feelings about William Shaw's death – his honesty had to be kept to himself. Kept even from Charlie. In Charlie's eyes, Nick was a better man.

CHAPTER ELEVEN

SARAH

DI Anderson didn't turn up until late afternoon. Sarah heard Kathleen warning the police officer in the hallway. It cut no ice with her that the man was a senior detective. Her voice came loud and clear through the closed door, her Irish accent pronounced and terse. 'She's been through an awful lot. Mind you don't go upsetting her more.'

Sarah prepared herself as the door behind her opened. Kathleen's dining room, that she used only for best, loaned for the interview. Sarah had her back towards the door, and was standing, staring out of a window at the narrow back garden. The realisation that Nick was there, alone with her in the room, struck her motionless. She heard his small intake of breath, and let out her own held breath.

'Hello, Sarah. We need to talk. My sergeant's outside finishing his cigarette. We've only got a few seconds before he'll be joining us.'

Sarah turned and gazed at him. 'Hello, Nick.' A moment in his presence and she was unnerved. Bleakly she wondered if he would ever lose this power over her. He looked tired, his dark eyes were solemn. Stubble emphasized his jawline, making him look remote, hard, more masculine and dangerous.

'The situation is, Sarah, that I can't stay on this case if anyone finds out about our past. I can come clean now and a new officer will step in, or we keep our involvement quiet and I just get on and do my job.'

'I won't say anything,' she quietly said. She moved a tremulous finger across her forehead. 'I don't want you to get in trouble.'

'Well, when my sergeant comes in, we'll be strangers. Okay?'

The ring of the doorbell broke the moment when Sarah might have said something more, like to ask him why he would want stay on the case. It must surely be difficult for him, as he must hate her.

By the time he returned, Sarah had control of her emotions. A further minute went by as Kathleen brought in a tray to put on the highly polished dining table. It held cups of tea and a plate of meat sandwiches. 'Sarah, you haven't eaten a thing since you've been here.' She gave Nick and the sergeant a look that said the food was not for them. Neither man showed any interest in what was on the table. Sergeant Bowden was getting comfortable, while Nick stood quietly by the door.

Nick closed the door once Kathleen departed, to give them privacy. Sarah sat down and put a spoon of sugar in one of the cups, stirred, and placed it in front of an empty chair where she thought he might sit. She caught a small smile on his face.

'What?' she asked.

He gave a slight shake of his head and the smile faded. Sarah realised her gaff. She put sugar in his cup automatically, because she knew how he liked his tea.

The sergeant was looking at her as she passed him a cup, having settled at the table and fetched out a notebook. Nick sat down and the interview began.

Nick spoke in a calming voice. 'Please accept our sincere condolences. I understand this is a terrible time, but getting a clear picture is crucial here, so if you can, we'd like you to talk us through last night. You phoned the police because you were concerned at your husband getting nuisance calls. Can you tell us a bit more about them?'

Sarah took a steadying breath. Her slim fingers touched the table. 'I don't know how many there were. He only told me about them when I came home on Wednesday and found him quite distressed. I know he reported them to you.'

'Yes, he did. He reported them to us on Wednesday. You say he was distressed? Was it only then?'

'No. I noticed a change in him when we got back from our honeymoon in September. He became quiet, sat for ages without talking. When I asked what was wrong he'd just say, "Nothing's wrong, Sarah." But I knew there was something. His mood would lift for a few days and then, bang, he'd go quiet again. So, Wednesday, when I came home and found him with his face white as a ghost and the phone in front of him, I made him tell me. He said he'd been getting calls most days, and then the notes. He thought it was one of his pupils messing about. I told him to go immediately and report it to the police. Yesterday... I mean the day before, he went and did that, but I don't know how long he'd had them.'

'You mean the letters? You didn't mention them in your initial call to the police.'

'No. It slipped my mind. Probably because I didn't see them. He wouldn't show me what they said.'

'He kept them from you?'

'No, he just didn't want me to see them.'

Nick raised an eyebrow at her. 'Is that not the same thing?' he asked in a supercilious tone.

Sarah felt her cheeks warm.

Sergeant Bowden chose that moment to cut in. 'How long

had you known your husband, before you married him, Mrs Shaw?'

Slightly rattled, Sarah was mute for a second. 'Sorry. It's just hard to... talk about anything. I met William for the first time last year, just before Christmas.'

An intake of breath from Nick interrupted her flow. She glanced at him, then quickly looked away. He was probably thinking that it wasn't that long after they broke up. She clasped her hands together for something to hold onto, then continued.

'I actually met him and his wife in the corridor as I was about to head in to the ward and start my new post. Shortly after, William wheeled Mary onto the ward. She was being admitted as a patient. The staff all knew them. Mary was a frequent patient. She had multiple sclerosis, and was declining. I didn't really know William then, of course, except as Mary's husband.

'In March, Mary died. Several of us went to her funeral. A few weeks later, William came to the hospital and we had a coffee together. At first I was reluctant. I felt it was too soon for him, but as William said, Mary had been ill for a long time. You have to understand it wasn't a case of a healthy wife dying suddenly. She'd been ill for years.' Sarah glanced at the sergeant, to see if he was judging her. When she saw nothing in his eyes, she continued. 'We were dating fully by the summer. By then we knew we wanted to be together and saw no reason to wait.'

'Clearly not,' Nick said, in a dry tone, causing Sarah to jolt. Her heartbeat picked up. Seeing his closed expression gave rise to the memory of the day she finished with him. His eyes had been filled with hurt until he closed off from her and walked away.

Sarah wanted to be anywhere else but in this room. She pushed herself back into the seat and heard once more the words he said to her that day.

'*I thought you loved me, Sarah. I thought we were happy. But clearly not.*'

Sarah tried to erase the memory fast.

'Thank you for sharing this with us, Mrs Shaw,' Nick said, a note of hardness in his tone. 'Apart from the letters and calls, did your husband have any other concerns? You said it might be one of his pupils messing about – did he say why a pupil might have been contacting him in this way?'

'No.'

'So no clue as to why? Was he being blackmailed, perhaps? Any money worries he told you about? And I'm afraid I must ask you this – do you know if your husband was involved with anyone else?'

A small gasp burst from her lips as she stared at him. 'We were virtually still on our honeymoon.'

He ignored her resentment. 'I'm sorry to have asked, but being newly married doesn't rule it out. It happens.'

'Yes, I know.' She sighed. 'But we didn't have a problem. You asked about money. After we married, we kept our saving accounts separate but started a joint account. The mortgage on William's house is paid, so the joint account was for our living costs.'

'So nothing else out of the ordinary as far as you're aware?'

She frowned and her eyes grew darker. 'Actually, there is something. A man knocked on the door a few nights ago. Tuesday, I think. I got a glimpse of him. Dark hair. Thin face. William went outside. I heard the man's raised voice. Just a couple of words. Like "stay away". Then William came in and closed the front door. Said the man had the wrong house.'

'And that was that? You didn't question it?'

Her eyes opened wide at his tone. Her stomach clenched. 'What would you have me do? Call him a liar?' She shook her head. 'I had no reason to think he was lying.'

'Anyone else you can think of that your husband didn't get

on with? Apart from this man,' he added dryly. 'Anyone from his first wife's family? Or his own family?'

'He has a sister.' Her voice altered. 'She didn't come to our wedding. I met her at Mary's funeral and she was a little hostile towards William, but he never explained it.'

'Something else he kept from you.'

Sarah stayed silent. She supposed she deserved the snipe. She had hurt him, without warning or even a proper explanation. It was a wonder he had any kindness left in him for her at all. She couldn't understand why he would even take this case. He had a legitimate excuse to be exempt from having anything to do with it. So why be on it? Did he want to help her? Was it their past making him feel he should?

Sergeant Bowden interrupted the silence. 'Any ex-spouse on your side we need worry about?'

She was tempted to thwart Nick, and expose the pretence of them being strangers, to see how he liked it. But she wouldn't. It might help to have him on her side. She shook her head.

The sergeant reached down by the side of his chair into a briefcase and brought out a large blue photo album, which he settled on the table. 'I've brought some of your things with me. I hope this won't be painful.'

Sarah glanced at it. 'This is William's album. I might not know everyone.'

'That's okay, just tell us who you do know.'

The first photographs were of William's parents, William, his sister and a dog, and several more of the dog.

'That was Toby, their dog,' she said. 'He died a few years ago.' And then: 'Sorry, I'm being foolish. I'm sure you don't want to hear about a dog.'

The next photos were of William and another woman. 'That's Mary, his first wife.'

The background in many of the pictures was inside their

home, and they captured the stages of her progressive illness almost cruelly. A Zimmer frame replaced a walking stick and a wheelchair replaced the Zimmer frame and her final incapacity was recorded in a photograph of a ceiling hoist above her bed.

On another page, the sergeant tapped a face. 'We met this woman when we went to your husband's school.'

'Yes, Amanda Black. She's one of the teachers. She used to come and see Mary on the ward.'

The last few pages of the album showed large photographs of Shaw with more pupils. The school uniform was different to the one at St Matthew's.

'Where's this school?' he asked.

'I'm not sure,' she answered. 'William said he and Mary moved to Bath after getting engaged. William is from Bristol, so I suppose it was closer to home.'

The sergeant put away the album, and then asked how well she really knew her husband. She gave a sad smile. 'Sometimes I feel I didn't know William at all.'

'You married him.'

'I know. I used to see William nearly every day when he came to see Mary, and in a strange way when I married him I felt I didn't get to know him any more. I mean, any better. I suppose it's a bit like working with someone and feeling you know them really well, then someone asks you what their favourite food or television programme is and you realise you don't have a clue.'

He nodded like he knew what she meant. 'You're a ward sister; is that right, Mrs Shaw?'

'Yes. For a year now.'

'Last night you were on duty. At what time did you start?'

'Eight o'clock.'

'So you left home at what time?'

'Seven-fifteen. Kathleen picked me up.'

'Did she go into your house?'

'No.'

'And your husband? He was all right then, was he?'

Sarah glanced at the sergeant, sharply. The question shouldn't be resented. She, of course, would be a suspect. 'Yes, he was very all right. He waved us off while putting out the bins.'

'The back door to your house was found open. Can you explain why it wouldn't have been locked?'

She shook her head. 'William must have forgotten to lock it.'

'Have you or your husband lost your house keys? Or has anybody else got a set, perhaps?'

'No. William's should be in the house, and mine are in my bag.'

'What time did your husband normally retire to bed?'

She shrugged. 'He had no set time. If there was a programme he wanted to watch he'd stay up. Other times he'd go to bed early to read.'

Nick cut into the conversation. 'The uniform you were wearing last night. Where is it now?'

Sarah gave him a sideways glare. So much for thinking him being on the case might be a help. He was making things worse for her.

'It's in Kathleen's washing. I was sick on it this morning. But it isn't washed yet.'

'We'll need to take it with us. In case of transfer evidence. You may have brought something to the scene or taken evidence away on your clothing.'

Sarah held up her hands to show him a faint blackness on her fingertips and glanced at the sergeant. 'I had my fingerprints taken before I saw William's body, so I understand.' She took a long, jerky breath and rubbed her fingers hard. 'Horrible stuff to get off.'

'Scanner was in use,' the sergeant said quietly to Nick. Nick murmured a reply, which Sarah didn't hear.

Sarah, all of sudden, felt deathly tired. William had died only last night. She had been to the mortuary early this morning. Then on returning to Kathleen's was made to drink soup, listen to her suggestions of trips to Asda and have fish and chips, before managing to escape to her bedroom where she was disturbed from a sleep by Kathleen touching her hair. She'd then had to meet with Issy Banks. And now this interview with Nick and his sergeant. She tuned out their voices. They had got all they were going to get from her. She wanted to be alone. There was nothing for her to feel guilty about. She had done what she should. What else could she do when faced with a hard decision? Forget what she knew? Like that was even possible.

The interview was hard. She was busy suppressing emotions. It had taken only a moment for her to be back at that place. The purple thing they covered him with, the scent of a thousand other deaths. They put it over his body. A low moan broke forth. 'So cold,' she whimpered. 'To be left like that alone.'

Sarah rose weakly to her legs. 'I'm too tired to talk anymore.'

Both men stood and the sergeant looked at her in concern, while Nick stared at the ground. 'We're sorry, Mrs Shaw, if we upset you.'

Sarah continued out of the room, too tired to say goodbye. Being in the same room as Nick was almost too much to bear. Maybe it would have been easier if a stranger was dealing with her husband's death. If she came clean about their relationship, then she wouldn't have to see him. Another officer, though, might unearth more about her than Nick had known. She would take her chances with Nick. When Nick loved her he had not known when she was evading the truth. He had been blinded by his feelings. But now he would be watching her closely. He once told her the ways he could tell when someone is lying: body language, face touches, fidgeting, eye contact. She knew he would not let up until he knew the reason for their breakup. And eventually she would have to tell him why she let him go.

CHAPTER TWELVE

NICK

The forensic mortuary was a new, purpose-built facility in a village six miles from the centre of Bristol. From outside it looked a nondescript, low-level modern building with a visitor's entrance and a staff entrance. What most people didn't notice was a vehicle yard with an entrance for the bodies. Inside, a high spec autopsy suite with an observation gallery kicked nondescript right out the door. It was a high and spacious room with plenty of space between each autopsy table, which were in a row along the length of the room. Identical looking steel cabinets with sink troughs, worktops and hosepipes created a unified appearance. The clean lines, bare surfaces, and shine of stainless steel added a clinical purity.

Nick would have preferred to see an old weighing scales beside one of the sinks – a crane set that measured in pounds and ounces, like the ones that were once used on a maternity ward to weigh babies in a large metal bowl – as a reminder of how it used to be done.

In the autopsy suite, the scavenger system that extracted atmospheric pollution would keep the air cool. Behind the observation window it was warm. But he shivered. Despite the warmth, he was cold. No sleep last night or the night before, and too much thinking about Sarah, had lowered his body's resistance and temperature. He had not taken Charlie's advice to get some shut-eye in preparation for this evening. He sat in an office where he wouldn't be disturbed, and thought about her. And these next few hours were likely to sorely tell on him.

His gaze went to the table below. The body on it was covered with a sheet. He turned as the door opened and Charlie joined him in the gallery, followed by Mark Steel and another man, who introduced himself as John Jenkins, the coroner's officer. The MCIT's exhibits officer was somewhere in the building, standing ready to record and bag any items off the body, along with an officer who would take photographs. William Shaw had very little on him in the bed.

Charlie sat next to him and Nick smelled fresh cigarette smoke. Charlie looked as haggard as Nick felt. Probably no sleep for him either.

Swing doors pushed open in the room below and the pathologist entered. His green scrubs and apron couldn't hide his identity as the size of his belly gave him away. Angus Doyle was a large man, born of a Scottish mother and an Irish father, who spoke with a London accent. He wore ordinary black wellingtons, unlike his followers who wore white. Any doubt that it was him beneath the mask disappeared as he turned and Nick saw how the man had secured his green trousers: the wide elastic of his underpants was turned over the back of them to stop them falling down. It was definitely Professor Doyle.

His voice boomed at them through the intercom speaker. 'Gentlemen. Welcome. Know where the door is if you haven't found it already. We don't want stomach contents emptied onto the floor up there.' He looked in the direction of Nick. 'Was that your fault over last night's caper, DI Anderson? Mrs Shaw, I mean?'

Mark Steel murmured in agreement with Doyle, which

Nick chose to ignore. Nick nodded. 'Sorry about that. She ran in before we could stop her.'

Charlie growled a deep cough and Doyle turned his attention to him.

'Every time I see you, Charlie, I hear that cough. Get it seen to. Otherwise it will be you on a slab.'

'Angus, if it's you dealing with me, just be sure you put earplugs in my ears. I don't want to hear any of that singalong music you love to listen to. Max Bygraves will kill me.'

'Not funny, Charlie. Look after yourself.'

Charlie quietly chuckled. He and the pathologist were of a similar age. Nick had heard him in the past talking to the professor like they were friends. He now made another joke. 'A bit of Doris Day, I wouldn't mind. If you can sort that out for me.'

The big man turned away from them and moved over to the table. He glanced at the assistants. 'We ready? Good. Let's begin.'

Nick glanced at the instruments: all shapes and sizes, and tools that a gardener or a carpenter would use. A pair of shears to cut through ribs, a circular saw for bone, and a chisel to lever the skullcap off. He hadn't eaten boiled eggs or cracked a walnut at Christmas since the first time he saw and heard them in use at a post-mortem. But before any of that could happen, the body had to be introduced, inspected, measured, weighed, photographed top to bottom, front to back. The preservation bags wrapping the hands and feet were carefully removed, ensuring forensic evidence was not altered or lost. Every speck of forensic evidence was vital, which is why the process took so long. Doyle dictated his findings every step of the way.

More than an hour later, one of the assistants lifted up a slim high-pressure hose to wash away the dried blood from the man's chest, neck and head.

Doyle scrutinised the now visible wound at the back of the

head. 'Exit wound is relatively small, but I expect it's done plenty of damage nonetheless.'

Nick stared at the screen providing a close-up. The wound was much lower down the head than he was expecting it to be.

'A steady hand has done this,' Doyle said. 'Feel the back of your head, gentlemen, where it meets the neck. That bony bump is the Atlas joint. In that spot is a bundle of nerve cells – the medulla oblongata. The lowest part of the brain. It plays a critical role in controlling autonomic activities, such as sneezing and breathing and heartbeat. While every part of the brain is important, life cannot be sustained without the work of the medulla oblongata. Put a bullet in that spot, it's game over in an instant.'

He glanced up at the viewing gallery, checking that his comments registered, before starting work on the main event. 'Right. Let's see inside, shall we?'

Nick needed to either stand up or sleep, or better yet visit the bathroom and take a short walk. The whirr of an X-ray machine was causing his eyelids to flicker, so he decided on a bathroom break. When he returned a similar noise was going on. A camera shutter at work. So he was back to hearing a hypnotic click. Click, flicker, click, flicker, click...

Doyle used forceps to prise open the mouth, and Nick could see a few fragments of teeth. Doyle picked out the ones that were loose and placed them in a dish. Taking a scalpel from the trolley he made an incision from behind the left ear, following the hairline all the way over to the right, cutting through scalp down to bone. He placed the instrument down and Nick braced himself.

Doyle stood at an angle with the man's mashed face resting firm against his big belly. He worked his fingers under the thick flap of skin and pulled. Moving his fingers in deeper he dragged it forward. The ripping, sucking sound of wet scalp leaving skull filled the room. Doyle's face turned red as he tugged harder, breathing heavily as he held on. Tough skin lifted and he was able to pull the scalp inside-out and fold it down over the face, so that hair from the head appeared to hang below the chin like a beard.

Doyle then put on a pair of protective goggles. A loud squeal jumped the nerves in Nick's teeth as the electric saw came to life, making him press his fingertips under the edge of the bench. Then it reached him. The smell of burning bone. He breathed through his barely open mouth until the skullcap was removed.

Doyle looked up. 'I'll leave that for the moment.'

Nick was puzzled, and then Doyle distracted him by whipping the sheet off the body. Nick could only stare in utter shock as he saw a woman's body.

What was happening? Where was Shaw?

Charlie grabbed his sleeve as he tried to get past him. 'Take it easy, Nick.'

'Take it easy! When the fuck did they make the switch?' Nick pulled away. 'What the fuck's going on?'

Doyle was smiling as he touched something on the woman's thigh. 'Ah! This is pretty. And very helpful. Someone will know her.'

Nick was stunned as he saw Doyle lower his head to inspect it. His face almost touching the skin. 'You need to see this, Inspector,' Doyle called to him.

Nick stared at the small butterfly tattooed in blue and felt his knees give way. He grabbed the table for support and saw Doyle's big finger prod the blue flesh. He couldn't breathe! Doyle picked up a scalpel and sliced through the skin. A delicate wing flapped and Nick felt himself falling through air. *You sick bastard! I'll kill you.*

'WAKE UP, YOU SILLY BUGGER! WAKE UP!'

Nick opened his eyes and saw Charlie and Mark looking down at him.

'You silly sod, you fell asleep, then nearly knocked yourself stupid falling off the bench.'

He raised his head off the floor and saw John, the coroner's officer, holding out a glass of water. 'How long was I asleep?'

'For most of it,' Doyle shouted through the speaker. 'And you snore damn loudly. Not to mention the bursts of profanity. Any blood up there, Charlie?'

'No, all good up here, Angus.'

Charlie helped him up and Nick's eyes were drawn to the table. William Shaw's body was there, and it had a penis. He stared a little too long, and then reddened at the look Charlie gave him.

Well, that was just great! All he needed to add to his embarrassment was for Charlie to think he was a voyeur as well as a silly sod.

Doyle peeled off his gloves, tossed them into the yellow biohazard bin by the sink, and washed his hands. He was finished and Nick had slept for most of it. At least two and a half hours of it, from the time on the clock.

Doyle was now looking at him over his mask. 'Well, Inspector, the cause of death is from a bullet passing from the mouth to the brainstem, resulting in immediate death at the scene. You'll have my preliminary findings within twenty-four hours, and my report sent to the coroner. No bullet was found, so it's probably embedded in the headboard.'

The officers individually thanked the pathologist, Nick going last to add in an apology. Doyle graciously accepted, wishing Nick a speedy resolution.

Nick wanted this case over with as fast as possible, and was intending on having someone to put in a cell, if not tomorrow, then the next day. He wanted his mind cleared of it so he could concentrate on her. He was not done yet. Not by a long shot. He still had plenty to do to put things right.

CHAPTER THIRTEEN

SARAH

Sarah turned off at Junction 17 of the M5. Driving in her old car, that Kathleen let her borrow. The ten-mile journey had been straightforward, but now brake lights winked at her. Twenty minutes later, after travelling at a snail's pace, she saw the reason. Christmas shoppers. Cars queuing to get into the car park on a Saturday. There were only two more weeks before Christmas, she realised.

The family she was going to see would not be celebrating Christmas this year. She wasn't looking forward to the visit, but she would rather that, or be stuck in traffic, than be stuck at Kathleen's listening to her conversations with Alexa.

Kathleen spoke to the machine like it was a friend, and had it playing Van Morrison and Danny O'Donoghue songs from the moment Sarah got up. Their names were imprinted in Sarah's mind from the number of times she heard Kathleen repeat them to the machine in response to Alexa saying, 'I'm sorry, I didn't quite get that.' Sarah had wanted to throw Alexa at the wall to shut Kathleen up.

Finally, she arrived and parked outside a bungalow on an estate that was reputed to be one of the largest in Europe. The curtains were drawn across each bay window, shutting out the world. Sarah walked up the short pavement. A dwarf conifer in a brown tub guarded the front door. She reluctantly rang the bell.

William's father opened the door. The man looked nothing like his son. Five foot one or two, small build and with a wrinkled bald head.

'Sarah?' he said, surprising her with his instant recognition of her. The small man blinked rapidly, either from habit or nerves. 'Come in.'

Sarah stepped into a brightly patterned hallway – red carpet on the floor, flowery wallpaper on the walls. A glass-panelled door to the left was open. William's mother sat in a blue winged armchair. Long and lean, her face like William's but older.

'Alice, look who's here.'

Alice stood up, topping Sarah's height by several inches. Her bony fingers shredded a flowered paper tissue.

'Put the kettle on, Ken.'

The small man went to the kitchen to do as he was told.

'Sit down, Sarah.'

Sarah did as she was told and sat at one end of the couch. She hadn't spoken to William's mother at the mortuary as they had only passed one another briefly in the corridor.

She looked around the room and found herself thinking that if colours were sounds, this room would be a cacophony of horrible noise. Flowers were the order of the day: large lemon and blue on the walls, smaller blue on the carpet and the curtains a repeat of the wallpaper pattern. The blue couch and armchair offered little relief. The blue was too strong.

She hadn't seen their home before. They met for the first time at a tea shop not long after she got together with William, the second occasion a restaurant, the time after that at her wedding.

She noticed the decorations piled in a box beside a white imitation tree, and cards on top of them. They were putting away all reminders of Christmas. Then the photographs in a different box on the coffee table. They were getting out all reminders of *him*.

Sarah sat quietly, wondering what she should call her mother-in-law, realising she had never directly addressed her. It would sound odd to call her Mrs Shaw and too familiar to call her Alice.

Ken returned with a tray. Full-matching set. Pink flowers on white. And teaspoons shined to a high polish. Alice Shaw served and Sarah sniffed the perfumed aroma of Earl Grey.

'When can we bury William?'

Sarah expected this question. 'The coroner's office will ring when they're ready to release his body.'

'Today?'

'Doubtful. More like a week, I would have thought.'

'How did he die?'

Again expected. 'He was... he was—'

'Would you like a biscuit?'

'Be quiet, Ken. Let her answer.'

Sarah felt sorry for the small, silenced man. 'He was shot,' she replied quietly.

Alice drew in a deep breath, her hands curling into fists around the paper handkerchief. 'Did he die quickly?'

Sarah blinked several times. 'A post-mortem was carried out last night, so I'm sure we'll have more details eventually.'

She looked unimpressed. 'Do they suspect anyone who could have done this to William? He was a gentle, kind man.'

Sarah placed her cup of Earl Grey down, still full. 'No, Mrs Shaw.'

She raised an almost hairless eyebrow at Sarah. 'You can't call me Mrs Shaw. Alice, or mother if you prefer. We're related, Sarah. I only wish you'd come into his life a lot sooner. He was thirty when he married Mary, and she ruined his life. He should have divorced her and met someone like you a lot sooner. He should have had children.' Her voice perceptibly broke, then she lifted her head high. 'But he didn't and now he's gone. All of him.'

Sarah slowly nodded. 'I know.'

'Have you spoken to Jane?'

Sarah shook her head. Surprised to be asked about her sister-in-law. 'No, I don't have her number, I'm afraid.'

The woman looked at her husband. 'Ken, give Jane's details to Sarah so she can get in touch.'

Ken crossed the room to a small bureau. He picked out a white envelope from a neat bundle and handed it to Sarah. 'That's her Christmas card. We won't be sending it now, but it has her address on it.' The man then took a biscuit and left the room.

Sarah sat quietly while William's mother discussed what arrangements she'd like for the funeral. A Catholic service, a burial at Holy Souls, and the hymns, though not 'Morning Has Broken' as it was sung at her brother's funeral. When it was time to leave, her voice turned firm. 'When you see Jane, will you remind her she has parents who have just lost their son. She hasn't phoned us since her father let her know.'

Sarah wondered why her mother-in-law didn't do this herself. It sounded like there'd been a falling out between Jane and her parents. She hoped, by being asked to do this, she wasn't being dragged into a family dispute. Before she left, Sarah popped her head around the kitchen door to say goodbye to her father-in-law. He had the window open and was placing broken biscuit on the windowsill, trying to entice a sparrow.

'Here, little birdie.'

Sarah's footsteps were audible on the lino, but he didn't turn round. 'Here, little birdie,' he said again, and Sarah saw the bird hop an inch in front of the man's fingers. She watched the bright-eyed bird peck before seeing the even brighter, tearful eyes of the man beside her.

Back in her car, Sarah shivered. She'd found watching Ken feeding birds pitiful, and hoped Jane Shaw was less like her mother, otherwise it would be another difficult visit.

Heading out of Bristol, and wanting to get it over with, she drove to Whitchurch, and easily found the street and house where Jane Shaw lived. A red-brick terrace, with the front door in need of a coat of paint, and a For Sale poster on the inside of the window advertising the Andrews Estate Agents.

Sarah knocked at the door and waited a time for it to open. Jane Shaw looked at her blankly. Her black T-shirt and track-suit bottoms were splattered with white paint. Her hair, in a tight topknot, skewered with a red pencil. No greeting given, she opened the front door wide, stepped aside, and let Sarah in.

The front room showed that mother and daughter were polar opposites. Not a flower or bright colour in sight. Instead, natural creams and beiges and polished bare floorboards. Tall thin twigs snaked with white lights in a large rattan vase.

Without a word, Jane led the way through another door to the top of a steep staircase, revealing that the house had a floor below street level as well as an upstairs. Sarah followed her down and entered a large kitchen, where she stopped still and stared aghast. It was this room that was being painted. The ceiling was wet and white – along with every single item in the room. The worktops, the fridge, the brown cooker, the pictures, chairs, table and floor had all been badly splashed. The sleeping cat had highlights in its black fur.

Sarah had never seen a worse job.

Jane picked up a scraper and started attacking the cream wallpaper. Within seconds, she had wrought havoc. Already too late to undo if this was just for show, just for her visitor, standing there aghast.

'Jane, would it be possible for you to stop that for a moment?'

The scraper stilled, but Jane continued to face the wall.

Sarah stared at the back of her head and wondered what was going on inside it. She had to be hurting. She had lost her only brother, and only sibling. From the little Sarah knew about her, Jane wasn't married or living with anyone. She had a job with the council, but Sarah didn't know any more than that. William never spoke about her.

Sarah saw him in her mind. His tall quiet presence, his quietness in bed, and quietness in the home, and his quiet keeping of his thoughts to himself. He had started to love her, though, and she guessed his feelings would have grown stronger. And yet they hadn't properly flourished, they hadn't been given enough time to get to truly know each other…

She turned her attention back to Jane, searching for something to say that wouldn't sound trite, but it was impossible when all she was trying to do was be polite to someone she barely knew. 'I'm sorry for your loss, Jane. It must have been a terrible shock to you.'

She didn't respond.

'I've been to see your parents. They gave me your address. They thought you might like a visit.'

Jane turned, and her face was disbelieving.

Sarah decided to be blunt. 'Would you like me to leave?'

Jane answered and Sarah was surprised. 'No. I'd rather you stayed.' She then perched on a stool. 'Why are you out visiting everyone? Surely it should be people visiting you.'

Sarah stepped nearer to her. 'I don't have many people who would visit. And I'm not in my own home. I'm at a work colleague's house. It felt better to go out than to be in someone else's home.'

'You're nothing like Mary,' she declared in a stark voice.

Sarah waited for her to say more, but when she remained

silent, Sarah said something equally stark. 'Why didn't you get on with him?'

She looked down at her paint-covered hands, then smiled cynically at Sarah. 'He obviously didn't tell you then.'

'No, he didn't. But I sensed a problem between you.'

She laughed harshly. 'Did you now?' Her arms tightly folded across her chest. Then quietly she said, 'They wanted my child.'

Sarah looked around as if expecting to see one. 'Your child?'

'Yes. Mary and William wanted my unborn child. I was pregnant and wanted a termination. I was thirty-four at the time and we'd made up our minds to not have children.' She let out a short, derisive laugh. 'He's now married with a child with another on the way. I went to see Mary to borrow some money and two evenings later William turned up with a proposal. Mary couldn't risk pregnancy with her health and William wanted a child. I said no. I didn't need to think about it. I didn't want to think about it. I told him to get out.'

Sarah's mouth dropped, and Jane nodded in recognition. 'It's a shock, isn't it? How many brothers do you know who'd ask their sisters for their baby? But that's not the reason I stopped speaking to him. The night he called here, after he left, I fell down those stairs. I'd shut the front door on him. Angry I suppose, and was careless. He came to see me in hospital. He thought I'd done it on purpose.'

Sarah was shocked that William never mentioned this, or his desire for a family. What a sad bunch, she thought, realising she was less alone than any of the people she'd seen today. She suspected that once William was buried she would not see her extended family anymore. But, for now, she would be a dutiful daughter-in-law and deliver her mother-in-law's message. 'Jane, your mother needs you, and I think so does your father.'

Sarah saw the slim throat swallow. 'Does he?'

'Yes, he does. I'd give him a call, get him over here to help you sort out this decorating.'

'Might do,' she said. Then she got off the stool and carried on scraping as if Sarah wasn't there.

Sarah was left to walk back up the stairs to the living room and out the front door on her own.

The drive back to Kathleen's was too short. It hadn't given her enough time to think about any of the things she'd learned. The most shocking was that William had wanted a child. When was he intending to tell her – his new wife, who should have known, should have been told? Had he planned to just spring it on her? Or had he just assumed she'd want the same?

His quietness had left so much unsaid. He never talked about his past. He never talked about the remembrance card he used as a bookmark. She never got to tell him about her past. She had badly wanted to tell him, so he would understand why she was there and see into her heart. There was no one she could tell any more.

CHAPTER FOURTEEN

NICK

'We should do a TIE on Mrs Shaw,' Paul Robson announced at the afternoon briefing, before they even got started. The thought sent a shiver down Nick's spine. He eyed the detective, wondering what was behind the outburst.

A trainee detective put a finger up, and Robson misinterpreted his query: 'Trace, Interview, Eliminate,' he informed the officer.

'I understand that,' the trainee said back, his fair skin flushed, a few acne spots highlighted on his young face. 'But we know she was working.'

'We still need to do a TIE. That way we'll know for sure. She could have had time to do it. My ex is a nurse. Hospitals are like small towns. Going from one ward to another you can walk a half mile and be gone ages without anyone noticing.' He smirked. 'I know that from first-hand experience. We used to sit in my car, even went for a drive once with a pharmacy collection of drugs in her lap. So it's possible for her to have done it. Have we done a background check on her yet?'

Nick had been trying to recall the trainee officer's name so he could reply. He settled for looking at him instead. 'DS

Robson is right. The wife is a suspect until eliminated. And, yes,' he turned now to Robson, 'background check has been done.' He didn't add that he had done one three years ago on an impulse, during a quiet moment when he was at work and had first started dating her. It was not something he was proud of nor previously felt the need to do on any other woman in his life. He had simply wanted to know everything about her faster than she was telling him. 'She's thirty years old. Mother deceased. Father unknown. No siblings. No previous marriages. She did her nursing degree at UWE Bristol, qualified aged twenty-one, then became a staff nurse and was promoted a year ago to a ward sister. Never been arrested or cautioned. An A-1 citizen. But a clean background doesn't stop us looking at her,' he added for Robson's benefit, hoping to shut the man up. 'Her uniform, what she was wearing Thursday night, has been sent for analysis. Charlie, if you can verify Mrs Shaw's movements from the time she got to work to when you turned up, that would be good. We haven't got a time of death yet to set enquiry parameters.'

'That's all very well,' Robson replied. 'But has she been swabbed for GSR? She could be scrubbing it off. And we all know how nurses like to scrub,' he added with another sly grin.

A paranoid idea suddenly consumed Nick. Was Robson's interest in pursuing this avenue more than professional diligence? Was he aware that Nick knew the victim's wife?

The sergeant behind Robson voiced his annoyance at Robson's last remark. 'Can we have less of the innuendoes, please. We're not all Neanderthals here, I hope.'

Nick relaxed. He was being daft. No one knew about him and Sarah. He would have showed her off to the world, but Sarah kept it strictly private. Which for her was easy. She seemed to have no friends. For him it was more difficult, because of people like Charlie – his only bloody real friend. But as it turned out, it had worked in his favour that it was kept private. Robson was thinking what every detective should think, that was all.

Issy, once again, came to the rescue. 'Sorry, but I don't think this should wait. We've got a lead.'

She glanced around the room at her colleagues, before her eyes settled on Nick. 'Okay. Long story short. A Mrs Lesley Page, a neighbour across the road, was disturbed from her bed at about nine-thirty. Her daughter, Maria, was having an asthma attack and was leaning out of her open window when she saw a schoolgirl outside the victim's house.'

Nick was surprised. He had wanted a suspect fast but hadn't thought to find one in a schoolgirl. But he would take what he could get. 'Does the daughter know who it was?'

Issy nodded. 'Yes. Amy Fox, the sixteen-year-old that you and Charlie saw upset at the school. The next bit's not so good. Amy's in hospital. No one was at her home address. I managed to speak to the head teacher, who gave me a number for a Miss Black. Apparently, after you left the school yesterday, Amy doubled up with severe stomach cramps. Miss Black went to the hospital with her. I briefly spoke to her. They kept Amy in for a D & C, after having a miscarriage. It's a routine surgical procedure they sometimes do when the miscarriage is incomplete.'

Charlie spoke up and gave some praise. 'Well done, Issy. We've got a person of interest, so good work.'

'Not unless she wears size tens, we don't,' Robson cut in. 'Let's not forget that or the soil on the kitchen floor, which Mark's team has now found upstairs in the bedroom as well.'

Nick gave him an amused stare. 'I don't think Mrs Shaw wears size tens either.'

'I'm just saying we need to remember it,' Robson snapped.

Nick made a show of looking at the wall of information on the whiteboards, especially the photographs of the shoe impressions. He had not forgotten they were there. Or any other detail in this case. The lights out. Back door unlocked. Red wax on bedside drawers. Anonymous letters and nuisance calls. A remembrance card with the name 'Ray'.

He was reminded to ask Issy about that. 'Issy, when you see Mrs Shaw next, ask who Ray is.'

She nodded. 'Will do.'

'What's she like, Issy?' Robson asked.

Nick saw the team turn their attention to Issy. They were all curious, by the look of it. She gave a small shrug. 'A little reserved. Quite calm. And very attractive.'

'No wailing and sobbing then?'

'No, she wasn't crying, Paul. She asked if she could have some of her clothes.'

'So really grieving then?'

Issy shrugged. 'It affects everyone differently, Paul. She seems a private sort so maybe does her crying when alone.'

'Or maybe no crying at all,' he added to get the last word in.

Nick wanted to punch Robson. Instead, he smiled, knowing it would irk the man more to have no one onside. The best thing Nick could do was ignore him. Or else highlight his valid opinion, because it might irk him equally well to have Nick's show of support when Robson clearly resented him.

He pointedly stared at the trainee detective, recalling his name. Ian Carter. 'TI Carter, DS Robson makes a valid point. There were 594 victims of homicide in the year ending March 2021, of which 114 were domestic homicides. Domestic homicide accounts for nearly twenty per cent of those murder cases. Mrs Shaw might well be newly married, but it didn't stop us asking her if her husband might have been seeing someone else. The testimony of neighbours and the teachers who knew the victim might reveal something interesting.'

Nick looked at the investigating officers dealing with the significant witness interviews, to remind them of some key facts. 'The man's first wife died only this year. Amy Fox's father was concerned his daughter's teacher was too "pally wally" with her. Was the victim a known philanderer and the new Mrs Shaw only just found out?'

He looked around the incident room, before resting his eyes on Paul Robson. 'Mrs Shaw said a man knocked at her door early in the week. She said he raised his voice. Just a couple of words to William Shaw. Like stay away. She said her husband told her the man had the wrong house.'

He paused before leaving them with a final speculation. 'Do we believe this? Or was it William Shaw telling this man to stay away? Is there an ex who wanted the victim out of the way?'

CHAPTER FIFTEEN

SARAH

Kathleen's tone was curt. 'Lunch is ruined. I was going to ring you, but I don't have your number.'

Sarah was startled, but hid her resentment. She placed the M&S bag on the kitchen table. She had decided to carry on driving and go into town after her visit with Jane, to give herself some thinking time. She bought herself some clothes and toiletries, and a pack of cotton pants to replace the ones she borrowed with new.

'Let's hope the same doesn't happen with dinner,' Kathleen now said.

She was standing at the kitchen sink, peeling potatoes and placing them in a pot of cold water. A frozen leg of lamb still in its plastic covering sat on the draining board, a bag of unpeeled carrots and a head of cabbage beside it. A Bird's Trifle Kit was on the counter, the ingredients still in the box waiting to be made. Sarah looked at Kathleen and then at the mountain of food she was preparing, and then had to look away. Where was she going with all this food? There were only three of them and Sarah couldn't eat a thing.

'I have to go back out, Kathleen. I'm going to Keynsham Police Station. I got a call from the policewoman who was here to say they want me to give a description of a man who came to the house on Tuesday so they can make an E-fit of him.'

Kathleen stared at the wall clock pointedly. 'Well, it's only quarter past two. Dinner won't be ready until five.'

Sarah eyed the frozen meat. It would stay that way for at least a few more hours. Unless she was intending to cook it from frozen, but that would take twice as long. It would be much later than five when dinner was ready.

Drying her hands on a tea cloth, she straightened and turned to Sarah. 'So where were you all morning?'

Sarah tensed. She was beginning to feel interrogated. 'I went to visit my in-laws and sister-in-law.'

'Is that the sister-in-law you don't like?'

Sarah was astonished. 'Where on earth did you get that idea from?'

'From you,' Kathleen replied bluntly. 'You said you thought she was a cold fish at Mary Shaw's funeral. And in the car one time you mentioned she didn't go to your wedding.'

The idea of Kathleen thinking these things about her... Resentment beat as loud as a large drum inside Sarah's head. The short jerky breath she managed was a direct result of her anger. She was not going to argue with Kathleen, especially as her mind was clearly not all right. In two days the woman had undergone several personality changes. How she sounded, how she talked, the constant change in energy, from standing still to rapid activity. It was almost as if her brain was being rewired every few hours to present a happy or angry Kathleen.

Sarah had found a third bedroom that morning, one with a double bed, next to Joe and Kathleen's room. Kathleen's uniforms were hanging in it on a clothes rail. She possibly used it when working night shifts to get away from the traffic noise.

But the bed was freshly made, so Sarah could have slept in there. So why put her in that other bedroom? Was Kathleen fantasising that Sarah was someone else? Sarah was beginning to think so...

She forced herself to speak calmly. 'Kathleen, please stop worrying about me. I know you care, but I can take care of myself. I've been doing it for years.'

Kathleen's cheeks turned instantly scarlet. Her mouth opened and closed like a fish. Her hands fluttered to her chest. Then her eyes filled with tears. 'I get on Joe's nerves all the time,' she said on the release of a ragged breath. 'He said to me I'd get on yours if I didn't back off. I'm sorry, Sarah, if that's the case.'

Sarah found it difficult to swallow. There was a deep unhappiness in Kathleen's face, but she couldn't involve herself in this woman's life. There were too many complications in her own. There was clearly some history in this home, but Sarah wasn't going to go looking for clues. Same as she wasn't going to look too closely at the personal objects and photographs around the place. Otherwise, Kathleen would swallow her whole. It was clear she was desperate to unburden, but she had chosen the wrong person in Sarah. Sarah needed to put all her energy into herself, to just get through each day. For how long she was there depended on how soon Issy could get her black coat. She had sent Issy a text listing the few items of clothing and toiletries she wanted, but hadn't heard back from her yet. She inwardly sighed. Regardless of Kathleen's strange behaviour, the woman was trying to do her a kindness. The fact that she misjudged the relationship between them was actually quite sad. Sarah could be kind at least. She could give Kathleen that.

'I don't have to rush off yet. I can stay for a cup of tea, and I'll be back in time for dinner.'

'That's grand,' Kathleen replied softly, before she went to put the kettle on. 'A cup of tea is what we need.'

Sarah slipped out of her brown coat, forgetting she was wearing the clothes Kathleen got out for her yesterday. She couldn't have visited her in-laws in Joe's tracksuit bottoms and top. She had put on the only jeans that would fit, which were properly skin-tight, and a black jumper that squashed her breasts. She folded her arms self-consciously and sat down before Kathleen could comment. And then, without thinking, she was so tired she blurted her biggest concern.

'I know the detective who came here, Kathleen.'

Kathleen glanced at her, and carried on getting mugs ready for the tea.

'I used to go out with him. He was playing the saxophone at a Christmas dance that was organised for the police, fire service and hospital staff. I went with another nurse. Debra Clark. She saw him first; spent half the evening trying to get his attention. It was only afterwards I found out he was a policeman. He was so good we thought he was part of a professional band. The last dance came on when, all of a sudden, he jumped down off the stage and walked towards us. You should have seen poor Deb's face when he asked *me* to dance.' A sad smile curved her lips. 'I should have said no to him then.'

'Why?' asked Kathleen. She switched the kettle off to silence the room, and quietly sat down at the table.

Sarah looked into her eyes. She couldn't hold back. 'Because it would have saved a lot of heartache in the end.'

'Yours or his?' she asked.

Sarah shook her head. 'His. Mine. Both of us, I suppose. He hates me now. I was the one who finished it. I hadn't seen Nick since that day until now.'

Kathleen sat silently for a few seconds before saying something that hurt. 'Well, you need to be careful then. If he hates you like you say he does, he might try to pin William's murder on you.'

Sarah's jaw dropped. Did the woman not have any filter on

what came out of her mouth? 'That's a bit extreme, don't you think?' she said in a gasp.

Kathleen shook her head. 'No, I don't. You're already a suspect. You were his wife. They took your uniform.'

'That's because I went into the house!'

Kathleen looked at her sagely. 'Maybe so, but I doubt that's the sole reason for their wanting it. When you asked me to drive you there, I didn't think you would go inside. They'll be looking at everything in your life, Sarah. Everything you say will be analysed. The policewoman who was here isn't your friend either. She'll have been watching you for any sign of guilt. If they don't find a suspect for William's murder, they'll look to you.'

Sarah gazed at her hard. The last thing she needed right now was to have Kathleen's unfiltered opinion. She needed to stop her right now. 'Do you really believe that, Kathleen?'

'Yes, I do.' Kathleen nodded firmly. 'They'll see what I see. That you're a young woman who doesn't give off the aura of someone who was in love, much less someone who is grieving.' She raised a hand as Sarah went to protest. 'Let me finish. I'm not judging you, Sarah. William came across as a kind gentle man, and it's fine to marry someone for that reason, but you need to be careful how you come across. Because being able to go out visiting people, and going to the shops two days after your husband is dead, is not the right impression to give.'

Sarah sat lost in thought. She didn't know whether to be grateful or angry with Kathleen for pointing this out. She felt like she was under a microscope right now, with Kathleen's magnified eye looking down at her.

Kathleen placed her hand over Sarah's and she tried not to flinch. She gazed at Sarah and gave a little shake of her head, as if Sarah had done something wrong. Sarah regretted confiding in her. Kathleen was too outspoken with her views.

'I know things, Sarah.'

Sarah looked at her worriedly. What the hell was she going to say now? Kathleen raised her head, as if to hold court and get Sarah's attention.

'I talked to Mary lots of times. William wasn't always kind.'

CHAPTER SIXTEEN

CHARLIE

Amy Fox was propped up in bed wearing a hospital gown. Her face was wan and her dirty blonde hair in need of a wash. Issy wrestled free a chair from a tightly stacked pile and brought it over to the bed. Charlie remained standing, staying on the far side of the bedside locker so as not to overwhelm her.

The girl eyed Issy curiously.

'Hello, Amy. My name is Issy Banks.'

'Are you one of the doctors?'

'No, I'm a policewoman. You met two of my colleagues at your school yesterday.' She jabbed her thumb towards Charlie. 'Charlie was one of them. We wanted to check that you're all right.'

The girl looked shocked. 'What d'you want with me?'

Charlie hoped Issy had rehearsed some pattern of questioning in her mind before arriving, because already the girl sounded defensive.

Issy smiled confidently. 'Just a little talk. To see how you are. We know how upset you were about Mr Shaw. It came as a shock.'

The girl nodded, her finger picking at a hole in the white blanket.

'Is that what happened to you? Are you here because of how upset you got?'

Amy's finger worked the hole bigger. 'It was a shock.'

Clever answer, Amy, Charlie thought. He saw her lick her lips and Issy got up to pour her some water. A sign above the bed read 'SIPS ONLY', but an empty teacup was in front of Amy on the table so it must be advice from yesterday.

Amy gulped the water. 'God, I'm thirsty. Hate water normally, but in here I'm drinking it like a goldfish.' She drained the glass. 'When I got back yesterday, I drank too much and was sick. They...' She shut up.

'Back from where?' Issy asked.

Her bitten fingernail now prodded a spot on her chin, testing to see if it was ready to squeeze. Smaller, scabbed ones told of the habit. She looked up, catching Issy staring.

'It ain't true what they're all thinking.'

'What are they all thinking, Amy?'

Amy eyed her scornfully. 'You know. Me!'

It was like trying to get a scalded cat to purr. Issy was good with cats. Charlie had seen her feed enough strays.

'What about you? What do they think?'

The girl's eyes darted over Issy's shoulders to see if anyone was in earshot. 'That I had the hots for Mr Shaw. What do they think I am? He's old enough to be my dad. I've got my own boyfriend. Mr Shaw was just kind to me. He was a really nice teacher. He showed me where Spain was on the map, 'cos I was gonna go out there and visit my mum... She went there when I was ten, to Costa Blanca to be a singer. Dad says she sings in all the bars.'

Charlie felt for her. She had an absent mum. Amy looked very small and vulnerable all of a sudden. 'What about your boyfriend?' Issy asked.

'Gone, inne? Didn't wanna know. Too scared to face me dad. No need to worry about it now, though.'

'I'm really sorry, Amy.'

The girl sniffed a healthy dollop of mucus. 'Best thing. Me dad woulda killed me. In one way it were a relief to see that blood drippin' outta me.'

Amy wiped her dripping nose with a paper tissue. Charlie used the moment to check on the time. He blinked at the message on his phone. It had been there a while, but he only just saw it. He eyed Issy suspiciously. She was always checking hers so she must have seen it. It was an alert to not visit Amy at her home address as there was new intel on the family. Was Issy ignoring the instruction because Amy was not at her home but in a hospital? His eyes bored holes into the back of her head. She needed to get to the point and be quick about it.

Reading his mind, or feeling his eyes, she asked the question. 'Amy, why were you outside Mr Shaw's house Thursday night?'

The girl's spiky lashes blinked fast. 'No. I wasn't!'

Wrong answer. 'You're sure?'

Amy stared angrily. 'You deaf? Said, didn't I?' She suddenly looked wary. 'It's me dad.'

Charlie turned and watched the man make his way to the bed. A bottle of orange squash was held in his hand, 80p on the 'Happy Shopper' label. He hadn't noticed Charlie. His eyes were all over Issy. Charlie used the opportunity to slip away and walk calmly towards the exit. He waited there for Issy, and saw through the glass panelled door as the man pawed at Issy's hand.

A moment later she walked out the door, her eyes wide with worry. 'He thinks I'm Amy's teacher. But Nick's going to go batshit crazy with me. I'm an idiot. I thought it would be a good idea. Nick would be pleased. Did you see him, Charlie?'

Charlie nodded. Yes, he did see Amy Fox's father. He also

saw what was as clear as the nose on Issy's face. She'd ignored the alert, because she'd wanted Nick to take a shine to her. He was aware they nearly got to first base a few years ago at the Christmas dance, and while boyfriends had come and gone, it was Nick who floated Issy's boat. She was right, though, to be concerned. Nick would fume over this blunder. Because while Amy might be a person of interest, her father was already known to the police.

* * *

Peter Metcalf, the facial identification technician, had packed away his laptop after his audience dispersed, by the time Charlie returned to the station. A printout of his work was up on the board. Mrs Shaw had good recollection and recognition skills and the artist had captured what he'd heard. An image of the man who visited her husband at their home.

The computer software involved in photo-fit had come a long way from the old technique, which consisted of photographs of real people jumbled together, with a selection of dozens of hairstyles, eyes, ears and noses to choose from. Because the images were so specific, witnesses found the process of identification very difficult. The new technique used images that were much more general.

Nick would have recognised the face, and then made the connection, which is why he issued the alert not to visit Amy Fox.

Dark hair, parted on the side, grown long over the man's ears. Narrow forehead, thick eyebrows and small hooded eyes over a thin nose and lips. His chin was small and round. The E-fit would be uploaded to the main terminal. There was no need. Barry Fox's photograph was already on file. He'd been a visitor several times to Keynsham Police Station, and to the one at Bath, before budget cuts closed it along with more than six hundred other stations across the country over the last decade. Cardboard cut-outs of uniformed police officers in places like shopping centres was meant to act as a deterrent. It didn't work on people like Fox.

He was an opportunist thief presenting himself over the years on vulnerable people's doorsteps as a salesman, a gasman and even a Mormon. Then he'd upped the stakes and become a burglar. Not a very good one, which is why he was caught. Two years ago, he was given a six-month prison sentence by a judge at Bristol Crown Court. Barry Fox, Charlie imagined, had been lying low since he was released.

Charlie went to find Nick to give him the news, and saw him at his desk. He approached Nick with his hands raised placatingly. 'We've got a problem,' he said. 'Issy just bumped into Barry Fox.'

'How?' Nick demanded.

'We went to the hospital to see Amy Fox.'

Nick's eyebrows rose to his hairline. 'You mean she talked you into going with her,' he countered with a blistering tone. 'Well, that's great. We just lost our element of surprise. Our number one suspect, and Issy just gave him a great big heads-up.'

Charlie defended her. 'He thinks Issy's a teacher, because his daughter introduced her as one.'

Nick scoffed at the idea. 'Barry Fox would smell a copper a mile away. He'll be like a rat up a drainpipe trying to get away. Let's just get this done fast, before he scarpers too far. Bloody Issy.'

The sudden quietening of colleagues alerted them, and turning round Charlie saw a warm-faced Issy standing at the door. Nick reined in his bad temper. He raised his hand in a placatory gesture. She looked miserable enough, without hearing him condemn her, and Nick had done far worse in his time. He was probably irritable because their first real lead was someone like Barry Fox, because while Fox had the cunning to get rid of footwear, or clothing, the man didn't have the nous to do this crime. He was liable to shoot off his own foot if he held a gun. And anyone who ever dealt with him would realise that. But the evidence was going to put him at the scene. Charlie was sure of it. The E-fit image was unmistakable. The odds of it being him knocking at the victim's door a few nights ago, and then his daughter sighted outside the property the night of the murder, meant he was involved somehow.

As for him being their number one suspect, Nick was being overhasty in that assumption. They needed to have all the facts first. Charlie wouldn't rain on Nick's parade by pointing this out, or spoil the team's motivation to get excited. Nick had shown in the past his uncanny ability for picking the most unlikely candidate to be the suspect.

Charlie might not be giving enough credence to Fox's more serous involvement, because while brave enough to enter a property where no one was home, he'd be a coward if there were occupants inside he risked waking. That said, he might have felt brave with a gun. He might have gone there to have a friendly chat with the teacher. His action that of a parent protecting their daughter. Only things got out of hand. The teacher might have threatened to call the police. Fox was cornered. The teacher had seen his face. The teacher ended up dead.

CHAPTER SEVENTEEN

SARAH

Joe Price put down the phone and carried on frying the eggs. A minute later he dished one onto each slice of toast. He put the two plates on the table with more rounds of toast and a pot of fresh tea.

Sarah smiled as she saw the neatly laid table. 'Looks good. I would have given you a hand if I'd known you were doing this.'

'You just eat it and I'll be pleased. Otherwise I'll have Kathleen onto me.'

She sat down dutifully and picked up the knife and fork. 'Was that her on the phone?'

'Yes. She needs some time on her own. Silly woman got herself all upset. A wander around Asda always sorts her out. She'll get lost in the aisles for hours. Buying God knows what.'

Sarah stared at the clean draining board. 'What happened to all the food? The lamb?'

'Back in the freezer. Making large meals is how she copes. Comes from being part of a large family. Although, Kathleen doesn't keep in touch with them anymore. She has brothers and sisters in Ireland she never sees.' Joe sighed. 'You've been a godsend, Sarah. Having you as a friend this last year has perked her up no end.'

Sarah felt guilty that Joe was unaware that his wife fabricated the friendship. It would hurt him to know the truth. Sarah knew next to nothing about Kathleen – not her age or birthday or anything about her personal life. Not what Joe did for a job. Or if they had children. She said nothing about it. She must apply the same behaviour with Joe as she did for Kathleen, and not become involved.

'Well, how come you stay so trim?'

He winked. 'I have a very deep lunch box, and across the road where I work a lot of ducks and other birds on the canal are well fed throughout the year.'

Sarah wished Joe didn't have to go to work. He had told her he would be going in about an hour, to work a night shift. She watched him neatly lay down his knife and fork by the side of the egg and toast, to pour them both tea. The simple meal was prepared and presented perfectly, and he'd not left mess behind, but cleaned and cleared as he went along. She was curious. 'Do you like cooking?'

He laughed. 'Well, I must have at one time. It used to be my job many moons ago.'

Sarah could easily imagine him working somewhere like a big hotel. He had an orderliness about him that had probably been taught. His eyes were resting on her as she glanced across the table. She had eaten the egg, but not the toast. She was not hungry.

'How are you coping, Sarah?'

'I don't know, Joe,' she answered truthfully. She gave a sad smile. 'I don't know if I ever really feel anything. I can't feel what's happened. The initial shock has gone, but that's the only time I felt something.'

He looked at her with concern. 'Maybe you're suppressing a part of yourself in order to cope. It would be no wonder if you were in some kind of deeper shock. I worked with a fella who lost his wife in a car accident. The very next day he came to work. To look at him you wouldn't think anything had happened out of the ordinary. He wasn't withdrawn, he was eating and talking, able to carry on as usual. Then he said he was going to get some supplies from out the back and stock up the shelves and he went up onto the roof and jumped straight off the building. Maybe you should see the doctor, Sarah. Just to be safe and sure you're not in some sort of mental lockdown.'

'Joe, I wish I was,' she answered fervently. 'But I think I've been like this all my life. Detached, when it comes to my own feelings. I can be kind and feel empathy for those around me. I feel those things as a nurse. But when I get close to feeling emotions that affect me, I run away fast.'

'It sounds to me like you've been hurt, or else never been shown love.'

Her throat tightened. Joe was a nice man, but he was not someone she could confide in. 'It's better that I run away, Joe. I can hurt people who get too close. Look at William.'

Joe shook his head hard. 'That's nonsense, Sarah. You're punishing yourself for what happened, because at the moment you're confused about how you feel. Maybe William was a safe bet. Maybe he was more like a father figure than a vibrant new husband. It doesn't mean that you're to blame because you can't feel any loss. Don't think that William got hurt because of you.'

Sarah sighed. She didn't believe that. If she hadn't married him, she was sure he would still be alive. Having her in his life was key to his ending. Which was not an answer Joe would understand.

The past always caught up with you. She would have told William what she had done. Probably when he told her he wanted children. He would have understood. It would have made sense to him, but that door had closed, and neither of them now could tell the other their secrets.

'I'll wait till Kathleen gets home. I don't want to leave you alone like this,' Joe said.

Sarah shook her head. 'There's no reason for you to go in late. I'm not going to do anything stupid, Joe. I'm not that sort of person. I'm stronger than I look.'

Joe looked undecided. 'From where I'm sitting you look like a lost child. I see the clothes Kathleen gave you fit.'

'Barely. The button on the jeans is digging in my stomach.'

Joe gave a small smile. 'They were like that on her, too. Wouldn't be told they were too tight for her. Mind, that was only puppy fat.'

Sarah returned the smile. Joe probably assumed she knew about this mysterious 'her', that his wife had told Sarah about their family. She let the remark pass. Sarah didn't get involved with families. Involvement led to knowing someone else's pain. She had one of her own once, but that was now in the past – a past only visited in her nightmares.

CHAPTER EIGHTEEN

NICK

At ten minutes to midnight the clock started the countdown on the time the police would have to detain the suspect, before they would have to release him. Barry Fox folded his forearms and puffed out his chest cockily. The duty solicitor appeared to have a head cold, sneezing and coughing into her handkerchief, tugging at the neckline of her blouse. The interview was being conducted by officers at Keynsham Police Station who had not visited the crime scene, as Fox was picked up from his home. It could not then be claimed, of any forensic evidence, that it was caused by cross-contamination.

Television dramas made it out that the senior detective was always the one interviewing the suspect, whereas in reality it was DCs and PCs who did the job, their techniques for questioning and retrieving information practised and fine-tuned. It was in no one's interest to have a senior officer do an interview when there were experts on hand who could do it properly.

But Nick would have dearly loved to be in that room. To smack one on Fox's weak chin, to get him to show a bit of respect to the woman representing him. Fox had slouched sideways so his shoulder pressed hers, forcing her to inch her chair to the furthest edge of the desk.

Nick had never hit a suspect in his life, but he'd been tempted. Despite all the courses on conflict management, on diffusing situations in a non-physical way, his hot-headed impulses rose to the surface on occasions.

The officers had been briefed by the interview advisor on interview strategies. Fox was in the TIE category. He lived in the vicinity – a half a mile away from the victim's home. He was associated with the victim, and they had an E-fit of him as the man who visited William Shaw at his home.

Nick was watching through a screen for the interview to begin, and waiting for a call from the search team to find out if they found footwear that would match the impressions found at the scene. They had all noted the brand-new white trainers Fox was wearing.

He saw Fox's eyes rest on the file the officer put down on the table. The officer sat down calmly and began. 'Mr Fox. Just to reassure you, Amy's safe and well and will be discharged tomorrow. In the absence of someone to take her home at the moment, they're keeping her in for one more night.'

Fox's tone was belligerent. 'Well, I'm not effin' stayin' 'ere tonight, so I can take her home.'

The officer nodded as if in agreement. 'Well, let's see how we get on first. You don't want her coming out if it gets too late.'

'Well I can go now then. Make sure that doesn't happen. All right?'

'We have some questions we need to ask you first, Mr Fox. You've been arrested on suspicion of being involved in a crime, which has already been explained. If we eliminate you from our enquiries, the sooner you can go. We would like you to give an account for your whereabouts on Thursday night.'

Fox answered quickly enough. 'Where I always go. The pub at the end of my road, for one or two before I go home.'

'Were you drinking alone or with friends?'

'Alone, the others were playin' darts.'

'These others, did they see you?'

A bored expression appeared on his face. 'Couldn't say, I wasn't lookin' at 'em.'

'What about the bar staff? Will they recall you being there?'

He shrugged, as if it wasn't his concern. 'Should do. I'm a regular customer.'

'And at what time would you say you left the pub, Mr Fox?'

'About half-nine. Same as always.'

'Then what did you do?'

'Walked home, what else?'

'You tell us, Mr Fox.'

'I walked home. Not likely to have got a bleedin' Uber, am I?'

'And where was your daughter Amy at this time?'

'Fast asleep in bed. Where else is she gonna be on a school night? I checked on her like any good father.'

Nick wished that Charlie would stop fidgeting next to him. The turning and swaying was distracting. Fox had just lied. Amy had been spotted outside her teacher's house at about nine-thirty.

'Go and have a smoke if you want,' Nick suggested under his breath. But Charlie stood still so Nick could focus again.

'I'd like you to cast your mind back to earlier in the week, Mr Fox. You visited Mr Shaw, Amy's schoolteacher, at his home. Can you tell us what that was about?'

'I could, but I won't. I don't want to slur the man's name now he's dead.'

'We know that you contacted the head teacher at Amy's school. It's been explained to us you had concerns.'

Fox bluffed his way. 'Well, that's what good parenting's for, isn't it?'

'So your visit was over concern for Amy, then?'

Fox cracked the knuckles on his left hand loudly. 'I was tellin' 'im to leave my girl alone. She was cryin'. Every time I'd try an' get 'er to talk, all she'd say is she wanted to see Mr Bleedin' Shaw. I put two and two together and paid 'im a visit.'

'Do you know why Amy is in hospital, Mr Fox?'

Nick was glad the other officer was keeping quiet, and allowing his partner to do the questioning. So far, the officer was doing a good job.

'I do now. I found out when I went to the hospital earlier.'

The officer held his gaze. 'So not before then?'

He shrugged. 'Not for definite I didn't. But you know what women are like. Messy cows. Leaves her stuff all over the bathroom. Including ten quid's worth she nicked from me.'

The officer feigned curiosity. 'What did Amy take ten pounds for?'

'You know, to buy one of those kits. To see if she were up the duff. Left it in the rubbish, like I'm blind and wouldn't see it.'

'When was this?'

'About four or five days ago. Same day I went to see the head teacher. Two blue lines effin' staring at me.'

'So you knew then that your daughter was pregnant, Mr Fox. It wasn't today you learned this, was it?'

Fox looked at his solicitor. 'Do I have to answer that?'

The solicitor looked resigned. 'You already have, Mr Fox.'

The officer backtracked to what was previously mentioned, keeping his voice at a low pitch so his words landed more powerfully. 'What did two and two add up to? You said you put two and two together and paid him a visit.'

Fox looked at him as if he were thick. 'She was up the duff. Stands to reason dunnit? Her crying, her pregnant, her wantin' to see 'im.'

The officer snared him right there. 'So you knew on Tuesday, when you went to see Mr Shaw that evening, that Amy was pregnant? You knew then, and suspected Amy was pregnant by her teacher? You went to see him to call him out on it, isn't that right, Mr Fox?'

Fox looked cornered. 'I ain't talking till I've spoken to my solicitor.'

The solicitor sighed heavily, probably wishing she was at home with some Lemsip and some company she didn't have to pay attention to.

'Now let us return to Thursday. You stated, Mr Fox, that Amy was in her bed when you got home from the pub, which isn't the truth. Amy was out of the house at that time, so you couldn't have seen her when you got in.'

The man's head jerked back, leaving his skinny throat exposed like a hen's. 'That stupid dozy mare...'

'We'll end the interview now, Mr Fox, to give you time to talk to your solicitor. I'm sure you're in need of a break. A cup of tea, perhaps? We'll sort out some beverages and food.'

Fox's eyes turned shifty. His voice nasty and hard. 'You do that, Officer. You do that like a good little policeman. Because I've got a lot more to tell about not so good policemen.'

About what? Nick wondered. He waited for Fox to say more, but the man folded his arms in a confident way, like he knew something that was going to help him.

Nick felt his insides sink, and hoped Fox was bluffing. If he walked, Nick would have to find a new suspect, which would cause him more of a problem. The longer this went on, the bigger the chance for Nick to be found out. And not just about the previous relationship.

If someone had seen him at the Shaw's house, before it became a known crime scene, it would be game over.

Because he had lied to Charlie about the time he got back. It had been much earlier in the day when he left London. He'd known when he arrived at the crime scene that Sarah had married. If someone knew that, it wouldn't take much of a leap to see it as a motive for killing the husband. This was another reason why he wanted to head up the case, so no one found this out.

His fall from grace, for someone like Robson, would be a lottery win. To see the handcuffs go on him and know Nick's career was over. For Charlie, it would be a serious blow to their friendship that might never recover. And Charlie, despite the grief Nick gave him, mattered.

He would just have to hope Fox didn't see anything.

CHAPTER NINETEEN

CHARLIE

On the south side of the city, in the privacy of his home, Charlie struggled for breath. He'd barely managed the drive back from work before doubling up with pain, hacking crap from his lungs and spewing vomit at the same time. His ribs ached fiercely, as did his stomach and the whole of his back. He took a hip flask from the side of the bed and took a hefty swig. He was relying on this to take away the last bit of pain. What the doctors prescribed him no longer worked. He needed something stronger. He would hate it if this bastard illness stopped him from working and from finishing this case with Nick.

He lay on a bed that was nearly as old as him. The feather mattress was now lumpy and sagging, but he couldn't part with it. It had been his aunt Charlotte's bed. She took him into her home when her sister died, when he was three. No children's services or social workers involved. Just like that. She brought him up, and became his mother.

Apart from Nick, she was the only person he ever had any regard for. He cared for Nick deeply. Not that Nick shared that sentiment. Nick would think him daft. It was something he didn't need to say, though there was plenty he would like say on another matter.

Nick had a sharp mind, but he wasn't using it if he thought Barry Fox guilty of this murder. It was laughable. Five minutes into the interview he was tripping over lies. Barry was more likely to have weaselled money out of William Shaw if he thought his daughter was pregnant by him.

Nick was out of sync. Charlie sensed it yesterday and again today when he told Nick he'd been with Issy to see Amy Fox in hospital, and knew something wasn't right about him. He wasn't asking for Charlie's opinion. Normally, by now, he would have used Charlie as a sounding board. They would have brainstormed ideas together. Nick hadn't even looked at Charlie yet, let alone stopped and properly spoken to him. After Fox's interview, Nick called it a night and left without so much as a backward glance.

Charlie regarded Nick like a surrogate son. He'd met Nick's real father years ago, when John Anderson reported his young wife missing. But neighbours put the police right. Nick's mother, who loved music and dancing and records, ran away. They had seen her get into a multi-coloured sleeper van with all her colourful friends, with her record player and records. None of them were surprised that she left her domineering husband, only that she left her son behind. Charlie had kept a distant eye on him ever since. On the pretext of checking for any news of the missing wife he'd call at the house occasionally, and would speak to the boy after a quick chat with the father. Each visit would lengthen in time from Nick getting Charlie to play football with him on the rough patch of green outside the house.

He felt a sting in his eyes, and brushed his forearm across them. He was a fool. Getting all emotional. Nick was probably just adjusting to being back. He'd burned the candle at both ends with his leaving do and hadn't had time to refresh. He just needed a good night's sleep, and a fresh look at it all tomorrow.

Charlie shouldn't worry so much. Certainly not about Nick doing his job.

And his other worry? Well, Nick would handle that as well. He wasn't a boy anymore. Of course he would cope. Charlie was just being overprotective. Which was fine, as long as he didn't become maudlin. They had Christmas to look forward to yet, so plenty of good times ahead.

His mind cleared, the pain had gone. He wasn't worried anymore. He let his body relax. His aunt Charlotte's shape hollowed into the mattress long before his, relaxed him finally into sleep with his memories of light kisses, while his nose buried deep in a pillow to catch the faint smell of rosewater.

CHAPTER TWENTY

NICK

Digging his keys from his pocket, Nick let himself into his old flat and saw the small cardboard box in the passageway. It must have been there on Thursday, but went unnoticed in his hurry to dump his luggage. He'd not been in the hallway long enough to notice it. And last night, after the post-mortem, he was asleep on his feet when he came in and found his way to bed. He hadn't had a proper look around yet. This morning he unzipped bags to find toiletries, a clean shirt and suit, and saw only the bathroom before he went out the front door. And now it was two o'clock Sunday morning.

He opened the box and saw a white envelope on top of the contents. Charlie's heavy scrawl was on the front of it. 'Welcome back. Catch up with a pint tomorrow.' Charlie had obviously expected Nick to arrive back early in the day, or he'd have put perishables in the fridge. Charlie was the only other person with a key to get in. He'd kept an eye on the flat while Nick was away, and had left him this welcome pack: milk, bread, coffee, sugar and butter.

The idea to rent it out hadn't crossed his mind. He'd been in a rush to get away and lick his wounds in private and hadn't thought beyond that. Somewhere in his mind he must have always been expecting to come back. Any longer away and he would have had to consider renting or selling it. His finances had taken a hit in the last year with paying for both his mortgage and the rent for the flat in London.

He flicked down the brass light switch in the hall and saw through the open door into the sitting room and the sagging couch, the standard lampshade with its green fringe, the low table with multiple coffee rings. It looked more spartan than he remembered, perhaps because there were no shoes on the floor, mugs on the table, or newspapers on the couch.

He carried the box to the kitchen, and saw Charlie had minded the place well. Nick wouldn't have thought to leave the fridge door open with the help of a teacloth. He probably left it with food inside that Charlie had to throw away. He needed to thank Charlie properly. He'd hardly kept in touch with him, except to post him a key and ask him to check on the flat occasionally. Charlie was probably at home sulking in his bed because Nick hadn't stayed to chat after Fox was interviewed.

He put Charlie's box on the counter, and turned the fridge on, hoping the milk hadn't already soured. He then went and had a look in the room next door. He'd slept in the double bed last night and not noticed it was made with a duvet cover and coloured sheets he didn't recognise. Charlie must have seen the bare linen cupboard and gone to fetch some from his. Nick vaguely remembered stripping the bed before heading for London. What he did with the unwashed linen was a blank. He may have put them in the washing machine with other unwashed bedding and Charlie found them gone mouldy. He would have to buy new linen, and towels as well. The one in the bathroom wasn't one of his. Charlie must have had a clear-out while tidying the place. But it would all have to wait. He'd pull out and hang up his other suits and a few shirts, but that would have to do. He needed sleep and a drink more than an organised wardrobe.

He returned to the kitchen and found a glass in a cupboard beside a bottle of Macallan, and poured himself a whisky – a large one that might help him relax. Managing with the light from the hallway and finding the kitchen more soothing in the dark, he sipped the drink and looked down onto the back windows of the houses opposite. His body turned tired and his mind emptied of everything else but her, and the year he just spent thinking of all the things he must have done wrong and all the ways he would put it right.

Had he taken her for granted, or not given back, or heard what she wanted? Had he been too selfish, too moody, or not exciting enough? Those were the reasons he attributed to her ending their relationship, and those were the behaviours he would change if she gave him the chance. If she had signalled that there was a problem, he would have done it back then.

Yesterday, when Sarah turned and faced him, she looked like a girl playing dress-up. The grey tracksuit engulfed her, making her look smaller. Her pale face and her big shadowed eyes showing her vulnerability. Seeing her like that gave rise to a memory he would never forget, of being in a wood and seeing another pair of eyes that had once stared at him like that – vulnerable and waiting for it all to end.

His father denied it ever happening – he would never have taken Nick hunting – and that it was just a dream. He got annoyed when Nick mentioned it. But Nick remembered being there. He'd worn wellingtons over his pyjama legs. He remembered being afraid, his head pushing into his father's thigh, and the hand moving across his face, pressing over his lips to keep them quiet. He'd seen between the splayed fingers her pale-brown coat – the blood vibrant and red and wet looking. He had watched her legs trembling, small shivers up each finely boned limb. The sound of the gun cocking had terrified her. She made one indecisive movement with her head and then she looked at him, her eyes clouding as she urinated on her legs and the mud – long seconds before she fell to the ground.

He learned something that day – that he could look at a death and do nothing to prevent it happening.

If Sarah had signalled that it was ending, it wouldn't have been as big a shock. The night before they had slept together. In the morning, they both went to work. Not a hint of what she was planning in her manner or in her eyes. It just ended with a curt full stop. A few hours later she was standing outside her front door, her forearms crossed, hands cupping elbows, telling him: *It's over.*

His mind hadn't been able to work it out. The suddenness of it. The level of disbelief he experienced brought back years of pain. And with it the insight that he'd avoided accepting for all those years, that his mother had not loved him. She had told him with *her* behaviour.

Nick had blamed his father for her leaving, believing that his preaching of the Bible and his attendance to the church is what drove her away. He was a curate, not even a minister, not even with a proper job, who believed prayer reformed everything. Nick remembered hating him when she left. Her few things were thrown away. Bits of jewellery, ornaments she had bought and any photographs with her in them, had all been shoved in a cardboard box and left out to get wet in the rain. The bin men collected it and Nick never had the chance to salvage anything.

But he was an adult when he realised he couldn't hide from the truth anymore. She could have taken him with her. She didn't have to leave him behind. She chose to. He remembered the last time he saw her put on her make-up. He'd climbed out of bed, wanting to see her, she'd been out when he came home from school. She was in her yellow dress, and a pink pretty scarf was tied in her hair. He remembered how her eyes didn't seem sad as she saw him watching her in the mirror. He remembered her lips pressing his cheek and the excuse she gave, as she confessed with a light laugh, 'I'm not very good at being a mother.'

Downstairs, he heard his father arguing with her not to go out again, then he heard the front door open and close. Her second coating of lipstick stayed on his face until his hot tears, and his cheek against the pillow, washed it away. But the hurt had stayed forever. Why had she not loved him?

He blinked hard, then stared into his own eyes reflected in the kitchen window, and wondered at the damage done to him. His mother? His father? Sarah? He should have learned by now to accept that sometimes there are no answers, and that he should stop looking for them. And he would if his mind would let him.

But his mind was that of a detective. There had to be another reason why Sarah ended it with him, that had nothing to do with his failings. Because her behaviour that day just didn't make sense. There was something that she was hiding. There was the truth.

CHAPTER TWENTY-ONE

SARAH

At eight o'clock on Sunday morning, Kathleen was stomping about rearranging furniture in the kitchen to fit in a large artificial Christmas tree she purchased from Asda last evening.

'Have you forgotten?' Joe asked. 'We have a perfectly good one in the attic.'

'Oh, don't be an old Scrooge.' She smiled. 'I can put that one in the sitting room.'

Joe relented and smiled in return. 'Well, it'll be nice, I suppose, to see the house all Christmassy. It's been a while.'

He went over to a kitchen cupboard and pulled out three mugs for him, Kathleen and Sarah, and switched on the kettle. 'I'll have this drink, and then I'm off to bed.'

From the logo on his shirt, Sarah now knew where he worked. On the worktop there was a bag of croissants, which he proceeded to slice and butter. Five minutes later, Sarah was sipping a mug of tea, and watching the activity of Kathleen with bemused eyes. She kept forgetting it was nearly Christmas. She would make sure she was gone before then, to give Kathleen and Joe back some normality. They should be allowed to enjoy themselves, without reminders of her there. And now might be the time to mention this.

'I'm thinking it's time to leave, to give you two back your lovely home,' she quietly stated. 'You don't want the police knocking at your door all the time. And when I was at Keynsham station yesterday, they said I'd get a number of visits in the next few days. They want me to look at photographs of my home to see if I can spot if anything was taken. Then there'll be a visitor from the coroner's office. The policewoman, Issy, is also going to call by again to see how I am. You don't need all that.'

Kathleen banged her mug on the counter, slopping tea down the side of the unit. 'What on earth are you suggesting? You can't be alone at Christmas! Joe and I wouldn't dream of letting you leave.'

Sarah protested. 'Kathleen, remember what I said yesterday. I'm used to looking after myself. And, to be honest with you, most Christmases I work. I prefer it.'

'Well, you can't work this one! The hospital wouldn't allow it after what's happened.'

'They will if I'm all right. They're too short-staffed to refuse.'

'Don't be ridiculous. They'll turn you around and send you home.'

Sarah stayed quiet. She would see about that. As soon as Kathleen left for work, Sarah would follow. She was going to see how she felt when she got there. She'd rather be useful than sit around all day with nothing to do. If people thought that odd, that was their concern. She needed to keep busy until her husband was buried. And then, she might stop.

Sarah used the keypad to let herself into the staff changing room. She didn't have her normal uniform with her because her dresses were in the wardrobe at her home, except for the one the police had taken from Kathleen's washing machine. She changed into some scrubs. She had her nurses' shoes, her fob watch, and ID, so wearing scrubs on the ward would be fine.

She heard Andy Brooke's voice as she neared the nurses' station. It was a surprise – she didn't know he was back. Andy had taken a sabbatical to work in Sydney. He was talking in a loud and excited voice to Kathleen, and Sarah stood still behind the wall to listen.

'I couldn't believe it! While my back is turned, the love of my life ups and marries the grieving widower. And now she's the widow, God love her. Talk about when the cat's away. I can't leave her alone for a minute without her causing all sorts of naughty gossip. So give me all the details now, and don't spare my feelings. I'm a big boy. How is she? And why is she at yours?'

Sarah pressed her hand over her mouth to stop herself from laughing. She forgave him. He was such a drama queen. She knew he'd have had the same conversation with her if it had been about someone else.

Sarah heard Kathleen's angry reply. 'It sounds as if you've already heard enough and I'll bet I can guess who from. It wasn't like that. She didn't marry him straight away. She waited six months.'

'Well, that's a decent enough interval, I s'pose. Give the man a chance to change the sheets and all that. And that wouldn't have happened if Mary hadn't fallen out of bed,' he said in a stage whisper. 'I mean her hospital bed, obviously, not the marital one.'

Sarah was no longer amused. She never heard a whisper, stage, Chinese or otherwise, of Mary falling out of bed. There was no report of that happening. Andy must be saying it to wind Kathleen up. He may as well have said Mary fell off her perch to make way for Sarah, because that was his meaning.

'Sarah is with me for the foreseeable future,' Kathleen

stated in a proud voice. Like she'd been given an award or some-thing, and Sarah was the prize. It made Sarah squirm again, like she had at Kathleen's home.

'Really? Why's that?' Andy asked. 'She has her other home.'

'What other home?' Kathleen asked, sounding put out that she hadn't known.

'Her flat. She still has her flat, according to Helen.'

Kathleen's reply was sharp. 'It's none of our business, is it?'

'No, I suppose not. But it's nice to know she'll be financially okay, and not have to worry.'

Sarah could hear hurt in Andy's response. His soft sigh. She waited until it all went quiet before stepping round the corner, and was relieved to see they were gone.

Dr Kumar stepped out from a side room. He was her favourite doctor – soft-spoken and unfailingly cheerful no matter what the circumstances.

His eyes clocked her and his lips curved into a sympathetic smile. He then took her by surprise by taking her hands in his. 'You shouldn't be here, Sarah, not in your condition.'

Sarah nearly burst out laughing, with relief she supposed from being with someone completely normal, but she didn't think Dr Kumar would appreciate it. He'd probably whisk her off to the psychiatric unit thinking she was having a breakdown. 'My husband has died, Doctor Kumar. I'm not pregnant.'

He shook his head at her flippancy. 'I meant the condition of you being in shock, Sarah.'

She looked back at him, a little shame-faced. 'I know you did. It's just easier to deflect kindness. Look, I'm not going to get in the way, and I don't want any fuss. I just need to keep busy.'

His eyes smiled kindly. 'I'm very sorry for your loss, Sarah. Very sorry.' Then he released her hands. 'I came out to find some help. I need to do a lumbar puncture. I'm suspecting Guil-lain-Barré syndrome.'

'Do you want me—'

'No. Absolutely not. I'd rather you went home, my dear.'

Sarah frowned at what she had discovered. She hadn't taken Dr Kumar's advice and she was still at the hospital, but wished now that she had left when he told her to. Instead, she checked pharmacy stock. She'd gone through the ordering book three times and come away from it with the same conclusion. One pot of diazepam and one pot of temazepam were missing. She had checked the drugs cupboards, and the drugs trolley, and counted the tubs that were unopened or in use.

She checked these medicines first because they had gone missing before. But it hadn't happened for a while. She rested her face in her hands, and decided she wouldn't deal with it. She didn't have the energy right now. She was officially on compassionate leave, and shouldn't even be there. She could pretend she didn't know about it.

Kathleen came into the treatment room and Sarah attempted a smile, but failed miserably.

'You should be at home,' Kathleen stated firmly. 'Not here. Doctor Kumar said he saw you. I'll kill Joe for letting you come.'

'Not his fault. He was asleep when I left.'

'Well, you're going home now. The police are coming here to have a chat with the staff, so you shouldn't be here. Not when you have the likes of Andy Brooke and Helen Tate on duty. It'll be another reason for them to gossip and you don't need to hear it.'

Sarah nodded. 'Thanks for the warning. I'm going to go straight home, and straight to bed. I'm tired, Kathleen. I shouldn't have come. It did me no good at all.'

CHAPTER TWENTY-TWO

CHARLIE

Charlie followed a tall, slim matron as she walked faster than a greyhound past bays holding patients. He smelled an amalgam of smells – from food to strong cleaning agents. He thought smoking was meant to damage the sense of smell. He was getting a whiff of poo also, and felt slightly sick.

She pointed him in the direction of a closed door. 'Take your time. I'll keep an eye on the ward.'

Charlie felt he should be thanking her for offering this service, but she was already trotting away.

He knocked and heard shouts from several voices inside the room, none of them welcoming. One of them was a clear order: 'Go away. We're having our lunch.'

He opened the door and popped his head round, his warrant card ready to show them. They all looked curious, and then were welcoming as he was offered a seat. Charlie saw Sarah Shaw's minder and nodded a greeting. 'Mrs Price.' To the others he said, 'Afternoon. Sorry to interrupt. I'm Detective Sergeant Bowden.'

A blonde nurse in a sky-blue dress stood up, and Charlie noticed the blob of pink nail polish dabbed at the bottom of a ladder in her tights. He recognised her as the nurse from the other night, who had fetched Sarah Shaw. She smiled and offered him coffee. 'Helen Tate. We already met.'

A spiky blond-haired nurse was staring at his colleagues. It gave Charlie a minute to gaze at them and to make eye contact with the pale-skinned nurse in the grey dress. He'd not properly looked at Kathleen Price. He'd never seen irises as pale as hers. She had her large hands wrapped around a cup. She placed it down on the low table, and took charge.

'How can we help, Sergeant?'

Charlie shrugged off his jacket, feeling the heat of the room. He took out his notebook and felt excitement emanating from his waiting audience.

'Well, as I'm sure you're aware we're investigating the murder of William Shaw. Many of you will have known him. I thought I'd start by introducing myself. I'm happy to see any of you individually, here or at the station. But, basically, I'm hoping to know more about the man. I believe his first wife was also a patient several times on this ward, so even something she may have shared with you might help.'

'Feel free to fire away,' the nurse with spiky hair suggested. 'I'm happy to sit here until the shift ends.'

'Mary practically lived here for the last six months of her life,' Helen Tate offered. 'We knew her really well.'

Charlie nodded encouragingly. 'Anything significant come to mind?'

The nurse shook her head. 'She was a bit of a stickler. Never satisfied with anything we did for her. Or maybe it was just with me.' She gave an impish grin. 'She was my English teacher at school. Even in my nurse's uniform I felt like a naughty pupil. The number of times I'd answer her with a "Yes, miss", "No, miss", I'm surprised she didn't ask for my homework.'

'The woman couldn't help herself,' Kathleen Price argued.

Helen Tate raised her eyebrows. 'She liked you, Kathleen, because you read her the Bible all the time. You didn't have to listen to her moans.'

'She didn't like me at all,' the spiky-haired nurse commented. 'Wasn't keen on being washed by a man. Which is fair do's. I'm all for diversity. Still, I was only saying this morning how surprised I was that hubby got married again so quickly.'

Charlie glanced at him. 'And you are?'

The nurse smiled. 'Who me? Sorry, I should have introduced myself. Andy Brooke.'

'So you must have been away, then, Andy. To not know William Shaw remarried.'

'Yes, Australia. I was away when Mary died, though that was less of a surprise. Soon as I have my flight money I'm going back. Got someone waiting for me out there.' He smiled shyly, and Charlie could see a sensitive soul, and secretly wished him good luck.

'While I, on the other hand, was surprised Mary died.'

Charlie stared at Helen Tate. 'What do you mean by that?'

She shrugged. 'You get these patients that tick along forever and every time they're ill you think "this is it", but next day you step on the ward and there they are sitting up in bed eating their Cornflakes. That's how it was with Mary.'

'Shut up, Helen,' Kathleen Price said sharply. 'You don't know what you're talking about. There'd been talk of moving her to ICU. It wasn't a surprise when she died. She was very ill.'

'I'm only saying it was for me. You saw my surprise at Mary being found dead on the floor.'

'Well don't,' Kathleen said forcefully.

'Chill, Kathleen. We all know you care. You did a good job laying her out so beautifully... after finding her like that.'

Kathleen stood up, not beating about the bush. 'I found her

dead because you didn't keep a watch on her. Too lazy. I wouldn't trust you to mind a dog.'

The silence in the room was deafening as she stormed out.

Helen Tate glanced at Charlie innocently. 'What did I say?'

Charlie looked around him. There were two nurses there who hadn't said a word. 'Am I missing something here, something I need to know about?' he asked them all.

No one answered. He stood up, getting ready to leave. He'd assign officers to have them all interviewed properly down at the station. He put his jacket on, put his notebook back in his pocket and stepped towards the door, when Helen's voice stopped him.

'Strange though... William and Mary Shaw dead in the same year. No one knows what's around the corner. Do they?'

Charlie glanced at her. She was someone he would definitely want to interview again.

An hour later, Charlie's head was stuffed with medical jargon. With the help of a modern matron, he had managed to map most of Sarah Shaw's movements during the timeframe of her husband's death. Charlie wanted the hours from eight to midnight accounted for, as he was at the hospital just before midnight to see Mrs Shaw.

What was proving helpful were the prescription charts collected by the modern matron from the various wards. She opened the first one.

'What are you checking for?' he asked her.

She pointed her finger at slim columns of boxes. 'This is where a nurse or a doctor has to sign. See the two letters in that box? That's the initials of the individual who signed. Then in the box below you have the time.' She moved her finger to the top of the column and Charlie saw boxes where the date was written. On the left-hand side of these columns the drugs were listed.

The matron opened the prescription charts to the night Sarah Shaw worked. She moved her finger on each one, stopping at various boxes, and Charlie saw 'SS' in black ink written several times, and the time when each drug was given. Sarah Shaw had signed her initials for the giving of these drugs on different wards. She was at the hospital during the hours he wanted accounted for, but not all the time was spent on her own ward.

'I'm confused,' he admitted. 'About why she's on other wards.'

'Well, that's because Sister Shaw is a highly experienced nurse. And sometimes the less experienced need a helping hand. Not every nurse, for example, can administer intravenous therapy through a Hickman line, or change a cannula. Sister Shaw would have gone to those wards to do those tasks, as well as to give medications.'

Charlie was satisfied. Her alibi was solid enough. With photocopies of the prescriptions under his arm he thanked the matron for her help. Outside in the cold fresh air he reached for his cigarettes. It had been a worthwhile visit. An interesting one. Especially hearing what Helen Tate said. *William and Mary Shaw dead in the same year...*

Her words had sent a shiver down Charlie's spine. Something didn't smell right about Mary Shaw's death. So maybe they should be looking at this hospital, and at all the people there who knew Mary and William Shaw. It would be a mammoth task he was about to land on Nick's shoulders. But instinct was pushing Charlie to look in that direction. He might even have met the killer – which sent another shiver down his spine.

CHAPTER TWENTY-THREE

NICK

Charlie was reading Professor Doyle's prelim report as Nick walked up to him.

'You had a chance to look at this yet?' he asked.

Nick shook his head. 'I only just walked in. What does it say?'

'Well, it tells you something – this is one very controlled killer. It takes a lot of control to get a gun inside someone's mouth.'

'You have control when you've got a gun in your hand, Charlie.'

'I disagree. A lot of people feel out of control when there's a weapon in their hand. Most of them use it because they panic or get scared. To get that close takes confidence. And this killer not only got close enough to shove a gun inside Shaw's mouth, but according to Doyle's report he interrupted him eating cake in bed.'

'What are you on about?'

'Undigested cake in his gullet. Doyle's written it here,' Charlie said, pointing at the words on the paper.

Nick took the PM report and read through it quickly. Then

he stepped away from the desk to make a call. He dialled Doyle's work number, hoping he was working on a Sunday. A minute later a receptionist put Nick through to Doyle's office.

'This is DI Anderson, Professor Doyle. I wonder if you have time to discuss a few things with me about your report.'

'Of course, Inspector. Fire away.'

'DS Bowden reckons the offender interrupted the victim while he was eating cake. Is that right?'

Doyle chuckled. 'Charlie Bowden can reckon on what he likes. But I deal with facts. And that isn't a fact. A lump of undigested sponge cake, chocolate flavour to be precise, was stuck in the top of his oesophagus. Whether he was eating it when the offender entered his bedroom is up to you to determine. I can only tell you that he didn't swallow it sufficiently to enter his stomach.'

'So what do you reckon, Professor?'

'That he died with a lump of cake still in his throat.'

'Wouldn't he have choked?'

'He did, Inspector,' Doyle replied dryly. 'On a bullet.'

Nick hung up and decided it would have to wait on further analysis. Also, he shouldn't argue with Charlie's assessment of the killer. Charlie was right. The killer was someone who really wanted to hurt Shaw. Nick needed Mark Steel to get back to them with *his* findings – forensics would tell them more. Maybe when all that crap was scraped off the floor in Fox's house there would be cake crumbs, or even a leftover cake in the kitchen with Fox's DNA drooled on it. Fox was just the type to wander into someone's home, chomping on a bit of cake while he rifled through their drawers.

Nick wanted Barry Fox for this murder. The man was perfect for it. But this report was disturbing. It aroused speculation. From the low conversations of the officers waiting for the briefing, they were getting an image of a gun pushing the cake into the man's mouth. Fox wasn't that inventive, or that brave. The rumbles of concern were saying as much.

A more pressing problem was their suspect in a cell at Keynsham Police Station. They couldn't keep Fox locked up indefinitely, not without charging him. He would have to be released on bail if further evidence wasn't forthcoming.

'Nick. This killer likes to play torture games, I think. Have you given any thought to what I said about Mary Shaw?'

Nick sighed. 'Can we just concentrate on this angle first, Charlie? Issy's going to be back any minute with an update on Amy Fox.'

'She's here now,' Issy said, coming into the room. She sank into a chair, and grinned at her colleagues. 'Amy admits she was outside her teacher's house. She went there because her teacher's wife is a nurse, and she needed help. But no one answered the door. She then got scared, thinking someone was behind her. She went back home and took some painkillers because she had a stomach ache, and saw her father was in bed.'

Nick was pleased because Barry Fox had said the opposite – that he checked on his daughter like any good father when he got home from the pub and found her in bed. So both were lying. Amy probably got scared from seeing her father there. The switch in opinion from Fox being innocent to guilty again was also a relief. Issy's input had jump-started new conversations – Fox was not out of the picture yet. He let them talk among themselves. He would start the briefing in a minute, though there wasn't much more to tell.

Charlie suddenly ran from the room, suspending the discussion.

Ten minutes later Nick headed into the toilets, his eyes sweeping along the open doors looking for the one that was shut. He banged on it hard. 'You in there?'

Vomit splashing a toilet bowl was Charlie's loud response.

He unlocked the door and struggled out, heading straight for a sink to wash his mouth, after which he raised his sickly face.

'I knew I shouldn't trust that pie.'

Nick watched him stagger across to the paper towels and his frustration rose. 'I was hoping you'd be there when we interview him again. We have him, Charlie!'

Charlie leaned over and gasped for breath, then rose unsteadily to a standing position. He spoke wearily. 'We don't have him, Nick. Fox is aptly named. He's cunning. But, while he isn't stupid, he hasn't got the balls for this. He has a yellow streak running down his spine. He's a small-time crook. Nothing more.'

Nick looked at his sergeant and felt cornered. He wasn't prepared to agree. Or lose. He had too much riding on the outcome.

'Go home, Charlie. I'll let you know how it goes.'

CHAPTER TWENTY-FOUR

SARAH

Joe didn't bat an eyelid when he walked into his kitchen and saw his wife at the kitchen table, and Sarah cooking at the stove. 'What is it? It smells good.'

Sarah turned and smiled at him. 'Spag bol. Nothing fancy. Just quick and easy.'

'I wouldn't mind a glass of wine,' Kathleen said. She rose from her chair, and took off her coat. She'd only been home a few minutes and, like Joe, didn't show surprise at finding Sarah cooking. 'I'll throw off my uniform, and fetch a bottle from the sitting room. I'll be back in a minute.'

Joe's kind face eased into a smile, and he squeezed Kathleen's arm as she walked by. 'That sounds nice,' he said.

Sarah was pleased, seeing them close like this. It would make it easier when she left tomorrow. She had decided on tomorrow because after her visit to the hospital she was worn out. She was making this meal by way of a small thank you, though it wasn't much and the ingredients were from Kathleen's kitchen.

Joe set about laying the table. 'This is nice,' he commented. 'And Kathleen did a lovely job on the tree. I'll have to dig the other one out now. It's been in the attic for years.'

Sarah turned from the cooker to look around the room. Their house was comfortable and roomy. The kitchen big enough to have a table and four chairs. Sarah had only sat in the sitting room once, with Issy Banks, and had been in the dining room only once with Nick and his sergeant. Which reminded her to text Issy and tell her not to worry about fetching all the items on the list. She'd bought some jeans and tops when she bought underwear. They would do her for now. She only wanted her black coat. Otherwise tomorrow she would be going nowhere.

Joe had turned the Christmas tree lights on, and Sarah felt a catch in her throat at all the pretty colours. She had only put a tree up twice in her life, and both times were when she was with Nick. He would have thought it strange that she didn't celebrate Christmas, so she put one up.

Kathleen had gone over the top with the tinsel, wrapping it around plants and picture frames. On the windowsill she had set a little wooden manger that looked old.

Kathleen returned with some red wine, and shortly after they sat down together and began the meal. Kathleen's face beamed. 'This is lovely, Sarah.'

An abrupt clanking of the letterbox made them jump, and then they laughed at their reaction.

Kathleen got up and went to the front door, calling over her shoulder at the same time, 'It's probably a Christmas card from a neighbour.'

A half-minute passed and she didn't return. And then they heard her give a small gasp. She walked back into the kitchen and handed Sarah a sheet of paper. 'I'm sorry I opened it before I realised it was for you.'

Sarah placed it on the table. She stared at it transfixed. The message had been put together in an amateurish way. Words had been cut out of a magazine or newspaper and glued to a sheet of white paper. The words were chilling.

I'M ON TO YOU. I HAVE PROOF.

Joe stared at it in astonishment. He rushed out of the kitchen and then ran past the window outside. A minute later, breathing fast, he returned. 'Couldn't see anyone,' he gasped. 'They must have bloody wings.' His hand reached for the telephone, but Kathleen halted him.

'Wait, Joe. Give Sarah a minute.'

'This needs to be reported, Kathleen.'

'We will. But Sarah doesn't need a zealous ex-boyfriend rushing round.'

Joe stared at her in confusion. 'I don't understand.'

'Sarah's ex-boyfriend is the policeman in charge of this case. They broke up. Sarah needs protecting, Joe. We know how the police work. I already warned Sarah they'll be looking at her for William's murder.'

Joe's voice rose. 'We've just sat here and heard it posted through the door. They're not going to think her guilty.'

'Your memory is short, Joe. They pointed the finger at us. Or have you forgotten?' She poured him some wine, and moved the glass into his hand, which Joe drank fast.

'You can protect her, can't you, Joe? You're a security guard.'

Joe's head rose in shock. 'For Tesco's! Not for someone whose life may be in danger. I'm Joe Price. Not bloody Bruce Willis.'

Sarah was sitting in a trance. Kathleen and Joe now noticed her, and Joe was first to react. 'You're as white as a sheet, Sarah. We need to lie you down.'

Sarah didn't resist. She felt dazed. Who would send her that message? What did it mean? Was she safe?

Kathleen followed behind Joe as he guided Sarah up the

stairs. She stood at the bedroom door while Joe settled her into the bed.

'I've made a decision,' Kathleen quietly said. 'I'm packing away Becky's things.'

Joe stood in the middle of the room and ran his hand over his greying hair. Then he slowly walked out. Sarah heard him open the door to his bedroom and then close it.

She glanced at Kathleen. 'Please don't empty this room for me.'

'Shush,' Kathleen said. 'I'll be back in a moment with some warm milk.'

In the silence that followed, Sarah thought she heard Joe crying.

Sarah opened her eyes and saw the milk beside her, and Kathleen sitting in a chair. Her whole manner had changed. She looked serene.

'Whose room is this, Kathleen?'

'Becky's,' she said softly.

Sarah sat up in the bed. It didn't feel right lying there with Kathleen telling her this.

'It was twelve years ago. And not a day goes by that I don't think about her. That I don't push my face in that wardrobe and breathe her in.'

Kathleen handed her a framed photograph that she'd had in her lap. Sarah stared at the image of the girl. She had curly dark hair. Her very blue eyes and very red lips were smiling.

'She was thirteen. A beautiful age, a beautiful child. Curious about everything. She'd be twenty-five now. I might have been a granny.'

'What happened? Was she ill...? I mean—?'

Kathleen rescued her. 'She was the healthiest child imagin-able. Full of life. Full of love, happiness – until she started secondary school. And then her life became a misery. I was back and forward to that school every other day, but they didn't want to know what my child was going through. Didn't want to acknowledge that what I said was true. Didn't want Mrs Price to keep knocking on their door. She was wilting away like an unwatered flower, and still they said there wasn't a problem.'

Sarah felt tears on her cheeks, but held her hands back from wiping them. She sat quiet and still, waiting for Kathleen to continue.

'It was a Monday morning. I came to wake her for school. I found her in bed, curled on her side with her eyes closed, as if she were asleep. I curled in behind her and held her against me, just holding her and feeling the weight of her in my arms. She had one hand tucked under her cheek; I didn't want to disturb it. I felt down under the cover for the other and in it she held my empty bottle of tablets. My angel had put herself to sleep.'

CHAPTER TWENTY-FIVE

NICK

A second interview with Barry Fox was about to begin. Nick watched through the viewing window as Fox drummed his fingers on the table, both hands in unison, showing his nerves. In contrast, the solicitor seemed more settled than yesterday and was sitting relaxed, a handkerchief no longer necessary.

An idea had formed in Nick's brain after Charlie went home. He wanted Fox questioned on the whereabouts of the gun. They wouldn't find a gun. But all that was needed was for it to be believed he had one. Unbeknown to Fox, the police had irrefutable evidence that put him inside the victim's home, not just in the kitchen where soil was found, but also in William Shaw's bedroom. His fingerprints were on the belt of a pair of trousers found on the floor. Nick had noticed them when he was there, and now he knew why – Fox's nicotine-stained fingers had been in the pockets. He had placed himself directly at the crime scene, so Nick would use that to his benefit.

The same two officers were conducting the interview, and Fox was reminded he was still under caution. The lead officer looked focused and ready to begin.

'Mr Fox. We have a forensic team searching your house. It would save a lot time and effort if you tell us where the gun is.'

Fox smiled at him. 'Can't tell you what I don't have. Hope they don't leave a mess behind.'

'Well, we know you were in the victim's home, Mr Fox. Your fingerprints were found on a trouser belt in the victim's bedroom.'

His smile disappeared. His hands gripped tightly together. Fox looked worried. 'Not saying I wasn't there. But *I* didn't kill him.'

The solicitor quickly whispered something into her client's ear, but Fox shrugged her off. 'I didn't kill him.'

The officer stared at him, staying silent.

Fox became unnerved. 'I'm tellin' you the truth. I didn't kill him.'

'So you keep saying, Mr Fox.'

'I'll say it for as long as I like. I did not kill him!'

'You lied about Thursday night. Your daughter was not at home at the time you say she was there. She was outside her teacher's house. Which I think you knew, because you were there too. Was she trying to stop you? Prevent you from killing her teacher?'

'I'm not denying I was there. I said it already, but I didn't lay a finger on him. He was dead already! D'you hear me? He was dead! I nicked his money, that's all I did. You prat!' Then he slapped the table hard. 'You won't find nothing in my house that will show you otherwise. I didn't go near him. He was in that bed dead before I got there! You need to be looking at someone else for this one, mate, 'cos I didn't do it!'

* * *

Nick returned to Kenneth Steele House, hoping to catch Naughton. He knocked the office door before entering the room. Superintendent Naughton, in the process of putting on his coat, smiled politely.

'I was about to head home,' he said. 'Did you want something, Inspector?'

Nick quickly brought him up to speed with where they were with Barry Fox.

Naughton was not a man given to casual chit-chat. His quietness was meaningful. He listened attentively and answered sincerely, but most of all he was constant. The same could be said for his appearance over the years. He still looked like a modern-day Viking, albeit an aged one, with his silver hair cut short against a large well-shaped skull, and his height and breadth of shoulder impressive in a dark grey suit.

Nick could do with a bit of talk for the sake of talk right now, and less of the constrained manner from the man. He needed Naughton onside.

Naughton seemed to be neither satisfied nor dissatisfied with developments to date. 'He hasn't confessed to it, has he?'

'No, sir.'

'So, we're waiting on forensic evidence? Or for the weapon to be found?'

'Yes, sir. But we have sufficient evidence at present to charge him.'

Naughton looked at him over his glasses. 'So you say. You have his fingerprints on a trouser belt.'

Nick was feeling the pressure. He should have waited until they had more to go on. He was hoping that cake crumbs would be found in Fox's home. 'Yes,' he confirmed. 'In the victim's bedroom. During the hours he was murdered. Fox admits to being there. He admits to stealing money from the trousers on the floor.'

'But not to murdering the victim.'

Nick had stymied himself by coming to Naughton too soon.

He should have had Fox tied up in a bow before he approached the superintendent.

'No. But he had motive and opportunity. He believed his daughter, Amy, was pregnant by William Shaw. He visited Shaw on the Tuesday to confront him about it. He then went back to the man's home on the Thursday to exact revenge. He lied during his interview.'

Naughton frowned at him. 'Lying doesn't necessarily make for murder. Stealing doesn't make him a murderer. I would have liked it backed up with more than you've got here. If not a confession, then further evidence.'

Nick looked at the wall clock. It was 9.15 p.m. At ten to midnight Barry Fox would have been in custody twenty-four hours. He should go before Naughton suggested releasing Fox on bail. Fox's wife lived in Spain, and he would probably hop on a plane from Bristol Airport if they let him out the door.

Naughton though was one step ahead of him and fully aware of how much time was left. 'So what you're asking is for me to authorise a further twelve hours?'

Nick nodded, then cleared his throat though nothing was wrong with it, to save on answering.

'Barry Fox,' Naughton now said, 'has never been known to carry a weapon. He's an unpleasant specimen at the best of times, but he would have to plan this and, quite honestly, I think he's as thick as two short planks. This seems a bit beyond his capabilities. Do we really see him with a gun?'

Nick didn't, but the idea he formed earlier gave him the opportunity to put forward a way to end this case. But it was a possibility he had to stop himself from jumping on too quickly. Instead, he gave a reasoned reply: 'It's too soon to say, sir. I wouldn't have thought it before, to be honest with you. He's an opportunist thief at heart. Charlie isn't buying it, I can tell you that. He doesn't think Fox has the balls for it.'

'But you're thinking it could be him.' Naughton looked at

him curiously. 'You've done profiling. What's your assessment so far?'

Nick could see Naughton wanted to explore why Nick was thinking this way. 'Power/control-orientated type,' he began. 'Someone who gains pleasure by the complete control of the victim. The killing isn't prerequisite. It may not necessarily be the intention.'

Naughton gave a short laugh. 'And this is Barry Fox?'

'This is the killer's profile we're talking about, if this is murder,' Nick expressed in an understated tone.

Naughton sat down on the edge of his desk with a severe frown between his eyes. His formerly calm demeanour was gone. 'Well, thank goodness we haven't given a press release yet,' he declared sharply in a loud voice.

Nick shook his head. 'Look, my first thought was this was a suicide. But we haven't found a gun. Barry Fox is the only suspect that we have that we know went into that house. So these are the possibilities: Fox went there and murdered him, or someone got there before Fox and did the deed, or Fox found him dead like he said he did and no one murdered him. Which comes back to my first thought – this was a suicide and the gun was there, and Fox sees an opportunity to take it?'

Naughton's jaw was clenched. He looked hard at Nick. 'What were you thinking,' he said between his gritted teeth, 'not raising this sooner? The victim will have been exposed to gunshot residue. We needed to check if his hands were clean.'

Nick nodded firmly, and then, as if it was an afterthought, he mentioned the autopsy report. 'It's the cake in the victim's throat that has me puzzled.'

He had to mention it. The one anomaly in this theory of suicide was that a man would eat cake and then shove a gun in his throat. To not mention it would appear strange. Because who would eat cake when they were about to kill themself?

'Blasted hell, Inspector. Make up your mind! Is this a murder or not?'

A strained silence followed Naughton's outburst. Nick let it be seen he was uncomfortable, while really he was settled. He had to keep the idea alive of Fox as a possibility. All he needed was for Naughton to believe Fox had either taken a gun to the scene to use, or taken one from it for gain, for all this to end.

Naughton stood up. He shook his head. 'Go home, Inspector. You're going to need your rest. Tomorrow, bright and early, you need to tidy up this mess, before it leaks to the press. This needs to be decided. A man's family think their loved one has been murdered. That is down to you. You're on the front line, leading this investigation. Everybody is calling it a murder. And now you're not sure. To be frank with you, this is a right royal cock up.'

Moments later, the door closed behind him. Naughton's annoyance was so marked that he hadn't bothered to usher Nick out of the office, but had vacated it himself. The dressing down had been severe. There was no telling what Naughton might do. Nick could turn up tomorrow and be off the case. And then where would he be? Where would Sarah be?

He needed to play it smarter. Forget what he knew. The groundwork was done. He just needed to be the detective leading the case. The dots were already joining. He had to remember when he saw Naughton tomorrow, to apologise, and if necessary to beg to stay on the case. The bigger picture was all that mattered. He was doing this for Sarah.

CHAPTER TWENTY-SIX

SARAH

Sarah had to splash her face with cold water before going down the stairs, after the phone call she just had with Issy. She'd been asked a personal question, and then been told some news.

Joe was on the phone, his hand rubbing the back of his neck agitatedly. Sarah busied herself putting the kettle on, and was halfway through filling it when she heard his raised voice.

'Look, Kathleen. I—' He snatched the phone from his ear and threw it on the table. He pressed his fingertips over his eyelids. 'She's on her way back. Can I make room in the fridge!' he exclaimed in outrage, and then Sarah saw his eyes and knew he was extremely angry. 'She doesn't think we have enough food or drink. You can't open a cupboard without food falling out.'

Sarah hid her unhappiness, while Joe started rearranging the food in the fridge, making space for his returning wife's shopping. She should have left when she woke at six. She could have avoided the problem of having a reception here. Alice Shaw phoned just after seven to let Sarah know she'd arranged for a memorial service to take place in three days' time. That alone had been a surprise. Sarah would rather wait for the release of her husband's body and do it properly and only once. A second surprise was when Kathleen jumped at the idea, and badgered Sarah to call Alice Shaw back and say a gathering could be held in her home. The arrangement was now sealed. Kathleen took off in haste with her purse in hand, which had upset Joe.

Sarah, of course, would reimburse them, but that was not the issue. Joe was having to turn his home over to strangers, to be used for a funeral gathering, without any say in the matter.

He spoke while he worked. 'I'm cross with Kathleen. You've been bulldozed into this. I don't know what she was thinking.'

Sarah was thinking the same for him. Kathleen hadn't consulted anyone, although she let Sarah think she had, and said Joe didn't mind. She felt queasy. Like she had motion sickness. She had a headache from all the tension, and in the last few moments it had spiked to a painful crescendo.

She leaned against the worktop. 'They've arrested a man,' she said quietly. 'He's not been charged, but they're questioning him.'

Joe pulled his head out of the fridge, and looked at her like a startled rabbit in headlights. Sarah supposed it had suddenly registered with him why he had an unexpected house guest. Why the police were contacting her. Her husband had been murdered.

His reaction settled. He nodded purposefully. 'Well, good. Now we can report the letter you got.'

Sarah glanced at the kitchen table. Joe had the presence of mind last night to place it in a clear plastic sleeve to protect it. She hadn't a clue who it was from, but she didn't feel safe. She should have reported it to Issy while she had her on the phone, but it had slipped her mind after the news she had been given. She would phone Issy back once she took something for this headache.

He took a step towards her. 'Kathleen never said how—'

'He was shot, Joe,' she interrupted. 'When I went to see the body, the sergeant confirmed what I already suspected. But no other details.'

'Jesus... I thought...' He stared at her, shocked. 'I thought a blow to the head maybe. But he was shot?' He stood rigidly, not saying anything for a few seconds, before releasing a deeply held breath. 'Are you making tea?' he asked.

She nodded, and the movement made her wince.

'What's up?'

'Headache. It's getting worse,' she admitted, holding her hand on top of her head to ease the pain.

Joe looked round the kitchen. 'She keeps paracetamol or the likes in one of these cupboards.' He opened one of them. Seeing no sign of the tablets, he opened the rest, moving objects out of his way in his search. Then he looked up and saw a Tupperware container on top of the units. He stood on a chair to get it down. Bandages, gauze, plasters, cough mixture, paracetamol, ibupro-fen. He took out the paracetamol and groaned. 'She told me the doctor wouldn't give her any more of these.'

Sarah walked over to see what he had found. Two grey tubs of tablets hidden beneath the top layer of medicines and bandages. She took them out of the Tupperware container. Printed on white labels was the name of the hospital pharmacy. The diazepam and temazepam had not been prescribed by Kathleen's GP, but had come from the ward where Kathleen worked.

Sarah didn't let on that they were stolen. She touched his hand. 'You can't blame her, Joe. She told me about Becky.'

Joe's chest heaved as he drew breath, and his eyes watered. 'You don't know the half of it. That shrine you're sleeping in replaced another one before it. That room is a constant reminder of our loss. We had a son who died three years before Becky was born.' He thumped his chest. 'She'll always be in here. Along with that little lamb. But I don't want to be reminded every waking hour that she's not coming back. I don't want to see her bed ready to sleep in, her clothes ready to wear, her hairbrush sitting on that dresser waiting to be used.' His fist rose to press his trembling mouth, to regain control. His voice sounded worn out. 'I don't think I can take it anymore. I've lost two children. And along with them, I lost Kathleen.'

Sarah, moved by his outpouring, did what came natural to her as a nurse. She put her arms around his back and let him lean against her until he regained his strength again.

They were sitting quietly, drinking tea, when Kathleen's key opened the front door. The container of medicines had been put away. Kathleen bustled into the kitchen loaded down with shopping bags. Joe stayed at the table and stared in dismay, the frivolity in his wife's voice already getting to him. The little yelps of excitement she made while pulling groceries out of bags. 'Oh, these are lovely,' she exclaimed of the fruit-shaped ice-cubes, skipping to the freezer like an excited child.

Sarah was equally dismayed. Kathleen had spent a fortune, and was behaving like it was a Christmas party and not a pre-funeral wake that that she was preparing for. She needed to put a stop to this. Alice Shaw would probably expect only sandwiches and tea, maybe a cake, not a banquet.

Joe beat her to it, slamming his hand on the table. 'Just stop it, will you?'

Kathleen jumped more from the sound of his anger than the struck table. Her eyes went wide with surprise.

Joe stood up. 'You need to go and see the doctor, because I'm not putting up with this, Kathleen. You're behaving unhinged, which is both disrespectful and hurtful to Sarah and me. A man has been arrested and is being questioned. Sarah's husband has been murdered, and you're behaving as if this is an excuse for a new life. Well, it's not happening, Kathleen. We got dealt a hard blow, but there is nothing we can do about it. We have to bear the weight and live on. But not through other people's lives. And not through Sarah's.'

The silence that fell in the kitchen was complete. Sarah held her breath as Joe stormed from the room and out the front door, and Kathleen then ran straight up the stairs. Sarah blinked to wipe away her tears and wished other people's pain didn't hurt. She realised she liked Joe and, to a degree, also Kathleen, after everything she'd learned. They had their daughter for thirteen years. It must have been heart-wrenching to lose her in that way. After losing a little boy too. No wonder Kathleen was reaching out. No wonder she kept that bedroom the same. She was desperate to fill the emptiness.

Sarah looked carefully at a photograph of Becky on the wall. She had spotted it earlier. Sarah noticed the school uniform, which hadn't altered much over the years. She did the maths in her head, and wondered if Kathleen had realised that William was teaching at the school when Becky was there.

She turned from the photograph and looked at all the food on the table. She closed the kitchen door, so as not to disturb Kathleen, and quietly got on with putting it all away. It shouldn't be Joe's or Kathleen's job to sort out fridge and food. William had been her husband. She needed to take responsibility for this event, to make sure it went calmly and smoothly, and put this home back in order afterwards.

A thought had gone through her head earlier, when she was sat at the table with Joe – Kathleen might have pressed for the reception to be here so Sarah would have to stay. She had been intending to leave today, but now she couldn't. The more she thought about it, the more likely it seemed. Kathleen was going to have to understand that when this event was over, Sarah would go. She was not staying to take Becky's place.

CHAPTER TWENTY-SEVEN

NICK

Nick suspected that if Naughton wasn't in the room he'd have heard a few jibes about this being psychobabble. He had heard it all before, but it never bothered him. During his postgraduate degree he'd been invited to Quantico, the FBI Academy in Virginia, and had attended tutorials given by the Behavioural Sciences Unit experts. He'd met the real Starlings and learned that Thomas Harris had sought the advice of the academy when writing *The Silence of the Lambs*.

'Typological profiling,' he said, 'is looking at behavioural evidence obtained at the scene.' He picked up a baton and pointed at the board. 'Personality type of an organised offender,' he said. 'These are the typical crime scene details of an organised non-social. The crime scene reflects overall control. Restraints used on victim. In many cases the victim will be tied up. In this case, a gun was used to immobilise Shaw. Victim forced to submit. Weapon absent. Body often hidden or moved from death scene. Overall, a planned offence.'

He paused as he saw Robson's eyes locked on him. Gelled brown hair added to Robson's good looks. He dressed in suits in preparation for bigger things to come. Nick knew the man was probably planning to challenge anything that didn't sound right. He carried on. 'Personal characteristics of perpetrator: Socially competent, manipulative. Average to above average IQ. Controlled mood during crime. Living with partner. Follows crime in news media. Souvenirs may be taken from the victim.' Nick swung the board around to show more writing on the other side. 'On this side, we have disorganised asocial. The disorganised person murders suddenly and spontaneously, without advance planning, and with no particular thought for avoiding detection, often using whatever weapon happens to be at hand. As a result, the investigation usually begins with many clues and a lot of evidence.'

'So what are you saying? Barry Fox is a bit of both?' Issy asked, with surprise in her voice. 'He obviously doesn't fit the socially competent type. And, yeah, he left his fingerprints and footprints at the scene, but he also planned bringing a gun.'

Nick folded his arms and sat on the edge of a table. He shrugged. 'I got a bollocking last night from our SIO,' he said to the team, as if Superintendent Naughton wasn't there with them in the room. 'And rightly so, because I can't make up my mind if this is murder or not. William Shaw's phone records, landline calls and mobile have been checked. We have not been able to identify a number for the anonymous caller. Mrs Shaw's number is down as the last caller on her husband's mobile and their landline. Seven times, to be precise, on the house phone. Shaw's finances have also been checked. No large, regular, or irregular sums of money unaccounted for have been withdrawn from his account. The two anonymous letters, which may be the key to all of this, haven't given us anything to go on. Background checks: clean licence, no cautions, no criminal record. From family we have Jane Shaw, his sister. Three years ago, she had a falling out with him while she was pregnant. She was planning to have a termination, when he suggested he could adopt the baby. However, she miscarried. They didn't get on particularly well after that. From friends we're hearing he was a popular man. A solid bloke. A good teacher. It begs the question, why then was he sent these letters?

'Ballistics say the perpetrator would have had maximum exposure to gunpowder residue if protective clothing wasn't worn. Mark Steel says the clothes piling up to be washed on Fox's bedroom floor had been left where dropped. The cuffs of Barry Fox's jeans have mud on them. His size ten boots, matching the impressions found, are in his home by his front door. The white trainers he was wearing when arrested – a present from his daughter Amy for his birthday.'

Mark Steel was nodding in agreement. Nick indicated that he should take the floor. 'Mark will give us an update on the forensic evidence.'

'Sure,' he said, coming up to the front to take Nick's place, while Nick went to stand by a window. 'I'm going to list what we have, then any questions can come later. A .45 calibre bullet was found embedded in the wall behind the headboard. Totally mashed up so we haven't been told its characteristics yet, but possibly a Colt. If we find the gun, it will have a blowback of blood on it. Perpetrator will also have been sprayed.

'The National Identification Bureau have found only one match against the fingerprints we filed, and they are Barry Fox's, but we do have fingerprints not accounted for after checking off family, but you know the score on that one. If they're on file with NIB we get a hit. Otherwise, it's pie in the sky.

'All evidence collected from the scene of the body has been analysed. The red wax found on the drawers... we found white candles in a drawer in the kitchen, but no red candles anywhere. Long hairs found on the victim's body and on the pillows belong to Sarah Shaw, the victim's wife. Fibres collected from the body consist of cotton threads from the sheet covering him. The sheet he lay on held hairs – his and hers; blood – his;

semen – his; and further cotton threads that were lemon coloured. Mrs Shaw's nightie – Mrs Shaw confirmed with Issy she had intercourse with her husband on Wednesday night.'

Nick jolted. He felt the air in his chest lock in. He opened the window beside him and a gale of cold air swept through the room.

Steel turned his head and raised his eyebrows at him. 'Bit parky for that, isn't it?'

Nick closed it. He could breathe again. He only hoped he hadn't betrayed his feelings on his face. What Steel had said left him wrung out. He glanced around the room and saw disdain on Robson's face. For a brief moment Robson's eyes betrayed *his* feelings, and Nick knew he would have to watch his back.

He straightened and walked back to his seat on the table as Steel finished, and no one had questions. He bet it would be less than a minute before Robson had one for him. He could see it brewing in his whole expression. He bet right – it was less than two seconds.

'Well, what about the cake in his throat?' Robson called out. 'Surely that's significant? Maybe if the killer thought Shaw was trying to have the best of both worlds, the message might be "You can't have your cake and eat it too".'

Nick smiled pleasantly. 'You might well be on the right track, but at the moment, Paul, anyone's guess is as good as the next. You see... here lies my problem.' He gazed at individual faces in the team. 'If this is a homicide, the cake is symbolic. What it represents, I'm not sure. A visible sign of something invisible, obviously.' He paused. 'Without this find, I'd be thinking Barry Fox went to that home with the intention to get money out of William Shaw. But instead, he finds the man dead and steals the suicide weapon.'

The room filled with a rumble of voices. Which is exactly what Nick anticipated happening – discussions about all the possibilities. For some it would be a disappointment that murder might be off the table. For others, it would be a relief to get back some normality to their lives and spend time with their families. He was mollified by Naughton's brief nod. Perhaps Naughton was agreeing with Nick's opinions.

A sergeant near the back put her hand in the air, trying to be heard over the din of noise. Nick quietened the team so Hilary Walker could speak. She was a neat attractive woman in her forties. He had worked with her a number of times, and hoped she wasn't going to be the first to voice an objection.

She spoke in a clear, calm voice. 'We have somebody you may want to take a look at. She came to our attention while interviewing the teachers at St Matthew's. Nothing concrete, but a lot of innuendo pointing to a relationship between her and William Shaw.'

Nick gave the sergeant an appreciative nod to show he welcomed the information, while he felt pure frustration within. He wanted them all to just stop looking, for the CPS to decide there was enough to charge Fox with murder, or the lesser offence of interfering with an investigation. It would salve Nick's conscience if they chose the latter. Fox would do some time, but then he should. He'd nicked a dead man's money, and thought he could get away with it.

Instead, Nick had to show willingness to interview this new lead, which would be a pointless exercise. While he was prepared to use Barry Fox in this way, he wouldn't do the same to an innocent woman.

CHAPTER TWENTY-EIGHT

CHARLIE

Amanda Black opened her front door with a ginger cat in her arms. She was the same woman who greeted them at the school, who had shown them into the head teacher's office. Her slightly bulbous eyes blinked at them in surprise. Charlie showed his police credentials, and introduced himself and Nick, even though they'd met before. She kept them at the front door for a moment before letting them in, her gaze on Nick. In his single-breasted black suit, pale-blue shirt and burgundy tie, he attracted women's looks. Charlie had seen it before.

The room she showed them to was like a gallery. Black-and-white photographs of movie scenes hung on white painted walls. Lauren Bacall and Humphrey Bogart, Paul Newman and Elizabeth Taylor, Audrey Hepburn, Katharine Hepburn, Charlie Chaplin. It was an attractive display, simple but effective, and a reminder that Amanda Black was a drama teacher who taught acting for a living.

A white console table against the far wall was entirely free of dust collectors apart from a single photograph of a man and woman. Charlie would come to that during the conversation, but would wait until they were sitting down.

His eyes rested on Nick, and saw the indifference on his face. He wondered why Nick wasn't jumping at the bit to get started. Charlie was ready to buy into the idea that Fox went to the victim's home and stole a gun, but he wasn't buying that this was suicide. Nick could not ignore what he highlighted. Cake in the man's throat, not even swallowed. He couldn't disregard that.

Charlie gave it a few more seconds and saw Nick still standing, making no effort to sit down, leaving it to Charlie to talk to the woman. She had been sitting for a minute and looked reasonably settled in her chair. Charlie apologised for their turning up unexpectedly. Then he turned to the reason for them being there.

'The photograph you have on your table is of you and William Shaw.'

'Yes.'

'Why is that?'

She frowned. 'We were friends. We worked together.'

'It's the only photograph in the room that isn't of a celebrity. It's curious, don't you think?'

Her eyes turned wary. 'Why are you asking about me and William?'

'Any information that comes our way during an investigation has to be checked. What's come to our attention is that there may have been more than a friendship between you and William Shaw.'

Nick chose that moment to butt in. 'Where were you on Thursday evening?' he asked bluntly.

Amanda looked startled and the cat meowed at being squeezed. 'Here.'

'Alone or with someone?'

'Alone... well, not entirely. I have Ember to keep me company.' Her hand smoothed the orange fur.

Nick smiled all teeth. 'I don't suppose Ember could verify that for us, could he or she?'

Her expression was confused, unsure if a joke had been made. 'No, of course not.'

'So, you were here alone? No one with you? Doing what?'

Her hand swept around the room as if it held the answers, and in a way it did. 'Telly, reading, marking a bit of homework.'

'In that order or all at once?'

She was becoming flustered by these quick-fire questions. Her eyelids blinking, she stuttered, 'I... I can't remember. Probably telly first and reading last. I always read last thing at night.'

'Was William Shaw your lover?'

A shallow breath escaped her. Amanda pulled a handkerchief from the sleeve of her pale-blue jumper, and Charlie wondered how long it would be before tears appeared. He felt uncomfortable at the way Nick was badgering her. They should have requested that she come to the station for a voluntary interview, as he suggested. But Nick thought it better to have a friendly chat with her at her home. This was not friendly.

Was it deliberate because he was fed up? Was this an inconvenience for his neatly thought-out theory? Charlie's gaze flickered over at him and saw the aloofness on his handsome face. It was a quality he'd always had that some people mistook for shyness. Nick wasn't shy, he'd just learned to harden his heart.

Her face went brick red. 'Is that necessary?'

It was obvious what she was asking – if this line of questioning was necessary – but Nick chose to ignore it. To ridicule her instead. 'For most people it is, but maybe not for you. You've got your cat.'

'How dare you.'

'He either was or wasn't.'

'So what if he was!' she stormed back. 'It's none of your business.'

Charlie needed to calm the situation. He'd formed no ideas

whether this woman was guilty or not, but she hadn't been read her rights. Anything useful she said might be negated in court.

Her laugh rang out, tinged with bitterness. 'I loved him while he was with Mary. I was there for him when she got ill. I thought we would end up together. And now he's...' She couldn't say the last word as a sob racked her.

'So what happened?' Charlie quickly asked, before Nick could open his mouth.

'*She* happened. He married her. He didn't love me like I thought he did.'

Charlie was relieved when Nick stayed quiet at the red flag just raised over Miss Black's head. Jealousy and revenge were strong motives and put her in the short list of suspects.

'Miss Black, we're going to leave you now, but we will wish to speak to you again. Someone will be in contact and you will be asked to attend a voluntary interview.'

Her face was shocked. 'Is that necessary? Mine and William's relationship stopped when Mary died. Why does it have to be dredged up?'

Charlie waited a beat, then said, 'This is an ongoing enquiry, Miss Black. So, I'm afraid it is necessary.'

They saw themselves out. Charlie got behind the wheel and drove in silence. They arrived back at the station just after eleven. Charlie drove the car around to the back of the building to the parking spaces for police vehicles that were out of public view.

He got out and leaned against the car door trying to ease the pain in his back, and after a moment he saw Nick step out of the vehicle.

Charlie didn't look at him when he spoke. 'For the first time since I've known you, I was ashamed of you. I understand the pressure you're under but that back there was downright brutal. I don't know what's ailing you, because you're not telling me anything. When did that happen, Nick, that you can't talk to me?'

Charlie got out his cigarettes. A deep phlegmy cough erupted from his chest as he lit up, and Nick sounded impatient.

'For Christ's sake give those things up.'

Charlie watched Nick walk away without giving an explanation. His hand shook as he held the cigarette. For the first time, he felt like he didn't know him.

CHAPTER TWENTY-NINE

SARAH

Sarah put her finger to her lips as she let Issy in the front door. She pointed at the ceiling and then put her palms together on the side of her head to indicate someone was sleeping. Issy's eyes glinted with humour and Sarah read her mind and shared the same thought. *Best they don't wake Kathleen.*

In a quiet voice, when safely in the kitchen with the door closed, she said, 'It's been a fraught morning. My mother-in-law has arranged for a memorial service for Thursday, and Kathleen offered to have the reception here, which has upset her husband.' Sarah sighed. 'The day has been slowly passing ever since, so it's nice that you're here.'

Issy's eyes were sympathetic. 'I thought you could do with an update.'

'Would you like some tea?' Sarah offered.

Issy shook her head. 'Let's talk first, in case we're interrupted, and then I'd love a cup.'

'Do you want to sit down?'

Issy seemed unsure, her expression troubled. 'Look, this is the situation... none of this is set in stone by the way. It's just... well, as you know we have a man we're questioning. He was in your home on the night your husband died. There's some doubt, however, as to whether he was involved in the death. Sarah, I don't think you've been asked this, but did William own a gun?'

Sarah raised surprised eyes. She answered without hesitation. 'No.'

Issy was nodding. 'Okay. Could he have had one without you being aware?'

Sarah tried to concentrate on what this meant, but images kept popping into her head. His quiet behaviour, the way he kept his thoughts to himself. She slowly nodded. 'It's possible, I suppose.'

Sarah rubbed her hands together as if they were cold.

Concern still showed in Issy's eyes. 'Are you okay?'

Sarah nodded. 'You're thinking suicide.'

Issy kept eye contact with her. 'We're not deciding on that yet, and we're not ruling out that this is an unlawful killing. But we need to think about who your husband was, and why someone would want to murder him. Or why he might decide to take his own life. We still don't know what those messages mean.' She pulled out a chair from the kitchen table. 'I've changed my mind. We should sit down. This is not easy.'

Sarah sat in the chair opposite. 'So you have no suspect then?'

'It's just...' Issy seemed to be struggling for the right words. 'We should be nailing someone by now or at least be having some idea of who it might be. Don't think we've given up. We do have other people to interview.'

Sarah heard the defensive note in Issy's voice and felt she should reassure her. 'Isn't it early days yet?'

Issy shrugged. 'Maybe. It's just another day is going by and we've got nothing concrete.' Her lips twisted in a half-smile. 'It's worrying, that's all. I'm an impatient copper. Hand me a suspect on a plate today, preferably one who is willing to plead guilty.'

Nick sprang to mind. Sarah had to stop herself from mentioning him. He'd been impatient at times when he was working on a difficult case. 'Well, let's hope it won't be long until someone does,' she said. 'Or it's decided that William's death wasn't at the hand of another.'

Issy smiled at her. 'I bet you're a good nurse. You make a difficult situation easier. You could have stood here and shouted at me after what I said.'

'That's not going to help, is it?'

'No. By the way, I got your text about your clothes. So you don't need anything apart from the coat?'

'I didn't, but now I do with this service coming up. I have a black skirt suit in the same wardrobe as the coat, if it's not too much trouble?'

'I'll let the inspector know. Which reminds me. I have a question to ask. There was a remembrance card in a book in your bedroom, in memory of Ray. Who was Ray?'

'William used that card as a bookmark. I noticed it when I moved in. Ray was someone he never mentioned.'

Issy glanced at her. 'You didn't ask?'

Sarah shook her head. 'I shouldn't have had to. I was waiting for him to tell me about his life. But we never went any further back than the time I nursed his wife, Mary.'

'That's sad. It makes it sound like you just slotted in after she died. Were you happy?'

There it was, the immediate pressure, when someone wanted to delve deeper. Issy was only looking out for her well-being, but Sarah couldn't open up. She couldn't answer truthfully. Otherwise, Issy would be wanting to question her seriously.

'I was relatively content. I wasn't looking for excitement when I married William. We were still only beginning to get to know one another.'

Issy stared away. Sarah knew she was surprised. She probably regarded Sarah as a newly-wed bride who'd been passionately in love with her new husband. Sarah had just trampled that image, but she wasn't going to pretend otherwise. It was a compliment to Issy that Sarah felt she could tell some truth.

Issy stood up, throwing her bag over her shoulder. 'Well, I suppose I should be getting back.'

Sarah didn't remind her about having a cup of tea. She liked Issy, but it was better if they didn't get too close. They had got close enough for Sarah. She would never be able to talk about things like happiness when it meant so many different things to others. But she was glad Issy visited. She had reminded Sarah of something she had to do.

CHAPTER THIRTY

NICK

Nick had made a detour to come and see the house again on his way home from work. He'd finished at five, early, after failing to achieve the desired result. Fox had been charged with burglary and released on bail. They could only keep him in custody for a maximum of thirty-six hours, unless a judge authorised a further seventy-two hours. Naughton didn't want to hear it. So Fox was now out.

Nick put on the coverall suit, overshoes, gloves and mask without being reminded this time. He signed his name in the logbook before opening the front door. There was no sign of life coming from anywhere within the house. He wasn't surprised to be the only one there, because the crime scene investigators work was mostly done. Mark Steel would say when they were pulling out for good. Turning on the lights he saw the floors were laminated and the doorways had been widened. Which must have been done to accommodate Mary Shaw's wheelchair.

He entered the kitchen, which was small, the walls painted a light blue. Black-grey aluminium dust coated the countertop and parts of the back door. He opened a wall cupboard and found it stocked with little jars of pesto, sun-dried tomatoes, and pots of different herbs. Deep jars of pasta shapes, brown rice and spaghetti lined up on a shelf beneath the cupboard. She was a good cook and he had often joked that he'd end up fat if he lived with her. But they never did live together properly. They never went public with their relationship. So that not even Charlie got to know about her. He wondered if Sarah's intention was always to keep him at arm's length.

He shut the cupboard and wandered into the dining area, a simple, small modern space with a black dome-shaped lamp hanging low over a round table. He imagined William Shaw sitting at the table eating with her. He walked out of the dining area and into the front room. Two deep bookcases packed tightly with books on every shelf filled the alcoves on each side of the fireplace. An assortment of stationery and various books were stacked in a pile on a sturdy wide table. He knew that William Shaw had been a geography teacher and guessed that this was his place of work in the evenings, after his day at school.

He sat down in a green armchair, relaxed his head back, and felt a hollow shape against his back in the upholstery. Had she sat here and watched him while he worked? He got up out of the chair and made his way upstairs. A turquoise bathroom, with the waste pipe beneath the sink removed in the search for evidence, looked as if a plumber had not finished the job. The tiled windowsill was covered with various bottles. Shampoos and body lotions and body sprays. It seemed ridiculous that he knew it was her toothbrush in the grey mug, but he did. She wouldn't use a proper toothbrush holder. He'd even gone out and bought her one, but she liked her toothbrush in a mug with a handle she could hold when she rinsed her mouth. He had teased her about it, and she had laughed.

'One thing you won't ever change about me, Anderson, is my toothbrush mug.'

He hadn't wanted to change a thing about her. Never since he first laid eyes on her had he met a woman he wanted more.

He left the bathroom and went into the bedroom. The base of the bed had been lifted onto its side and rested against a wall, and the headboard and mattress had gone to a laboratory. The other night it had been William Shaw's bedroom. Now he saw it as *theirs*. He stared around the room, and knew he would never be free of her. Here – this place – would bind them forever. He could not undo any of what happened here. He could only keep going until safely in the clear. Fox can't have seen anything, or he'd have said by now. So hopefully it would soon be plain sailing.

He went over to the wardrobe to find the items he was there for – the text from Issy said a black skirt suit and black coat. It should be an easy find. He parted some hangers before he saw the little lavender bag, which he had never understood, imagining only old ladies using them. But she had a thing about clothes not smelling, wearing them only once before washing. She was hygienic to a fault, almost an obsession to never let them smell of any bodily odour.

He moved hangers along the rail, checking every dark item of clothing, then checking again, before accepting there was no black suit and no black coat in the wardrobe. He was about to close the doors when he noticed a small brown handbag at the bottom of the wardrobe. The zip was undone and the contents protruded untidily from the opening. He crouched down to tidy it. He wasn't expecting shoes to be aligned after investigators finished their search, but if they emptied out bags he would hope they would at least put back the contents properly.

A passport had some damage to a page where it had not been closed before being put back in the bag. The page had torn, probably from catching on the zip. He examined it and saw it was Sarah's and it was still in her maiden name – James. He closed it and placed it down while he tidied the rest of the

contents. He returned store cards that were in the folds of a
letter from Vision Express to a small leather purse. He put the
top on a lipstick that had smeared a Lloyds Bank statement. He
unattached the teeth of a comb from a Boots card. He gathered
loose photographs – random scenery pictures – and put them
back in a worn photograph envelope. At the bottom of the bag
he found a booklet of stamps. He put them in one of the inner
compartments of the purse when he saw a passport-size photograph protruding from a card pocket. He eased it out and as his
eyes fixed on the image he reacted instinctively and flung it out
of his hand.

'Holy hell,' he whispered.

He breathed raggedly and loudly. He retrieved the photograph from where it had landed on a shoe. Why hadn't he
thought about this? She was bound to have old photographs. He
wondered how Mark Steel's team had missed finding it. It
wasn't that well-hidden. A handbag in a wardrobe they had
taken time to empty, but failed to see what he saw quite quickly.

A thought struck him. He went still and stared at the
wardrobe. Had someone taken the black suit and coat before he
got there? Was the search of the bag recent? In the last few
hours? He needed to ask Issy if she had collected the clothes.
He pulled out his mobile and texted.

He held up the photograph and studied her face next to his.
She was kissing his cheek while he stared at the camera. They
had gone into a Tesco's to buy some wine and he had pulled her
into a photo booth. He cut one of the photographs off the strip
to keep in his wallet and gave the rest to her. He had thought
himself a good detective, but finding this made him wonder
what other evidence he might have missed. It was unlikely
she'd have online photos, Sarah wasn't one for social media.
Not even Facebook. She couldn't see why people would want
to post to the world at large everything they were doing every
minute of the day. He turned off the light in the bedroom, then

on the landing, and was back in the hallway when Issy's text arrived.

> *No. I thought you were. Maybe Paul fetched them to save you the bother.*

He turned off the light and opened the front door. The officer outside was chatty. 'Think we've got rain coming. My kids want snow but it's not cold enough yet.'

Nick took the logbook from him. He hadn't taken notice when he signed it earlier of the last name written before he wrote his. *DS Robson.*

He handed the logbook back and wished the officer a good evening.

He wondered if this was it. If his world was about to come crashing down. If his freedom and job were about to be taken, his reputation forever ruined. The thought that it could be Robson taking him down stuck in his throat.

Should he prepare himself? It would only be a matter of hours before someone contacted him if Robson had found other photos. The man would be racing to blab his information.

Nick was going home. He wasn't going to hide. If they wanted him they knew where to find him. At his home with a bottle whisky, where he would wait to see just what was coming.

CHAPTER THIRTY-ONE

NICK

Sarah was standing beneath the streetlight outside his house, fidgeting nervously as he walked towards her. Her dark hair glinted from a light fall of rain, and her face shone.

He unlocked and opened the front door. 'Come in.'

She walked ahead of him up the stairs and then waited while he unlocked the second door. 'I took a chance that you might still live here,' she said.

'Yeah, it made sense not to sell. Buying back in Bath would be a non-starter. I was lucky to get the mortgage I got six years ago.'

She gave an amused smile at the opened suitcases on the floor in the small hallway. 'Do you intend to use this area as your wardrobe?'

Nick moved the luggage nearer to the wall with his foot. He led the way to his sitting room, and removed a newspaper from the armchair. 'I haven't had time to unpack. It will get sorted as and when I need anything. I found this quick enough.' He held up the bottle of Macallan. 'You want a drop?'

She nodded, slipping out of her brown coat, and he found it difficult to swallow. She wore skin-tight blue jeans and an equally tight black jumper. She folded her arms self-consciously and sat down, shivering.

'Kathleen lent me these. They were her daughter's. I bought a few clothes, but I couldn't find the bag they were in.'

Nick found a glass on the table and headed to the kitchen to wash it. On his own, he leaned over the sink and breathed deeply. Having her here was all wrong. Being alone with her was stupid. His need to keep a distance was being sorely challenged.

He lingered at the kitchen sink and then dropped the glass when she spoke beside him. It shattered against the white enamel and before he could stop her, her hands were in the sink picking up the broken pieces. He heard her wince and saw a pearl of blood bloom from her little finger. 'Here.' He grabbed her finger and ran it under cold water, but blood continued to come. 'You've got a bit of glass in it.'

'Sorry, I just wondered if you needed help,' she said breathlessly.

'It will stop if I...' He bent his head and sucked her finger, feeling carefully with the tip of his tongue for the glass. Then he spat into the sink. 'There, it's out.'

Sarah looked at her finger, then sucked it herself, her eyes darker with pain. The small kitchen suddenly seemed smaller and Nick felt trapped and retaliated with his only form of defence – anger. 'Why are you here?'

Her pale skin flushed, her lips trembled and he felt on the brink of exploding. 'You shouldn't be! I'm investigating your husband's death. It's my job to find out who did it. You being here is definitely not a good idea. Anything you need to say should be said through your family liaison officer.'

Her eyes shot open and she stuttered. 'I'm sorry. I just needed to see you... I just... I'm sorry. I'll go.'

'Cut the crap, Sarah.'

She turned to walk away. 'This isn't the time. I shouldn't have come.'

He stepped past her, making it impossible for her to leave. 'What did you want?'

Sarah nervously licked her lips. 'I'm sorry. I'm sorry if I hurt you. That's what I wanted to say.'

He felt his gut burning with anger. She had no idea of how much she had hurt him. No idea that she was still hurting him standing there. 'Why did you marry him? Why? Just tell me that.' Which was only a cover for the real questions he wanted to ask, such as why she had broken off with him? What was she hiding that made her do that?

Sarah shook her head, then looked at him with brimming eyes. 'I can't explain. I was lonely, I suppose.'

He laughed unkindly in her face. 'Well, why didn't you get yourself a cat?'

A few seconds later he heard the front door bang and her feet running along the pavement on the street below. She was lying. Everything he was doing was for her, yet she continued to lie. He lifted his head and shouted up at the ceiling. All his frustration and pain and emptiness expressed in his heated words. 'Damn you, Sarah, for being in my life!'

CHAPTER THIRTY-TWO

CHARLIE

Charlie was drawing deep breaths and his hands were gripped tightly together when Naughton came upon him alone in the office.

'You praying, Charlie, or practising some deep breathing exercise?'

Charlie waited a second for the pain to ease, breathing out slowly. 'I was thinking,' he said.

Naughton raised his eyebrows. 'Well, it looked like it was straining you. My advice, stop thinking so hard. You don't want to blow a gasket in your head.'

Charlie breathed normally. 'It helps clear my head, if you must know.'

'Well, that shouldn't take long,' Naughton quipped.

'Funny, Richard. Very funny. What are you after? Thought you'd be gone home.'

'When are you going to come for Sunday lunch? Margaret keeps asking. I needed to get that in, in case I forgot. She's yearning to lecture and mother you.'

Charlie smiled. 'Tell her soon. And tell her, her husband doesn't deserve her. She should have married me.'

Naughton laughed, unguarded and informal in front of Charlie. He was not a man without warmth, far from it, but it was warmth constrained beneath a deeply reserved nature. But Charlie had known him a long time now. He and Richard had played rugby together in the under sixteens for Bath. Neither of them had been very good.

He wondered why Naughton had sought him out.

'I'm perturbed, Charlie. DI Anderson didn't mention an important point at the morning brief, that Barry Fox was uncontaminated by gunpowder residue. Unless it's a mere fluke and he was amazingly careful, he should have shown positive just from handling the gun if he took it. Unless he was wearing gloves and knew what he was doing.'

'I kind of assumed that was the case. About Fox, I mean,' Charlie replied, though he hadn't known it until now. 'I suspect that's why it wasn't mentioned.'

'Did he mind being called in?'

Charlie shook his head. 'Good as gold,' he replied. He wasn't going to tell him that Nick was in a tetchy mood.

'I'm surprised Nick came back. The Met wanted to keep him, you know. He did some good work for them while he was there. Some very senior officers were making offers that were hard to refuse. A promotion for one.'

'He's a Bath boy, Richard. He knows where he wants to be.'

'The thing is, Charlie, I'm not seeing that. He's all over the place with this case. He had Barry Fox locked up for thirty-six hours; I had the review officer snapping at my heels, then he wanted a three-day lie down. Another seventy-two hours! For what? What's he hoping to achieve? Fox is under surveillance. If he's going to try and hide evidence he'll get caught in the act. You know him, Charlie, better than anyone. What's your opinion of it?'

Charlie could well understand Naughton's frustration. They were nearing the end of day four and what did they have?

Barry Fox and Amanda Black. But only one of them felt like a real suspect. William Shaw's murder was personal. Why not just shoot him in the head? Why feed him cake? A tiny amount of cake crumbs had been found on the victim's neck and chest, but nowhere else in the house. Charlie couldn't help thinking the cake being brought to the murder scene was significant. Had Amanda Black fed it to him as a form of foreplay before pulling a gun on him? Had she felt discarded after being there for him, and then for him to choose another woman? Charlie felt that the motive was still too far out of reach. The two anonymous letters might be the reason the man was dead. But maybe not. He wanted to protect Nick, but they should have been unravelling clues and hauling in all the possibilities.

He answered carefully. 'I think we should be looking at the hospital. I don't know enough yet. But Mary Shaw died in hospital, and something didn't feel right when I was questioning staff.'

Naughton raised a silver eyebrow. 'Well, she died in a hospital because she was ill. Surely if there was any sign of it being suspicious, someone would have noticed something. What you're saying doesn't make sense.'

'Neither does William Shaw's death, which is why I think we need to be looking at hers too. Like I say, I don't know enough yet. It's a hunch, Richard.'

Naughton sighed, sounding mildly exasperated. 'Charlie, at the moment we don't know enough about anything. I think – and I'm sure you'd agree – a hunch that her death is suspicious is not a good enough reason to point the finger at a hospital.'

Charlie looked at the photograph he'd been studying of William Shaw. With a sheet draped low over his hips, his bare torso, long lean rib cage and concave abdomen, his head at an angle and arms loose at his sides... he reminded Charlie of The Pietà in St Peter's, Rome.

Maybe Naughton was right, but Charlie's hunches weren't

normally wrong. He'd have to investigate in his own time, and on the quiet. He didn't want to raise even more doubt about Nick's ability to handle this case.

Charlie nodded. 'Anderson would agree with you. He's smart, and on occasion he sees a solution blindingly fast. Just got to kick him now and again when he won't shift.'

'You're fond of him, aren't you?' Naughton said.

'Someone's gotta love the bugger. His mother ran out on him when he was seven. And his father... a disciplinarian from what I remember of him. Liked praying a lot. Nick turned out all right, considering his home circumstances. He graduated with a first-class honours degree in psychology. He has other talents as well,' Charlie proclaimed like a proud parent.

Naughton smiled. 'I often wonder why some nice woman hasn't cornered you, Charlie. And I agree with you. Nick's certainly talented. I've seen him play.'

Charlie was surprised. 'Didn't know you knew he played.'

'Yes. Saw him play in The Bell on Walcot Street. Went with one of my sons.'

Charlie felt suddenly lightheaded and swayed on his feet.

'Do you need to sit down?' Naughton said, concern on his face.

Charlie breathed in deeply to clear his head. 'No, I'm good. It's the heat in this place.' He shrugged off his jacket and stood up straight. 'Must be getting too old for this job. Becoming a right old war-horse, me.'

Something went quiet in Naughton's manner, and Charlie needed to quickly reassure him that both him and Nick were all right to do the job. 'It's late. You should be home with Margaret. And don't worry about Anderson. He'll have this case wrapped up sooner than we can down a pint.'

Naughton looked doubtful. 'I hope you're right, Charlie. But what I'm saying is, keep an eye on him.' His careful tone revealed he was aware he was putting Charlie in an awkward position. 'Just that, Charlie, that's all.'

Charlie nodded. He knew it was pointless to argue that Naughton had no grounds for asking this. Nick had not been performing at his best. He'd have to wait for the right moment to have a word with Nick, to enlighten him about how he was coming across without breaking Naughton's confidence.

But, for now, he was too tired. Now all he could think of was his bed.

CHAPTER THIRTY-THREE

SARAH

Sarah could feel the tense atmosphere as she walked into the kitchen. Both Joe and Kathleen had told her off last night for going out. Sarah was clearly not forgiven, judging from the look on Kathleen's face. Sarah breathed in as she saw her preparing to rant again.

'What on earth possessed you? Joe was out searching the streets for you. He drove everywhere, getting more worried by the hour.'

'Do you want me to leave?' Sarah asked over the rim of her mug.

Kathleen's eyes couldn't get any rounder. 'What sort of remark is that? Of course I don't want you to leave. I just want you to let us know when you decide to up and go out of the house to God knows where for hours on end.'

'I needed to see Nick,' Sarah said.

'Could you not have told us, instead of having us worried sick?'

Sarah slumped back in her chair. 'Oh, for goodness' sake. I don't need this. I wanted to see him and that's that.' She let out a long sigh. 'I'm sorry if you were worried, I didn't think. And if it's any consolation I got just as big an ear bashing last night.'

Kathleen's anger fell away. 'Did he upset you?'

Sarah smiled sadly. 'He's got the right to, Kathleen. I walked all over his feelings and I expected to make it all right with a simple sorry.'

'That's history, Sarah. It doesn't give him the right to hurt you. Look, listen to me, girl. You don't need any of this. You'll end up getting more hurt. You have to remember the police will still be looking at you.'

'Actually, they won't,' Sarah informed her. 'They're thinking this is possibly suicide.'

'What?'

Kathleen was shocked, and Sarah was glad to push her off the track of always thinking of her as a suspect. It wasn't helpful to her situation to be constantly reminded of this. It was controlling, and perturbing, and not very nice.

'Well, maybe they're right,' Kathleen said softly.

Sarah was surprised Kathleen was ready to believe so quickly. What happened to her surety that William was killed by whoever had been phoning him?

'Maybe William had something to feel guilty about that he couldn't live with. Someone may have been reminding him with those phone calls.'

'Like what?'

Kathleen shrugged. 'I don't know. I told you Mary said he wasn't always kind.'

Sarah watched her, trying to work out if she knew something. She caught Kathleen glancing at her before looking away. Sarah decided she would tell a white lie. 'When I was on the ward on Sunday, I never told you, but I heard Andy and Helen talking about Mary having a fall out of bed. It sounded like it happened the night Mary died.'

Kathleen turned her eyes to Sarah, and she noticed the very

pale, almost washed-out blue, irises. Close up, she could see a white ring around each iris and wondered how long they'd been forming, and whether Kathleen had high cholesterol or heart disease.

'Don't be listening to gossip, especially from the likes of Helen Tate. I wouldn't pay attention to anything she says. I've seen the way she is. She hides a nasty streak.'

Sarah was intrigued. Kathleen sounded genuine. 'What do you mean?'

She curled her lip as if tasting something unpalatable. 'She plays tricks on people. Have you never noticed?'

Sarah shook her head.

Kathleen sighed. 'Well, next time you work with her notice the little things. They soon add up. The night Mary died, she was all questions afterwards. When was the last time someone went into Mary's room? Who were her visitors? Did anyone notice the time they left?'

'Why? Who were her visitors?' Sarah asked.

'Why?' Kathleen's voice was bitter. 'So she could unnerve everyone. Mary's husband visited, like always, and Father McCarthy came and said prayers with her.'

'It seems odd, don't you think? That she'd ask about visitors?'

'No. I don't think it's odd. The only odd thing is that no one else seems to notice the things she does, and then talk about them to upset people, for the fun of it.'

Sarah backed off. The morning had barely begun, and Kathleen was already in bad form. She needed to get her out of her bad mood, not make it worse. Sarah was curious, though, that Kathleen didn't outright deny that it happened, or say Helen lied. She'd not said Mary didn't have a fall, only that Sarah shouldn't listen to gossip.

Which was not reassuring.

CHAPTER THIRTY-FOUR

CHARLIE

Charlie thumbed the pages of the hospital newsletter looking at pictures rather than words to engage his mind. The waiting room, even at this early hour, was already full, and the air seemed inadequate to fill the lungs of the waiting individuals as collective sighs were heard every time a nurse appeared and called someone from the salmon chairs. He had read the whiteboard and knew there was more than one doctor to see all these people, but he wanted to know when his doctor was going to start; when was a name from the blue chairs going to be called?

For the last half hour he'd been trying to guess the order that the people around him would be called. The man opposite, sitting on the edge of his seat, obviously thought it would be him first, but then again it could be the younger man beside him with all the paraphernalia of a long comfortable wait – a newspaper and a flask. He sighed inwardly, looking at the wall clock and then at his wristwatch. Both instruments agreed that it was 9.05 a.m. Every minute he was kept waiting was a minute more that he would be late for work. He sat up straight as he saw a nurse coming towards him.

She smiled politely. 'We're so sorry to keep you waiting.

Doctor Maine is going to be another half hour, but he's asked me to give his apologies, and asks if you can please kindly wait. He really does want to see you today.'

Charlie sighed and got to his feet. 'I'll be back in half an hour,' he said. He might as well do something useful with the time. Like visit Ted Parry. It wasn't a simple fall he'd had, by all accounts. He'd been kept in hospital.

Ted looked as fat as ever as he lay on top of his hospital bed, his large abdomen pushing up his hairy chest and his blown-out face ruddy with warmth. He looked pleased to see Charlie. 'This is a surprise.'

'Yeah, well, I thought I'd pop in for five minutes and see how you are. So how are you doing? Fallen for any of these nurses yet?'

Ted scowled at him. 'Ha ha. Bloody fallen enough for one year. I'll sodding sue the council for making them steps so slippery.'

'You should have taken more water with it,' Charlie joked. Then he saw Ted's eyes quickly lowering. 'Oh, I see. Not so far off the mark, am I?'

'It was a long day. I only had the one. Rushing out of the pub is what did it, after I got called to come in. I wasn't drunk.'

Charlie saw Ted was getting upset. 'It's okay, Ted, your secret's safe with me. Do you good to be in here for a while, get you on the wagon.'

He nodded, agreeing. 'Best I've felt in years. Gonna make a resolution to get fit. Might even take up a bit of sport.'

Charlie looked at the covered bed frame hiding his damaged leg. He lifted the sheet and cringed as he saw the cylindrical cage trapping Ted's leg, held firmly with steel nails driven below his knee and ankle. The cage moved and Charlie winced. It didn't seem to bother Ted.

'Not for a while you won't,' Charlie said, feeling queasy from looking at it. 'Got to go, Ted. I need some air.'

'Don't blame you. It gives me the willies seeing it. You take care and I'll see you again.'

As he walked through the ward, Charlie stopped a nurse. 'I wonder if you could help me. I'm trying to find the ward or the names of doctors who look after patients with illnesses like multiple sclerosis.'

She looked at him strangely until Charlie showed his warrant card. 'Sorry. I should have explained. I'm a police officer on duty, and I'm at a loss where to start.'

'Well, you could try Doctor Phillips. He's on the ward now.'

Charlie glanced back at the patients' beds. 'But isn't this orthopaedics, for things like broken legs?'

She nodded. 'Yes, it is. But sometimes people have other illnesses, besides broken bones, that need treating by different specialities. I'll have a word with Doctor Phillips, and see if he can see you. Could you tell me your name please, so I can say who's asking?'

'Yes, of course. Detective Sergeant Bowden.'

A short while later a tall, slender man approached him. Dr Phillips' skull was large and Charlie thought it must house a large brain.

'Hello, I understand you'd like to see me?'

Charlie's mouth felt dry from the guilt of doing this behind Naughton's back. 'Yes, if you have time. I wanted to ask about a patient who passed away in March. Her name was Mary Shaw.'

'I know that name. Let's talk in my office. I'm heading there now.'

Charlie nodded, and followed the doctor halfway across the hospital, trying not to show he was panting as he waited for him to open the office door. The doctor invited him to sit down, and Charlie sank into the chair exhausted. The doctor then walked over to a sink and splashed his face with water, the back of his white shirt criss-crossed with creases, the plain navy tie not tucked properly under his collar as if the man had put it on in a hurry.

'Been up all night and I'm buggered. But then I don't have to tell you – you get the same in your job.' Drying himself on a paper towel he moved back to his desk and finally sat down. 'Okay, so what exactly are you after?'

Charlie wasn't sure where to start, but he needed to clarify first he was with the right person. 'Can I just ask, were you Mary Shaw's doctor?'

Dr Phillips smiled. 'I wouldn't have had you follow me here if that wasn't the case. Yes, I was Mary's consultant.'

'Can I ask how ill she was? What exactly she died of? I only know the basics of her illness, what I was told by the head teacher at the school where she used to work.'

'MS. Multiple sclerosis. It's a degenerative disease of the nerve fibres within the spinal cord and brain. The cause is unknown, but it has a higher incidence in females and usually has its onset between twenty and forty years of age. Mary was twenty-seven when she was diagnosed. The disease is characterised by remissions and relapses, but these are variable and unpredictable. Early symptoms include tingling sensations, numbness, weakness in limbs, blurring of vision, depression. Mary had all these symptoms by the time she was thirty-two.'

'I've known people with MS, but I didn't think it killed you. An ex-colleague of mine, now retired, has it and he's in his seventies.'

The doctor nodded. 'MS itself is rarely fatal. Life expectancy is five to seven years lower than average. Patients in remission can be without symptoms for years. For some a relapse can be mild, while for others there is an occurrence of new symptoms or worsening of old symptoms. But complications may arise from severe MS. Mary developed bladder infections, chest infections, swallowing difficulties. On top of that she had cardiovascular disease. She was a heavy smoker when she could light one herself. It was a miserable time for her those last few weeks.'

Miserable years, Charlie thought, feeling like he'd just had a biology lesson. 'What actually caused her death?'

'Respiratory failure first, I should think, leading on to cardiac arrest. Mary was already gone when the nurse went in to check on her. We were considering moving her to ITU the morning before she died, but we had no ITU beds. And it wouldn't have been the right choice anyway. Mary had a DNR in her notes. I mean, we were actively treating her symptoms. But I had a funny feeling that last morning I saw her. There was no physical change since the previous day, but I saw it in her eyes. While we were holding on, she was letting go.'

'So you weren't surprised when she died?'

'No, not really. I wasn't expecting her to die that night, but there was no real surprise that she did. She was relatively young, but also very ill.'

'Post-mortem didn't reveal anything untoward, then?' Charlie asked.

'She didn't have one.'

Charlie was surprised. 'Why not?'

'Because she'd been in hospital for several weeks. We already knew what her diagnosis was. She had hypostatic pneumonia and one of several complications can arise from it: the collapse of a lung, septicaemia or empyema. The coroner would have decided on a PM if a doctor wasn't treating her during her last illness.'

'The DNR? This means you don't save them.'

'No. The directive now has more letters for complete clarity. DNACPR. It means do not attempt cardiopulmonary resuscitation. A DNR does not mean do not treat. It's a request to not have CPR if your heart stops or you stop breathing.'

'And who would know this?'

'Everyone who treated her. They would have to know about it.'

'So a fall wouldn't have made a difference?'

'A fall of what? I don't understand.'

'A fall from her bed, I presumed, if she was found on the floor,' Charlie replied.

The doctor was clearly surprised. He stared at Charlie in confusion. 'I thought you were meaning a fall in blood pressure or something. I have no recollection of a physical fall, and it's not something I would likely forget if the patient then died.'

Charlie realised he was treading on dangerous ground. If he admitted to the doctor what he'd been told by the nursing staff, without the sanction of Naughton or Nick, he'd be opening a can of worms and be kicked off the case into the bargain.

He back-pedalled fast. 'Maybe it was a fall in the past they were discussing. Come to think of it, they never said the word fall, they said floor.' Charlie was aware he was sounding like a bumbling idiot, and couldn't wait to get out of there. 'I've confused myself several times today. Sorry if I alarmed you.'

Dr Phillips stood up from behind his desk with a poker face, his manner less congenial as he showed Charlie out. 'Perhaps next time, Sergeant, an appointment should be made. I might then have had a clue what this meeting was about.'

Charlie flushed, and was still feeling the embarrassment fifteen minutes later when seated in Dr Maine's office, his mind going over the visit he'd just had with Dr Phillips. He was sweating from hurrying to his appointment, which he'd been late for by forty-five minutes. It was now twenty past ten. He didn't want to check his phone to see how many missed calls or texts he had asking for his whereabouts.

'How are you, Charlie?' Dr Maine asked him.

'Fine,' Charlie said. 'Just been to see a mate on one of the wards. Broken his leg. They've got it trapped in some cage trying to hold the bone in place while it knits. Poor sod. He'll probably be in here a few more weeks yet.'

'So, you're fine are you?'

Charlie shrugged. 'Apart from the pain. I could do with something stronger, but otherwise pretty okay.'

Dr Maine tapped his finger on Charlie's notes. 'I have your CT scan result. It's not great news, I'm afraid.'

He opened the folder, and Charlie tried to tune out what was being said to him. A SOL. From across the doctor's desk he could see it written in bold black capitals. He didn't have one problem. He had another too – a space-occupying lesion.

'Do you understand everything I've just said, Charlie?'

He did – he knew what those three letters meant. It was taking up a bit of space. Pushing aside a bit of brain that he needed. The bit that controls his walking, talking, his breathing... 'Yes. I've got a SOL in my head,' he heard himself casually answering. 'A fuss, more like. I've got more important things I need to be thinking about. We've got a murderer in Bath, in case you didn't know. I have to help catch him before I get stuck in some hospital bed.'

Dr Maine looked long and steadily at him. 'You have options, Charlie. You don't need to do this alone.'

Charlie leaned back in the chair and closed his eyes. Finally, when he was ready, he opened them and stared at the man who had been not only his doctor, but a friend as well. A kind man who befriended Charlie when he had to tell him what the future held.

'You know something, Doc? I learned something a long time ago. There are no options when it comes for you. There is only the decision about how you face it. My plan is to carry on as normal. So if you would kindly write me a prescription, I need to get back to work.'

CHAPTER THIRTY-FIVE

NICK

An eruption of noise interrupted the meeting. Nick turned and saw Charlie using his back and elbows to hold open the door as his hands were otherwise occupied with carrying a large white box. He was complaining loudly to anyone and everyone in earshot.

'Bloody stupid place to put a door,' he bellowed. 'Nearly dropped the lot.' He carried the box over to the table where they made hot drinks. 'I'll just check the cakes are safe,' he said, plonking down the cardboard box and lifting the lid. 'No harm done, they're okay.'

Nick sighed with exasperation. There might have been top-ranking officers present but Charlie would still behave this way. He said what he said without a care in the world for propriety. But this was his charm and just one of the reasons on a long list of others why Nick had loved the man so long.

'That's it, arrive late and then take your time about it,' he lightly jeered.

Charlie raised his eyes. 'You won't be moaning when you taste what I brought in. Coffee Battenberg and Maids of Honour. Bet the big boys weren't as kind.'

Nick smiled. 'No, they weren't. Too busy to sit around eating cakes.'

A mocking 'Ah' was hailed at him from Issy Banks. 'Our hearts bleed for you.' To the back of the room she called out, 'Charlie, didn't you get any Orange Madeira this time?'

Charlie shrugged his shoulders apologetically. 'They didn't have any.'

Nick clapped his hands to get their attention. 'That'll do, you pair of reprobates. Let's get back on track. Charlie, one important thing you missed: Miss Black was interviewed at nine this morning and is now no longer a person of interest.'

'How come?'

Charlie was disappointed. Nick knew he'd been wanting Miss Black to be a strong suspect. He told him what he'd just relayed to the rest of the team.

'Apart from watching TV and marking homework, she sent emails from her home computer. One to the head teacher to inform him she was arranging a school trip, one to an art gallery to ask what date would be best to visit with thirty pupils. She also ordered a rug and four bed pillows from Amazon. But the most important detail she forgot to mention was that she had a home delivery from Tesco's. She took photographs of the times and dates the emails were sent, and showed them at her interview. DS Robson has gone to her home to check her computer, and her Tesco delivery has been verified. The driver arrived at eight forty-five and departed at eight fifty-five. So it sounds like she's in the clear.'

'How is she in the clear? We don't have a time of death.'

'We do now, Charlie. Professor Doyle puts time of death between eight and ten p.m. So the old boy two doors down from William Shaw's home probably heard right that a gun fired at about eight-thirty.'

'Do we know yet if the victim had gunpowder residue on his hands?'

Nick sighed, knowing where Charlie was going with this. He was wanting proof this was a suicide. 'Tests showed he had it on his arms, his chest, his face and hands. So, yes.'

Charlie stared at him. 'But it's not really "yes", is it? At that close proximity, it's a given he'd test positive.' Then he turned his head to stare out of the window.

Nick didn't reply. His mind was caught up with Charlie's scrawny neck. He took his first proper look at Charlie and felt concern. He had lost weight by the look of things, and his brown jacket was hanging off him. He hadn't seemed to have aged until this moment. He saw the face of an old man, rather than someone in his fifties.

The briefing ended a few minutes later. Nick waited until the team were helping themselves to teas, coffees and Charlie's cakes before he went to speak to him. 'Here, I brought you a tea and a cake before they all disappear.'

Charlie took one of the mugs from Nick's hand and placed it on the windowsill, while Nick placed his own and the cake beside it. 'Bloody 'ell. Must be my birthday for you to wait on me.'

'Thought you could do with a pick-me-up. How come you were late?'

'I had a doctor's appointment at nine. Didn't think I'd be there all morning. Anyway, he's told me what's wrong.' Charlie pulled out his cigarette packet. 'These.'

Nick felt his stomach tighten. 'You mean...'

'No, not that! It's called Bronchiole something. Had to have one of those tubes put down me gullet. The nice doctor wants me to try patches, and for me to give up the fags. I told him I'd end up overdosing.'

'So it's not serious then?' Nick asked, watching for the answer on Charlie's face.

'Well, I probably won't see ninety, but who wants to anyway?'

'You won't see sixty if you ignore your doctor's advice.'

'Oh, here we go, a reformed smoker. Okay, I'll try the patches if you play at the Christmas do.'

'Are you serious? I haven't got time for all that.'

'Bob Taylor, Ed Nixon, Tall Jim, and Shaun Walker – I already promised them you would.'

Nick glanced around the room, spotting the four officers, and Tall Jim gave him a thumbs up. 'Cheers, Charlie, I haven't played in more than a year.'

Charlie's ginger eyebrows rose. 'Stop being a prima donna. They've not asked, because you're too surly to approach. I'll tell you something else as well: it will mean something to this lot. You've been treating them like you barely know them. Hard to believe, but some of them regard you as more than a colleague. Shaun used to be your mate.'

'For Chrissake, Charlie. I'll have a catch up with them when we're less busy.' Playing for a Christmas dance was the last thing he needed right now. It was a huge reminder of where he'd met Sarah.

'Might I remind you, Nick, you're always busy.' Charlie's eyes were serious. 'You could do with making time for friends.'

Nick rocked back on his heels. 'Bloody got you. That's enough.'

Charlie hesitated, seeming to consider what he was about to say, his feet shuffling as if preparing to move away. Then he held still and locked eyes with Nick. 'Well, then talk to me, Nick. Tell me something's not wrong.'

Nick answered in a voice as nonchalant as he could muster. 'There isn't anything wrong, Charlie. There's only you thinking there is.'

Charlie walked away, and Nick saw the cake still on the windowsill. He felt sick with nerves all of a sudden. He was so close to ending this case. It was only the likes of Charlie and one or two others holding it back from happening. If Naughton would come to the decision that this wasn't a murder, but a tragic death instead, this team could disassemble. Nick could behave naturally again, and recoup Charlie's trust.

He had to win this, even if it meant briefly losing Charlie. If Charlie knew what was at stake, he'd roll over. He'd want Nick to win.

CHAPTER THIRTY-SIX

SARAH

Sarah wasn't sure she would be able to do this, until she found herself standing at the entrance to the hospital. She wanted to check if her worry was unfounded. It was the right time to have come. Kathleen was at home and the late shift were still on duty.

She smoothed her hair as she pushed the heavy door open and allowed it to click shut behind her. Andy Brooke was first to see her. He raised one blond plucked eyebrow and greeted her with a wide smile.

'I thought I smelled something beautiful! What are you doing here?'

'I needed to get out for a while. Thought I'd come by for a quick hello. Who's on duty?'

'Helen, but she's just finishing. Beth's doing the supper trolley on her own.' He nodded his head towards a side room. 'Because me and the agency nurse are in with Mr Harris. He died an hour ago. Poor Tim looks like he's having a breakdown. Don't think he's ever had a patient die before.'

Sarah was surprised. She would have thought the young

doctor was able to cope better than that. 'Shall I see if he's okay?'

Andy shook his head. 'No. You don't need to be seeing any dead bodies.'

'I'm perfectly capable of seeing a dead body without it affecting me, Andy.'

'Well, aren't you the tough one?' said Helen from behind her.

Sarah turned to face her. 'Not really, Helen. I'm no more resilient than any of you. We're nurses. We deal with things differently. Anyway, it was nice to come out for some fresh air.' She smiled. 'I'm getting mollycoddled by Kathleen.'

'You don't surprise me,' Helen replied. 'She's very protective of you.'

Sarah saw a glint of something bright in Helen's mouth and didn't realise she was staring until Helen suddenly poked out her gold studded tongue and wiggled it suggestively. 'Like it?'

'Yes, but I wouldn't want one myself.'

'You should try it. Gives men a real thrill.'

'Also breaks your teeth, darling. I've had to have two crowns,' Andy said.

'That's because you talk too much.'

The call bell rang and Andy went off to answer it, while Helen stayed. 'How are you coping?' she asked.

'I'm all right. The waiting for answers is what's difficult. I heard something that I wanted to discuss with you, if you have a moment. About Mary.'

Helen raised an eyebrow. 'You're the second person to bring up that name today.'

'Am I?'

'Yes, a police sergeant phoned me. In fact, I have appointment with him later on. I—'

Sarah jumped as the door behind them banged and Tim Summers shot out of the office.

'Where is it? I can't find it!' he half-shouted at Helen.

Helen approached him calmly. 'It'll be safe somewhere, Tim. You're obviously not looking in the right places. Let me find it for you.' Then softly tutting she went to find whatever was lost.

The doctor looked pale, his eyes behind his glasses blinking anxiously. He looked about to cry. Sarah was bewildered. She had never seen him upset before. Andy was right. He did look like he was about to have a breakdown.

'Whatever's the matter?' she asked.

Tim took off his glasses and pinched the bridge of his nose. 'Don't know. Reaction, I suppose. I can't think straight until I know for sure.'

'Know what?'

'Stupid thing to do,' he whispered miserably. His hands trembled badly as he raised them to his face. 'I'll be struck off. I might go to prison for this.'

'I don't know what you've done, Tim. You need to tell me,' Sarah replied.

'Helen asked me to write him up for different antibiotics,' he said, after regaining control of himself. 'I was going to anyway; he was threatening pneumonia and wasn't responding to the ones he was on. But we couldn't find his prescription chart. I knew all the drugs he was on from his notes; I'd written the prescription in the first place, so I decided I'd go ahead and give him the new antibiotic. He started coughing, holding his chest, wheezing. I pressed the emergency bell, then ran to get adrenaline. Helen and I worked on him until the crash team arrived.' Tim rubbed his face hard, keeping his hands pressed against his face as he continued. 'Helen thinks he was allergic to the penicillin, but I don't remember ever seeing that.'

'Are you talking about Mr Harris, Tim?'

He nodded. 'Yes. I have to find the prescription chart to give to the crash team.'

Sarah tried to comfort him. He'd had a terrible shock. A patient had died on him, and he thought it was his fault. She stayed with him while they waited for Helen to return, and when she did, she was smiling.

Helen sighed heartily, and waved the prescription chart in front of him. 'You'll be relieved to know I was wrong.'

Tim took it from her and stared at the front cover. He turned the page and his eyes travelled rapidly down and across. He checked the front page again and scanned the contents once more. He raised shocked eyes. 'He doesn't have any known allergies. Oh, thank God.' Then he started to cry.

By the time Sarah calmed him, and while he wrote and signed for the drugs he had given, Helen had gone from the ward. Sarah remembered what Kathleen had said that morning. *She plays tricks on people. For the fun of it.* She was wondering if this is what had just happened to Tim Summers. Had Helen played a cruel trick on him?

If true, Sarah was relieved she hadn't got further with asking her questions about Mary. She couldn't trust her to tell the truth. She wondered, though, why a sergeant was asking.

CHAPTER THIRTY-SEVEN

SARAH

Sarah headed in the direction of the Security Staff office. She had her ID in her handbag, but they would know her anyway which should make it easy to get what she wanted. She was not leaving this hospital until she had an answer. She caught her breath before knocking at the door. She could do this. It wasn't like she was breaking the law.

Shane Maddison opened the door and Sarah was pleased it was him on duty. He was a doctor's son and worked at the hospital between his term times. He was in his third year at Cambridge and was extremely well mannered.

'Sister Shaw,' he said.

Sarah smiled politely. 'Sorry to bother you, Shane, but could you give me a key to the Medical Records office please?'

'Yes, I'm sure I can, but it would be better if I unlock it for you. For security reasons.'

'I will bring it straight back, and make doubly sure that I lock it when I leave.'

'It's no problem for me to do that for you.'

Sarah didn't want him with her. She wanted to look at this

file on her own. 'Well, I need to go to the ward first, then pop to the loo.' She pulled a face. 'I have a bit of a tummy ache.'

As expected, Shane became politely efficient. He went over and unlocked the key cabinet on the wall, and ran his finger down the list of departments on the sheet of paper on the inside of the cabinet door, before choosing a key. 'I'll see you back here then when you're done.'

Sarah nodded, then headed to the south wing. Medical records were kept in storage in an office along a corridor with other offices that were all closed for the night. The light in the ceiling was low wattage and rather dim. There wasn't a sound to be heard. She felt a little jittery, and was starting to perspire, which was silly. She had been in this corridor hundreds of times. It was only quiet like this because it was night-time.

She unlocked the right door, and placed the key in her pocket to keep it safe. She took her coat off before stepping into the room and turning on the lights, feeling instantly better for not being so warm. She closed the door, then opened it again, to make sure she wasn't locked inside.

Shelves from floor to ceiling with narrow passages between ran down the length of the room. She hoped she wouldn't have to use one of the metal step stools. The files were in alphabetical order. Surnames beginning with S were in row seven at eye level, above the Ts. She pulled out the first file on the shelf and was pleased to see first names also in alphabetical order. She soon found the name Shaw, and then Mary after Maria and Marie.

She removed the elastic bands from around the bundle of manila folders and checked the date of birth to be sure it was the right one. Then sitting on the floor, between two walls of shelves, she opened the most recent folder containing Mary Shaw's patient notes. She checked the last entries made by the doctors, before looking at the entries by nursing staff. Sarah read quickly through the familiar handwriting of colleagues. She read the last five days of Mary's nursing care, the physiotherapist and occupational therapist notes. Nowhere in any of it was there any mention of a fall.

So why had Andy Brooke said it? And why hadn't Kathleen denied it?

Sarah closed the notes and pulled the elastic bands over the bundle of folders to secure them together. She stood up and put Mary's file back on the shelf. There was nothing here for her to find. Should she put what she heard down to a hypersensitivity to hearing her name coupled with Mary's? Mary's death made to sound dramatic to make way for the new bride? Or did Andy say what Helen and Kathleen knew for sure, that Mary had fallen out of bed?

She breathed in deeply. She couldn't decide, but she would now take the key back to Shane. She went to the door and pressed down the handle and pulled, but it didn't open. She tried it again, then tried moving the handle upwards, but it only pressed down. She went to get the key out of her pocket but she couldn't see her coat. She went to where she was sitting, but it wasn't there. She checked in each narrow passage, then on the desks and cabinets, beneath chairs, and the entire floor space. It wasn't in the office. When she took it off, she must have put it down on the floor outside the door when checking it didn't lock her in.

Coming back to the door, she looked for the keyhole. There wasn't one. There was only one on the outside of the door. She tried opening it again, this time using her shoulder to push, and felt a miniscule movement. She shoved harder, with the same result.

Sarah went still. The door was locked. She fought down a feeling of panic. Had someone gone into her coat pocket to get the key? She heard faint footsteps, and banged on the door hard. 'Hello? Can you hear me? Can you open this door, please?' She heard silence. She held her breath and listened hard. Then called loudly again. 'Hello! Is there someone outside this door? I'm locked in here, so can you please let me out!'

No one answered. With a trembling hand she turned off the lights and got down on her stomach, pressing her head to the side, putting her eye to the tiny gap between the bottom of the door and the floor. She could see only darkness, but could feel air coming at her face. She stared, then she gasped. Her teeth hit the floor as she turned her head sharply, moving frantically away from what she saw. She had seen darkness until it moved and let in the light. Fear filled her mouth. She had been looking at shoes... right outside the door.

Sarah pulled her knees up to her chest and stayed quiet. Who was trying to frighten her? Who was out there? She was such a fool. She already had someone send her a message, which she still hadn't told the police about. She had come here oblivious to any danger she might be in, oblivious to being followed.

Sarah raised her head to feel for her bag. Her phone was in it. She wasn't going to hesitate. She was calling the police. She groped in the dark, using the flat of her hand, then out of necessity turned the lights back on. She looked around her. It wasn't visible anywhere. This was ridiculous. Was she that absent-minded? She didn't recall putting her bag down.

In frustration, she banged at the door and kicked it with her shoes. Then she screamed, 'Let me out. Let me out. Let me out.'

Her hands were shaking from anger, and from slapping them against the door. Her legs were ready to give way. She sank back to the floor and curled into a ball. Anxiety was making her breathe too fast, she could hear her pulse in her ears. The turbulent flow of blood in the tiny vessels was muffling her hearing to other sounds. She would be safe in here. Someone would eventually come. She now wanted the door to stay locked. There was nowhere to escape from here.

She would pretend no one was there. She could do that.

She could make herself think she was somewhere else. Somewhere no one could find her. She squeezed her eyes tight and listened to the hum in her ears. Then a hand touched her shoulder and Sarah screamed in terror. Her mind paralyzed with fear. Her hands flailed wildly against legs. She head-butted the thighs and tried to bite, teeth scraping material as she tried to find flesh, screeching and screaming and panicking with all her might.

It was the taking of her hands, the pull on them to stand her up, that brought her back from the brink of collapse.

It was Shane.

He was as shocked as her, his eyes round in alarm, as he breathed hard. When he led her outside the room, her bag and coat were on the floor. She shakily put her hand in the coat pocket and found the key. 'I don't understand,' she stammered. 'It was locked.'

Shane shook his head. 'It was jammed. I think by the strap of your bag. I think it got dragged under the edge of the door and wedged it closed. I had to pull it away before I could open it.'

Sarah stared at the inch-wide leather strap of her handbag. She knew that wasn't what happened. She had seen darkness at the bottom of the door before those shoes moved.

'When I saw your coat on the floor, I should have checked you were in there first, but I thought you might have dropped it there and gone looking for a bathroom. I went to find you, to make sure you were all right.'

'But you would have heard me banging and shouting.'

'I did. All the way down the corridor I heard you, and hurried back. Are you all right, Sister Shaw? Do you want me to call someone for you?'

Sarah shook her head. 'I'll be fine, Shane. I just got a silly fright. I'm sorry if I gave you one.' She handed him the key. 'Thank you for coming to my rescue.'

Sarah waited while he locked the door, and was glad he was beside her to walk with her until she was back at the entrance. She felt fearful as she made her way out of the building. She couldn't shake the feeling that someone had deliberately locked her in.

CHAPTER THIRTY-EIGHT

SARAH

Sarah closed the front door quietly and placed the front door key back in the bowl with other keys. She concentrated on the silence. The downstairs lights were on, but maybe Joe and Kathleen were in bed. She heard a spoon tap lightly against a cup, and then Joe's voice. 'We're in the kitchen, Sarah.'

Sarah tried to gauge the tone of his voice. He sounded tired, but it was difficult to tell without seeing his face if he was annoyed or merely speaking quietly. She couldn't stand in the hallway any longer. She pressed her lips together firmly to compose herself before speaking. 'Okay. Just hanging up my coat.'

She hung it over Joe's jacket, and then went into the kitchen. The tension in the room was fit to burst. Kathleen had her coat on. Her curly, dark hair, flattened against her head, was damp either with rain or sweat. As she stared at Kathleen's bright pale eyes and flushed cheeks she felt a weight in her chest, and had to force herself to breathe deeply to expand it.

In the five days of living with her, Sarah had undergone several changes of feelings towards Kathleen. The constant vying of happiness and sadness was aching her heart, and as much as she didn't want to get involved in her life, getting to know her was making it difficult not to care.

They stood at the far end of the kitchen, Kathleen's arms folded, tucked tightly across her chest as if to hold what she was feeling inside herself. Joe leaned against the draining board. He gestured to a chair and Sarah sat down.

His face was strained. Sarah waited. Intending to stay this way for however long it took for them to go quietly about their business or up to bed, her conscience got the better of her. She felt guilty for worrying them. They were supporting her, looking after her, and trying to keep her safe in their home.

Joe drew a sharp breath. Sarah didn't want to hear anything bad, and quickly offered an apology. 'I'm sorry. I did leave you a note though.'

He sighed heavily. 'Silly getting so upset, aren't I?'

Sarah felt her eyes prickle. She could see repeated little swallows in Joe's throat. He coughed to clear it. 'Yes. We found it just now. The wind must have blown it down on the floor when Kathleen opened the front door.'

Sarah frowned. She thought she tucked it tightly under the bowl.

'She went to the shops and when she came back you were gone. She's been out looking for you ever since.'

Sarah glanced at the kitchen clock. She went out at five and now it was quarter to ten. 'Well, I'm home now. I'm safe. Please don't be getting upset.'

Joe gazed at her. His voice was weary. 'Sarah, this is no joking matter. Your husband has been murdered, or possibly not from what Kathleen says, but we don't know that yet. And you've received a letter that the police don't even know about. I don't want you to leave this house alone again. Preferably not at all. I'm sorry to be a scaremonger, but we don't know what you're dealing with.'

Sarah agreed with him. She was reminded of her frightening ordeal at the hospital, and wished she wasn't. She had been in mortal fear. Something she had never experienced in her life before. 'I'm going to be calling the police first thing in the morning, Joe. The only reason for not calling now is I don't want to speak to them about tonight until I feel calmer.'

Joe blinked at her, his grey eyes anxious. 'What happened tonight?'

Sarah's chest heaved, and before she knew it, she was blubbering like a baby, her eyes and nose streaming as she let go her tears from knowing she was safe now. Kathleen folded her into her arms, shooshing her gently until she was calm. Joe placed a mug of tea in front of her, which she picked up with shaking hands and drank greedily. The tension in the room had gone, and Sarah was relieved to feel a weight lift from her.

'Are you trying to give me a heart attack or a divorce from Kathleen? I'll get a rollicking from her when you're not listening for letting tonight happen.' He smiled at them both to show he was only teasing.

Kathleen rested her elbows on the table, her chin on her hands. Sarah was grateful she was calm, and wasn't forcing her to say straight away what happened. Breathing easier, she wiped her face with her fingers.

'I went to the hospital and I got locked in a room and couldn't get out. And I don't know if it was done deliberately.'

Joe sat down so that Sarah was sitting between them. It had been an instinctive behaviour and she was reminded of how much he had lost. She patted his hand. 'I'm okay now, and I might be wrong. The security guy who let me out said my handbag had wedged the door shut.'

Kathleen sighed, but it was a soft sound and her voice was low and not rushed. 'Why did you go to the hospital? What room were you locked in?'

'I just wanted to touch base, and say hello.'

'Who did you see?'

'Doctor Summers, Andy, and Helen.'

Kathleen huffed loudly. 'Did she lock you in a room?'

'No, Kathleen. She wasn't there when that happened. But I think you might be right about what you said... Tim was upset because he thought he'd made a mistake and given the wrong antibiotic, but he couldn't find the prescription chart to check. Helen put the idea in his head, and then it was her who found it, and then Tim realised he hadn't made a mistake and then he cried.'

'That sounds exactly like her. I'm glad you were there to see it for yourself, Sarah. And you were there for poor Tim.'

'Again, I might be wrong. Helen might be completely innocent.'

Kathleen seemed to shiver beside her as she breathed in quickly. 'You're not. But that's for another day. We'll monitor her together. She won't be able to hide her behaviour with you watching as well.'

Sarah nodded firmly. 'No, she won't.' She glanced from her to Joe. 'I promise I won't leave this house without either of you. You won't have to go out searching for me again.'

'You're safe now. That's all that matters,' Kathleen said. 'But listen, Sarah. I know you're an independent young woman, but maybe you should think of staying here longer. I know you plan on leaving after Thursday, but until you know what's happening with William, wouldn't you be safer here?'

Sarah felt an uneasiness creep over her. Sadly, she wasn't surprised by the offer. Kathleen was trying to hold on to her. But Sarah longed for solitude.

'Kathleen, the person who sent me that message knows I'm here. You and Joe both work. So whether I'm here or someplace else there'll be times when I'm alone. I need to do this. No one is going to scare me enough that I can't even go home.'

Sarah didn't mean to her marital home, but to her flat. She could feel Kathleen's disappointment, and reassured her that this wasn't goodbye. 'Me being here has given you and me a chance to get to know one another. So that's a good thing.'

'It's the best thing,' Kathleen said, smiling with eyes that were too bright, which just strengthened Sarah's resolve to continue as planned. Even if she had to face a few difficulties with Kathleen getting emotional, she would go.

CHAPTER THIRTY-NINE

NICK

The outside of his father's house hadn't changed much since Nick was a child. The wooden framed windows had never been replaced and the front door was still dark brown. The house was rented as far as Nick knew, and had something to do with the church. John Anderson had never had a paid job – his was a church volunteer job, so maybe it had been handed to him on a plate for him and his young family. And, for a short time, there was happiness in that home.

John's young wife had loved music and dancing and her records were played night and day, much to the annoyance of some of the neighbours, but she hadn't cared. Nick loved his mother's wilfulness and her daring to be different to all the ordinary people around them. He had loved coming home from school and seeing the multi-coloured sleeper vans parked outside the house and meeting all her colourful friends, watching them drink and smoke and hearing her laugh at the things they said.

When she left, the house was stripped of all memories of her. Her name was never mentioned again, and on the few occasions that Nick broached the subject with his father, trying to find out where she had gone, he was brought up to his room where he was expected to pray for forgiveness for questioning his father's right to privacy.

When Nick joined the police force one of the first things he tried to do was track her down, with both technology and legwork. He looked for her under her married name, her maiden name and her mother's maiden name, but she had vanished off the face of the earth. She had run away from John Anderson and she wasn't going to be found. Sometimes in his dreams she was with him and his father in the woods that day, wearing a fawn coat. The few cousins he located thought she might have gone to America, because of her love of Elvis Presley.

His home had changed after she left. Silence or prayers were expected and crucifixes and holy images had been put up all over the walls. The music and the laughter was banished into one small cardboard box, and for a long time after Nick had wished that his father had put him in one of them so that he could disappear as well.

The passenger door opened and Issy climbed back into the car with two bags of crisps, a packet of Jammie Dodgers, and a can of Coke. 'I'm not buying their sandwiches at this time of night, even if they are reduced. They've probably been sitting there since yesterday. You sure you didn't want anything?'

Nick shook his head. He took one final look at the house opposite the shop, knowing he would have to call in there some-time, then started the engine. 'Are you sure you don't mind coming?'

She shook her head. 'No, not now I've got something to eat. How come you're taking the call?'

He shrugged. 'I was out driving when I heard it called in. Uniform have already attended, but I thought it would be a nice surprise if we turn up.'

'Nick, do you think this is wise?' Her voice sounded concerned. 'I mean... he was only released yesterday.'

'Yes, and look how he's behaving. If he wants me to stay off his back, he shouldn't draw my attention.'

Nick was regretting the impulse to call her, along with the rash decision he'd made to do what he was doing now. He should turn the car around and drop her back at her home, and then go home himself. He'd been out since seven, burning up fuel to get rid of his frustration and fear, thinking about how to stop it, but it was still with him, thumping his heart in his chest... and now he was plagued by something else. Guilt. Of all the feelings he expected, guilt wasn't one of them. He could now expect to wake up in the mornings, put on his clothes, and go to work and know he would never feel the same again. For dishonouring the uniform he was trained to wear, he would never feel he was a police officer anymore.

He'd turned the engine off a couple of times to just sit and think. He thought back to the scene, to the moment of finding that photograph of him and Sarah. He couldn't settle until he could be sure that Robson hadn't found others before he got there. When he arrived at work this morning he'd expected to be hauled into an interview room, but no one approached him or gave him a look. But he wasn't eased. He was positive he'd overlooked something.

He accepted the Polo mint Issy offered, it might stop him grinding his teeth. She said something he didn't catch. 'What was that?'

She had a mouth full of biscuit and garbled her response. 'Shr'own good.'

Nick swallowed the dregs of the can of Coke she handed him. 'What's for my own good?'

'What I just said. That we don't go there. Let uniform deal with it.'

Nick carried on driving. He had another reason for going there.

An ambulance car and police car were parked outside the property. Nick went up to the police officer standing at the door. 'How's the situation?'

'It's fine now, sir. It was when we got here. Neighbour who called it in said she was worried by the shouting and the girl screaming. A paramedic has checked her over. She doesn't need taking in.'

'What's the father saying?' Nick asked.

'Usual. She hit it on a cupboard.'

'And her?'

'Same as her father.'

Nick rang the bell. Amy answered the door in a towelling dressing gown over pyjama bottoms. A small dressing covered her left cheek, and she had the beginnings of a black eye. She looked nervous as she saw Issy.

'I was just going to bed.'

Issy saw Nick's subtle nod to continue. 'Sorry, Amy, but we'd like to see your dad.'

'He won't want that,' she whispered.

'We won't be long, Amy. We just want to check everything's all right.'

Amy stared at them anxiously, and jumped when she heard the angry voice coming from the back of the house. 'Shut the effin' door and tell who's there to piss off. You're lettin' in the bleedin' cold.'

Nick stepped forward, moving the now shivering girl along the hallway. 'Why don't you go back to bed while we speak with your dad?'

Barry Fox was in the living room lying on his couch. He was guzzling a can of Foster's, until he caught sight of his visitor.

'What are *you* doing here?' he spluttered, wiping his chin of beer. He then saw Issy. 'Oh, I see. You were pretendin' to be a bleedin' teacher?'

'Not true, Mr Fox. I never introduced myself as a teacher,' Issy replied.

The man got off the couch. He was taller than Nick. But Nick would outmatch him in strength any day. One smack and the man would go down. The small living room, aside from the furniture being filthy, had dirty dishes and empty cans littered across the floor, and cigarette butts were stubbed out on an overflowing dinner plate.

Fox put down his beer. 'So what d'you want with being 'ere?'

Nick sat down on the couch and made himself comfortable.

'Make yourself at home, why don't you?'

Nick took the opportunity to wind him up, and put a cushion behind his head.

Fox scowled. 'Don't get too comfortable, Anderson. You'll be leaving in a second.'

Nick frowned at him as if confused. 'Is that so? The way I see it, you're on bail. You've been charged with burglary, and on the very next day the police have been called to your home.' Nick sighed. 'You hit your daughter tonight, Mr Fox. We will be reporting our concerns to social services.'

'I never did. She hit it on a cupboard.'

'Do you mind if I go and talk to Amy?' Issy asked.

Fox turned to her. 'Do what you bleedin' like.'

Issy disappeared from the room, leaving the two men alone. Fox sat down and then a moment later smirked at Nick. 'I know your game. I worried you.'

'When was that?'

'At my interview. When I said I had a lot more to tell. You would have been watching from behind a screen.'

Nick eyed him coolly. 'And do you?'

Fox gave an indifferent shrug. 'Thing is, you only got to say that to get a rise and see which one is a bent cop. They soon start squirming.'

Nick wondered if he shot off the couch and twisted the man's arm behind his back, bringing him to his knees hard enough for his face to hit the carpet, he could get away with it before Issy returned. But at that moment Issy appeared. She gave Nick a subtle shake of her head to indicate Amy hadn't changed her story.

Nick rose to his feet. He winked at Fox, and pointed a finger gun at him. 'You stay seated, Mr Fox. We'll see ourselves out. But don't get too comfortable. You'll be residing elsewhere soon.'

CHAPTER FORTY

CHARLIE

Charlie was taking his jacket off when Nick approached him, looking agitated. 'You'll want to put that back on, and find Issy. Sarah Shaw was sent an anonymous message.'

Charlie walked towards the hot drinks table and heard Nick rudely call out. 'Lost your sense of direction, Charlie? The way out is that way.'

Charlie turned, and folded his arms like he was trying to keep patient. 'I'm waiting for Issy.'

'I asked you to find her.'

Charlie saw quick surprise form on their colleagues' faces as they heard the bite in Nick's voice, but he ignored it. 'You want me to go into the ladies for her? Because that's where she is.'

Issy gave a small cough from the door. 'Sorry, I heard my name. Everything okay?'

Nick turned his attention to her. 'You're going with Charlie to see Sarah Shaw. She's received an anonymous letter.'

Issy nodded. 'I know. I just spoke to her on the phone. Paul gave me her suit and coat. I'm taking them to her.'

When Nick looked back at him, Charlie stared serenely at

his senior officer while he called to Issy. 'I'll see you outside, Issy. I'm just getting us a coffee.'

* * *

Kathleen Price stood in the doorway holding a large bloodied knife, momentarily startling Charlie and Issy.

'Sorry. I'm doing liver. She's as pale as a ghost. I wouldn't be surprised if she had no iron in her,' the woman said in a tone that managed to convey that it was their fault.

She let them in and called up the stairs, and a second later Sarah Shaw came down. Issy handed her the suit and black coat and they waited while she hung them with the Prices' coats. Charlie stared at the young woman, and was reminded of the black-and-white photographs he saw at Miss Black's. She bore a striking likeness to the actress, Natalie Wood, especially in the film *West Side Story*, with her shoulder-length dark hair and brown eyes.

Charlie and Issy were led into the kitchen, where Mr Price sat at a table with the letter in front of him protected in a plastic sleeve.

'I wanted to report it straight away,' Mr Price said, 'but I was convinced otherwise; Kathleen was worried you lot would keep her under lock and key.' Charlie saw the man glance at Mrs Shaw affectionately as he continued, 'With her ex—'

Charlie's heart jolted. Instinct made him react faster than he could think. He interrupted before Issy got the gist of what he thought Joe Price was about to say. Thankfully, she was talking to Mrs Price. 'What do you mean straight away? When did the letter arrive?'

'Sunday evening. We were sitting here having dinner when it was posted through the letterbox.'

'It's Wednesday. Why haven't you reported it sooner?' Issy

asked, reassuring Charlie she'd missed the reason Mr Price just gave.

'A lot's happened since then,' murmured Mrs Price, putting down the knife on the draining board and leaving what she was doing to join in the conversation.

'Like what?' Issy asked.

'Like Sarah getting locked in a room at the hospital yesterday evening.'

Sarah Shaw gasped. 'Kathleen! You can't say that! I told you the security guard said my handbag wedged it shut.' She gazed at Issy. 'Last night I was shaken because I couldn't open the door, but it makes sense this morning what he said. I'd left my bag on the floor outside the room, and when I pulled the door closed the strap got caught under the door. With me then trying to push it open, more of the strap wedged and the security man had to pull it free before he could open it.'

Kathleen held up her hands. 'Okay, I take it back.'

Charlie reached across the table and dragged the plastic sleeve towards him. He turned it around to read it, and Issy came and stood beside him.

She made a sound of disgust. 'Err... what is this? It looks like something you'd see in a low budget film.'

'Did any of you touch it?' Charlie asked.

Sarah Shaw nodded. 'All three of us.'

'No. I didn't,' Mr Price corrected. 'I used the meat tongs to pick it up and slide it into the sleeve.'

'Does the message mean anything to you, Mrs Shaw?'

She shook her head. 'No, but it's trying to make me look guilty of something.'

'And has anything else happened while you've been staying here? Any sense of being watched or being followed?'

'No, but it's this that unnerved me last evening, because I thought someone was trying to frighten me when I couldn't open the door.'

'We'll get someone to check if there're any security cameras by the room you were in, if you tell us the location.'

'Medical Records,' she replied.

'Okay,' Charlie said as he stood up. 'We'll take this with us. What about an envelope?'

Mrs Shaw shook her head. 'There wasn't one.'

'I opened it,' Kathleen Price said, flustered as his gaze rested on her. 'It was just a plain envelope with no name on it.'

'Well, how do you know it was for Mrs Shaw?'

'Well, I... I just assumed... I didn't think it would be for Joe or me.' Her neck and cheeks were flushed, her hands crushed together as she stood there nervously. 'The envelope's in a drawer. I didn't throw it away.' She rushed to get it, and returned with a plain brown envelope.

Charlie took it from her and glanced at her reassuringly. 'You were probably right to assume. We've got Mrs Shaw's fingerprints, we'll have someone contact you so we can take a set of yours, for elimination purposes. Then let's hope we find some different ones.'

'What did Mr Price mean by us lot would keep her under lock and key?' Issy asked as soon as Charlie started driving.

'What you on about?'

'You heard him, Charlie. He said they didn't report it because Kathleen was worried you lot would keep her under lock and key.'

'Nothing. He meant nothing,' Charlie answered.

'But—'

'Leave it, Issy. Just leave it.'

'Oh, I see. So when he said "with her ex", he meant nothing? Who was he talking about?'

Charlie glanced sideways, saw the hurt expression on her face and sighed. 'When Nick was questioning her, he kept asking her about any ex-boyfriends she had that might have wanted her husband out of the way. That's probably what Mr Price meant.'

Issy stared at him. 'I didn't get the feeling it was over something like that. It felt more proprietary. A bit personal. I don't know. It was just...'

Charlie shook his head. 'Big word for you, Issy.'

'I know a lot of big words, Charlie. I choose not to use them.'

Charlie took his hand off the wheel and gently squeezed her hand. 'I know how intelligent you are. You'll make sergeant at a lot younger age than I was.'

She was quiet for a moment, then she murmured, 'I'm not sure I like her anymore.'

Charlie spent the remainder of the journey with his insides churning. Issy wasn't a fool, but he prayed she wasn't thinking the same as him. That Nick was the ex. He had seen a guarded look in Sarah Shaw's eyes a split second before he interrupted Mr Price, and in the same moment the penny dropped for him. She was guarded because she was aware Charlie didn't know about them. Either she or Nick decided to keep it quiet from everyone. Though Mr Price had known, so maybe she slipped up and mentioned her ex to him. The ex had to be Nick, otherwise where was the problem if it had been another officer she dated. Another officer wouldn't be leading this investigation so her past life wouldn't have mattered.

Nick's behaviour was because of her. Sarah Shaw. There was history between them, he was sure. Was it a fling between them or something more? Was she the reason he went to London so suddenly? Charlie went to see him one evening, just before he went – not that Charlie had known at the time that Nick was going – and found him sitting in his flat as miserable as sin. Charlie hadn't stayed long, as he was not getting much in the way of a response to questions he asked about his well-being. Was it her that made him like that? Had Sarah Shaw got under his skin?

It hurt Charlie that Nick could behave so cavalier about something that could end his career. If he knew the woman, he had no business being on the case. What scared Charlie most was that he would take this risk. Because why would he? Unless he had a good reason. Or hadn't gotten over her? Which could be worse. His feelings would get in the way, and make him blind where he should be vigilant.

Nick's owns words shot through Charlie's brain. *Is there an ex who wanted the victim out of the way?* He actually said this to the whole team.

Charlie's breath stuttered in his throat causing a sob-like sound, making Issy turn to look at him.

He muttered something unintelligible through tight lips and shook his head to indicate he was okay. While in his mind he was decrying Nick's behaviour.

Bloody man. Bloody fool. What the hell are you doing?

CHAPTER FORTY-ONE

NICK

Nick followed the procession of vehicles in front, but decided not to follow them into the gated car park. He didn't want to get boxed in, in case they were needed back at the station. He parked on the road, and Charlie fished out his cigarettes. As he started to open the car door, Nick stopped him. 'Smoke it in here. It's too cold out there.'

Charlie wound down the window and lit up. 'Never expected this many. Imagine what it'll be like when it's the funeral. The head teacher said he was very popular.'

The white roof of St Bernadette's Church evoked an image of a medieval nun's wimple. Yet its distinctive design was starkly modern. Nick watched the people getting out of cars. While some were dressed in black, others were in jeans and jackets, and a few were carrying flowers.

'I wonder if he loved her,' Charlie said. 'The first Mrs Shaw.'

Nick shrugged. 'Why wouldn't he?'

'Well, he didn't waste any time. I imagine it's hard to be a carer for a relatively young wife. It's not like they were old.'

Nick didn't comment and Charlie carried on. 'It's true

though, isn't it? Six months down the line he's married someone new.'

Nick felt a tightening in his stomach, and wished Charlie would belt up.

'But then seeing her last night, I'm not surprised,' Charlie rambled. 'A very pretty woman. And she's got a calmness about her that must be nice to live with.'

Nick got out of the car. If he didn't know better, he'd think Charlie was needling him.

A few minutes later the two of them went into the church. The pews at the front were filled, while at the back they were sparsely dotted, apart from a bench with pupils from St Matthew's school. Amy Fox was among them, a dressing still on her face. The priest, a small man with sparse hair and a pink scalp, waited for everyone to settle.

Nick stayed at the back with Charlie and let his eyes wander over the gatherers. Sarah was wearing the suit Robson had fetched from her home. She turned her head and he saw her pale face and dark eyes giving her a look of vulnerability he'd seen in her a few times before. He was reminded of that day in the woods. And the guilt he carried. If only he had made a noise. One tiny movement would have been enough to save her. But he hadn't and the deer had died. A beautiful animal shot by his father. She brought out the same guilt in him. And deep down inside, where he buried stuff he didn't want to dwell on, he knew why. He had sensed a loneliness that he hadn't wanted to see, in case he had to free her.

He lowered his eyes. His attention was returned to the altar as the priest said, 'Take your memories of William Shaw into your hearts and let peace now comfort you. He was a man who touched many lives with strengths and gifts and love. And as we celebrate the life of our dearly departed brother, we must cherish these memories of him and hold them special.'

When the service ended the congregation moved out of the

church. Nick waited for them to pass, then made his way out through the entrance porch. A man was shaking hands with each person as they passed him. What the hell was he doing here? Then he saw the priest talking to him and knew. He was here as an aide. Probably to carry the priest's Bible and holy water.

Seeing no way of avoiding him, he walked over. In a black suit and collarless white shirt, the man looked like a priest. Nick knew he wasn't. But he was a man who had dedicated his life to the church, not to the main man Himself, but to a building that made him feel holier-than-thou.

He turned at Nick's approach and, showing no surprise, smiled pleasantly. 'Nicholas, I didn't know you were back. I take it that it's recent?'

Nick met his father's eyes. 'Yesterday,' he lied. 'I got back yesterday.'

'I take it you were coming to see me?'

'I'm busy at the moment.'

John Anderson raised one dark eyebrow. 'Not too busy for your father, I hope?'

Nick looked away. 'No, not too busy for that.'

'Good.' John Anderson smiled again. 'Come to supper this evening.'

'That might not be possible. I'm on a case.'

'Well, when you have time then. It would be good to catch up.'

Nick saw Charlie waving and had an excuse to leave. 'I've got to go. I'm needed over there.'

Charlie was beside some flowers. Nick looked down and saw a colourful wreath from Shaw's parents, and a simple message inscribed on a flowery card: *In memory of William.* Beside it was a single white rose tied with a white ribbon, and with it a wholly different kind of message. *In memory of your lies. For R & R… May they now rest in peace.*

Charlie discreetly found a latex glove from his jacket, and used it as an evidence bag to put the card inside. Nick stood there, and knew right then that the situation had just gone pear-shaped. How was he going to convince anyone now that this was suicide?

CHAPTER FORTY-TWO

SARAH

Sarah closed the door and leaned against it, adjusting to the sudden silence. The noise in the dining room and kitchen had been intolerable, each voice grating louder and louder like fingernails on a blackboard. Everywhere mouths seemed to be opened. She'd become dizzy, seeing only red and black, until she couldn't breathe.

She'd had to get out of there. Andy Brooke hadn't shut up since he'd arrived; he was carrying on as if he was at an ordinary party, carelessly forgetting it was meant to be a wake. Why Kathleen invited him, she didn't know. Every time Sarah had glanced at him, his blue eyes, made bluer by tinted contact lenses, had been wide open and glued on Nick, like a lovesick puppy.

Now it was silent. She took gulps of air, trying to ignore the throbbing pain at her temples. She wanted to go home, not to the house that she shared with William, but to her small flat that would be blissfully empty of people. She wanted to live there again. William's house was never really hers. It was Mary's home. She thought about her life before William, what she had and what she gave up on. She hadn't settled for William. It so happened he came along at the moment she had the worst news of her life. That it was him she saw in the corridor, right after she was told, seemed predestined. He had been wheeling his wife to the ward, and Sarah was the new ward sister. He had seen her upset face and gave her his handkerchief.

The door was tapped softly, and with an inward groan she saw Kathleen come in with a mug of tea and some paracetamol.

'Take these, drink this, and then go on up to bed. Andy's gone home in a taxi, thank God. I invited him because I thought you could do with some of your colleagues here. I wish I hadn't. He didn't stop batting his eyelashes at your policeman friend out there.'

Sarah took the tea and tablets. As she swallowed each one she was reminded of the medicines Kathleen had stolen from the ward. She was positive Joe hadn't yet said anything to his wife. He was probably waiting until this day was over, or until Sarah was gone. Sarah couldn't say anything either. She was a guest in their house and Kathleen had done so much for her. Even if she sometimes got it wrong, like inviting people like Andy, she did it for Sarah. She would keep quiet about the discovery, and pretend she didn't know.

Another knock came on the door and Joe popped his head round. 'Have we got any more sugar?'

Kathleen glared at him with annoyance. 'Can you never find anything without my help?'

The two of them left the room and Sarah sighed with relief. She was causing friction by staying here – the sooner she left the better. For Kathleen's sake. The woman had stepped back into a role that had been taken away from her. She was mothering her, as if Sarah was her daughter. Saying things as if they were true – *we'll decorate your bedroom. Make it look nice and new.*

Sarah sat down in Joe's armchair, closed her eyes and let silence soothe her.

'Oh, you're in here!'

Sarah jolted at the sudden intrusion. She hadn't heard the door open this time.

'Some of your guests are leaving. I think you should come and say goodbye to them.'

The pain in her head bounced back in full as she looked at William's sister. The dark trouser suit she wore gave her a stern appearance. 'I'm sorry, I needed some quiet,' Sarah said.

'Well why don't you go home?'

Sarah's cheeks flushed at the rude tone. 'I hardly think that's appropriate at the moment, do you?'

'I didn't think it appropriate for William to remarry so soon, but he did,' she answered coolly.

The flashes of red and black shimmered before Sarah's eyes again. She couldn't stay here. She needed to get up and walk out of this room.

'You do realise why he married you? You haven't been under any illusions that it was because he loved you. He wanted a child and you were picked. He probably had you picked out even before Mary died.'

Sarah managed to get to her feet, but Jane hadn't finished with her yet.

'I have another reason for coming in here to see you. I won't beat around the bush. I've had to put my home up for sale. I think in all fairness your time with William doesn't justify you getting his house. I think that as his sister, I should receive something. Unless of course you'll have another mouth to feed.'

Sarah felt her hands begin to shake, her skin turn clammy. She wanted Jane to stop staring at her stomach, as if the answer was there. She had never told it to anyone, she had only ever said it in her head, and it hurt that she was going to say it now. 'I can't have children.'

Jane's mouth opened wide. Her eyes fairly sparkled. And then a cruel laughter, probably not intended for Sarah but for her brother, spilled out of her mouth. 'Poor stupid William. First he marries an invalid and then he marries a barren. He can't have known, otherwise he wouldn't have married you. Poor mother, she's been hanging on to that thread of hope. Well, you won't be flavour of the month when I tell her.'

'What's going on, Jane?' Alice Shaw demanded from the open doorway. 'What are you laughing about? This is a gathering in memory of your brother!'

Jane stared at her mother in such a way that for a moment Sarah felt sorry for her. Her eyes revealed an angry tough exterior to hide her pain. 'I suppose you wish it was in my memory, Mother, instead of William's.'

The slap was delivered before Sarah could intervene. The mark on Jane's cheek was livid. Jane didn't try to cover it. She delivered her retaliation in words: 'Sarah's not pregnant. She can't even have children.'

Sarah didn't hear or see if her mother-in-law made any comment, she was too busy registering the shock she saw on Nick's face as he entered the room. He hadn't masked it quickly enough.

'I think you ladies should take this conversation elsewhere. Sarah doesn't need this right now.'

Nick closed the door after them and she turned her back on him, not wanting him to see her face. She wanted him to leave the room with them, so that she could leave too. She wanted to grab her coat and bag and walk out of this house, and not have to see any of these people again. She couldn't bear pity. Anything else but that.

She kept her back to Nick and was glad when there was another knock on the door. He didn't respond and the knock was repeated harder, before the door opened.

'I'm busy, Charlie. It can wait.'

'Can't, I'm afraid. We're needed urgently elsewhere.'

Sarah heard him sigh, and then the door quietly close after him.

CHAPTER FORTY-THREE

CHARLIE

A police car was parked outside the semi-detached Edwardian house. Charlie recognised the nurse sitting in the back. On the other side of the road was a Rapid Response Vehicle. Blue-and-white tape crossed the gateway. Charlie and Nick ducked under it and walked up the stone steps to the open front door and were greeted by a uniformed officer and a lone paramedic standing inside the small porch. A female body lay a few feet away from them on the hall floor.

'Have you been through the house?' Nick asked the police officer.

'Yes, sir, no one else is on the property. My colleague is in an alleyway at the back to secure any entrance through the garden. We had to use a battering ram to open the front door.'

The paramedic was writing up paperwork, using a clip-board. He spoke to Nick. 'On arrival to premises, recognition of life extinct at 13.43. Body in a state of decomposition. Significant head injury observed.'

The two detectives covered their shoes with plastic slipovers, pulled on latex gloves, and stepped into the horse-shoe-shaped hall. Charlie looked at the dead woman. She was on her front in her nurse's uniform. Her right arm was squashed under her chest, her left down by her side. Approximately three-feet away from the body, a pool of vomit stained the floor. The left side of her face and left arm were discoloured a blotchy purple black. Her hair was matted with congealed blood. A milk eye stared sightlessly through the stiff strands. He ignored the pungent smell, akin to rotten fruit, and touched a gloved finger to her arm and felt the skin move unnaturally.

Charlie was in shock, which was rare for him. He felt desperately sorry for the waste of young life. He felt guilty. Could he have prevented it? He could still see her smiling as she said, 'We already met.'

Charlie listened as the police officer explained the situation. 'The man outside phoned it in. He came over to see her after being at a funeral. He knocked and then looked through the letterbox and saw her lying there. He said her name is Helen Tate.'

Nick glanced through the hall door at the man in the car. 'What's the man's name? I recognise him.'

'Andy Brooke.'

'He was at Mrs Price's house,' Charlie said quietly. 'He's a nurse.'

Nick looked down at the body. 'Is this Helen Tate, Charlie?'

Charlie nodded. 'She was pretty a few days ago.' He noticed her shoes were not on her feet, and wondered if she'd slipped in her nylons. The mosaic tiles on the floor looked cold and hard. He looked at the paramedic. 'Do you think she slipped?'

He shook his head. 'I think she fell from up there,' he said, pointing to the top of the stairs. 'She has movement in the bones in her face. Her jaw is fractured, and her right arm looks like it could be out of the socket.'

'Wouldn't she be lying at the bottom of the stairs if that was the case?' Charlie asked.

'Yes, if she tumbled down them,' the paramedic agreed. 'I

think she went over the banister. She might have leaned over it to be sick. The vomit's still wet, but it's at least a day old. It's drying.'

Charlie hoped it was instant if that was the case, and that she hadn't lain there conscious and knowing she was dying. He had a sick feeling inside him about this death. Had it occurred yesterday or on the Tuesday when he had an appointment with her? He'd wanted to talk to her some more about Mary Shaw. If he'd been on time for their appointment would she still be alive? He'd arrived late and knocked on the door. When it didn't open he didn't pursue it further.

In silent agreement, they moved into the living room and saw a coal effect fire full on. It was no wonder the smell was strong, the house was like an oven. Charlie went over to turn it off. He took off his jacket, tying the arms around his waist to leave his hands free as they continued their search.

'Nice pad she's got. Certainly seems to have a bit of money. Unless it's all on HP,' Nick remarked.

A pale-pink Christmas tree with pink fairy lights glowing stood in the far corner against rich burgundy wallpaper with gold leaf. A brown leather three-seater and two-seater formed an L-shape on a dragon red rug, and a Queen Anne style coffee table was positioned between them. Behind the couches against the wall, a display cabinet with three glass doors and a mirrored top section held matching crystal glasses and smaller ornaments. Facing the couches was a corner entertainment unit with a Sky box and DVD player, and a widescreen TV. A DVD of *The Bodyguard* sat beside the telly. Her nursing shoes were on the floor by a sofa.

They left the room and went into the kitchen. Good quality units in pure white were professionally installed from floor to ceiling, with enough electrical gadgets and equipment on the worktops to keep the most adventurous cook happy. The polished chrome glinting against the blue tiles looked unused.

The fridge was empty save for two tins of flavoured SlimFast, a bottle of Prosecco, and the remains of a pizza in a takeaway box.

'Definitely got a nice pad here, Charlie. I wonder if she rents with someone.'

Charlie walked out of the room and Nick followed. A door on the other side of the hall was open. The room was used as a study with medical books and black box files on the shelves, and an Apple Mac laptop on a desk. Nick lifted a file down and unclipped it. Salary slips and P6os from the hospital. In another box were household documents, purchases, guarantees and instruction manuals for electrical items.

Nick was busy looking in a third box. 'This is interesting stuff, Charlie. It looks like a patient's notes.'

'Bet it's not as interesting as what I've got,' Charlie replied.

Nick turned and saw Charlie had opened a drawer in a small sideboard. In his hands he had a packet of photographs. He shook them out onto the desk and used a pencil to spread them. They were all of William Shaw. He'd been photographed in the street, in the car park at his school, standing at his front door, and what was obvious in all of them was that he was unaware of them being taken.

'We need CSI here,' Nick said.

Two hours later, Helen Tate's house was busy with crime scene investigators. Her body had been removed to a mortuary, diminishing some of the smell. Steel's team was working fast and Charlie watched one officer examine the staircase banister and measure the height of the stair rods. Others were busy dusting for prints with their twirling brushes. Nick and Charlie had searched upstairs while they waited for the teams to arrive. There were two bedrooms and a bathroom, but only one bedroom looked properly occupied, despite clothes being in both wardrobes, and there was only one electric toothbrush in the bathroom.

Charlie wondered what was going through Nick's head. The hospital documentation he found was medical notes of a patient. Since when did nurses bring a patient's notes home with them? The photographs Charlie found put her as a substantial suspect for the murder of William Shaw.

Charlie found Nick in the kitchen. He had some updates to give. 'Doyle rang. He doesn't think he'll get time today, so more likely tomorrow morning for the post-mortem. He'll give us a call later to fix a time. Wiltshire police have informed the parents. They got a little background information. The property belongs to them, their daughter just lived here. The idea was she would rent it with another nurse but never got around to getting someone else to live here.'

Nick carried on poking around in drawers while Charlie watched him. 'So what are you thinking, Nick?'

Nick stilled. Then he straightened and sighed heavily. 'You know what I'm thinking, Charlie. The same as what you're thinking. That I screwed up. I wanted it to be Fox because he's a piece of work, but it wouldn't stick, and I kept thinking suicide. Now we have a dead nurse, because I was too mule-headed to think I could be wrong.'

Charlie watched him carefully while he talked, and wondered if it was smoke and mirrors. He couldn't be sure he was getting the truth until he had it out with him about Sarah Shaw. He wouldn't do that right now, not until they knew if Helen Tate's death was suspicious. His gut was telling him it was murder. But who would kill Helen if it was her who killed William Shaw?

CHAPTER FORTY-FOUR

NICK

Nick called an emergency briefing to inform the officers of Helen Tate's death. For the remainder of the afternoon and into the early evening there was a buzz of activity that allowed no time for easy conversation or joking while they investigated all the possibilities. A second board was set up in the incident room, with Helen Tate's name at the top. Until the post-mortem gave them cause of death, Nick hadn't wanted to write it. They were, however, preparing for a murder investigation.

The case they thought nearly over had now escalated with the find of those photographs. Nick was only staying focused through sheer willpower. His throat tightened with anxiety. He didn't know what he was hoping for any more – for Doyle to declare it an accident or suspicious.

If not for the photos that Charlie found, her death might have been thought an accident, but now everyone was aware the situation didn't look normal. How could he look upon this situation as normal? Where had his decency gone?

He jumped as Issy put a hand on his shoulder. Then he forced a laugh. 'Sorry, I was miles away.'

'Superintendent Naughton suggested we get some rest,

because we could be starting a new investigation tomorrow. Some of us are going to the pub while we can.'

Issy chose a pub in Bath more local for the group getting home, while officers living nearer Bristol stayed closer to their own local. They walked past the pub Nick would have chosen in Abbey Green, past the ancient plane tree in the centre of the square known as The Hanging Tree, where public executions were reputed to have taken place. As a boy his macabre curiosity would have him looking up at the branches for ring marks left from the rub of the ropes.

The Cork was busy to the point of being uncomfortable. Or maybe it was just him getting old. At his place at the table Nick had been jolted by passing customers and had beer spilt on his suit as glasses were carried over him. The music was blaring too loudly to allow for conversation, so Nick simply stared at the officers present, watching their behaviour.

Shaun Walker was picking beneath a fingernail with a matchstick. Tall Jim, Bob, and Ed were having to put mouths to ears every time one of them said something to the other. Nick wondered if the four officers had come for a drink to press-gang him into playing in the band for the upcoming Christmas dance, not trusting Charlie's reassurance that he would. The only one Nick ever socialised with was Shaun Walker. Shaun wouldn't be out of place in a rugby lineout, wearing a number 4 or 5 shirt. His looks were a deterrent to any criminal, but Nick knew he didn't have the aggressive nature to go with his size. He had been a good mate at one time, but Nick had let the friend-ship lapse.

He was the better musical talent out of the four, playing keyboard and piano, though Bob wasn't bad as a drummer, and with Tall Jim and Ed on guitars they had to be half-decent to get the gig, even if they *were* playing for free for colleagues and friends.

Issy was carefully removing a label from a beer bottle. Ian Carter, the trainee, was selectively choosing from a Bombay mix and bobbing along to 'I Wish It Could Be Christmas Everyday', and Charlie was leaning back in a chair, holding himself in a stiff manner. Nick knew he'd offended him with the way he spoke to him yesterday. He'd never disrespected him or been ignorant with him like he was after their visit to Miss Black.

He caught Issy watching him, and glanced away. She'd be better off turning her attention elsewhere, instead of hoping for him to notice her. He wasn't free. He couldn't be with her. A scabby thought entered his mind. He was a cuckoo waiting to move in on a dead man's nest. Her husband wasn't even buried, which summed up how low he'd fallen. He wished he'd stayed in London, and never found out he could become this person. He had been a better man there. He had his reasons for his behaviour, but that didn't stop it from being wrong.

'Did you leave any broken hearts behind or are you still nursing the one you went with?' Shaun hollered at him across the table. He didn't see the start Nick gave as he continued his not so sensitive probing. 'Have to say you look a damned sight better than you did when you left here. You were more often pissed than sober when I saw you. She must have done a right number on you. Said that to Charlie. Told him I'd never seen you like that before. Said when you left it would do you good, give you a chance to get over her and visit a new nest. Tell me... did you?'

Nick didn't know whether to laugh, growl or thump Shaun's head. The man was unbelievable; he'd always had the knack of ploughing in, stating what he thought whether good or bad, private or sensitive information, and all without any offence intended.

Nick settled for a grin. 'Plenty. Enough to make *your* brown eyes green.'

'Good,' Shaun chortled. The big man's eyes were full of merriment, his bald, brown head bobbing forward in mirth. 'That's what I like to hear. Now I got to see if you're still up to scratch. Make sure you're not treating it like one of your old girl-friends – a five-minute fumble and still not reaching the high notes.' He grinned slyly. 'Make my eyes turn green... As if,' he scoffed. 'So now you're back, are you going to carry on behaving like a bloody hermit?'

Underneath the banter, Nick sensed a note of disappoint-ment. 'I'm not,' he answered defensively.

'Yeah, you are,' Shaun argued back. 'The entire year before you left, the only time I saw you was at work. Do you know when we last had a social night out before you went away?'

Nick didn't.

'Three years ago, almost to the day, and that was only because we were both playing at that do. You met someone around then and didn't even introduce me. And the only reason I knew is because when you did finally raise your head from the love nest, you were like a bear with a sore head. It was all over and I never even got to say hello to her.'

'It wasn't like that, Shaun. It was—'

'Well, bloody prove it and turn up at this do.'

Nick shook his head at him lightly. 'Shaun, I'll let you know.'

He checked his watch: 8.00 p.m. He had been in the pub for an hour and wondered if he should make an effort to talk to Charlie. There was a wall between them at the moment, which was Nick's doing, but he'd like Charlie to know he still cared while he had the chance. Especially if things started to go south for him. When it would then be too late.

Charlie stood up, and Nick saw he was leaving. He should offer to drive him home as he'd only drunk half a shandy. It would give him the opportunity to say something. Charlie moved out from the table and Nick reached out for him as he stumbled. He was about to make a joke in case Charlie was embarrassed, but Charlie was suddenly on the floor. Nick went into shock as he saw Charlie's body start to jerk. Issy pushed him aside so she could get to Charlie and slide her scarf under his head to prevent him injuring himself. Coming out of a trance, Nick saw the others on their feet. Tall Jim had a phone to his ear, Ed was making some space on the floor, getting people to stand back. Nick was too scared to do anything.

Charlie came to before the paramedics arrived, but they took him out to the ambulance to check him over. While the others went home, Nick went and got his car and hung about for what seemed like forever before the back doors opened. He stepped forward in case Charlie fell down the steps of the ambulance. But he was steady on his feet and looked okay again. When they got in Nick's car, Charlie told him again he was fine.

'It was just a faint.'

'So how come you had a fit?'

Charlie shook his head. 'It wasn't a real fit. They explained it was a momentary drop in blood pressure with not enough oxygen to the brain.'

Nick was relieved. 'Well, you bloody scared me.'

'I should have paid more attention to what Shaun said to me. I don't remember him saying it. He was right, wasn't he? You left because of a woman.'

'Wrong, Charlie,' Nick replied. 'You know me. Love 'em and leave 'em.'

'Can you pull over?' Charlie asked.

Nick glanced at him. 'Why? Are you feeling sick?'

'Just pull over, please.'

Nick did as he was asked. He turned to check on him and found Charlie facing him. Before he could say anything,

Charlie locked eyes on him. 'Maybe I'm wrong, and only you can say, but I get a feeling you're in deep water, and it's to do with Sarah Shaw.'

Nick stayed silent and saw the worry grow in Charlie's eyes and his jaw quiver, and he felt a pang of guilt. His behaviour had come at a price. It had hurt Charlie. There was nothing he could do to change that. Except to stay quiet. If he told him everything, he would add more pain.

Charlie looked at him knowingly. 'You're not going to tell me, are you?'

Nick met his gaze.

'Jesus, Nick.' His voice was pleading. 'Walk away now and bury this. Do whatever you have to, because it'll take you down. Everything you worked for... You'll get caught! And I can't be the one to catch you.'

A tear slipped from Charlie's eye.

Nick had to look away.

CHAPTER FORTY-FIVE

SARAH

Sarah took one more glance around the room and knew she would never forget her stay. She would never watch another Harrison Ford film without remembering the poster up on the wall. She would never go to a pebbled beach again without searching for a large pebble like this one on the bookcase. She'd sensed the presence of the dead girl surrounding her; had found herself touching the hairbrush, opening the wardrobe and inhaling the scent. She'd felt as if the girl was watching over her. She picked up her belongings and stepped out of the room.

Kathleen was in the kitchen frying onions. Bloody steaks sat on three plates with jacket potatoes. It was gone nine. Sarah couldn't believe she was cooking, with all the leftover food they had from the reception. Tinfoil covered plates, piled on top of one another inside the fridge, and more on the worktop.

'Ready in a few seconds. Open that wine, will you, Sarah?'

'How did you know it was me behind you?'

Kathleen smiled over her shoulder. 'You always have that gorgeous smell; even over this I can smell you.'

'It's just body lotion. I've been using it for years. Molton Brown. I'll buy you some.'

'As soon as you walk on the ward we know you're there. Helen Tate, the spiteful cow, said you were like the Pied Piper of Hamelin with all the doctors following your scent.'

Sarah set about opening the wine. 'You really don't like her, do you?'

Kathleen flattened the onions against the pan squashing out their juices. 'No, I don't, but not just because of you.' She lifted the pan off the ring and hollered up at the ceiling. 'Come down, Joe, it's ready.'

There was no sound from overhead and Kathleen clicked her tongue. 'He's going deaf.' She walked out of the kitchen. 'JOSEPH...!' Her face showed shock when she returned. 'Why are your things by the front door?'

Sarah felt her mouth go dry. 'I'm going home, Kathleen.'

'Home?' Kathleen blinked several times. 'You can't go home, back to that house. It will be awful for you.'

'I'm not going there. I'm going back to my flat. I kept it.'

Kathleen sniffed. 'So Andy told me.'

'I was going to sell it after my honeymoon, but haven't really had the chance to.' Sarah gazed at her earnestly. 'After the initial shock, I didn't feel able to stay there but now I need to. I can't stay here forever. You know that. It wouldn't be fair on you or Joe.'

'What are you talking about? We love having you here. This is the happiest I've been since...' Kathleen's voice broke as tears pooled in her eyes.

Sarah sighed. 'I can't take her place. And you don't really want me to. I can't stay, Kathleen.'

Kathleen's hand darted towards the Christmas tree in the corner of the kitchen. 'But it's nearly Christmas. I've got loads of food and wine; we're going to go to Mass on Christmas Eve.'

'We can still go, Kathleen. I'm not going away, only home.'

'But this is your home now. Joe and I are your family.' Her eyes were tormented. 'If it's that policeman, you can bring him home here. Joe and I won't mind you seeing him. You can invite him for Christmas. We're modern. We're not going to worry if he stays over.'

'That will do, Kathleen!' Joe said in a voice that brooked no argument. His face was pale. 'Sarah needs to go.'

Kathleen whirled on him, waving the hot spatula at him. 'It's your fault! She's going because she thinks you want her to.'

'I'm not!' Sarah protested loudly.

'She's going because she knows you're becoming dependent on her. She's not our daughter. She's not *Becky*.'

Kathleen wrapped her arms around herself. Her cry filled with grief. 'But she could be. She could be. I couldn't love her more.'

Joe hugged his wife and moved her over to a chair. Sarah poured her some wine, which Kathleen gulped down. A moment later she stood up. 'Well, she's having her dinner before she goes.'

An hour later, the kitchen was cleaned up and Sarah ordered a taxi while Kathleen went upstairs. The main light was off leaving only a table lamp and the Christmas tree lights to illuminate the room. Sarah had looked at every one of the tree hangings. All simple things like stars, Father Christmases made out of red foil and whole eggshells, a cotton wool snowman and a paper angel on the top. Every item was handmade. Every item marked a year of Becky Price's life. Nursery and school day treasures that Kathleen lovingly cherished.

A dozen photographs sat on the sideboard. Sarah gazed at them, trying to see the unhappiness the child felt, but all she saw were shining eyes, and a head of dark curly hair. She looked loved and cared for. She'd had a lot to live for until she got broken.

Kathleen's face was puffy and her eyes dull when she

walked back into the kitchen. 'Do you have time for a sherry before you go?'

Sarah nodded. 'Please.'

Kathleen opened the blue bottle she'd bought for Christmas Day and poured two glasses. 'Joe thinks I'm turning into an alcoholic.'

Sarah smiled sympathetically. 'He loves you... he worries about you. He needs you, Kathleen.'

Kathleen's chin sunk low on her chest, her head shaking as if in denial, her voice filled with despair. 'And what about me? What do I need? What did I ever do to deserve this life?'

Sarah swallowed painfully. 'Joe told me. He told me about... about before Becky.'

Kathleen heaved, her lips pressing hard. 'Well, Sarah, it can't get any worse, can it? God dished out all my pain in one go. He was generous, I'll say that for him; and greedy, very greedy. Takes my baby boy, and then my darling Becky.' She stood up, wiping her eyes with her forearm, and smiled. 'I've got something for you. I was going to give it to you on Christmas Day, but I want you to have it now.'

She handed Sarah a slim, black jewel case and watched as she opened it. Inside was a beautiful bracelet. Sarah had never seen anything like it before. She didn't know if it was made of gold or silver. She couldn't see any other colours except blue and yellow – delicately linked blue flowers with yellow centres.

'This was Becky's. I want you to have it. The flowers are forget-me-nots.'

Sarah was speechless. 'I... I can't, Kathleen.'

Kathleen folded Sarah's slim fingers over the bracelet. 'Of course you can. This is so you won't forget me. You know I'd do anything for you. Remember that, Sarah, won't you?'

CHAPTER FORTY-SIX

NICK

Nick attended Helen Tate's post-mortem without Charlie. He'd sent him a text, telling him to get a check-up with his GP. He might have only fainted, but there could be an underlying cause of his blood pressure dropping.

Nick stared down at the body on the table. She was still dressed in her nurse's uniform. The exhibits officer was waiting for the clothing to be handed to him. Professor Doyle pointed to her ankles, and the photographer took several close-up shots. Doyle picked up forceps and the exhibits officer got an evidence bag at the ready to receive whatever Doyle had found. Nick couldn't hear them, and realised the intercom speaker wasn't on. He pressed some buttons and then heard Doyle speak.

'We'll remove the tights now.'

'Professor Doyle,' Nick said. 'I'm afraid I didn't hear what was being said. The intercom wasn't on.'

Doyle glanced up at him. 'We found some woollen fibres on her tights.'

Nick shut up. It was going to be a long morning if every thread was going to be tweezered off the clothing. He switched his mind back to yesterday, and what he heard. Why had she never told him? Had she thought it would have made a difference to how he felt about her? Children had not figured in his mind. Did she think he wouldn't have wanted her because she couldn't have them? Jane Shaw said something cruel, that her brother wouldn't have married Sarah if he'd known. Had Sarah told him? And if she did, how did he react?

Why had he been so blind? Looking back on his time with her, he could see now that there were many occasions where she seemed to go into herself. He remembered cajoling her out from her quiet places, but not once did he step inside with her to see just why she went there. If he had taken the time to discover what she kept from him, none of what happened would have taken place. He would not be investigating the death of her husband or be feeling a hatchet hanging over his neck.

His brain was in overdrive. Regardless of what Charlie had said, why would anyone else think anything was suspicious about him and Sarah? There was nothing to find out about them unless it was verbalised by him or her. They had nothing of each other's personal items in their homes. He had a key ring, and one small photo from a strip taken in a photo booth, but that was it. If they'd found anything in hers, it would have been mentioned immediately. He had no reason to feel so unsettled, no one would be tapping his shoulder. When it was over, he could put this behind him, and help her to move on. He would put his psychology degree to good use for once. He would spend hours talking her through everything.

He focused his mind back to what Doyle was doing and was surprised at how far he'd progressed. The body was undressed. Patches of greenish-reddish skin patterned her neck and jaw and her features were becoming unrecognisable. She was twenty-six years old and was going to be cut open to find out why she died so young. She was X-rayed from head to toe, and several broken bones were found. Her right shoulder and arm, the top of her head, eye socket, jaw and nasal bone where she must have face planted the floor. One of the assistants removed a stud from her tongue and another from her navel. The intimate objects were placed in a bag, to eventually be given to the family.

Doyle started. He made the usual 'Y' incision, drawing the scalpel from above her collarbones, across the chest and down to her pubis. He used a bone cutter to open up her rib cage and the noise was like nuts being cracked. He next went about the business of examining the internal organs. He dropped wet handfuls of innards into large metal bowls. When he sliced open the stomach, he sniffed deeply like a hound dog searching for a scent. Nick grimaced, and had to look away from the glistening visceral mass.

He left the autopsy suite feeling more than just tired. He hadn't got a clue about what he'd just seen or was now meant to know. Doyle, he realised, hadn't given him any verdict. He'd just said he'd be running some tests. Nick was going to look a prize idiot returning to the station with no information.

At five past three, Doyle telephoned. Nick was surprised. He hadn't expected to hear anything further from Doyle today.

'I thought I smelt something and I was right. Wine – a very good activator to get a drug quickly through the bloodstream, especially if it was a sparkling wine. Chlordiazepoxide, or Librium if you like, was taken.'

'You mean Valium?'

'Same family. Ten to twenty minutes after taking it she would have got groggy. Drowsiness is the primary symptom. You can usually detect substantial amounts in the blood, and steadily decreasing amounts up to twenty-five hours after swallowing.'

'Is this giving us a timeframe for her death?'

'Don't get confused here, DI Anderson. My finding was from her urine. The drug can be detected in this for up to a hundred and twenty hours after taking it. I suspect it was put in the wine she was drinking. It's a good choice of drug to relax someone.'

'But there was no wine found at the scene. Some in the fridge, but no opened bottles around.'

'So I'm told.'

'Is that what killed her?'

'No. And she probably would have been fine next day, especially as she had a healthy vomit not long after consumption. She might only have needed to sleep it off with no other treatment. No, it was the fall. She sustained a depressed fracture of the skull causing it to fragment and drive inwards. Direct injury was caused to the cranial contents. Death was instantaneous.'

Nick ground the mobile phone against his ear trying to block out the background noise of other officers talking on phones. 'Are we talking an accident, then?'

'She has broken fingernails and bruises to the inside of her knees.'

Nick didn't let on he hadn't seen them, that he hadn't paid attention. But he was able to work out what Doyle was implying. 'She was holding on,' he suggested. 'She gets to the top of the stairs, leans too far over the banister, then feels herself falling and grabs on for dear life?'

'The holding on to dear life is probably true, but what she also has is black fibres of wool around each ankle—'

'Sorry, Professor,' Nick interrupted. 'I'm not getting this at all.'

'Well, let me finish then. The fibres were on her tights. In my opinion, they snagged onto the nylon when her ankles were held by a person wearing black woollen gloves.'

'Couldn't she have got them wearing woollen slippers or boots with woollen insides?'

Doyle sighed and Nick felt his ears turn red. He was clearly meant to know already what Doyle was trying to explain.

'She could have, or even from a woollen blanket. But none of that would leave bruising in a pattern consistent with fingers and thumbs around each ankle. Or did you forget about that?'

The call ended. Nick put away his phone. He needed to give his head a good shake and get his act together. This was the second time he'd behaved like a fool in front of Doyle. He became aware of Charlie and Issy staring at him as they awaited the verdict.

'We're now officially treating Helen Tate's death as murder,' he quietly told them. 'I'm calling an emergency briefing for four o'clock. In the meantime, I want you, Issy, to go and see Sarah Shaw. See if she has anything to say about Helen Tate. We need to know why she had photos of William Shaw. Was it because she simply fancied him or did she have something on him? Did she send the anonymous letters to William Shaw and make those calls to him?

'Charlie, I want you to pay a flying visit to the hospital. Talk only to officials to inform them of her death. Get them to let you have a look inside her locker. We still haven't found the gun that killed William Shaw. If, and I stress this, *if* Fox is innocent of taking it, should we be looking at Helen Tate for the murder of William Shaw?'

Charlie gave him a disquieting look. 'So, we're shifting the focus to her. Even though we know she was working a night shift?'

Nick moved his gaze from Charlie's face to Issy's and saw hers was frowning at him. He was irritated by both of them. Why couldn't they just work with this? He feigned confusion.

'Why wouldn't we?'

Neither of them answered, which gave Nick some breathing space, and some hope that they were simply questioning his direction and didn't have an answer... because they didn't know what to ask.

He gazed at Issy. 'Be mindful. Mrs Shaw will realise we're changing our opinion back to her husband being murdered.'

Issy nodded. 'I'll be sensitive with her. Don't worry.'

He was reassured, and smiled. 'Thanks, Issy. I know I can rely on that.'

CHAPTER FORTY-SEVEN

SARAH

The opened envelope was still in her hands. She used the tips of her fingernails to pull the sheet of paper free, careful not to touch the glossy cut out words: YOU'RE NOT SAFE.

Sarah shuddered at the thought of what might happen. She stared at the locked front door, as if it was to blame. She had planned to take a short walk, and now felt unable to go anywhere. This morning when she woke, she felt the benefits of being here instead of at Kathleen's, but that was now gone. She was frightened something would happen if she didn't leave straight away.

The envelope had been posted through her front door. Someone had come up the stairs to her flat while she was in the shower. They had known when she was at Kathleen's, and knew that she was now here. They wouldn't know this unless she had been followed. The incident at the hospital... she was convinced now that the door was locked and not jammed. She should have listened to Kathleen's advice and stayed with her and Joe, at least until she could work out why she was sent the first letter.

The sharp knock on her door sent her body into shock. She

sat terrified to move lest someone hear her. She stopped breathing, waiting for them to leave. The door was knocked again and unable to stop herself she squealed.

'Sarah!'

Uncontrollable trembling consumed her. She was slow to stand. Her limbs having no power to move.

'Sarah! Open the door! It's me, Issy.'

She breathed in raggedly. Nausea swirled through her stomach, threatening to force contents up her throat. She needed to control her fear. Her eyes darted to the letter. She wasn't ready yet to show it to Issy. Issy would take control of the situation, she might take her back to Kathleen and Sarah would be left in limbo, not knowing what to do. If she caved in now, she would be frightened to stand on her own again. And that was something she couldn't allow. She had managed on her own in worse situations far more frightening than this.

She put the letter on the armchair and placed a cushion over it, and went slowly to the front door. 'Hang on a sec... I'm coming.'

The policewoman's eyes darted over her, and Sarah gave her an excuse for why she cried out and was slow opening the door. 'I had terrible pins and needles in my leg and foot when I stood up. It's gone now.'

Issy looked around the kitchen while Sarah made them tea. Sarah was pleased every surface gleamed. She didn't want Issy to find fault with her home. Issy took the mug Sarah handed to her and walked back into the living room. Sarah sensed some hostility. Something had changed in the relationship.

Issy stood by the window. 'I didn't know you had left your colleague's home,' she said.

Sarah heard a stiffness in her tone, and wondered if she was meant to have told her. 'I came here last night. I needed to get back to some kind of normal. I'd intruded on their home long enough.'

'If you'd informed us, I'd have told you that you can now go back to your house. The investigators are done with their search.'

'It doesn't feel like my house,' Sarah quietly said. 'This feels more my home. When the funeral is over I'm going to speak with my in-laws and tell them they can have it. I don't want it.'

Issy sat down on the sofa. Sarah was in the armchair with the cushion and letter behind her back.

'I have some news to give you, which isn't pleasant, I'm afraid. I must ask that you don't discuss it with anyone as it hasn't been released to the media yet. Helen Tate was found dead yesterday in her home. We're investigating her death as murder.'

Sarah didn't realise she was breathing loud and fast until Issy patted her hand. 'Sorry, I didn't mean to alarm you. Can I get you some water?'

Sarah stared at her blankly, and then managed to shake her head. Issy gave her a few moments to settle and then sat back on the sofa.

'What was your relationship with Helen Tate?' Issy asked.

Sarah tried to focus, and not think too far ahead. 'Work colleagues.'

'Were you friends?'

'No. We were only ever work colleagues.'

'Do you know if she had a boyfriend or if she had any particular friends?'

'The only one I can think of is Andy. He works with us.'

'Andy Brooke?'

'Yes, but he's not a boyfriend. Andy is gay.'

'Do you know if Helen ever showed an interest in your husband?'

'Wha—' Sarah started to say, but Issy spoke over her.

'Did you ever sense this, Sarah?'

Sarah shook her head. 'No. Why?'

'In her home, we found photographs of your husband. They show he wasn't aware of them being taken. Which makes us wonder if it was Helen Tate who was phoning him and sending him letters. Did he ever mention her name?'

'No. Never!'

'Are you aware your husband was having an affair while he was married to his first wife?'

Sarah held out a hand in protest. 'Why are you telling me this?'

'I'm wondering if he had form for this, and whether he carried on having affairs when he married you. It would have been a terrible shock to discover this. You said you weren't looking for excitement when you married William. You were still only beginning to get to know one another, so it would have been a knock to your confidence to find out he was looking elsewhere so early on in the marriage.'

Sarah's heart was pounding. She could barely articulate what to say. 'What are you...? What does this...? I don't understand. What are you trying to say?'

'I'm just wondering if you had cause to dislike Helen Tate.'

Sarah stared at her astonished. She was sure Issy Banks had just crossed more than one line in her job. Baiting her like this was not support. It was bordering on harassment. 'I want you to leave, please.'

Issy stood without argument. She walked as far as the door, and then said, 'We are linking her death with your husband's, as we no longer think his was suicide.'

Sarah stayed in the armchair after Issy's departure in an abject state. She had no idea what had changed between her and Issy, but she was glad she hadn't shown her the letter as she suspected she wouldn't have received sympathy.

She rose out of her chair and went into her bedroom. From her wardrobe she took her old suitcase. She placed it on the bed and unclipped the latches. The contents soothed her. They reminded her she was strong. She could survive this episode in her life. Nothing could truly hurt her anymore. She was protected by her experiences from the past. What was now happening would just be something to add. She would see this as a chapter in her life, now gone. And then, she would take her suitcase and move on.

One day she might not have to hide anything. She might not have to feel so alone. Or pretend she was someone else.

CHAPTER FORTY-EIGHT

NICK

The briefing was delayed by an hour at Naughton's request, and Nick now knew why. The meeting room was more crowded than on the morning after William Shaw's death. Detectives and uniformed officers had been called in from Wiltshire and Gloucester. At the back of the room Superintendent Naughton stood shoulder to shoulder with Assistant Chief Constable Hugo Wright, a man who had long since distanced himself from the days when his name had sent him into battle against kids who taunted him over it. His appearance was immaculate and his shoulder pips and jacket buttons shiny bright. He acknowledged Nick's presence with a quick impersonal nod and indicated he should proceed.

Nick had hoped Naughton would stand beside him for the briefing, but Naughton seemed to be taking a back seat. He was leaving his deputy to stand alone, perhaps for a reason. Nick would now have to show how committed he was to finding the person or persons responsible for these murders. The room was quiet. Nick broke the silence.

'Before we begin, is everyone up to speed with where we are in the investigation?'

No one raised a hand, and head nods were given by some of the newcomers.

'It's been eight days since William Shaw's murder. The person who did this will be under enormous pressure. Maybe struggling with guilt, remorse. In order to do what they did, they may be behaving out of character. Their family might be noticing a change in them.

'At the memorial service yesterday, Sergeant Bowden found a single white flower with a message for William Shaw. White roses usually symbolise purity, humility, innocence. The message we think was directed at him: "In memory of your lies. For R and R." Does this link to the remembrance card found in Shaw's home? We don't know who Ray is. We need to ask his parents and sister about that name.

'We need to tie up all loose ends. Pay a visit to Amy Fox. She said no one answered the door when she went to her teacher's home. She then got scared, thinking someone was behind her. We need to establish the details. Was someone else there, or was it her father she saw?

'The surveillance on Barry Fox continues. We can't afford to completely eliminate him. He might not have had the stomach to cold-bloodedly kill Shaw, but he might have had the gumption to get someone else to do it for him. The search for the murder weapon is ongoing. Sergeant Bowden has just been to the hospital to check Helen Tate's locker. I'm hoping he might have something to share.'

'I don't, I'm afraid,' Charlie responded. He was standing near to the door, and the officers were able to see and hear him clearly. 'The Chief Executive opened it personally. I secured the contents in evidence bags: Two blue nurses' dresses. A pair of black slip-on shoes. A pair of dark tights. A tin of deodorant, a container of talc, a box of tampons, spare toothbrush and tooth-paste, a hairbrush and two pairs of knickers. No gun. The manager re-locked the locker. She didn't want other nurses to see it empty.'

Nick noticed Charlie's clipped tone, reeling off every item like he was making the point that it was a waste of his time. Nick responded positively. 'Okay, so no luck there. But we have discovered finds elsewhere. Mark Steel will be joining us shortly to tell us what they found at her home.'

Charlie interrupted. 'Can we go back to the hospital for a second. I want to talk about Mary Shaw.'

'Okay. Sure.' Nick nodded.

'She had a DNR in her patient notes. She didn't have a post-mortem – I'm not happy about it.'

'Coroner was, Charlie, otherwise there would have been one.'

'Yeah, well I'm not.' His brown eyes were serious. 'Helen Tate made a point of telling me the first Mrs Shaw and William Shaw have both died this year. And now, Helen Tate is dead. What's more, I made an appointment to go and see her Tuesday evening, to talk about it some more. I got there a bit late, twenty past eight. Only she didn't answer the door, and now I'm thinking she was already dead. I think the proximity of the three deaths is something we should seriously look into. Mary Shaw should be exhumed.'

Nick noticed Charlie looking distressed. He hadn't told anyone about the appointment. He should have said about it. This line of enquiry should have been raised as an action. He wasn't going to tell him off now, but he wouldn't be pleased with his answer. 'I don't think we'll get permission for that, Charlie.'

'I agree,' Superintendent Naughton called out from the back of the room. Nick was happy he was in agreement. 'But I also agree with you, Charlie. I think we should be looking at the hospital. But discreetly. We have a nurse's death to investigate. It stands to reason we'll be wanting to talk to staff.'

Nick inwardly sighed. This case was never going to end, with so many other avenues being pursued. He was grateful an exhumation wasn't on the cards, as it would slow everything down even more.

Robson interrupted his thoughts. 'What about people close to Shaw?' he called out.

'Who do you have in mind, Paul?'

'His wife, for one. Maybe she killed Helen Tate because the nurse killed her husband, or because Helen Tate knew Sarah Shaw killed him.'

Nick felt his heart stop as he waited for Robson's next comment.

Naughton came to his rescue. 'Did you read something in the statements to suggest that, DS Robson?' he asked.

Robson shook his head.

'Well, when you do, then it might be useful. It's not helpful at this time.'

Robson's olive skin grew darker as he flushed. 'I'm just saying the second Mrs Shaw knew them all,' he declared.

Charlie butted in. 'I checked Mrs Shaw's alibi. I spent several hours at the hospital and brought back confirmation of her whereabouts. If you see something out of order in them, be my guest and check again.'

'Just stating a fact, Charlie, that's all,' was Robson's suave reply. He then smirked, which worried Nick. It was like he had a dirty little secret he was keeping to himself.

Issy then delivered a damaging blow. 'I have to say I'm less sure about her than I was. She's no longer at the Price's house. She's staying at her old address, which is a flat. There's something off about her that I hadn't picked up before.'

Nick wondered if the beat of his heart was visible through his shirt. The sensation was causing him to worry he was about to have a heart attack. He felt the urge to sit down to see if it passed. He felt trapped standing there and was never more grateful when Mark Steel entered the room.

Nick raised a hand, and waved him up to the front. The crime scene manager carried a plastic box. He placed it on a desk and poked a finger up under his silver-framed glasses to rub at his eye. He stifled a yawn, and only then acknowledged the large audience. 'Sorry, folks, it's been a busy twenty-four hours.'

He unclipped the lid from the box, which contained A4-size glossy photographs. 'I'll use the magnet board,' he said to Nick.

Nick could barely nod his head, the tension in his neck was so great. While Mark put photographs of the evidence up on the board, Nick sat down in a chair with officers at the front so that the only person he faced was the crime scene manager.

'We found two magazines in a shoebox in a wardrobe in Helen Tate's bedroom. You can see in the photographs letters cut out from different pages from the magazines. They are a match to the letters stuck on the sheet of paper sent to Mrs Shaw. I'M ON TO YOU. I HAVE PROOF. Exactly nineteen letters have been cut out from various pages.'

'Any other interesting finds?' Naughton asked.

'So far, only this and what DI Anderson and DS Bowden found. Medical notes of a patient, and a collection of photographs of William Shaw in a Boots photo envelope. It might be nothing, but one of the investigators mentioned a DVD of *The Bodyguard* next to the television. A character in the film was sending Whitney Houston letters in a similar fashion to the one sent to Mrs Shaw. So maybe the idea was taken from that.' He paused. 'The medical notes are a copy of a prescription chart. Noel Harris is the patient. The last date drugs were administered was on Tuesday at 16:20. I phoned the hospital and asked to be put through to patients' admissions. Noel Harris died in hospital on Tuesday.'

Nick took his place out front again. He was ready to carry on. His heartbeat had settled to a regular rhythm, and some of the tension in his neck eased. 'Helen Tate was seen alive on Tuesday. She was at work. She finished her shift at five thirty and presumably went home. We know that Sergeant Bowden knocked on her door at eight twenty and received no answer.

'We need to find out everything we possibly can about Helen Tate. We need to look at her phone records, finances, social media presence. House-to-house enquiries – we need to ask about any visitors. A long shot – but was anyone seen outside her home around that time wearing a pair of black woollen gloves?

'We need to know why she had a patient's medical notes. Particularly as they were in current use and this patient died on Tuesday, which is the day she must have taken them. She was watching William Shaw to take photographs of him, did someone then watch her?'

'Seems unusual to have printed copies of photos at her age,' Issy announced. 'Everyone my age normally keeps them on their phone. Also, wouldn't Boots have raised an eyebrow at clandestine photos of one person?'

Mark Steel answered her question. 'They're digital, Issy, so can be done instantly at a photo kiosk in-store. But I'm looking into that as I was surprised as well.'

Nick gave it moment for more comments, but at the silence he continued. 'Are we looking for one offender – the same person killing both victims? Did Helen Tate murder William Shaw, and then someone different murder her? We need to check, double-check every person we have interviewed. Are we looking for a man or a woman for this?

'Our enquiry will be focusing on the link between these two victims, and possibly a third victim, Mary Shaw. That information does not get shared. Let's not muddy the waters asking about Noel Harris' death either. We put that on the backburner for now. We will start with just routine questions with hospital staff, and take it from there.'

As the officers talked among themselves, Naughton came up to the front and spoke quietly to Nick. 'You've got a lot of legwork ahead and Shaw's murderer is moving away fast.' He sighed. 'I have to say at this point that I wish we were further on in this investigation. I'm appointing a second deputy SIO to share the load.'

Nick felt warmth rise in his neck. 'With respect, sir, are you asking that I step down? Because if that is what you want I would rather you stated it clearly.'

Naughton shook his head. 'I'm not asking that, but I am asking that you question your own ability, and if you feel this is too big to handle, then tell me now and I'll have someone take over.'

Nick felt the hatchet make a tiny connection with his skin. He had a sudden urge to walk away and let them discover what they might on their own. A part of him wanted to say yes, that it was way too big to handle, but the consequences didn't just affect him. The need to hold onto the reins was too important. 'Thank you, but I want to carry on.'

As Naughton moved away, Nick glanced around the room, trying to identify who might be the new deputy SIO. He saw Robson knee-deep in conversation with Issy, which was no surprise. Robson was determined to make Sarah Shaw a suspect.

CHAPTER FORTY-NINE

CHARLIE

Angus Doyle was studying Charlie with a mixture of curiosity and concern. 'Did you raise this with the SIO?'

Charlie sighed. 'I did, and he said permission wouldn't be given.'

'Well, he's right. You'd need more than a hunch for this to be granted.'

'It's more than a hunch, Angus. It's a burning gut feeling. Three people who knew each other: Mary Shaw, William Shaw and Helen Tate. Three people who have died in a short span of time. I don't think it's unreasonable to be suspicious. The worst it can do—'

'Is bring more pain to her family. That's what it can do! Are you prepared for that?' He took a deep breath and sat down. 'I have to say I think it's a hare-brained idea. I carry out on average a hundred and fifty post-mortems a year and have a guess at how many of those result in an undetermined cause?'

Charlie wasn't sure. 'A lot? A few?'

Doyle held up his forefinger. 'One per cent. One per cent, Charlie.'

'That's the whole point. Mary Shaw didn't have one!'

'Lots of ill people don't have post-mortems, Charlie. And trust me, exhumation autopsies are rare. And very complex. There's no guarantee, when a body is exhumed, that a post-mortem will tell you if death was unlawful.'

'Do you not think it's worth a try?'

'A try? I think you're better off looking for answers from the living.' His gaze became more concerned. 'What's going on, Charlie? Why aren't you talking this over with DI Anderson? You and him are close.'

Charlie shrugged. 'I thought I'd come to the expert.'

'You thought that, did you? I've never known you to come to me before.'

Charlie decided to lighten the mood. 'I didn't want to look an idiot in front of him. I don't mind with you. And now I have, I'll be off. And it will be the living I'll be speaking to next, because there's a nurse I'd like to see.'

Angus eyed him less seriously. His expression was amused. 'Oh, yes, pretty is she?'

'That's for me to know and for you to find out.' Charlie gave a smug smile. 'Tatty bye for now. Let's hope we don't meet again too soon.'

* * *

Charlie followed Sarah Shaw, and then sat down on a comfortable couch when invited. Her manner seemed detached, and it troubled him. It didn't seem to be coming from a place of unfriendliness. Her dark eyes showed her torment. He wondered if it was from grief. Or perhaps Issy had upset her. Maybe she hadn't been her usual kind self. She'd taken a dislike to her since their visit to the Prices' home.

'How are you?'

She gave him a sweet smile. 'I'm okay. Been a strange day though.'

Charlie nodded. 'Hearing about Helen Tate. Being so young and being a colleague... Do you feel safe?'

Sarah looked at him like he'd asked something strange. She sighed like she had the world on her shoulders. 'I'm trying not to think anything, to be honest. I can't go back to Kathleen's. It's just too...'

'I get it,' he said. 'She's quite a force. I live alone and I'm not sure I could cope with being in someone's home in these circumstances. I prefer it quiet.'

'Me too.'

'Issy said you were here. This is where you used to live.'

'Yes. There wasn't time before getting married to decide what to do with it. I probably would have sold it, but I'm glad now I didn't. I'm letting William's family have the house. I'm sorry if I was meant to have informed the police that I came here, I just didn't think.'

'You had a lot on your plate yesterday.'

She nodded. 'And you as well. Helen is why you and the inspector had to leave urgently. Your job must be very hard to deal with sometimes. You see things that are deeply sad and harrowing.'

'It's true. Sometimes we do. But then the job takes over and you push through. I do anyway. Mostly.' He shrugged lightly. 'There isn't another job I'd want to do.'

'Me neither. I like being a nurse. I miss not being on the ward now.'

'Which brings me to why I'm here. Helen Tate.'

Sarah's eyes turned wary. 'What about her?'

'You're a ward sister. You know how hospitals work. Why would she have a photocopy of a patient's drug chart in her home?' Sarah's mouth opened in surprise. Charlie could see it was a genuine reaction. It made him more comfortable with discussing this with her. 'The patient in question died on your ward on Tuesday.'

Sarah stared at him as if struck dumb, her mouth still open. It took her a moment to speak. 'Noel Harris. I was there after he died. Helen was going off duty. The doctor dealing with the death was terribly upset. He couldn't find the prescription chart. Helen found it for him before she went home. I have no idea why she would have a copy of it. I saw the original and there was nothing wrong in it.'

'What do you mean?'

'An error. Like the wrong drug had been given. Doctor Summers thought the patient had reacted to medication and that it was the cause of death, but when the chart was found it showed he had no allergies.'

'So why would she bother photocopying it?'

Sarah shook her head. 'I don't know. Maybe she copied it without looking at it. She might have thought the patient had allergies and she should keep a copy in case there was an enquiry.'

'Or perhaps to have something on the doctor she could blackmail him with? How upset was he?'

She closed her eyes as if she didn't want to say. 'He cried with relief,' she said quietly. 'He thought he might go to prison or be struck off until he realised he hadn't made a mistake.'

Charlie made himself at home in Sarah's kitchen and made them both some tea. He had managed while he was there to keep his mind off his concerns about her and Nick. He liked her, he realised, and he could see why Nick would like her. She gave little away, but her company was restful, and her character seemed compassionate.

He wished he could see a few weeks ahead and know if everything would be all right for Nick. Waiting for something serious to be discovered filled him with dread. And Charlie didn't know how much more energy he had. In the last half hour, he had discovered a possible motive for Helen Tate's murder, but it felt wrong to run with it if the doctor was innocent, and was already upset for thinking he had done something wrong.

The old Nick wouldn't want that, he'd err on the side of caution if there was any unanswered doubt. But that was then, this was now, and the old Nick wouldn't have sent him on a wild goose chase to look for a gun in Helen Tate's locker. Every step forward was taking him further away from the man he knew and Charlie just hoped at the end of it all the old Nick would appear again. He missed him, and wanted to see him again before it was too late. He just wanted the chance to remind him of who he had been to Charlie, so that he could work towards being that again. He just needed to find that moral fortitude that was so much a part of him. It was still there in him, because traits like that didn't just disappear.

If Nick could just come clean with him then maybe Charlie could help. He would do anything for Nick, but until he knew the problem all he could was watch his back. Charlie couldn't imagine what would happen if things didn't go well for Nick. He wished he could do more. He owed Nick that. He owed him for keeping something back that Nick should have been told years ago. And that was beginning to deeply trouble him. Charlie had to put that right. And soon. And hope Nick could forgive him not telling him.

At the time, he didn't think it would be of help. But withholding the information shouldn't have been Charlie's decision to make. Nick should have known then what Charlie discovered, even if it had led to nowhere.

He'd had the right to know everything when it came to his mother.

CHAPTER FIFTY

NICK

A quick pint to welcome new colleagues had turned into a session. The atmosphere was warm, not only in temperature, but also in comradeship. The beer had been flowing at a steady rate since nine o'clock and the noise coming from the officers had increased as time passed. Nick laughed just as hard as the rest of them, finally able to relax, the demons in his mind given a heave-ho to leave him be.

Issy placed a fourth pint in front of him. 'You look miles away,' she whispered in his ear. 'Sleep catching up on you?'

'I'll outlast you any day, Banks,' he mocked.

'Yeah, yeah in your dreams,' she jeered back. Her face was flushed with alcohol, and merriment danced in her eyes as she leaned back in her chair.

'Did you get any crisps, Issy?' Ian Carter asked.

'You are a sad sod, Ian,' Issy said. 'Food is all you think about.'

His eyes suddenly glinted boldly and the trainee detective showed a whole new side of himself that was anything but bashful. 'But, Issy, I'm a man who's hungry *for lurve*, and you never even offer a nibble.'

'I'll nibble your face off if you get any closer,' she snapped as she stood back up. 'Well, that's it, I'm off. Some of us need to have our thinking caps on tomorrow.' She gave a quick salute to most of them and a flirtatious wink to Nick as she staggered past them to get to the door.

The group broke up shortly after that and at 11 p.m. Nick got a lift back to Bath. The Wetherspoons' pub was only a few minutes' walk from Bristol Temple Meads railway station and he could have got a train. After four pints and no supper he was in no fit state to drive. The PCSO who drove offered to drop him off at his home, but Nick assured him the city centre would be fine.

He stepped into the small taxi hut beside the old Bath Police Station, which was now University of Bath buildings. His career had started there, which is why he'd ended up buying a flat in the city. On the opposite side of the road was a One Stop shop with a yellow phone on the wall outside to call the police after hours. A city without a station, and officers without a base. They had an office at a different site where the officers had their lockers and their computers, and they responded from there. They were equipped with handheld devices that were essentially mobile police stations with mobile access to systems and processes. And the rumour was that it was all about to change again. A police station was going to be given back to the city, which Nick was all for. The public used to be able to go into a police station and feel like they were being protected and were being listened to. Police officers liked to feel proud of their station. He knew he did when he was starting out. He had loved walking into that station, knowing he was there to protect the community.

He'd have to get a taxi to work in the morning, but the evening had made it worthwhile. He was numb and free of worry, and at this precise moment he loved his job. He was about to tell the taxi driver as much until he heard the truculent tone in the man's voice.

'You see that photograph? That's one of my mates. Now out of a job, I might add.'

Nick peered out of the window expecting to see a billboard.

'On the seat beside you. Bloody disgrace,' the driver said heatedly. 'Giving a front page to something like that when there's real crimes being committed.'

Nick picked up a copy of the local newspaper and stared at the named and shamed drink-driver. In between streetlights he read the article. The driver heard the rustle of the paper.

'Don't you agree with me?' he said.

Nick murmured as if agreeing, but privately thinking he'd attended too many RTAs, seen too many broken bodies, and heard too many times the same lie: *I only had one... for the road.*

'Now I'm not saying you gotta take liberties, but a couple can't hurt. You gotta live a bit. But the police always come down on the good guys, or rather where the money's made easiest, speeding tickets and the like. Me, I see it all from this cab, the ones that are miserable, the worriers and the weirdoes. Getting a few too many of them in Bath lately: a teacher last week, a nurse this week. Trouble is you could be carrying them in the back and you wouldn't know it. Police are about as good as a burst rugby ball on match day. The wind's gone out of them as soon as something big happens. You mark my words, they'll be running round with their tails between their legs another year from now and still be no closer to getting who did it. Don't you agree?'

'On what? Teachers and nurses being weirdoes?'

'You what?' the driver said. Then he laughed. 'Oh, I see, yeah, well that might be true as well. No, I'm on about the police being no good.'

Nick was tempted to tell him what his job was, but as the taxi drove along the familiar road he saw a light on in the upstairs window of the flat where she used to live. Eight days ago he had rang her bell and received no answer, because she hadn't been living there. He asked the driver to pull over, and found himself almost perversely giving a tip.

The man smiled. 'Good talking to you. I can see you're a man who knows what's right and wrong. Take care now.'

Nick stared up at the window. Sarah was in there. Issy had said it at the briefing. He checked the name beside the second doorbell and saw her name was still there: Sarah James. He rang and quickly stepped away from the door, his intention to leave immediately, then found himself boldly pressing the bell again.

He heard a crackle, and then he heard her voice from the intercom. 'It's me,' he said. The front door buzzed and he pushed it open.

She was in pyjamas and her hair fell forward partially covering her sleepy face. Shit! He'd woken her. 'Sorry I saw the light on. I thought you were awake. Just thought I'd check and see how you are.'

'At nearly midnight? Well, I haven't turned into a pumpkin yet.' She smiled sleepily. 'I felt safer leaving the light on. Do you want some coffee?'

'Please.'

He followed her into the small living room. Everything was just as he remembered. Dusky-pink couch and armchairs, heavy cream curtains hanging at the windows, and the same chocolate sheepskin on the floor. He'd lain on that a few times. She turned on the gas fire and told him to sit down.

A few minutes later she returned with coffee and a plate of cheese and crackers. She knelt at the coffee table, serving him first, and then sat on the floor with her knees drawn up to her chin. He sat on the couch trying to keep his eyes off her pink painted toenails and helped himself to a slice of melting Brie. He cleared his throat a few times intending to say something, but as he had no idea about what, he sipped coffee and ate cheese instead. She leaned back against an armchair and their silence was comfortable. It was new. He couldn't remember being quiet with her before. In his mind, he could see himself being loud and energetic, trying to impress her. He remembered her smiling and occasionally giggling, and lots of hand holding and touching while out walking together. And in the evenings, a quiet drink in a pub off the beaten track, out in the countryside, and then back here to her flat or to his.

They had spent two years together and had shared their time with no one else. He had thought they were happy by themselves. Their time had been full of passion and love and he had thought it was enough. But he had judged it wrong. Had she always known that their time together would end?

He held the warm coffee mug in his hands and closed his eyes. He was so comfortable.

He didn't feel his feet being lifted off the carpet or a duvet being pulled over him. He didn't feel her fingers touch his hair. But he dreamed of her.

CHAPTER FIFTY-ONE

CHARLIE

It was five fifteen a.m. and the building was quiet and still when Charlie arrived at work. He'd given up on getting any sleep after tossing and turning in bed all night and seeing on the alarm clock it was four in the morning. The night crew were mainly sat at computers, double-checking information, checking for discrepancies, logging enquiries, completing tasks, carrying on the work. No one raised their head.

Charlie made himself a strong coffee and didn't disturb their peace. He sat at an empty desk, then saw Mark Steel through an office window. He wondered if the man had started work early or not gone home. He was an odd bod at times, his incessant attention to obscure details often had him talking to himself as he asked and answered his own questions. Charlie took his coffee with him and went to see what he was up to. He saw photographs up on the monitor, and beside the computer several Boots photo CDs.

'Found any more of Shaw?' he asked.

Mark shook his head. 'No. I was checking these to see if I could find the CD of the photographs you found. It looks like she gets all her photos done on a CD, but I can't find that one.

She has other photographs on her iPad and her phone. Just seems a bit random having them developed this way without a CD.'

'Maybe it'll be in the room she used for a study.'

Mark shook his head. 'No. In all the cupboards and other drawers she kept things very orderly. Things were lined up neatly, folded away tidily – a place for everything. The drawer you found them in held pens, Sellotape, scissors, envelopes, paperclips. Stationery equipment, everything methodical. It wasn't a bits and bobs drawer. She didn't have one of those.'

Charlie was intrigued. He had found those photographs in Helen Tate's house very easily. First thing in the drawer he'd pulled out, on top of everything else. There were no other wallets of photographs either. He wandered back to the desk where he had been sat and picked up the briefcase he'd put by the chair. It still held William Shaw's photograph album. He took it out of the case and placed it on the desk. He'd been meaning to do this since his visit with Nick to interview Sarah Shaw, but kept forgetting. It was the photographs at the back of the album that he was interested in, the ones of the pupils and Shaw from when he was at his previous school. Charlie hadn't noticed before because he hadn't been looking for her, but there she was right beside him. Mary Hicks, before she became Mary Shaw, was a pretty woman.

Charlie left the room and made his way to the Holmes Room. 'Can you find out Mary Shaw's date of birth? Then run the name Mary Hicks,' he asked an officer.

Ten minutes later an incident report came up on a screen. The officer opened the file and Charlie watched as the information downloaded. It was dated March 17, 2007. Charlie felt his heart give a good thump. He had heard that day and month only recently. He got out his notebook and hastily flicked through. He found it. Mary Shaw died on the seventeenth of March. He stared back at the screen and read on and felt his heart tapping hard as phrases jumped out at him.

Road traffic accident, Mary Hicks driver of the vehicle, carrying one passenger. Victim on road, male baby, unresponsive. Death at the scene.

'Jesus!' he whispered. 'Print me a copy, please.'

At six a.m. Charlie got into his car with the report folded in his pocket. By the time Nick and the rest of the team arrived for work and sorted themselves out, Charlie should almost have arrived at his destination. He had a two-hour forty-five minute drive ahead of him.

He was going south-east to Gillingham in Kent, an area he'd been to when he was a boy – a day trip he'd taken with his aunt Charlotte. It had been Navy Day. They spent the day at Chatham Dockyards and Charlie had explored warships and submarines, while soaking up the atmosphere and excitement of being with crowds of other people looking up at tall ships and hundreds of flying flags. They'd had a lemonade in a pub garden before their long journey back, and he remembered lying down on the back seat of Aunt Charlotte's car for a comfortable ride home. Today his visit would be very different.

Medway Police Station was on a busy road opposite an Asda superstore. Charlie took the liberty of parking there and used the pedestrian crossing to get safely over to the large terracotta-coloured building. At the reception desk a smartly dressed woman with short grey hair was waiting to be seen. She smiled politely at Charlie. Then unexpectedly offered to let him go before her. 'You look like you need to speak to someone more urgently than me.'

Charlie wondered what he looked like. His tie was loosened and his jacket a bit crumpled. 'No, I'm fine. Just had a long drive from Bath.'

Her eyes opened in surprise. 'How very odd. I'm here to talk to someone about a letter I've received from Bath. It's a little unsettling.'

'Well, I'm a police officer in Bath.'

The woman stared at him with an expression of wonder. Her interest in him becoming intense. 'This might sound off the wall, but I do believe we were meant to meet.'

She moved away from the desk. 'Would it be possible to have a really quick word before I speak to someone here?'

'Okay,' Charlie agreed, hoping it wasn't going to take long.

She walked to where there were seats. Charlie reluctantly followed. She held out her hand to shake his, before she sat down. 'My name's Harriet Hoffman. I'm a psychologist. If after I've spoken to an officer here, I don't feel... well, that they're taking it seriously, would you mind if I call you? The person who wrote the letter lives in Bath.'

Charlie pulled out his wallet and found her his business card. 'This has my work mobile number, but I'm sure if it's serious they'll sort it out here.'

'I hope so,' she replied, and handed him her business card. 'Just in case you wish to check my credentials.' She gave a small worried sigh. 'I don't wish to appear an alarmist, but this is the first time I've come to a police station to report *a feeling*. Please let me assure you, I don't give into flights of fancy.'

Charlie didn't doubt it. Everything about her looked sensible. From her clothes to her shoes and business card, which he glanced at before putting in his pocket. Dr Harriet Hoffmann, (PsyD). Even her tone of voice, calmly expressing the reason for her being there – *a feeling* – made her sound sensible.

Charlie respected her frankness. 'Instinct is a feeling that you have that something is the case,' he said. 'I learned that from a dictionary when I joined the police. I love that sentence. It's my motto when I start doubting myself.'

She glanced at him appreciatively. 'Thank you. I brought spare copies of the letter. May I give you one?'

Charlie nodded, hoping that this was all she required. Dr Hoffmann was better off letting Medway Police deal with the situation. Let them take it up with Avon and Somerset if concerned.

She pulled a wide envelope from her bag and handed it to him. 'There's a copy inside it. I'd be interested in your opinion.'

'I'll read it when I can. Might not be today. I'm on a mission.'

'Thanks. When I received it on Thursday, it bothered me immediately. I haven't seen this patient in years. Since they were a young teenager. I was transported back in time, to a day much like this one, cloudy with the threat of rain. I'd been seeing the patient for six weeks before a word was spoken.' She gave a wry smile. 'I got one very small conversation about *clouds*. Rain was coming, and clothes smelled damp dried indoors. And then all contact stopped. My patient went missing that day, along with a jack-in-the-box from my office.'

Charlie felt some sympathy. You could never shake the worry of a missing kid.

'I should have sensed a bigger picture. That what I was dealing with wasn't all down to having a tragic death in the family. My instinct,' – she gave a short, disparaging laugh – 'my *feeling* didn't kick in until that day. But when it did, I wanted to know what social services were doing, whether there were any prior concerns about the family. The state of the school uniform – frayed collar and cuffs grimed in dirt. Grey socks hanging heels over the back of scuffed shoes. Unwashed and uncared for – it was only fit for a bin. What I saw, I realised, was the norm. Not just the aftermath of a recent tragedy.'

So far, Charlie hadn't heard anything out of the norm. Uncommunicative teenager and grubby school uniform – that had been him.

She glanced at Charlie, and gave a resigned sigh. 'I can see in your expression what you're thinking. Where's the problem?'

Charlie was taken back. He'd always thought he had a poker face. He gave her the truth. 'I am thinking that. Bearing in mind, I don't know your patient. But from what I've heard, I'm not picking up anything alarming.'

'Ex-patient,' she replied. 'When I received the letter on Thursday I could think of no reason why I would get one after all these years. Unless it was to get my attention. Was I being blamed for what happened to this family? Transference some- times happens when a patient attaches anger and hostility onto their therapist. If this is what is happening, after all this time – a stored-up resentment might be about to come my way. The mood of the letter is dark. There's talk of crime, of people dead, of no one punished. It's like I've been told something bad has happened or is about to happen. And there's no remorse. It doesn't give details. It gives a glimpse into a very dark room where something is happening, but I can see nothing at all. I can only feel something there.'

Charlie felt a shiver run across his chest. He took back what he said. It sounded like Dr Hoffmann was right to have a feeling.

'The postmark on the envelope's from Bath, but there's no return address on the letter. But I can give a name,' she said.

Charlie frowned. Surely it was on the letter. Otherwise how did the doctor know who it was from. Unless it was redacted for confidentiality reasons.

She saw his confused expression. 'You'll see what I mean when you read the letter.'

Charlie rose to his feet and waited for her to join him. He offered his hand to say goodbye. 'Well, good luck. I hope things works out okay.'

She smiled warmly. 'Thanks for talking to me. I'm glad now I came to report it. At least to have it on record. I don't know what this patient wants or is hoping for or has done or is intending. It could be just a letter to elicit a reaction. Or it could be leading up to an admission.'

She looked him in the eye. 'I don't want to wait for that to happen. I don't want to put this off to another day. Because I really don't need to read something when it has already happened and too late to do anything. Especially if it is something bad.'

An officer came to the window and Charlie left her to speak in private, and a moment later a second officer attended to him. Charlie was able to return his mind to the reason he was there. Charlie showed his warrant card and asked to speak to the duty sergeant. Twenty minutes later he was drinking tea and waiting for the officer assigned to help.

Sergeant Beverly Thompson was a striking blonde. Taller than him, probably in her mid-forties. She was carrying a blue file and gave Charlie a toothy smile. 'Was I meant to know you were coming?'

'No. It was a spur of the moment decision made at around half five this morning when I ran the name Mary Hicks and discovered she'd been involved in a traffic accident.'

'Before I let you look at the file I'll give you the run down. I was a DC on this case. As you can imagine it's one I remember quite well. Always do when it's a babe, and such a tiny one. He was three months old. His mother was Monica Marah. She was pushing the little boy in his pushchair. The accident happened on a busy main road – I'll show you on a map where it happened in a minute. Mary Hicks, a teacher, was driving down it. Monica Marah stepped out into the road without looking for oncoming vehicles. The baby and his pushchair were taken fifty feet down the road. Miss Hicks didn't have a chance to slow down. The mother just stepped out in front of the car.'

'Any witnesses?' Charlie asked.

'It was raining so not many pedestrians about. Other drivers saw the accident, but none could give a clear account. It's a very busy road, so traffic in the opposite direction kept moving.'

'Was the mother hurt?'

The sergeant's mouth twisted into a bitter smile. 'It was her blood on the road. The officer attending the scene first thought it was her knocked down. She had blood on her hands and was scrabbling on her knees. It was only when he picked her up that he realised she was crawling through broken glass from a whisky bottle that must have got thrown out from the basket of the pushchair. All the time he was helping her, the pushchair went unnoticed lying on its side fifty feet down the road, the little baby in it was dead.

'We had to wait until the next day to talk to her. She wasn't sober enough until then. I wanted the Crown Prosecution Service to press charges. She should have been done for murder. The coroner's verdict was misadventure. A misfortune, he called it, and she got off scot-free.'

'And Mary Hicks?'

'Probably left with nightmares for the rest of her life.'

CHAPTER FIFTY-TWO

NICK

Seagulls were circling overhead for breakfast, their screeches piercing Nick's ears. He was moving his feet slowly to lessen the pounding in his head. The aspirin that he had found in his jacket pocket had yet to work, and the icy bite in the air was making his nose and ears ache. He closed his mouth to keep his teeth warm and was relieved to see Issy marching towards him.

It wasn't her presence that pleased him; it was the sight of the two Costa coffee cups in her hands. His mouth tasted foul and his teeth were like rough wool. He hadn't helped himself to coffee at Sarah's. It had been shock enough to wake up on her couch this morning. He'd crept along to her bedroom and looked through the gap in the door. She was sleeping, lying on her side, hair spread across a pillow, hands uncurled and relaxed and a pale breast uncovered and bare. He'd quickly tiptoed back to the kitchen and splashed his face at the sink with cold water before using those silent moments to slip away.

'Are they both for you, or can I have one?'

'One's for Ian, but I'll tell him I forgot. He's got a hangover.'

Nick grunted a reply, and sipped the coffee, but couldn't taste the boiling liquid.

'You look rough,' Issy said, stating the obvious. 'Aren't they the same clothes you had on last night?'

'Fell asleep on the couch and thought it was later than it was when I woke. You think anyone's got a spare shirt I could borrow?'

She frowned at him. 'I'll ask. I'll bet you still haven't given Charlie back the one you borrowed from him.'

'I haven't washed it yet.'

'I'll find you a razor as well. You look like a frigging bear.'

'Yeah, well let's hope Naughton doesn't need to talk to me until I've had a makeover.' He drank some more liquid and sighed wearily. 'I am so not looking forward to this day.'

The team were now looking at Helen Tate as a possible suspect, and he would have to go along with it. They would run the same checks on her as they had on Sarah, to establish if she had the opportunity to leave the hospital undetected to commit the crime. Robson would probably suggest they re-check Sarah's alibi while they were at it. Nick was definitely not assigning the task to him. It would be better if Charlie did it, especially as he'd already gone through the proper channels to obtain the information on Sarah.

Issy handed him two paracetamols. 'I'll head in and start asking around for a shirt.' She wrinkled her nose. 'You'll need to be more presentable for the hospital.'

Nick looked at her blankly, then he sighed heavily. He remembered. Him and Charlie were visiting the hospital this morning. The interview coordinator had sorted out timeslots for the doctors and nurses that would work with their shift pattern. It was not the intention of the police to cause needless disruption at the hospital. They were simply visiting to gather information about the former staff nurse, Helen Tate. That the interview coordinator had been canny enough to ask for the names of staff who had worked on the ward on March 17 was neither here nor there. They didn't need to mention Mary Shaw.

Nearly half an hour later, Nick had washed and shaved himself with a pink razor and cleaned his teeth with Issy's spare toothbrush. The shirt he was wearing was a white police shirt that she'd borrowed from someone, but he was grateful and it would do. He drank the bottle of water she gave him as well, but it didn't change how he felt. He couldn't concentrate on anything.

Being in Sarah's company last night brought home to him how fragile were their chances of a future together. He pictured himself going to prison. While she... He couldn't think about it. It scared him.

Nine days ago when he returned to Bath his only thought had been to drop off his luggage and then go and surprise her. His first port of call was her flat. The neighbour downstairs said she had left. That she had married a teacher. That she had a new address. The neighbour had given it to him, and numb with shock he had driven away.

He drove blindly to the hospital and enquired if she was on duty. *She's on a night shift*, he was told. He wanted to stop then. But he found he couldn't. He felt deceived in the worst possible way. How could she possibly fall in love and marry someone so quickly? She who was so cautious, who liked to take things slow? He would have sold his flat so they could live together properly if he'd had the chance.

He'd parked down by the river, trying to feel something other than numb. He watched the flow of the water on the outside of the bend where the current was at its fastest, and thought to get out of the car and just put his legs in the water and see if fate took him...

It was the rain that stopped him. One of life's little ironies – he thought it too wet to leave the car. He sat in the dry, listening to the creaking and the groaning of the trees and the rush of the dark green water.

When he left, it was reluctantly. The night air had chilled him. He drove carefully along streets towards where she lived and passed her car, parked on a road that was not hers. He parked on her street, and saw lads doing wheelies on motorcycles. They didn't notice him. The house looked quiet. Instinct drew him around to the back. From a pocket in his jacket he found a pair of disposable shoe covers. He put them on and used his elbow to press down the handle on the back door. It opened and let him in to a kitchen. He waited to check that all was silent. He made no sound as he climbed the stairs.

In that moment, everything in his life changed.

When he returned to his car and drove away, Sarah's car had gone.

He'd carried an idea inside him for the last nine days – if he had stayed by the river – time might not have passed, night might not have come.

Nick put his tie and jacket on, and checked his appearance. He looked presentable. He went in search of Charlie. He looked around the room, and couldn't see him anywhere. 'Has Charlie come in yet?' he asked the officer standing next to him.

A shake of the head was the response. Nick hoped Charlie hadn't had another faint, and that he'd gone to see a doctor yesterday. He got out his phone and sent him a text to ask if everything was all right. Then Issy let him know he should go. The two other interviewers had already left. The hospital was expecting him to be there at nine. Nick peered around the room again. Still no sign of Charlie. He couldn't delay any longer.

'Okay, Issy. You're with me.'

Nick pretended not to notice her happy smile. He'd taken advantage of her feelings already. The least he could do was to try and be a decent person while he carried out this sham of being a noble detective. It wasn't much, but anything that made him feel even a fraction less corrupted was worth trying.

CHAPTER FIFTY-THREE

CHARLIE

Charlie banged the door with the side of his fist again. He was sure someone was home. Then he heard a voice. 'All right, all right, keep your hair on.'

Monica Marah looked ancient, though she was probably younger than him. She had a baby fifteen years ago. Her thinning grey hair straggled over her worn-out face and Charlie grimaced as he saw her revolting yellow teeth.

A cigarette clung to her lip even as she spoke. 'What d'you want?' Charlie showed her his warrant card and watched her grey eyebrows lift. 'Thought you'd turn up some time. Come on in.'

He followed her tiny frame, smelling her as she moved. Cigarette smoke, alcohol and, he was sure, dry urine was left in her wake. He felt his shoe squash into something soft and lifted it up to see. His nose wrinkled, as he smelled the faeces. He wiped his shoe against the newspaper beside it and she saw him do it.

'Cats! Poop everywhere. Give us your shoe and I'll clean it.'

In the kitchen Charlie stood on one foot while she rinsed the sole of his shoe over the dishes in the sink. He saw a brown blob fall into a cup and then she wiped his shoe with a grimy teacloth. She sat down. After briefly examining a chair, Charlie did the same. The green jumper she wore had small burns down its front and Charlie wondered how often she fell asleep with a cigarette in her mouth.

She waved a bottle of gin at him. 'Too early for you or what?'

Charlie shook his head. 'Too early.'

She pointed at the cooker. 'Make yourself a brew if yer want.'

'I'm okay,' he answered, wondering how she could think of offering him any beverage after witnessing her hygiene standards.

'Please yourself,' she said, then poured a large measure of gin into a cracked mug. She drank it back. 'Gotta have something to warm you up,' she cackled. 'Apart from shitty cats. So am I gonna have to drag it out of you or what? Where is she?'

'Where's who?' Charlie asked.

The cigarette bobbed up and down as she talked. 'Me daughter, of course. Jess!'

Charlie wished he could have a drink. Instead he lit up.

She smiled her horrible yellow teeth. 'Thought you were one. Hear it in your voice.'

'I haven't come about your daughter.'

'Oh, what then?'

Charlie didn't know where to start. Sergeant Beverly Thompson had given him the address, and he'd come here with the notion that it might help him somehow to solve the murders back in Bath. But sitting beside her, he saw it was a daft idea. Her brain was addled by alcohol. She was barely able to hold a mug in her unsteady hands.

'Where is your daughter?'

Her scrawny neck stretched as her chin lifted. 'Dunno. Didn't come home, did she?'

'When was this? I take it you rang the police?'

''Course I did.' She poured another mug of gin. 'Thirteen, fourteen... you lose track. One day rolls into another. I'd try again but my phone's been cut off for years.'

Charlie felt a surge of frustration. He should call Nick and tell him where he was, otherwise he'd be sending someone to check on him. 'Mind if I use your bathroom?'

'Be my guest, love. It's up the stairs.'

He watched where he walked and went back along the hallway. The sitting room door was open. It was furnished with an old couch with ancient blankets shoved up to one end, indicating where she might sleep, and empty gin bottles vied for a place on a floor littered with more faeces-smeared newspapers. Of the offending cats he neither heard nor saw them. No doubt they were out getting fresh air.

Some unframed photographs left on the mantelpiece to gather dust showed her and presumably her husband when they were younger. He didn't see pictures of her baby boy or of her daughter, though.

He went up the stairs, keeping hands off the banister and wall. In her bedroom, filthy linen gave off a rank sweaty smell, and in the bathroom a towel was bent over a rail, literally stiffened with dirt. A grimy bar of soap left cracked and dried sat on a ledge above a toilet bowl that was so stained it stilled the need in Charlie to urinate.

The door to the last room he visited was stuck and needed a push. At first glance Charlie thought the cardboard box on the floor beside the single bed was a place where her cats slept, but he realised it wasn't when he saw a baby's blanket and bottle. The lemon blanket was tatty and dirty, the plastic drinking bottle stained black inside with a brown teat on top.

Charlie felt emotional. The thought of the little baby sleeping in a box. He presumed this was where the daughter slept as well. He sat on the thin mattress on the single bed, and stared down at the floor. Something wasn't right. Why had the daughter left the box there?

He went back downstairs and found her slumped at the kitchen table. Charlie stubbed out her burning cigarette and wondered how she'd not set fire to the place. He gave her shoulder a nudge to wake her up.

'Mrs Marah. When did your daughter leave home?'

She sat up and he could see her calmly thinking. Her eyes looked sober. 'She left after the baby died. I buried one child, and then my daughter went too. I was a reckless mother. I haven't seen her since then.'

Charlie had to pity her. He didn't know why she drank. She might have had reason. This sober look in her face hadn't blotted out the memory of what she had lost. Maybe that's why the box was still there. To remind her of what she let happen.

They were settled into a room that was used by doctors. A sink and examination table gave it away. They'd been provided with a jug of water and two plastic tumblers, and chairs that were reasonably comfortable. The first person on their list was outside the door. Issy went to let her in.

Debra Clark was in uniform. She smelt fresh and looked groomed for work. Nick had a feeling he'd seen her somewhere before.

'Have we met before?' he asked.

She smiled at him impishly. 'You were playing in a band at a Christmas dance. Me and my friend were there.'

Nick smiled politely, then quickly changed the subject. He could almost feel Issy burning with curiosity beside him. Her eyes were filled with questions. 'Well, thank you for seeing us. We appreciate you taking the time. Before we begin, are you aware of why we're here?'

'Yes. It was on the news. And from walking through the hospital. I've never seen so many managers about the place. I think they're out en masse to do a welfare check with staff.'

'Yes, I can imagine a lot of people will be upset. For us, this is simply the quickest way to gather information about your former colleague.'

She checked the fob watch pinned to her dress. 'Will it take long? I start work at eleven.'

'You'll be fine,' Nick said. 'It's only ten to ten.'

'I know. I've been waiting since ten past nine.' She frowned. 'You are aware I don't work on the ward where Helen worked? I used to, but now I do paediatrics.'

'Sorry for keeping you. And, yes, we're aware of that, but you used to work with Helen?'

'Yes. I was there for a couple of years.'

Nick showed an interest as if this was news to him. 'Ah, so you may have known William Shaw?'

'Mary's husband. Yes. I read about him in the newspaper. It's so sad. He was really nice.'

'It's tragic,' Issy said, nodding at her. Nick was pleased that she had picked up on what he was trying to do. 'His wife dies, and then his life is taken. That sort of thing must affect you. You probably just hoped for him to be all right after losing his wife, and then you read about him in a paper.'

She shifted nervously in the chair, her eyes moving from Nick to Issy. 'Yes. I did think that. I was on duty when Mary died. I was on the night shift. I haven't worked on that ward since.'

'Why's that, Debra?' Nick asked.

She looked slightly startled. She put her hand up to her mouth, took a deep breath... Then shook her head. 'No real reason. I had annual leave, and then I got a job on paeds.'

'Was it a difficult shift?' Issy asked in a sympathetic voice.

'Not really. I got there my usual time – ten to eight. I like to make sure the milk's been put on for the night drinks. At eight we went in for the report. I was allocated one end of the ward. We got on with the work.'

Nick opened his notebook as if searching for something.

Issy reached across and tapped her finger on a snail he'd doodled in the margin. She murmured as if agreeing about something. Nick looked at the nurse. 'Who else was on duty?'

His question had thrown her. It was apparent in the immediate tension in her face. 'Um, Helen Tate. Kathleen Price, a healthcare assistant. Oh, and a bank staff nurse.'

'What's her name?'

She shook her head. 'Can't remember. We get a lot of bank nurses come on the ward. Staffing Solutions will know who she is.'

'Who cared for Mary Shaw?'

Her eyes flicked back and forward from his face to Issy's. 'We all did. I popped my head around the door after we had handover and I could see she had company. She had the priest with her. Helen gave her night medication. The bank nurse was put with Helen, so they would have done the turns and the nursing.' She licked her pale lips. 'At about eleven the main lights were turned off. We had a cup of tea then. And then, just before midnight, Kathleen found her. She'd gone in her sleep.'

Nick decided to end the conversation there. He thanked her for her help. When she closed the door behind her, Issy said, 'I can't even remember what I did yesterday. Yet she recalls every detail of Mary Shaw's last night some nine months later. Did you notice how she answered the question? Lights out and then we had tea. Making sure we heard every minute accounted for and that staff were together.'

Nick was nodding. 'It might be worth chatting to the bank nurse. Ring this Staffing Solutions. See if you can get her name.'

Next up was Kathleen Price. Her cheeks were flushed and her upper lip was perspiring. Nick offered her some water.

'Thank you. I will.'

Nick was conscious of her looking at him intently, and hoped Sarah hadn't revealed anything to the woman. She stopped staring at him when Issy said hello to her.

'Hello again, Issy. You get around in your job. And today you're with the boss.'

Kathleen drank the glass of water, and then settled her hands across her lap. She had a manner that was slightly off-putting, and an overassertive tone to her voice. Nick decided he'd use the conversation with Debra Clark to start up this one. He mirrored her body behaviour and rested his hands in his lap.

'We just had a chat with one of the nurses who was on duty the night Mary Shaw died.'

Her pale eyes went back to his. She answered in a matter-of-fact voice. 'Well, that would have been Debra then, because Helen Tate is no longer with us. And Sally Hunt, the bank staff nurse, has just had her baby.'

'Would you mind telling us about your shift that day?'

'Not at all. The ward was busy. By that, I mean it was full. We had the handover. We were told there was no change in Mary. There'd been some talk about moving her to ITU, because she needed constant oxygen and regular suction of secretions, but that wasn't new. She had her husband and Father McCarthy with her so I went and sorted out other patients.

'We were nearly finished at our end so I went and helped with Helen's patients. Helen said they'd already been into Mary. I then got busy with changing a wet bed. When the work-load was finished, we had a cup tea. I decided I'd check on Mary. It was me who found her dead.'

'Did she...? Had she died peacefully?'

She looked him directly in the eye. 'I doubt it. I expect she died very frightened and alone.'

Nick frowned at her. 'Why do you think that?'

'Because I found her on the floor. Her nightdress was soaking from a jug of water she'd knocked down.'

Nick wondered if Charlie had heard this, and if this was the reason he was suspicious. 'So she had a fall? What did the doctor say?'

She shook her head at him. 'He didn't. He didn't know. Helen didn't inform him. She helped me put Mary on the bed, and I washed and prepared her for the mortuary. Helen kept asking who was the last to see her – it should have been her if she was nursing her properly. She was a very lazy person, and that's all I'll say.'

Nick was surprised when she stood up. She had meant that's all she would say to them, not just about Helen. She was out of the room before he could thank her.

Issy let out a big sigh. 'Jesus. No sympathy for Helen Tate was there? Charlie might be right. They both seemed like they were hiding something. God, she's overpowering. She was like a guard dog over Shaw's widow when I went there. You know, I was thinking, there could be another angle on this: if Mary Shaw was helped on her way, her killer might already be dead.'

'Well, Helen Tate is dead.'

'Not thinking of her. I was referring to William Shaw. He might have killed his wife. And Helen Tate might have known about it. Might be the reason she was photographing him.'

Nick's head felt full of possibilities, but that's all they were – possibilities. 'Why would he? Why not wait until she just died of her illness?'

'Beats me. Maybe he was in a hurry. Maybe she had a will? Or life insurance? Or maybe he had another woman waiting impatiently in the wings.'

'You mean Sarah Shaw,' Nick replied, not wanting her to think he wasn't open to suggestions.

'Yes. She might even have been in on it. Maybe that was the meaning of the message sent to her. Helen Tate was on to her. She had proof.'

Nick stretched his long arms up in the air. 'Maybe. Possibly. Still don't know anything though.'

'Not going to on an empty stomach either. I've had no breakfast. What say we order a McDonald's. I could eat a double quarter pounder with cheese and fries, and maybe a doughnut or something.'

'Jesus, Banks, for someone skinny you certainly pack it away.'

Issy clasped her slim waist. 'This body is a temple and it needs to be treated like one.'

'You're treating it more like a dustbin if you put all that in you.' He stood up and pretended like before not to notice she was flirting again. 'Come on, I'll buy you a sandwich. We've got time. If they're all as quick as Mrs Price, we'll have too much time on our hands today.' He heard her small sigh, and gave her a look like a father might give a sulky child. 'All right. I'll add a doughnut as well.'

She stopped still and looked like she was going to stamp her foot.

'What?'

Issy folded her arms. 'Are you playing at this thing tonight or not?'

Nick blinked in surprise. Was that tonight? Damn! He'd forgotten about it. He was about to refuse when he remembered the deal he'd made with himself. Anything to feel less corrupted. He'd do it for Charlie, if nothing else. 'I can't promise. If I can I will.'

CHAPTER FIFTY-FIVE

CHARLIE

Charlie parked on the road outside Chatham Cemetery. He walked through the open black gates and made his way to the area where children were buried. It was a place that was easy to find. Small stone angels stood guard over many of the graves, eyelids closed as if sleeping, and wings spread in protection. It was silent, but he imagined there had been much weeping done over these small graves. He had to walk round more than two dozen of them before he found the one in which Monica Marah's son was buried.

A patch of unkempt grass covered the small plot. There wasn't even a plastic flower to brighten it up. It lay in stark contrast to the other graves buried beneath mountains of fresh flowers and small personal objects.

A small grey block not much bigger than a house brick held his details:

Ray Marah
Born 9 Dec 2006
Died 17 March 2007

Charlie felt his breath catch. Both dates were significant. William Shaw died on the anniversary of the day that the child was born and Mary Shaw had died on the anniversary of the child's death. The baby was three months old. Mary Hicks had been driving the car that killed the boy. There was most definitely a connection here. William Shaw used a remembrance card as a bookmark with the name Ray on. The motive, he could only think, avengement. To harm the person responsible. But why the deaths of William Shaw and Helen Tate?

Charlie pulled out his phone and saw two texts from Nick. He wasn't going to tell him yet what he had found. He wanted to do some more research first, so he sent him a reassuring message to explain his absence.

He'd already found a bed and breakfast so he could stay the night. He wasn't driving back today. Charlie wondered if he could persuade Beverly Thompson to join him for a drink and maybe some food. He sat down on a bench and called Medway Police Station and asked to speak to her. Perhaps she could give him some answers to his questions and then he'd see if she was free this evening. He liked listening to her voice. A minute later he was talking to her.

He described the school uniform that the pupils were wearing in the photograph that was different to the one at St Matthew's. Sarah Shaw hadn't known where her husband and his first wife taught before moving to Bath, but perhaps it was in Kent.

'I can give you the name of a school that wear the colours green and gold. If you give me some time, I'll find out the name of the head teacher in 2007,' she replied.

Charlie smiled at her cheerfulness. 'Thanks, Beverly. That would be great.'

He put his phone away. He glanced once more at the grave, then made his way out of the cemetery. A short while later he was checked into a room that was clean and quiet, and with a notice on the back of the door. No smoking and no hot food in the rooms. Then Beverly rang.

'Charlie, have you got a pen and paper or do you want me to text it to you? I've got a name, phone number and address.'

'I'll write it, save you texting.'

He jotted down the details and heard her give a small sigh. 'Sounds like you could do with finishing work soon.'

She laughed. 'I am, thank goodness. I'm leaving in the next minute. I've got my son's party to sort out. I've got a bunch of ten-year-olds coming to my house at four o'clock. It's now ten to and I'm not home. My husband will let them run riot if I'm not there. He's a bigger kid than they are.'

Charlie thanked her and let her get off the phone. He was disappointed, but sensing she had a happy life made up for it and gave him a good feeling. She seemed like a nice person.

He stood quietly by the window, noticing the sky got dark here earlier than it did in Bath. He tapped his fingers on the windowpane. Restless, without something to do. Back home he'd still be working. Though he didn't think of it as work or his job. He wasn't able to compartmentalise what he did for a living and how he lived the rest of the time. The two were inseparable. The police was his life, moulded together, fused into one.

The rhythm of the quiet beats calmed him. He could think of nothing that he would change if he lived his life again. He was lucky to have had the life he had. He might have ended up on the other side of the law but for his aunt Charlotte. She'd taken him out of school when he was fifteen and got him a job with her brother when she could see him becoming unruly. Charlie never told her it was from receiving unjust corporal punishment from a man who liked using a cane.

He worked for three years with a bunch of hardened brick-ies, and they helped him change his behaviour. They taught him about fairness. A spate of petty thieving was taking place at the site they were working on, anything from a bag of cement to a wheelbarrow, and even a door unscrewed from its hinges. When the thefts got personal, such as money going from pockets, a watch, a small transistor radio, Charlie set out traps – literally. Mousetraps in every coat pocket. They found the culprit; a twenty-year-old who yelped when he was caught. Charlie fully expected him to receive a beating from his uncle Brian and the other men, but he didn't get one.

Instead, the labourers formed two columns shoulder to shoulder as straight as any military operation, with Uncle Brian standing at the end of the human corridor. The culprit was made to walk the length, and as he passed each man, a back was turned on him. Uncle Brian took from the man his prized tool – a trowel. From that day, Charlie earned the nickname Sherlock. The men had said he was worse than a copper always sniffing around, but a future was formed for him. He saw a fairness in justice.

Charlie turned away from the window, pondering his evening. He debated ringing Dr Hoffman to see if she would like to join him. She could tell him how she got on with the police. His thoughts turned to the envelope folded in his pocket. He ought to look at it first, before calling. If he had free time to go out he could spare a few minutes to read it.

He moved a carrier bag off the small armchair. He'd bought some basic toiletries in a petrol station on the same road as the guest house. He'd wash his socks and underwear in the small sink before bed and let them dry overnight on the radiator. And he'd wear his vest to sleep in. It was only for one night, hardly a hardship.

He fetched the envelope out of his jacket and his glasses from his breast pocket, and then settled to read Dr Hoffmann's letter.

Dear Dr Hoffmann,

It's been many years since I wrote to you. Don't feel confused at not remembering a letter. You never received it. I wrote it all down for you – my thoughts – like you suggested me to. I was going to tell you so much. But you didn't deserve to know my thoughts so I never sent the letter to you.

I must confess to something long overdue, and apologise for taking 'Jack'. I know you'll remember that. The red lacquered box on your windowsill. I'm not a thief, but like a magpie I was drawn to its shine.

Well another year has passed since I last saw you, and I thought you might like to know how things are. This one has been particularly difficult. It feels like the past is catching up with me, and I can never quite run from it. Impending doom accompanies me and makes me question if our fate is decided long before we meet it. The face of the past holding us to account. Marking the date of when to come to claim for our misdeeds.

I keep having the same nightmare. I'm crying, thinking that I'm alone, sitting against a wall. The window above me is open, which is how I hear them. They don't know I'm there. They think they are safe to say what they want... I have to stuff my fist in my mouth so that I don't make a sound. What they say is so cruel. I vomit when they finish speaking. The vest in my hand is soaked, and I have to wash it. But it is the only one I have...

I can't erase that memory, because I have nothing good to replace it with.

No one got punished.

Do you know what's really sad? It's that you haven't got a clue what I'm on about. But then aren't all psychologists the same? Unless the patient tells them exactly what they're thinking, it's all just guessing. I'm not trying to switch seats with you. It just annoys me that you get paid loads of money when you don't really know how to fix anyone. No one really knows *how the mind thinks, because the mind is too clever to understand. You people just like to pretend you do.*

You had your chance to help and a fat lot of good that did. With your cookies and your lemonades like it was a medicine. And you were Mary fucking Poppins!

Forgive my profanity, Dr Hoffmann, but your therapy didn't help one iota. You should have asked me what else I saw in the clouds. You never once asked about my mother. Or about what happened.

Have you ever kissed cold lips, Dr Hoffmann? Or tried to uncurl frozen fingers? Have you ever held death in your arms? You wouldn't like it. The coldness comes through no matter what you do.

They gave me a couple of minutes to say goodbye. Then they all came in, standing at the doorway like a posse ready to seize me if I ran. It was comical really. Him stuffed under my jumper like a chicken I was trying to steal from a shop. But then it got nasty. One of them pulled his legs while another dug down my jumper and grabbed his head. In the end, I had to let go. There were too many of them. And they were hurting him.

I watched the coffin going down and I wanted to tear off the lid and let in the light. None of those people understood what I was trying to do. They looked at my muddy knees and hands as if I was deranged. When it was over people hurried away to get out of the rain. They wanted to get on with their lives. Get back to normal.

But how can you when the normal is a lie?

But here's something for you to know that is real – They're dead. They all fall down... Fate came to claim them.

I feel no guilt whatsoever. Yet, that also feels normal. Lately I wonder if what I have done was the wrong decision. Did they ever feel they should be punished? Is what they did the worse crime? I wanted to tell someone, but I never could.

Their secrets will lie with them in a box. But I think the real reason I contacted you was to ask a question.

Was everything that happened my fault?

Yours truly

Jack-in-the-box

(I think this an appropriate valediction)

Charlie now knew what Dr Hoffmann meant. The real name of the author wasn't on the letter. She was right in saying it was unsettling, but there was nothing stated clearly and in detail, to say if a crime was or about to be committed. It sounded like the patient was reaching out, in a mental health crisis, and should really be having therapy.

Charlie folded the letter away in his pocket, then leaned forward to get up from the chair, and wished he hadn't. The slight stretching rendered him with impossible pain. On his feet, tears spilling down his cheeks, his insides were agony, almost making it impossible for him to move, but he knew he had to. He needed to get to the bathroom. His tablets were there. He coughed and saw blood splatter the small basin. He needed help. He struggled back to the room and collapsed on the single bed, grabbed his phone and dialled 999.

CHAPTER FIFTY-SIX

SARAH

Sarah avoided looking at Nick. She felt her face warm at the memory of the morning. She hadn't been sleeping as deeply as he must have thought, and heard him breathing at the door. She had been aware of him watching her and that her breast was bare.

Issy was sitting close to the wall. She had said hello, but it was a formal greeting. The officer who rang her said they'd be happy to have someone come and see her at home, but that if she preferred, he could arrange a time for her to be seen at the hospital. The police were there chatting to staff to gather information about Helen Tate. She'd opted for that. Four o'clock would suit her fine. She had not stepped foot outside the flat since getting the letter, and the longer she stayed inside the more nervous she would become.

Nick took charge. 'As you know from Issy, we're conducting a murder enquiry into Helen Tate. But we're also running a separate, quiet, enquiry about a patient who died on the ward.'

Sarah filled with dread. Was this about Mr Harris? Was Tim in trouble?

'We know you weren't on duty at the time, but it would be good to have your input on a very delicate matter. We're conscious an investigation by the police into a death in a hospital is not good for public confidence. So we would rather do it this way, quietly, to see if there's any reason for concern. The patient in question was Mary Shaw.'

Sarah was conscious of Issy watching her closely. Was she expecting to see guilt written in her face? Kathleen was right. Issy was not a friend. 'I don't know what to say... Are you thinking she was murdered?'

He shook his head. 'No. We're not thinking that. One of our sergeants raised a concern after talking to staff. He thinks he picked up on some subtext relating to her death. This morning Issy and I spoke with two staff members, and one of them said Mary Shaw was found dead on the floor, and that the doctor wasn't informed that she'd had a fall. She was put back in bed and nothing was reported.'

Sarah coughed as her breath caught in her throat.

Issy poured her a glass of water. 'Here, drink this. Your face has gone red.'

Sarah stared at her. Issy's tone was uncaring. She didn't know what she had done to cause it. They had initially got on so well. She gulped the water, then spluttered. Nick gave her his handkerchief.

She wiped her face. 'Sorry. I'll wash it and have it returned to you.'

'There's no need. Keep it. Please.'

Sarah wasn't sure what to say. Who had told them this? It can't have been Kathleen, otherwise why not tell her? If she knew it happened, why not admit it? Why hide it? Unless to protect someone? Is that what she was doing? But what was she supposed to say to them now?

'By the way,' Issy said. 'I meant to let you know there is a camera in the corridor near Medical Records. But nothing to worry about. The only time someone was outside the door was when the security man came. He was right. Your bag jammed it.'

Sarah was apprehensive about the change in Issy's tone. It sounded kind. Why was Issy telling her this now?

'What were you doing there? You're surely not at work at the moment, are you?'

'No. I was just checking I'd completed something from when I finished work so abruptly. A patient died the night my husband died. I had just carried out last offices when Sergeant Bowden arrived. I couldn't remember if I completed the nurse documentation.'

Nick interjected in a slightly cool tone. 'Issy, can we get back to this, please?'

Issy held up her hand. 'Sorry. I got sidetracked. I just wanted to reassure Sarah that she's safe.'

Sarah relaxed the grip on her fingers beneath the desk. She felt light-headed. Had she put Mary Shaw's file away properly? Did Issy know that she just lied and was waiting to trip her up? She cleared her throat. 'The night Mary died I wasn't working. The following morning, I was on an early shift. Helen Tate told me Mary had died. I didn't hear anything about a fall.'

'Can you recall anything unusual about any of the staff?'

Her eyes returned to Nick. 'No. Everything was normal.'

His expression was pensive. 'Thank you, Mrs Shaw. If we need to talk to you again, we'll be in touch.'

Sarah closed the office door. She stood outside it wishing the hurt would go away. Her hands trembled as she raised them to her face. Each time she saw him, she hurt a little more. She was desperately wanting to run away but equally desperate to stay. From a young age she had denied herself feeling love. She experienced it briefly for such a short time.

Life lessons were better learned when she denied herself any emotional connections. But it made it tougher to live with the memories. Like the warmth against her body, the feel of skin on skin, a kiss in the dark to give comfort and take comfort. But it was the truth that was unbearable to live with.

The knowledge she could never tell anyone.

CHAPTER FIFTY-SEVEN

NICK

Helen Tate's alibi checked out. She did not leave the ward for the entire shift. She had even sat in the office for her break. Other staff members on the night shift confirmed her presence. She did not murder William Shaw.

The team, thankfully, were not looking at Nick in the hope he'd come up with another angle. Most officers had the look of people wanting to go home. It was six o'clock, and some were planning to go to the Christmas dance.

Nick stopped by his place on the way back from the hospital, and while Issy sat in the car he ran in for a change of clothes, his washbag, and saxophone case. He saw the grin on her face and hoped his performance later would be worth it. He was gifted at playing most single-reed woodwind instruments – his father thought his musical talent was genetically inherited from his mother's side – but to perform really well Nick had to feel emotionally connected. What he was feeling right now was guilt. He joined the police to feel a sense of belonging with people who would eventually feel like a family. The situation he was in had betrayed all of that... he had lost the right to belong. And he had to accept that there was no turning back. He chose to do what he did – no one forced him.

The atmosphere in the incident room was one of excitement. He turned a blind eye to the cans of beer being passed around the room. He only hoped Naughton wouldn't walk in and catch them. He relaxed; they were off duty. He just wished Charlie was here. He pulled out his phone. Charlie answered on the first ring.

'Have you enjoyed your duvet day, Charlie? That's a first for you. You'll be asking for a four-day work week next.'

Charlie laughed. 'You need to move with the times. It's a growing trend among stressed out Brits.'

Nick was forced to laugh back. Charlie must have been feeling unwell to take a day off. 'You lazy bugger you. We haven't got time for you to lie in bed. So what are you up to now?'

'I'm in bed!'

'So that's it? You're staying put? You conned me into playing and now you're bailing.'

Charlie laughed heartily. 'Well, I'm blowed. Knew it was in you to be nice.'

Nick's sigh was heartfelt. 'I shouldn't be. We're scraping the bottom of the barrel at the moment. I keep expecting Naughton to take me off the case. He's putting in a second deputy SIO, but I haven't met anyone yet.'

'Yeah? Well, it's nothing to worry about. It's a big case. Do me a favour: play something nice for me. None of that heavy jazz stuff.'

'Any particular request?' Nick asked sarcastically.

Charlie started to hum it.

'Jesus, Charlie. Don't sing it to me. The others can hear you.'

'I can't remember the title. Something like "Red Valentine".'

Nick laughed kindly. 'You old softy. You mean, "My Funny Valentine". Have you forgotten it's a Christmas do?'

'No. Play it anyway. Least you can do, seeing as I'm missing out. I'm too comfortable to get out of this bed.'

'Yeah, well you stay there if that's the case. And we'll definitely have a catch up pint tomorrow.'

'About time,' Charlie remarked. Then: 'Nick. I, um...Well, I was going to say I...' He gave a self-deprecating laugh. 'Articulate, aren't I?'

Nick jeered him. 'Yeah. A right Bamber Gascoigne. What's up?'

Charlie laughed. 'Nothing at all. It'll wait. I'll tell you tomorrow. Nighty night.'

Nick put his phone away. A moment later, he turned to the door as Ian gave an ear-piercing wolf whistle. Tall Jim and Issy were standing there: Jim in black suit and black tie, and Issy in a red-velvet dress.

'I'm in heaven,' Ian groaned. Since the night in the pub, the young copper's inhibitions seemed to have vanished. It would seem Issy had unleashed a young lion. 'I'm all yours, baby. Take me!' He marched towards the pair and Issy covered her face, but he ignored her and planted a loud kiss on Jim's cheek.

'Mind the suit man,' Jim cried. 'I don't want you mucking it up with your grubby hands.'

Issy smiled at Nick and he felt an odd little catch in his throat. She was beautiful. There was no doubt about it; Issy Banks was beautiful. He just wished he fancied her.

'We need a photo,' Jim said.

'I'll do it,' Robson called across the room. He pulled out his phone and started snapping the twosome. Issy played to the audience and showed her thigh through the slit in her dress.

Ian showed all the lust of youth as he stared at Issy's legs, his head and shoulders angled sideways for a better view. As Issy became bolder, he whooped excitedly and nearly fell off his chair, and dropped his can of beer into his lap. 'Shit!' he cried, quickly wiping himself.

Everyone fell about laughing as Ian jumped up flapping his hands at his trousers. Nick joined in with them but immediately felt the sounds in his throat die as Robson's eyes locked on his and he spoke quietly only to him.

'I throw away the photographs that are just of scenery. Pointless keeping them. They don't tell you anything.'

Nick felt the hatchet on his neck draw blood. He could imagine the feel of it in his mind, and if he put his hand there he was sure he would see his fingers coated with red.

The photographs. He had missed the relevance of there only being photographs of scenery in her handbag. Robson had left them behind because they didn't mean anything. He took only what would wreak havoc on Nick's career.

Nick stared at him with flinty eyes. He was not running. He would not give Robson the satisfaction of that.

CHAPTER FIFTY-EIGHT

CHARLIE

The call from Nick had cheered him. He was glad he fumbled his words. What he had to say was too serious to start talking about over the phone. Nick was sounding like his old self again. Socialising with his old colleagues and playing his sax was a sign that maybe he had sorted out whatever he'd got mixed up in. He had just needed to remember his job.

Reassured, Charlie settled contentedly in the hospital bed, floating on morphine. A bag of blood was being dripped into his arm and the doctor he'd seen in casualty was sitting beside him. She had a pretty face, open and kind.

'Feeling better?'

Charlie smiled. 'Much.'

'We've had your X-rays back.'

Charlie patted her hand. 'Don't worry about them. My doctor in Bath has already spoken with me. I have an appointment on the third of January.'

With her other hand she now patted his. 'Good. You're not bleeding inside; that was just a small blood vessel that popped when you coughed. We're giving you blood because you're anaemic. Rest tonight and tomorrow and you'll be all right.'

'We'll see,' Charlie said.

She pretended to look cross. 'What d'you mean, we'll see? So all this concern for you is unnecessary. I can now stop worrying about you.' She shook her head in mild exasperation. 'Your heart rate was thrashing. You were pale, cold and clammy. You know what that tells me, Charlie? You were in agony. So why don't you stay a few days? What's the big rush?'

Charlie tapped the side of his nose. 'Got a killer to catch.'

The doctor smiled at him, probably thinking he was a policeman who was reliving his heydays. She probably thought only young coppers like Nick ever chased the bad guys and that poor old buggers like him sorted out the little old ladies who needed help crossing roads. He didn't mind. Not about what she thought, nor who caught this killer. As long as it was soon. He was smiling now, but a couple of hours ago he had been in agony. The pain had come out of the blue. This was what scared him. He couldn't prepare for it. There had been no warning and he knew it could happen again. His time was running out.

Good job he never got time to phone Dr Hoffmann and made any arrangement to meet. Poor woman might have been sat somewhere waiting for him, wondering why he hadn't turned up. Tomorrow he would discharge himself. He was hoping to see a Mr Peel, a retired head teacher of the school where William Shaw and the then Mary Hicks used to teach. He thought of Nick, and wished he was down here with him. They could have gone to the pub and watched the footie. He was going to get such a surprise tomorrow when he heard what Charlie had discovered. This was the biggest lead they had. Charlie would tell Naughton it was Nick's idea to send him here. That it was Nick who discovered the connection. He wanted Naughton to see what Charlie saw in him. Someone who normally had his mind twenty-four seven on the job.

His eyes fixed on the window and the black moody sky outside, and for once didn't mind the thought of rain. It was all going to work out all right. Charlie closed his eyes with a smile on his face. And dreamed, of all things, of the smell of damp clothes dried indoors...

CHAPTER FIFTY-NINE

NICK

Issy stepped back up onto the stage. The band had just had a ten-minute break. Nick had been shocked when she joined them – he had no idea she could sing. She picked up the microphone. 'Are you all having a good time?' The crowd clapped loudly, wolf whistles coming from around the room. 'Good, because you're going to have more. Let me reintroduce for you, The Boys in Blue. Please welcome back Jim Reed, Ed Nixon, Bob Taylor, Shaun Walker, Nick Anderson.' The clap got louder and harder as Shaun stood up.

He ran his fingers up and down the keys, his beautiful teeth showing as he smiled brightly and waved to the crowd. 'Thank you, thank you, thank you, and now put your hands together for Issy Banks. Michelle Pfeiffer took lessons from Issy, so ladies keep hold of your gentlemen, and gentlemen keep hold of yourselves, 'cos the little lady is about to set you on fire. Take it away, Issy.'

Issy positioned herself by the piano. 'This next song is for someone who doesn't know I care, so I might just come right on down there and find myself somebody new.'

Ian Carter was looking up at her from the dance floor. 'Is it for me?' he shouted.

She smiled down at him. 'Shut up, Ian. It's not for you. So here we go, folks. Sing along if you want. You all know it. It's called, "Makin' Whoopee".'

Shaun's fingers touched the piano keys and began the intro. Then Issy opened her mouth and in a husky drawl, betraying no nerves, slowly, seductively purred through each word: *Another bride, another June. Another sunny honeymoon. Another season, another reason. For Makin' Whoopee...*

She turned cat-like and dragged her nails slowly across the back of Shaun's shoulders. She held the audience enraptured. Nick could see they were loving the duet, and wasn't surprised. Her breathy voice was captivating. She had clearly practiced this number with Shaun and all the little movements that went with it. In a moment that was almost missed, it was so elegantly performed, Shaun lifted her to sit on top of the upright piano. She crossed her legs and sat side-saddle, and all the while singing.

Nick clapped till his hands stung. She had made the evening a success, and he was so glad to have seen it. He was proud to be performing with each of them, and for the first time in a long time, felt he was exactly where he should be.

At quarter to twelve, Nick picked up his own microphone. His dark hair was damp and his face flushed from the heat of the lights and the alcohol he had put away.

'This next number is for someone who can't be here tonight. I'm hoping Issy knows the words. It's called, "My Funny Valentine".'

Nick thought of Charlie as he played. Of the first time he saw him, standing outside on the pavement, smoking. His bright hair glowing red like a fire in the sun. Nick was seven. Charlie had been speaking to neighbours about Nick's mother. He caught sight of Nick watching him from the upstairs window and gestured to the ball in the small front garden. Outside the gate was where all the kids played on a wide patch of grass, and for a short while Nick and him played football.

When Nick finished, the crowd clapped, and Shaun gave him a thumbs up. He grinned, and Nick grinned back.

They were forced to play on for another ten minutes, and then it was over. Nick caught Issy by the waist as she passed him, his eyes glazed with alcohol. 'You are totally amazing. You were brilliant.'

'You played for another woman, Nick, and don't deny it!' she challenged angrily.

Nick's handsome face was comical as it screwed up in confusion. 'Whoa! What you on about, Issy?'

'That song! "My Funny Valentine"!'

Nick threw back his head laughing. 'You daft woman, that was for Charlie!'

Before he could stop her she was kissing him, her mouth pressing hard against his, putting everything into the kiss, to convey what she was feeling. Then she realised his lips weren't moving, his hands weren't touching and he was backing away. He was only close because her arms were still around him. He was waiting for her to let go.

She sprang back and Nick saw the hurt in her eyes.

'Issy. I didn't mean for... I'm sorry...'

'No, I know you didn't. It was my mistake.'

'A big one, Issy,' Paul Robson suddenly said. He had appeared on the stage without warning. 'He's not interested in you. He's not interested in any of us. He's been keeping us all in the dark.'

Nick turned and saw that behind Robson, Ed, Bob, Jim, and Shaun had pieces of paper in their hands. Their faces were grim. He looked back at Robson and saw photocopies of photographs in his hands. Robson had let him know earlier with that sneaky remark that it was him who searched Sarah's handbag when he went to collect her suit. He probably left it untidy deliberately for Nick to find. Well, he refused to bow his head and let him bring the hatchet down any further. He'd had his quota of Nick's blood. The imaginary blood line drawn across the back of his neck was barely a scratch.

Shaun's eyes were searching Nick's for an answer. He had the look of a disappointed man. 'Nice one, Nick,' he said bitterly.

'You don't understand, Shaun,' Nick tried to explain.

Shaun picked up his black jacket. 'Oh, I understand. You're swimming around in muddy water and we've now got to save you. We're your mates, Nick, not just people you work with. You want my advice; go fuck her. And while you're at it, fuck off this case.'

'Will someone tell me what's going on?' Issy angrily demanded.

Robson handed her the photographs. 'I found a few holiday snaps. And kissy kissy ones done in a photo booth. Lover boy here is involved with Shaw's wife. Now all we need to know is whether he is involved in her husband's death.'

Below them at the foot of the stage Superintendent Naughton was standing. And from the look on his face he wasn't there to congratulate them on their performance. Robson had already shown him the pictures.

'I need to speak to you, DI Anderson, and I need to speak to you now.'

Nick stared at the sea of faces surrounding him for a couple of seconds before whipping his hand forward and giving a theatrical bow. Then, at a speed no one anticipated, he was off the stage, weaving through more than two hundred people and gone from sight.

* * *

The light was still on and for a moment he hesitated. This was the line he could choose not to cross. Explanations could be given, arguments had, disciplinary action taken. It was not too late to save his career so long as he didn't cross this line. But then how would he save her?

He pressed the bell.

Her hair was wet and gleaming and the scents of soap and shampoo rose from her warm washed skin. He leaned against the doorjamb with his jacket over his shoulder, hooked on his thumb. He didn't want to talk and he didn't want to think of why he shouldn't be here. Yet his thoughts refused to clear.

He closed his eyes and turned to leave, but she was faster and moved forward and caught him by the tie. Her mouth touched his – just a press of softness and a feel of warmth. He groaned and she pressed firmer and this time he tasted moistness. Then more boldly she teased his bottom lip with her teeth and tongue and from that moment every reason why he shouldn't be here was gone from his mind. He swivelled her around, kicking the front door shut with his foot, and pressed her hard against it. The urgency of his need to touch her was almost making him rough as he pulled material from her shoulders to see her nakedness underneath.

He groaned again as her mouth moved under his and he kissed her like a starving man. He remembered every taste of her, only now it was almost too much. He quickly pulled back.

'I can't,' he said harshly. 'It's been a while. I don't know if I can control myself.'

She reached up and pressed fingers to his lips, telling him without words not to worry. Then she stepped back and loosened the belt of her dressing gown, allowing it to fall to the ground. For the longest second he simply stared at her, and then going down on one knee he searched for the butterfly that Doyle had cut open with a scalpel in his nightmare. Tattooed in blue and nestled on the top of her thigh, he kissed it tenderly.

Feeling as if his very soul had come home, he held her close and rested his hot face against her stomach. She shivered and made a tiny sound in her throat.

'We should stop,' he whispered.

Sarah waited until he looked up and saw the clear message in her eyes, and then she whispered back, 'We will... afterwards.'

CHAPTER SIXTY

CHARLIE

The new blood in Charlie's body was giving him energy. He found himself wanting to go for a long walk and fill his lungs with fresh air. He was looking forward to going home, to having a pint with Nick, and as soon as this visit was over that's where he'd be heading.

He parked behind the disabled parking space and got out. The house was early Victorian with big square windows and a steep roof. It was the type of family home Charlie would have liked if he'd had a family. Andrew Peel, trim and with a grey goatee beard, opened the door and ushered him quickly inside and along the hall into an airy colourful room, oil paintings and prints of famous artists' work against white walls. Charlie didn't know who painted what, he just recognised them as famous.

Mr Peel shut the door. 'If my father hears talking, he'll keep shouting down the stairs wanting to know who's here.' He glanced up at the ceiling. 'He's not very well – hasn't been for a number of years. When you phoned, I'm sorry I couldn't talk for long, he was just having his breakfast.' He gave a weak smile. 'We have smoked salmon and scrambled egg on a Sunday.' He pointed at the couch. 'Sorry, sit down.'

'I won't keep you too long, Mr Peel, and I'm sorry to have called so early. I'm heading back to Bath after this.'

'Good time to travel; not so much traffic. You'll be back in Bath before noon. D'you want a cup of tea or coffee before we begin?'

Charlie shook his head. 'Just had breakfast.'

Andrew Peel sat down. 'How can I help?'

'It's about Mary Hicks and William Shaw. They both used to teach at your school.'

'Yes, that's right. Got William's Christmas card up on the mantle.'

Charlie tried to warn him as, clearly, he was unaware. 'There's no easy way to tell you this news, but I'm afraid it's not very pleasant. I'm sorry to tell you, William was found dead in his home. He was murdered.'

The man stood up. 'Jesus, no! And so soon after losing poor Mary as well. What sort of world are we living in?' He walked over to a low table against a wall, poured amber liquid from a decanter into a glass, and drank it back. 'Would you like a tot of rum?'

Charlie smiled. 'Love one, but I can't.'

The man sat back down. 'I needed it. Hell of a shock you've just given me. Have they got the person who did this?'

Charlie shook his head. 'We're still looking, which is why I'm down in this neck of the woods. We've been looking back on their past and yesterday discovered the accident Mary was involved in in 2007. Do you recall it, Mr Peel?'

Peel gazed up at the ceiling. 'As if it were yesterday. It was a truly horrible accident and I felt so sorry for William and Mary. They'd just been out to celebrate their engagement – such a tragic day. Mary was distraught. The two of them were wracked with guilt. All the teachers rallied round to offer them support, but with the baby's sister at the school it was a nightmare.'

Charlie stared at him keenly. 'His sister was a pupil at the school?'

'Yes. After it happened she just sat in the playground on her own. Wouldn't let anyone console her. The day after the accident her mother let her come to school, and of course we couldn't send her home. It was truly a horrible time.'

'I saw Mrs Marah yesterday; she mentioned a daughter. She said she left home after the baby was buried.'

Peel stood up again and poured himself another rum 'Yes, that's right. She ran away. Mrs Marah was not a very capable woman. She'd send her daughter to school sometimes without a wash. Or keep her off school to do errands for her or mind the baby. The daughter missed a lot of school. As you can imagine it was an awful time for everyone. We were not surprised when Mary and William decided to look for new posts. The social worker arranged for the daughter to have counselling, but I'm not sure if it did any good. I've never forgotten Jess Marah; I still feel guilt over her running away. She was only a child herself.'

'Where did she run?'

'No one knows. She never came back.'

'What was she like?'

'Quiet. Self-conscious probably. Her clothes were never very clean. I've a school photo of her in one of the albums. I'll show you.'

There was suddenly a loud banging on the floor overhead and Mr Peel looked apologetic. 'Sorry, he'll be wanting the bathroom or something. Can you give me ten minutes?'

When he returned Charlie was handed a large photograph. He'd seen it before in the back of William Shaw's album. Peel also handed him a magnifying glass.

'Be easier with this. She's standing in the back row, second from the left.'

Charlie held the glass over the girl's pale face and stared

intently at the shape of it, trying to ignore the messy hair half covering her cheeks. Then he stared at the eyes, and slowly, and then not so slowly, his heart began to thud.

CHAPTER SIXTY-ONE

SARAH

Sarah didn't want the day to start. She kept her eyes closed and felt Nick ease out of the bed. He padded quietly out of the room and to the kitchen. He had held her in his arms all night and made love to her again. The only words they shared were intimate ones. But now she was awake, they needed to talk.

A few minutes later he returned to the room and placed a mug on the bedside drawers. He spoke softly. 'It's half past ten, sleepyhead. I'm popping out, but I'll be back soon. I've made you some coffee.'

Sarah's mouth watered at the thought of fluid. She pretended to be sleepy and mumbled an acknowledgement. She waited until she heard him leave and then got out of bed. She wanted to be dressed before he returned. She needed only a quick shower after her bath late last night. She found clean clothes and brought them and the coffee to the bathroom.

After drying and dressing, she cleaned her teeth and brushed her hair, and was wondering why he had gone out. She hoped it was not to buy breakfast. She opened the bathroom door and heard the flat still silent. He was not back yet. She would make her bed, and then some more coffee while waiting.

Sarah walked into the bedroom and jumped back in fright, catching her elbow sharply against the door. The pain went right through to her groin. 'Bloody hell, Kathleen!' she gasped in a strangled voice. 'You frightened the life out of me.'

She cradled her elbow in her hand. It was smarting beneath her sleeve. She'd wait until the pain eased before she checked if it was bleeding. Kathleen was on the far side of the bed by the wardrobe, staring at the floor.

'How did you get in?' Sarah asked in a shocked voice.

'The door was off the latch. I've closed it.'

Nick must have done it thinking she would fall back asleep. 'Why are you here?'

Kathleen had yet to look at her, she seemed more interested in the floor. Sarah had a horrible feeling and walked around to where Kathleen was standing. The lid of her suitcase was open. It had been like that for the past two days. She took comfort from being able to see her things. Nick had slept on her side of the bed and hadn't noticed it. Sarah gazed down at the contents. They looked disturbed.

'I think you should come back to mine, Sarah. You'll feel safer there.'

Sarah's stomach knotted. Something dawned on her – it might have been Kathleen who sent her that note. To frighten her into coming back.

'I know why you married him, Sarah. I know what he did.'

Sarah bent down to tidy the clothes and saw the letter she had written to Dr Hoffman when she was a teenager, the one she wrote before she ran away but never sent. She hadn't felt the doctor deserved to know what she wrote. Her emotions had been raw. But it was the truth of everything that happened. In the end Sarah decided not to share it with her. Dr Hoffman should have asked more questions. She must have been surprised when she received a letter from Sarah after all these years, and must be wondering why.

Watching William reading his book in bed beside her had made her reach out to the doctor. She had sensed that he was never going to tell her about the name on the card he used as a bookmark and, in that moment, she felt she had to tell someone. What she wrote was true, but she never got to the point of revealing what was a lie.

It was hard to know why she married him until she confronted all of the truth about herself. She deceived William by not telling him who she was. She hadn't seen a glimmer of recognition in his eyes. In those first few months after ending it with Nick she went from despair to feeling oddly remote. William would visit Mary every day and she saw his caring and kindliness to his wife. When they started dating she had remained detached, yet she could picture herself smiling at him kindly and holding his hand, so he never saw her impassiveness.

Sarah had felt nothing very deeply for him when she married him, and little or no sorrow when she attended his memorial service. Yet her marriage had been soothing to her. She had felt comforted by the knowledge that he knew about Ray even if he never spoke of him, that another person in the world remembered his existence. She had been shocked by his death, like a door had closed to her past.

She grazed her finger on the edge of the lacquered box, but she wouldn't let jack out. She didn't want him to see Kathleen's scary face. She closed the case lid, but didn't lock it. She stood back up. 'Kathleen, you need to go.'

'Mary told me. She didn't realise that what she was telling me was about you. Then you started on the ward. She met you briefly in the corridor, and she recognised you. She was a very clever lady. She told me your name wasn't Sarah James. I told her she was wrong. She could hold a pen then, and she showed me how the letters of your new name made your real one. Jess Marah. Not quite an anagram, she said, but close. There's only two a's in Jess Marah, three in Sarah James.'

Sarah turned her back on Kathleen. Her heart was thumping. 'Kathleen, please leave now,' she said in a choked voice. 'This is upsetting me.'

'Sure, I'm not surprised. You've had a lot to cope with on your own. But things will be different now. You don't need to be alone any longer.'

Sarah turned and faced her. She was angry with her for forcing her to do this now. 'Did you send me that letter to say I'm not safe?'

Kathleen looked at her with pale sorrowful eyes. 'I did, my darling, because you're not safe. The police will find out, and they'll lock you away.'

Sarah stared down at her hand and saw a smear of blood on her fingers. 'How could you? Did you send me the first one?'

Kathleen's eyes went wide. 'No! That was Helen Tate! And it wasn't for you, Sarah. It was sent to me!'

Sarah automatically stepped back from her. She felt disorientated. 'Why?' she whispered in a short sharp sigh.

Kathleen clasped her hands in front of her chest in a pleading gesture. 'Because she knew I'd taken a few tablets. She was letting me know. She sent that note to my home, where Joe would have seen it if you'd not been there.'

Sarah felt reality slipping away from her. 'Did you hurt her?'

Kathleen pulled her shoulders back and raised a stubborn face. 'I did,' she said, showing no regret for what she had done. 'She hurt too many people to be allowed to get away with it any longer.'

'You should go,' Sarah said bluntly.

Kathleen hung her head. Sarah needed her to leave. She wanted her gone before Nick came back.

Kathleen's head slowly lifted and her eyes were searching. 'Are you judging me, Sarah? After all I've done for you!'

A painful memory chose this moment to return, and Sarah

could hear her mother's voice. *After all I've done! You stand there and cry!*

'After all you've done for me! How is that, Kathleen? You tried to trap me. You want a replacement daughter. You put me in Becky's room!'

'I kept you safe!'

'How?'

'By keeping your secret safe. By being here now to take you home. By not letting Mary tell anyone else!'

Kathleen lowered herself awkwardly into a crouch. She had to spread her feet wide to support herself. She opened the lid of the suitcase and lifted out a baby's cardigan. 'I know about your little brother.'

Sarah stared at her transfixed. Her words took a moment to sink in. 'Did you push Mary out of the bed?' she gasped.

Kathleen looked horrified. 'No!' she cried. She gazed longingly at Sarah. 'No,' she insisted in a stronger voice. 'She was on the floor when I found her. Father McCarthy must have left the side down. I just saw her... something made me leave her there. Afterwards we put her back in it. Father McCarthy would have found it very difficult to know he'd let a patient fall out of bed. I didn't kill her... I just didn't help her live.' Her voice cracked as she continued. 'Because I had another reason that I think Mary would have understood. She didn't help Becky. She did nothing to stop Helen Tate tormenting my child. She didn't challenge Helen's behaviour at all. Helen was the same way as a teenager. Intent on destroying people's lives. And people didn't see it.'

Sarah was bewildered. Her loss had interwoven with Kathleen's loss. Helen Tate, Becky's tormentor at school. Mary Shaw, their teacher. Kathleen the mother who kept going back and forward to the school every other day, who kept knocking on their door wanting them to acknowledge what she said was true. Why would Mary Shaw tell Kathleen anything?

'It must have been very hard for Mary to be on the ward,'

Kathleen continued. 'Her being reminded of her past by you, by Helen, and by me. I told her I couldn't forgive her for Becky but that I'd be kind to her because of what she'd already suffered.'

A tear escaped her eye. Sarah watched it roll down her cheek and onto the cardigan. She needed to get Kathleen out of here. She needed to stop her from touching Ray's clothes. She pulled the cardigan from her hand and picked up the case from the floor.

A light knocking came at the front door. Sarah stared at Kathleen in shock. 'Stay here!' she ordered. 'Stay very quiet until I get rid of him.'

CHAPTER SIXTY-TWO

NICK

Nick put the finishing touches to the small artificial Christmas tree in the corner of her living room. He switched on the fairy lights. 'Ta-da,' he sang happily. 'So, what do you think?'

Nick walked towards Sarah and kissed her long and hard until she gently pushed him away, saying that's all he wanted her for. It wasn't, but for a moment it made him think that she might really believe it. He mustn't rush her; after what she'd been through she was probably still reeling. Well, he could slow it down. They had serious stuff they had to talk about. He had to decide when he was going to tell her. They should leave the city to have this conversation, taking her car and not his. Because it was only a matter of time before the police came knocking at her door.

'Well, let me have a look at it then.'

Sarah examined the tree as he stood behind her. He rested his hands lightly on her shoulders. He turned her around to face him and examined her appearance. The clothes she was wearing were suitable for a walk in the country. He'd suggest a hat and warm jacket. It was cold out there.

She looked up at him. 'I've got to go out soon. Do you want another coffee before you go?'

'What? I thought we were going to spend the day together.'

'Can't, I'm afraid. I'm going to see Kathleen and help her prepare lunch. I'm having dinner with her and Joe. She'll be running round like a mad thing if I don't help her.'

Nick fought back his disappointment as he tried to understand. 'But I thought... I mean... well, after last night... Sarah, we need to talk.'

She eased away from him and went and stood by the window. 'I want you to go, Nick. Last night doesn't change anything... but I'm grateful... it helped me get through the night.'

Nick was cold all of a sudden, a shivery feeling swirling through his chest, and a lump the size of a brick wedged in his throat. She didn't know what he knew. These were simply her feelings about him. 'Grateful? Is that all it meant to you?'

She glanced at him. 'Yes. I'm grateful for your tenderness... your warmth; I needed that.'

'My warmth, my tenderness... that's all it was?'

'Don't get heavy on me, Nick,' she said quietly.

'Well, then don't shut me out!' He hesitated, not knowing how to argue this, and then he struck on where he thought the problem lay. 'Is this because you can't have children, because if it is it doesn't matter, not to me, unless of course you want them? It's you I want.'

He touched her shoulder and she shrank away as if he'd burned her.

'And that's the problem, Nick. We broke up because I don't love you.'

This was all wrong! She was just afraid because he was a police officer.

'You're lying. You don't mean it, Sarah. You finished with me for another reason. I don't know what that is yet. But I know what you did. I've been protecting you. But we have to work together to keep you safe!'

'I don't know what you think I did, but I didn't ask you to protect me. I didn't ask for you to love me. I can't love you back! I'm sorry, but you need to understand that!'

Silence fell between them at the enormity of what she said. The only sound, if such a sound existed, was the shattering of his heart. He couldn't hear it. But he could feel it. His insides were ripping apart with the pain. She actually did mean it. She didn't love him. He had to leave now while he was still able to, while he could still put one foot in front of the other. But he couldn't leave without warning her.

'Sarah, they know about us. They'll put two and two together soon, and they'll come after you.'

She turned her head away. 'Let them,' she quietly said.

CHAPTER SIXTY-THREE

CHARLIE

Charlie wiped his brow after parking the car. The high-speed drive had shaken him. On the motorway the speedometer clocked ninety-five before Charlie saw blue flashing lights in the mirror. He had wanted to ignore them and would have done but for the fact their vehicle was faster. Another five minutes and he'd have been off the motorway. At less than a quarter of a mile from Junction 18.

Every part of his body ached. The roads of the M25, the M3 and the M4 had passed under the wheels of his car without him noticing. He'd sat bolt upright for the entire journey, continuously trying to ring anyone he could get. None of the team had arrived for work yet, so he'd tried their homes. Issy's mobile and landline were on but she wasn't answering. Robson didn't have a clue where Nick was and he'd caused Charlie to hang up because he started going on about Nick being in trouble for running off last night. Trying Naughton, he got told by the desk duty sergeant that the superintendent was over at headquarters with Assistant Chief Hugo Wright in some urgent meeting. And as for Nick, he was simply not available. Well, after today he'd kill him. His mobile was switched off, his answerphone was on but he wasn't picking up. Charlie had asked control to send a car round to his place and knock him up. To his surprise they'd already done that, but there was no one at home.

Charlie had pulled onto the hard shoulder, in no mood to be detained.

Five minutes later the police car speeded towards Bath with blue lights flashing, accompanying Charlie's car. They saw him down into the city before departing.

Standing outside the house Charlie knew he should wait for another officer, but he couldn't. Pain had jabbed him more than a few times on the journey. His illness wasn't wasting time and neither would he. He entered the property and stood still in the high-ceilinged hallway, careful not to make a sound. His hands were clammy, his heart beating hard as he climbed the stairs, when he suddenly stopped mid-step at seeing the door opening at the top. In further shock, he saw Nick coming down the stairs. What the hell was he doing here?

Nick merely glanced at him and said, 'So you found me?'

Charlie motioned him to silence. He jabbed his finger frantically at his lips, and held his palm almost against Nick's face, warning him to stay put.

Nick ignored him. 'So that's why you're here.' His voice was loud in anger. 'Well, I'm not doing it! You're on your own there.'

'Shush!' Charlie whispered fiercely. Then abruptly he stopped the warning. 'Shit!' Charlie stared past him up the stairs. Nick turned and saw Sarah standing halfway down them. A rag doll hung limply in her hand.

'You better come up,' she said.

Nick moved towards her. 'We don't need to, Sarah. Go back inside.'

Charlie looked at Nick. His face was pale. He was shaken and not fit to do this. 'Wait outside, Nick.'

Again Charlie was ignored. Nick climbed the stairs instead.

He followed Sarah and Charlie followed Nick. Sarah led them into the room where Charlie sat the other day. Nick went and stared out the window.

All three of them stood in the cosy warm living room and Charlie saw a small shabby suitcase open on the sofa. The case was full of baby things: knitted jackets and booties. Dummies and rattles and soft toys. He remembered the cardboard box on the floor beside the single bed. The tatty lemon blanket and stained drinking bottle.

Charlie found his voice. 'Sarah, I've been to see your mother.'

Nick turned from the window to Sarah in confusion. 'You told me your mother was dead.'

'Nick,' Charlie calmly said. 'Keep quiet. Let me do the talking.'

'How was she?' Sarah asked.

'She said you ran away. I went to see your old head teacher, Mr Peel. He told me what happened. The police told me about how your little brother was killed in an accident. Mary Hicks, your teacher, was driving.'

Her eyes glazed in anguish. Charlie didn't want to notice this. He liked her, which made it hard enough already. 'Which is why I know you'll understand why I must ask you to come with us.'

She smiled sadly and corrected him. 'The police have never known what really happened. I married William, knowing exactly who he was. My teacher who killed Ray. I heard him and Mary discuss it, that she should say she was driving and not him. He'd had a drink you see, while Mary hadn't. He didn't think Ray would amount to much, coming from a family like mine. That my clothes were unclean and I was unwashed.' She smiled tearfully at Charlie. 'I didn't love him, but he was the only person who still knew of Ray's existence. Not counting my mother. I wanted him to know who I was, what Ray meant to me.'

Nick's face was white. His voice was choked. 'Why didn't you tell me you had a brother?'

'Nick,' she said softly. 'It'll be all right. Don't worry.' Her chin trembled. 'I have a confession to make—'

'Don't, Sarah! Don't say anything.'

'I know what I said hurt you, Nick. But it wasn't true. I said it to get you to leave. I do love you...'

Charlie needed Nick to keep it together. The man looked about to cry. This was hard on all of them, but Nick needed to be strong. 'Sarah, I'm going to ask you to come with us now. Nick will get you a coat.'

'We can run, Sarah,' Nick exclaimed. 'Charlie won't stop us. We'll take your car.'

'Sarah doesn't have a car,' a voice said from the doorway.

Charlie swivelled his eyes to the woman. 'Mrs Price! What are you—?' Charlie stopped speaking, his mouth suddenly gone dry. Kathleen Price had a gun in her hand, a serious looking revolver, and Nick wasn't even aware. He was focusing on Sarah, urgently conversing with her. Charlie was confused, and deeply concerned. Kathleen Price looked far too calm.

'She won't be going anywhere with either of you.'

Nick turned at hearing the dictatorial tone in her voice. 'Would you mind leaving? This has nothing to do with you.'

Charlie flinched. For Christ's sake. When was Nick going to notice? He was squaring up to the woman. Charlie had to warn him. 'Stay back, Nick! She has a gun!'

She aimed the gun at Nick, and ordered Charlie further into the room. 'I want you both in my line of sight.' She flicked her gaze to Sarah. 'You're an awfully naïve girl. I've been listening the whole time. Sarah, they're here to arrest you.'

'I know that, Kathleen, but I'm not worried. I haven't done anything wrong.'

'You've said plenty wrong, you foolish girl. You've given them motive.'

Nick wasn't looking at the gun being aimed at him. He wasn't taking it seriously. His eyes were only on Sarah. 'I saw your car,' he said to her. 'You parked it on a road that isn't yours. I went into your house, and upstairs I saw what you had done.'

Charlie wanted to gag him. He inched closer to him. 'It wasn't her, Nick,' he quietly and firmly said.

'But I saw her car. And afterwards it was gone. It's parked outside on the street now. It's her number plate.'

Sarah Shaw had worked it out. Charlie could see it in her expression. 'It isn't my car anymore, Nick. I sold it to Kathleen.'

CHAPTER SIXTY-FOUR

NICK AND CHARLIE

Nick was shocked. His mouth hung open, his eyes turned wide. He inhaled a shaky breath. 'I should have checked. Charlie, I should have checked! Sarah told us she got a lift! I thought she lied or came back somehow. Christ!' he cried in a harsh whisper.

Price moved closer to them. She was nodding her head in agreement. 'I didn't park when we arrived at the hospital. Sarah got out and went in. I turned around and went back to him. No one noticed I wasn't there. I missed some of the handover, but I said I was with a patient.

'I gave him every chance,' she said in a self-righteous tone. 'I sent him a remembrance card with the little boy's name on it, and the letters, and made the calls. They had killed a baby, and they had lied. Mary told me everything. About the girl whose brother they accidently killed. About how they discussed the life he might have had in the family that was his. About how it wasn't her who was driving that day, but him. *Him*, one drink over the limit, while Mary was sober.'

Kathleen paused and looked at the gun, without it seeming to bother her that she was holding it and pointing it at a man.

'This is Joe's gun that he brought back from the Falklands War. He kept it in a tin for forty years. I brought it with me when I went to see William. I made him aware of what he had done by bringing him a cake on the day that it should have been Sarah's brother's birthday if he had lived. I let him blow out the candle. Then I silenced his lying tongue. A false witness will not go unpunished. William and Mary were very arrogant to think it didn't matter who they hurt. My darling daughter. Sarah's little brother. Both now gone. Ray and Rebecca. May they rest in peace. God love them.

'Helen Tate never recognised me, unlike Mary, who recognised Sarah. But I knew who she was. The ringleader of all those other spiteful girls who made Becky's life so unhappy. I planted those photos in Helen's home. I knew it was her who sent the letter. I saw the cut up magazines. When it arrived at my home I had told poor Sarah it was for her. Well, everything's sorted now. None of them can hurt anyone anymore.'

Kathleen gazed sorrowfully at Sarah. 'I guessed why you married him. Though you give a different reason – it had to have been for revenge. After what they said, you must have wanted that.'

Sarah shook her head as the tears fell. 'I never wanted any of this,' she murmured. 'You're wrong to think I wanted revenge. William was my last connection to Ray, other than my mother. The only person to blame is my mother. What they said was true. Ray slept in a cardboard box. My mother wasn't fit to look after a child.'

Charlie needed to distract the woman so that Nick could get Sarah to safety. The revelation of hearing about her daughter – the white flower. For R & R. For Ray and Rebecca. He saw a movement from the corner of his eye – Nick was reaching his hand out to Sarah Shaw. Price reacted in an instant.

She jerked the gun up, anger filling her eyes as she glowered at Nick. 'She doesn't need you! She needs people who care for her. Who love her like me and Joe. She has a home with us. So you can now just back away. Because she doesn't want you!'

Charlie wished he had a radio on him so he could send a silent SOS. Where the hell was the other officer? Probably waiting outside on the pavement. He knew he had to keep Kathleen talking. Until help arrived he needed to keep Nick well back from her. No way was she ready to relinquish that gun. He could see her fist tightening in anger, her finger tensing over the trigger on a gun he now recognised as a Ballester-Molina, a weapon used mainly by Argentine officers. Charlie needed to calm her. The lightest pressure and that gun would go off.

'We can sort this out, you know. So that nothing bad happens to you. You just need to put the gun down, and then we can sit down and talk.'

Kathleen laughed at him harshly. 'Every possible bad thing has happened already. There is nothing worse that can happen to me.'

Charlie looked pointedly at the gun in her hand. 'If that thing goes off, Sarah could get hurt, or could put a hole in this lovesick fool beside me.' Charlie glanced at Nick. 'How are you doing, Nick?'

Nick could feel a burning pain at the back of his eyes. He was hurting from hearing her words. He didn't deserve her love. After everything she had gone through, he had believed her guilty of murdering her husband. His gaze kept straying to the suitcase of baby's clothes. He had been so keen to impress her with a Christmas tree that he hadn't even noticed it sat there when he returned.

'I'm an idiot, Charlie. What I've put you all through. I manipulated everything to control the situation.' He sighed in despair. 'I'm so sorry. I've behaved unforgivably to you.'

Charlie gripped his forearm. 'Calm down, Nick. We can talk about it afterwards.'

Nick breathed in deeply, and got a grip of himself. He needed to cause a diversion to get Charlie and Sarah out of there. The love he feels for these two people – nothing else mattered at this moment. Certainly not him. He summed up the woman before him. She was an unknown quantity. None of them knew what Kathleen would do. Any tension at this moment could make her antagonism worse. Nick saw her looking at Sarah, her features softening.

'Talk to me, Sarah,' she softly pleaded. 'Let me help you. Sure, you were only a child when this all happened to you. You lost your brother and then you ran away from home.'

Nick saw tears in Sarah's eyes. Her voice was eerily calm. 'You can't help me, Kathleen. And you're wrong.' She shook her head. 'Ray was my baby. My son. I was fourteen and pregnant by a boy who was seventeen. Mother took me to Ireland, where I had him.' Her eyes briefly shone. 'My midwife took a photo of him... the only one I have. The sun was shining so brightly on that winter day it blazed through the window. The midwife said a ray of sunshine had come to welcome him.

'I went back to school in the February and was made to say I had a baby brother. But it was me who birthed him and nursed him and loved him. Because he was mine. It's true what you say, Kathleen. There is nothing worse that can happen after you bury your child.'

Sarah's eyes were pools of pain as she held up the yellow rag doll. 'I made this for him. They wouldn't let me give it to him. I tried to get them to open the coffin, but they refused. He was so little. He'd never been in the dark on his own. He was always with me...'

Nick realised he was crying when he felt the wetness on his jaw. He had to help her.

Sarah smiled at him now, a sad little smile, and scrunched

up her nose as if embarrassed. 'Pretty shitty, eh? Being that young, it wasn't good for my body. I can't have any more children, Nick.'

Nick could feel the muscle in his chest squeezing. He was hurting for Sarah and angry at Kathleen for holding them hostage. He noticed Charlie had managed to inch his way to the window. Hopefully he was seeing help arrive. By now, Naughton or Robson must have figured out where he'd be. Robson would be itching to arrest him.

Nick raised his hand in a soothing manner and spoke to Kathleen. 'Mrs Price. We've all been here a while. Can you please put that gun down? I don't know about you, but I could use a drink.'

'I'm sorry,' she said. 'It's too late for that.'

His hand froze and his stomach flipped over as she switched direction and aimed the gun at Charlie.

'Please lower the gun, Mrs Price.'

Charlie moved towards her.

'Stay back, Charlie!'

He moved again.

'Charlie, stay back!'

Charlie gently shook his head. 'Give me the gun, Kathleen! You don't want to hurt anyone.'

'Stay back. I'm warning you!' she snarled.

Nick could see determination in her eyes. There was no time to think. He rushed forwards and the gun exploded. He saw the instant flash of flame, felt the assault of sound through his ears, and smelt the cordite. Pain seared in his shoulder. And in a blur, he saw her take aim again. He lowered his head and lunged at her. His fingers brushed against the material of her coat... He needed to grab her arms. She stepped back and avoided his grasp. He raised his shoulders and head ready to go again and at the same time... saw the gun pointed at him.

He stared into her eyes, waiting for it to explode a second

time. He expected to fall down, but he was still standing. *She couldn't do it. She couldn't shoot again!*

He turned around and saw Charlie on the floor. His eyes were wide open with surprise and he was trying to smile.

Nick looked back and saw Mrs Price running out the door and Sarah chasing her. He shouted after her to come back! 'Let her run, Sarah!'

Nick fell to his knees, holding his shoulder, in pain and shock.

'Nick.'

Too weak to run after her.

'Nick.'

He needed to get back up.

'Nick!'

'Shut up, Charlie. I need to get up and go after her.'

'Nick, I need you.'

'I can't, Charlie. I'm bloody injured.'

Then Charlie groaned.

Nick turned his head, and focused on Charlie. *Why was the silly bugger still on the floor?* Then he saw Charlie's frightened eyes and knew.

Swiftly he crawled over to him, and knelt next to him. 'Where are you hurt, Charlie?'

Charlie lay on his back. He felt cold. Couldn't feel much else, just this shivery coldness creeping through. Then he saw Nick's face and felt safe. 'I'm not hurt, Nick. I'm just cold.'

Nick carefully raised Charlie's head and rested it on a cushion he grabbed from the sofa. He saw the red spreading over Charlie's shirt and pulled it open.

'You're bleeding, Charlie. I gotta get you help.' He ripped the sleeve off his own shirt, tearing it clean away from the injured shoulder, and pressed it against Charlie's chest. 'You're gonna have to do this. I gotta get help. Are you listening, Charlie? Press it!'

'I need to tell you something, Nick.' Charlie's voice quavered, as if afraid.

Nick stared at him sternly. 'It'll wait!'

'Can't wait,' he replied.

Nick could see the red leaking through the cotton sleeve and tried desperate humour to shut him up. 'If you're about to tell me where your cigarette card collection is, I already know you keep 'em under your bed.'

'I gotta tell you something about your mother, Nick.'

Nick looked poleaxed by this revelation. His expression marked with astonishment. He gave a shuddering breath and bit his bottom lip to keep check of his emotions. He stared wide-eyed at Charlie and found humour, again, helped him focus on the much more urgent situation in hand. His voice was tight with ironic amusement. 'Shit, Charlie. You pick your time to deliver news.'

Words came slowly out of Charlie's mouth. A tear ran down the side of his temple. 'A year after your mum went missing, I came by your house. It being the anniversary. Your neighbour on the left had a birthday banner up at the window. He was out front when I was leaving. Going off to London to celebrate his sixtieth. I wished him happy birthday. He said, it'll be better than last year, which he spent in casualty after slicing his thumb with a Stanley knife. His wife joined him and joked she'd never hear the end of it. Had to cancel the barbeque. I reminded him about the year before, the day he saw your mum driving off in a campervan. He looked perplexed. They both did, and said it couldn't have been on his birthday then. Must have been the day before.'

Charlie's voice choked and Nick tried to stop him talking. 'Shush. Rest. You can tell me later.'

Charlie panted. 'Let me finish. I checked with the other neighbours, the one on the right and the one beside, and they were adamant that the anniversary date was correct. That was the day they saw your mum go. The discrepancy bugged me. I checked every detail of the man's story. The time he was in the hospital. He wasn't at home the time the other neighbours saw her go. But he said he saw her. His was the statement that gave the most details. Yellow dress. Pink scarf in her hair. Record player in her arms. I never stopped questioning it, Nick, with your neighbours and with your father, but I could never get any further. Your father wasn't there to see her leave. You were at school. I didn't tell you, Nick. 'Cause I didn't want you hurt more. But I had no right to keep it from you. I'm truly sorry, Nick.'

Nick couldn't process what he was feeling. His shock was blunted from being acutely aware of how seriously injured Charlie was. The bullet that hit him hit Charlie as well. It got him in the chest. The cloth he was pressing was seeped in blood. 'I gotta get a towel or something, Charlie. To plug you up. Gotta get an ambulance.'

'Hush,' Charlie said. His voice soft, and relaxed. 'One'll be on the way. Gunshot will have been heard.' He reached up and pulled Nick's hand from his chest and held it instead against his face. 'Let it bleed, Nick. I don't want to die in hospital. I don't want to die in one of those places.'

'Shut up, Charlie! You're not gonna die.'

'I am, Nick, and not because of a little bullet. My lungs were already shot to pieces... I want to go this way... much nicer. You, me... my boy...'

'Shut up, Charlie, and let me sort you out.'

His tears dripped on to Charlie's face. 'You're not gonna die, because I'm not gonna let you get out of buying me a pint. I know your game. Play dead so you don't have to put your hand in your pocket.'

'Have one for me... won't you?' Charlie whispered.

Nick swiped his hand across his face so he could see into

Charlie's eyes. 'You can drink with me, you old miser, and that's an order.'

'I won't be there, Nick... I'm sorry.'

'You bloody well will be. You hear me!'

Charlie didn't respond.

His hand was no longer holding Nick's.

Nick stared at his lifeless body. He touched Charlie's face and felt the warm skin. A few minutes ago Charlie had gripped his arm strongly.

A pain so unbearably crushing locked his throat, until finally, his shoulders heaving, his neck convulsing, the sounds were freed from his mouth.

Time stopped while Nick sat there. He registered all the people coming into the house. He wasn't ready to leave him. He needed to tell him something first. He bent his head and kissed his friend. 'Damn, Charlie. What am I going to do?' he softly said. 'I love you, you old bugger. I didn't even tell you what you meant to me. You were the best thing that happened to me... You taught me to be better. And I will be again, Charlie. I promise you.'

CHAPTER SIXTY-FIVE

NICK

Heavy grey clouds covered the sky and rain pelted the windscreen. Nick held a brown envelope in his hand. It was delivered to his home that morning, but he mostly knew what the contents would say. Shaun had kept him in the loop. Kathleen Price was undergoing a psychiatric evaluation. In the envelope was a copy of the transcript of her interview. He pulled it out, noticing it was barely half a page long. He started reading. In his mind, he heard the voices.

Issy Banks: Before we begin, do you need anything, Kathleen?

Kathleen Price: No, I'm all right. Is Sarah okay? She didn't come home for Christmas. All day I waited.

Issy Banks: Do you understand what's happened, Kathleen?

Kathleen Price: Yes. Yes, I understand. I said it was too soon. She should never have married him.

Issy Banks: Do you mean William?

Kathleen Price: Oh, he's not around anymore. Have you met him?

Issy Banks: What about Mary?

Kathleen Price: Well, it's obvious – the poor creature is out of her misery.

Issy Banks: Kathleen, do you know why you're here?

Kathleen Price: Yes. I'm looking for Sarah. Do you know where my daughter is?

Issy Banks: Kathleen, I'm going to get our doctor to see you. Do you understand?

Nick finished reading. It was obvious the woman was in the throes of a breakdown. He placed the transcript back in the envelope. His hand was trembling. The guilt he felt was with him day and night. He hadn't seen any of his colleagues since Charlie's death more than a fortnight ago, but he knew they'd be working round the clock to assess the damage. Looking for withheld evidence, or witness statements that weren't followed up. Any actions that could have prevented Helen Tate being murdered.

He rested his head against the seat. Believing Sarah was guilty would weigh on him. He'd been seized by fear at the thought of her being captured. When he left the Shaw house the night of the murder he sat for hours in his car while he thought of how he could protect her. He'd deliberately arrived late to the crime scene to make it look like he'd only just arrived in the city. And it had all been unnecessary. She didn't do it.

No one had managed to contact her since she gave her statement. She had disappeared. Nick wondered where she could have gone. Having learned of her history, maybe she went back to where she lived between leaving her home at just fifteen until she started training as a nurse. Nick didn't want to imagine how she coped with that. It was hard enough imagining her out there alone. But he would leave her be. Perhaps if he hadn't focused on all the reasons for why she finished with him, and instead on dealing with his own demons, he would have returned more able to help her as a friend, instead of behaving like a juvenile despot.

At thirty-five he still had some growing up to do. While Sarah had grown up a long time ago. When Price was arrested, she had Sarah's birth certificate in her possessions. She hadn't lied about who she was. She just never mentioned who she once was. She changed her name by deed poll at the age of eighteen and started her life again.

In Charlie's jacket pocket they found a business card for a Dr Hoffmann. When an officer contacted her, the surprise was that she had not only met Charlie a day before his death, but she had met Sarah as a patient years ago. The doctor had received a letter from an ex-patient who lived in Bath. She couldn't a hundred per cent confirm the name of the patient as the letter was signed using a codename – Jack-in-the-box – but she was otherwise certain of who it must be. Jess Marah. A teenager she saw back in 2007.

He placed the envelope on the seat beside him. There was another document in it but he wasn't going it take it out. He had no intention of reading Charlie's autopsy report. Doyle had performed the post-mortem and he'd rung Nick after it was over.

'Weeks, Nick. That's all he had. He had a massive tumour that was inoperable. Charlie wouldn't have wanted a slow death.'

Nick could understand that, but deep down he felt Charlie would have liked just a little more time to have one more Christmas, drink one last pint, smoke one last cigarette, if he'd had a choice. He only hoped Charlie didn't go, thinking he needed forgiving. Charlie had nothing to be sorry for. What he did showed Nick how much Charlie loved him. Nick wasn't ready to address what Charlie told him. But he would, eventually, look to find out what was true.

He picked up the flowers and got out of the car. He was going to see his friend. He hadn't said goodbye to him yet. The funeral had taken place on New Year's Eve but Nick didn't go. He hadn't had the strength. He knew Charlie would understand.

As he walked into the cemetery he looked up and saw Superintendent Naughton coming towards him. His grey eyes were sad.

'Just wanted to say hello.'

Nick showed the flowers. 'Just wanted to say goodbye.'

Naughton was waiting for him when he came back out through the gates twenty minutes later.

'Just wanted to check you're okay. How's the shoulder?'

'Sore, but no long-term damage. The bullet just grazed my skin before it hit Charlie. So antibiotics and dressings.'

'And how are *you*?'

Nick took a shallow breath. 'Getting there. Getting out of this business as well.'

'Bad move, Anderson. It will follow you. You've got to work through this.'

'What? And get someone else killed?'

'That wasn't your fault, Anderson. Charlie was the one who put you at risk. He went in there thinking Mrs Shaw had murdered her husband. Therefore, she might have had a gun. The fact that the real killer was there was bad luck. But Charlie wasn't thinking straight.'

'Oh, yes he was. He was looking after me! He probably thought he could take her in and then let me know what she'd done. He was protecting me. I was the one not thinking straight, not him.'

'Trust me, Anderson – you most definitely were not thinking straight. I've no doubt about that. But I think Charlie took a chance because he was ill. But I'll tell you something, if he's looking down right now he'll kick himself for taking that chance. This is the last thing in the world he'd want.'

'Charlie will understand.'

'No, he won't. He was proud of you. Told me so himself. In fact, I'd go as far as to say he loved you like a son. So think about it, Anderson. Are you going to walk away and let Charlie down?'

Nick wanted so badly to lean on someone. He shook his head. 'I already let him down.'

'Charlie was a good judge of character and he knew you. You've got to face this inquiry, take whatever they dish out and rise up again. You single-handedly misdirected an investigation. Nearly outsmarted a whole team. And Charlie knew that too.'

Nick wanted to hide his face in shame. 'And that's what the force needs is it? A corrupt cop?'

'I don't condone what you did one bit. But I do think of what you could do if your mind had been set on actually catching a suspect.'

'You knew him, didn't you? Charlie. Why didn't he ever go higher? When you think of what he alone uncovered, every angle he pursued was right on the money.'

Naughton's voice turned mellow. 'He could have. He didn't want it. He didn't need it. He did what he liked doing best. Catching villains, and showing young officers how it should be done.'

Naughton walked away, and Nick knew he had to do one more thing. He walked back into the cemetery to Charlie's grave. He needed to be near his friend as he did this. Charlie once said to him to throw away what he was holding onto, as only then would he cast off the chains. Nick was going to take a gamble and hope that what he was holding onto, if set free, would one day want to come back.

The rain overhead was stopping and a tiny ray of sun was struggling to shine through. He took the broken angel out of his pocket and felt its weight one last time, feeling its contours and the rough edge where the second wing had once been. He closed his hand over it, and aiming towards the horizon of cloud he flung the broken angel free.

CHAPTER SIXTY-SIX

SARAH

Sarah watched him from a distance. Nick looked vulnerable standing there at the grave alone. It was hard not to go over and comfort him. He would be confused by her absence. But she needed to stay away. They both needed time to heal.

She had hurt him badly with the way she broke up with him. It had tortured her to have to stand there and be cruel to him. She had waited for him outside her front door, and not let him in. After two years of dating she finished their relationship out on the street. Saw him throw his key ring down on the pavement. Neither of them were expecting the day to end as it did. She had not let him know about the result she was waiting on – she had expected it to be something they could fix. Not something that would explode all hope from her heart.

Structural damage occurred during the first delivery...

She had wanted to run out of the room and unhear what the doctor said and pretend it was untrue. But it *was* true, and she could never offer Nick all of herself... ever. So she had to be cruel. He would never have finished with her and she would always have felt guilty. Despite what he may have said, Nick wanted children. She remembered the occasional wistful expression cross his face when they passed parents with prams. When they went for walks through Victoria Park, he somehow always managed to detour to the duck pond where they would sit on a bench and watch toddlers throw peas and pieces of bread. He would laugh about the waddling toddlers trying to chase the much faster waddling ducks, and laugh even louder when he saw their pudgy hands pushing the offerings into their open little mouths.

She may have weakened and not been able to carry it through if not for the second shock that day. When she recognised William and Mary in the corridor, it barely registered – she was reeling from the news she had just received. William had seen how shaken she was and offered to sit with her. She had waited for him to recognise her. But he never knew who she was. Not then or after. Not even when he showed her a photograph in the back of an album, a school where he was a teacher, and she was a pupil standing in the back row.

She declined his offer, and shortly afterwards she went to the ward to start her shift. He was there and Mary was a patient, and it seemed fitting that they should be present on the day she found out she would never conceive again, as well as on the day her first and only baby should die. Their presence strangely comforted her.

The question she asked Dr Hoffmann had gone through her mind many times in the last two weeks – not that the doctor could have given her an answer, even if she'd had one, without a forwarding address. It was a rhetorical question: *Was everything that happened her fault?* Or was there a blueprint of people's fortune, ready to go at birth, somewhere out there in the universe?

Sarah would like to know the answer. She would like to think she had no hand in it, because the logical part of her brain was telling her the answer was *yes*. If she had not slept with a boy, her mother would never have needed to mind her baby. William would never have driven into the pushchair that day. He and Mary might never have moved schools. Kathleen would have spoken with a different teacher, and maybe it would have been handled differently. Rebecca and Helen and William might still be alive. Mary might have died in a bed and not on a floor. She wouldn't have married William. Nick wouldn't have sabotaged his career. *She* would have been able to get pregnant.

Your body hadn't finished growing and was not yet fully mature.

She could think about what William had done to Mary, making her take the blame, and could see he had weaknesses, but she saw it as his price to pay for his inability to be a stronger person. He would have known that, he'd been an intelligent man.

She had used him, she supposed, but was it to help her get over Nick? Or had she used her misfortune to end with Nick so she could be free to dwell on her past with someone *from* her past? A more brutal question, that made her want to distance herself from her thoughts, was whether she had decided this path right from the beginning when she saw him in the corridor. Could a need to avenge her baby's death have been buried in her mind, making her do this? When he asked her to marry him, he never told her he wanted children, but if he had, would she have let him know that she couldn't?

The thought lodged in her mind. She hoped she was a better person than that. She didn't want to see herself as a bitter and vengeful woman. She *was* better than that. Otherwise, she would have enjoyed his torment over the phone calls and not advised him to go to the police. She wouldn't have worried about him falling down stairs when he didn't answer her calls.

It was hard to know what she had been after from him. Maybe a life she felt she deserved, formed of more loneliness. She had run from her past, an immature child, changing her name to get rid of the memory of Jess. And then, all grown up, she had become a nurse, but what she failed to do was live. She isolated herself from people, she rejected a man who loved her and whom she loved. Not giving him a choice. Or the truth. She could have told Nick about her past. She could have shared it with others. It was not so shocking it had to stay secret. Teenager has baby, grandmother claims it as hers. It can only have been for one reason – punishing herself to punish her mother.

In her memories, her entire childhood had been focused only on those few short months of motherhood. She had so many fragmented memories – the smell of cigarette smoke and floral room spray, the smell of alcohol and the stain of red wine, a dirty house and a pitiful cardboard box.

For her to ever have a chance of moving on, she had to face what she had run from. She would never be Jess again, but neither would she deny her existence. She needed to search for memories from before. The distant echo of laughter, Coca-Cola and chips on a Friday, telling silly jokes to each other in bed, and the only way to do that was to go back to where she left them – with her mother.

She was turning thirty-one this year, was fourteen when she fell pregnant, and fifteen when she ran away. It was too many years to punish them both. Her mother, for all her faults, probably thought it for the best. She was not educated enough to know the damage she was causing. She would have looked on Jess as a child and felt she had no choice. She would have looked to the bottle to help her through.

Sarah took a sharp intake of breath to steady her turbulent thoughts.

What had she gained? And what had Kathleen hoped for?

To fill the emptiness, she supposed. Sarah wished she had found another way so as not to bring sadness to another family, and not to leave Joe alone. She sent a letter to Joe to tell him how sorry she was for coming into their lives, and that she would be there for him if he ever needed a shoulder to lean on. She enclosed Rebecca's bracelet with the letter. The forget-me-not flowers should be with those who had loved her. To remember her by.

From the inside pocket of her coat she took out the photograph of Ray. She touched the tiny face, as red as a beetroot, and felt her eyes brim. Despite everything, despite other people's pain and loss, she could not wish him away. Not ever. She had waited so long to be able to acknowledge him, to feel the sense of connection that came over her the minute she revealed that she was his mother. She would never want that taken away now. She could now show his image and say... he was mine. During his few precious weeks of life he had been desperately loved by her. She would never want to wish that time away.

She dried her tears and placed the photograph back in her pocket. She held the memory of her arms wrapped around her baby. She would hold onto that. The days ahead wouldn't be easy. She would visit her mother and try to get to know her again. She would try and focus on a happier future and less on an unhappy past.

Images appeared in her head and she couldn't help the tug of hope that came with them. If she was brave enough, there were children who needed to be adopted – who needed a home. She could provide them with that, and she could teach them things. To teenagers especially, she could tell them of the perils of running away... She wouldn't expose them to all her experiences, just enough about what being on the streets really meant. Small things: nowhere to brush your teeth or get a shower or charge a phone. Nowhere to sleep that wasn't dangerous.

She would protect them from making the same mistakes as her.

She looked across to the graves. She wanted to tell Nick what she felt. What she had always felt from the moment he jumped off that stage and asked her to dance. If he turned and stared in her direction, she would take it as a sign. Her heart began to thump as he turned from the grave, ready to leave. She held her breath. He did not look her way. The sun then shone in her eyes and blinded her. She couldn't see him, and waited anxiously for him to appear. She had no right to want this, but her heart wouldn't listen to her body, and maybe it was right that she should feel the bittersweet pain. She had made him leave her twice. Now she had to wait and see if fate intervened. If it didn't, she had no regrets. In her life she had loved deeply.

The sun disappeared behind a cloud, and she caught a movement beneath a tree. A smile tugged at her lips. There he was, walking out of the gates. She touched her lips to her finger-tips and blew him a kiss. And no doubt it was her imagination, but it seemed to her that he turned his head slightly.

She would always be there from now on. Keeping an eye, making sure that he didn't get too unhappy or into trouble again. Isn't that why she gave him an angel in the first place? Nick needed a guardian angel to watch over him. And care about him the way Sarah did. She had never stopped loving him. Despite making her heart try. She had only paused...

A LETTER FROM LIZ

Dear reader,

I want to say a huge thank you for choosing to read *The Nurse's Secret*. If you did enjoy it, and want to keep up to date with all my latest releases, just sign up at the following link. Your email address will never be shared and you can unsubscribe at any time.

www.bookouture.com/liz-lawler

I hope you loved *The Nurse's Secret* and if you did I would be very grateful if you could write a review. I'd love to hear what you think, and it makes such a difference helping new readers to discover one of my books for the first time. I was inspired to write this story after listening to a different story my father told me many years ago. If he were alive today he'd be aged 107. I don't know if it was a made-up story or if it was true. He was a great storyteller, and with this particular story the tale often changed. But the version that intrigued me most was during the 1930s. It was about a newlywed couple who were driving to their honeymoon. He was a policeman and she was a teacher. On the backseat of the car was her brown leather suitcase and in it there was evidence that she had committed a crime. I think the evidence was in the form of a letter, but there my own memory fails me. When my father told me this story I must have been about ten. But what I do remember is that the wife was taking the evidence with her to get rid of it, and her husband was completely unaware!

I love hearing from my readers – you can get in touch on my Facebook page, through Twitter, Goodreads. If I'm late in responding please never think it's because I don't care or that I've ignored your name. It's only because I'm absent for a little while writing.

Thanks,

Liz Lawler

 facebook.com/liz.lawler.90
twitter.com/authorlizlawler

ACKNOWLEDGEMENTS

All the wonderful, hard-working and talented people who helped me to write the book disappear from my mind until I type the final full stop. Then when I read the story back I see all their special inputs – the questions I asked are all answered. The 'what ifs' and 'what happens' written in the pages. The errors corrected, the sentences smoother. The cover designed with absolute care. So many things go into making a book appealing, to give it the best chance of finding a way into your hands. So my deep gratitude goes to some very special people:

I'd like to thank Dr Peter Forster MBBS FRCA for sharing his expert knowledge. You cure my worries and make it all better! I will be forever indebted to you. Any mistakes are, of course, mine.

I would also like to thank Detective Inspector Kurt Swallow for reading this through a policeman's eyes. My police characters wouldn't know what to do without you to guide them. Your input has been invaluable!

A very special thank you to my incredible editor, Natasha Harding. Your support has been absolutely perfect. It's been a privilege to work with you.

An equally special thank you to Alexandra Holmes, head of editorial management, Sarah Hardy, book publicist, and the entire brilliant Bookouture team. Thank you to every one of you for everything you do!

My deepest thanks to my agent, Rory Scarfe, and The Blair

Partnership team always there to root me on. Fingers crossed, only fifteen more to go, Rory...

My thanks to Martyn Folkes, and brother-in-law Kevin Stephenson for reading the first draft! To my brothers and sisters for being there always. My sister Bee Mundy for promising to take me to Barcelona for research for the next one!

To the loves and lights of my life: Mike, Lorcs, Katie, Alex, Harriet, Bradley, Darcie, Dolly, Arthur, Nathaniel, Cooper, Buddy, Cleo, Millie. I can't wait to come out to play...

To mum, my constant inspiration...

And finally a very warm thank you to the readers and reviewers who have taken the time to read my stories.